"Hallie Jo spins an intriguing story, rich in symbolism, purposely embedding God's plan for humanity. She weaves implications of historical biblical accounts into her characters with events familiar to people of faith. Her imagination merges with her awareness of spiritual matters and guides her readers down a path that leads to faith in a higher being who loves and cares about his subjects. Her thoughtful conclusions at the end of her book offer readers who identified with her interesting characters good reason to adopt the truths that surface, as God intended them, to trust Jesus as their personal redeemer. While the setting suggests a medieval tone, the reader hears a clear call to rely upon sound biblical doctrine. A good read for those who cherish allegory and poetry. An amazing work from a young woman of immense faith."

—**Karen Jordan**, speaker and author of *Words That Change Everything*

Dedicated to "the Resistance" of the real world. Christians who face pain and even death for refusing to forsake Jesus Christ, the True Lord of Lords. You will receive an eternal reward for your faith. I pray that I can be as strong in Him as you.

*But before all this, they will lay hands on you and persecute you. They will deliver you to synagogues and prisons, and you will be brought before kings and governors, and all on account of My name. This will result in you being witnesses to them. But make up your mind not to worry beforehand how you will defend yourselves. For I will give you words and wisdom that none of your adversaries will be able to resist or contradict. You will be betrayed even by parents, brothers, relatives and friends, and they will put some of you to death. All men will hate you because of Me. But not a hair on your head will perish. By standing firm you will gain life.*

*- Luke 21:12-19 -*

# THE PROMISE

## Hallie Jo

Carpenter's Son Publishing

The Promise

©2017 by Hallie Jo

Published by Carpenter's Son Publishing, Franklin, Tennessee

Published in association with Larry Carpenter of Christian Book Services, LLC of Franklin, Tennessee

Cover Design by Suzanne Lawing

Copy Edit and Interior Layout Design by Adept Content Solutions

ISBN: 978-1-946889-05-8

Printed in the United States of America

# CONTENTS

## CHAPTER ONE

# THROUGH THE NIGHT

He woke in the dead of night to the sound of his own screams. He sat up in a cold sweat, skin crawling. His heavy breathing echoed through the massive chamber.

The guards stationed in the hallway banged on the heavy doors. "Are you all right, Lord Nazar?"

*If he dares to open that door without permission I shall have his head. Doesn't he know who I am?* his thoughts raged.

He took deep breaths to steady his heart rate. "I'm perfectly fine!" he roared, followed by a stream of profanity and, "Get me my general! Now!"

As he rushed to make himself presentable, he felt a spirit of terror overshadow him: the dream.

He combed his wet hair. He was running out of time. They were getting impatient. But they had given him a dream. This could change everything.

He rummaged madly through his things until he finally found what he was looking for: a journal. Two of his assassins had gotten it from a successful raid two years ago. He flipped to the page seen in his dream. The words stared boldly back at him.

How had he missed this?

*The witch has a daughter.*
*Find her.*

An inhuman snarl of a laugh welled up from deep inside him, causing fear and twisted exhilaration to shiver down his spine.

❧

The young man replayed the orders given to him at dawn the previous day. After a week of searching, they had finally found her. He dismounted his horse and dropped to one knee. He silently took some hay in his hand and let it slip through his fingers. It was perfect. He turned to the blond woman beside him. "This will do nicely."

The woman nodded, lifted the top off the lantern, and offered it to the hay. It quickly took the flame.

❧

"What's wrong, Star?" Andrea asked, leaning down to rub the jet-black stallion. Tensing up, he refused to take another step and tucked his normally proud tail down. Something was definitely wrong.

"Easy, easy, boy," she soothed.

She looked around. Nothing.

*Wait. What was that?* She squinted.

Smoke. There was a big fire headed their way. Right toward the house. She had to warn everyone. "Go!" Star was only too happy to get out of there.

As she neared the farmhouse, she was met by Judd.

"Andrea, how many times do I have to tell you something before you get it through your thick skull?"

She tried to interrupt but he just kept throwing his fit, drunk again. "You cannot ride that stupid horse until after you get all your chores done. Have you even mucked the stalls yet?"

"Yes, sir, but that is not the point—"

"Oh really? Well, have you milked the goat?"

"I did, but listen—"

"Did you ever fix those halters like I told you to?"

"Please, just listen—"

"Don't get sassy with me! You live in *my* house—"

This time she was the one to cut in. "Stop!" she practically screamed. It startled him enough that she could get a word in.

"Listen, there is a fire coming this way! It has already hit the hay field in the far south east corner."

He was immediately concerned. "How big? Is it headed this way? And if this is some stupid trick—"

"I'm not sure how big it is, but it is definitely headed this way." She started toward their nearest neighbor, who was a mile away.

"Where are you going?"

"I must warn the neighbors. Maybe they will help." Before he could protest, Andrea spurred Star into a gallop.

Andrea forced herself to calm down as she rode. She was almost nineteen—and he was not even her father—yet he still treated her like a child. Andrea sighed away some of the anger and urged Star to hurry.

She slid to a stop in front of the neighbor's house, slipped off her mount's back, and knocked on the sturdy door to the stone house.

Lisa opened the door. When she saw Andrea, the color drained from her face and she slammed the door.

"Lisa! Please!" she said as she banged on the door. "There is a fire coming!"

The woman opened the door a crack. Her voice, though forceful, held a slight tremble. "Go away! I don't want any trouble."

"But there's a fire!" Andrea was at a loss for words.

"Thank you for the warning. Now go!" The door slammed shut and she heard the wooden bar slide into place, locking her out.

*What is wrong with Lisa?* Andrea thought. *Well, there is no time for this now. I have to go warn Mark.*

A few moments later, her horse skidded to a stop in front of Mark's house. Andrea slid off Star's back and held the reigns in one hand as she raised her other hand to knock. Someone grabbed her wrist and covered her mouth. Her muffled scream was never heard. She let go of the reins and kicked and fought and screamed. None of it mattered. The man was firm, but didn't hurt her.

"Don't fight. You will only hurt yourself," said a calm, sweet voice. His words were like dripping honey. "I'm going to let go of you. You are going to get on your horse, and ride northwest. Be swift. Don't stop for anyone or anything. Once you get to the mountains, look for a stream. Follow it north into the mountains and in the center of the stream you will find an old tree that starts out as one, then divides into two. Its branches twist back together, forming a large oval. The tree resembles a weeping willow.

"I'm going to let go now. Don't scream, or your life will be in danger. He who has ears, let him hear."

He let go and she jerked away. She whirled around and backed away toward Star.

The man was huge. He was muscular, and well over six feet tall. His strong yet compassionate brown eyes looked almost golden and she felt as if she didn't dare look into them. His hair was wavy and so blond it almost looked white, and his handsome face showed no expression.

She screamed for Mark.

Star reared, squealing at the sound of the scream. Andrea attempted to mount her terrified horse. Star sensed her fear and sidestepped away.

The door flew open and Mark appeared. "You!"

Andrea ran to him. "Mark! You have to help me!"

Mark slapped her.

Greatly startled, it nearly knocked her off her feet. She lifted a trembling hand to her stinging face, mouth agape.

"Don't look at me like that!" he cried. "I don't know what you did, but I am not going to get myself marked too! I am turning you in." He reached for her arm.

She stumbled back. The stranger stuck out a leg and the pursuing Mark fell to the ground.

The stranger turned to the horse and spoke sharply. "Peace!"

Star froze. You could still see the whites of his eyes, but he froze.

Before she knew what was happening, the stranger swept Andrea up with surprising ease and set her gently in the saddle.

"Don't move!" Mark was on his feet. His face red with rage, oblivious to the stranger.

"He who has ears, let him hear," said the calm, steady voice.

The stranger then slapped the horse on the rump. Star bolted.

Andrea's instincts kicked in and she leaned forward and grabbed two fistfuls of mane. She squeezed her eyes shut and fought with all her strength to stay on. She looked back only once to see one very angry Mark.

The stranger was gone.

಄಄

"Wynn."

The stranger turned around to face the voice behind him. "Yes, Baros?"

Yosim was baros of the guardians. He stood at twelve feet tall with glowing bronze skin, a brilliant sword hanging at his side. His eyes were golden and his hair was wavy like Wynn's, but a silvery white. His ageless face was handsome and strong.

"Wynn, you were ordered to not physically interfere unless it was absolutely necessary." His voice was in no way harsh or demanding, but compassionate.

"I'm truly sorry, Baros," Wynn said, now his regular twelve foot height and in shining white robes like Yosim. "I feared for her safety. But I did show myself as a human. And I didn't allow the man to see me."

Baros Yosim's face relaxed a little. "Good." He put a hand on his friend and fellow warrior's shoulder. "But she must choose to fulfill her calling. You may guide and direct her, but don't intervene in physical matters unless her life is threatened. Even then, don't be seen. The time is not yet right."

Wynn nodded, then hesitated. "What if she does not accept her path? What if she fails?"

The question pained the baros. "She cannot be forced. Guide her, but ultimately, the choice is hers alone. All will be given to her if she chooses to take it." He sighed. "If she fails, it will be because she allowed herself to, and another will replace her in due time." He brightened a little. "But take heart, friend. The Maker knows best and is aware of His choice."

಄಄

A tall, slender figure with raven black hair made sure all the ink wells were full. She wiped her snowy white hands clean on a rag. Her extravagant braid started at the top of her head and made its way to her waist. It had never been cut.

"Musa?" asked Riven from the entryway to the ancient room.

"Yes?" she answered.

"If you are ready, we are here."

"Send everyone in."

Soon a group of twenty adults of every gender, age, and race was seated on the floor in Yopac Raj. Musa passed out blank paper and the section of the book from which they would be making copies.

"Before we begin," she said, "Riven has an announcement to make. This will be announced again in the Zann Raj at the nightly gathering, but I believe this will encourage you as we work."

The tall Darrionite stood. "The last round of copies that we made has been successfully smuggled to Kimble. We delivered fifty copies to the Lovers there."

Everyone cheered.

Once it was quiet, Riven continued. "We also managed to get copies into the hands of three different printers—whose names and locations I will not disclose for their safety—who will make sure that Lovers in their area get to them."

Riven sat as everyone cheered once more.

Musa now sat in the circle with the others, ready to write. "So, let us start from the beginning."

And everyone began to work.

*Before the ages, before time began,*
*No sun nor moon was, exist did no man;*
*The Great Light Alone lived and brought forth life;*
*Light and Holy Son made the Courts of Light.*

*Light made worshipers—beautiful and strong,*
*To bring Him glory through wonderful song;*
*Placed over the rest was Nyese-Vinai,*
*Of all these beings, to lift Light's Name high.*

*In Nyese-Vinai hot jealousy raged—*
*For Light's Holy Throne war would soon be waged;*
*Nyese-Vinai led worshipers astray,*
*Though some for Light's truth decided to stay.*

*Since Nyese-Vinai acted jealously,*
*He was called Lavin—meaning jealousy;*
*It was jealousy that paved Lavin's path,*
*He would use the same to again stir wrath.*

෧∽෧

She rode through the night in a daze. The full moon and its blanket of stars were her only light, confusion and complete exhaustion her only feelings. Star never slowed his pace, and she never tried to stop him. She was not sure what was going on. Not sure why she still ran. She knew by the stars that they were headed northwest. Hopefully, whatever she was running from was not there.

Yes, something was wrong with Mark, Lisa, and that stranger. But all she really knew was that she didn't know anything.

Star finally slowed to a still-hurried, but gentle gait.

෧∽෧

Wynn followed just above them, unseen. The horse sensed his presence. In fact, that was the only reason why the stallion kept going through the long hours of the night. He knew Andrea's complete exhaustion and confusion were the only things that kept her from turning the horse around. He had to make sure that she arrived safely. All would be made known to her once she got there.

His beautiful voice pierced the night's stillness in a song in a language not known to the ears of men. *Lythrainial*—the Tongue of the Courts.

Andrea didn't hear it with mortal ears, but her spirit was calmed. The confusion slipped away for a season, and she drifted to sleep, draped over the slow-moving horse.

"Well done, Star." Wynn landed in front of the horse and folded his wings, in the form of a human, but still unseen. He led the horse at a slow and gentle pace, occasionally using a giant hand to steady the sleeping girl. He kept the horse heading northwest.

At the break of dawn, he stopped the horse, and placed the girl under the shelter of a tree. The horse plodded over to the stream for a drink. The poor beast deserved that much.

"Rest and regain your strength, Andrea," Wynn whispered, "for your journey has only just begun."

## CHAPTER TWO

# MARKED

G reen sunlight splashed through the leaves and across Andrea's face. Her eyes fluttered open to a tree towering over her. How did she get here? Where was *here?*

Star. The fire. Lisa. The stranger. Mark. The ride through the night.

It all came back to her. She jumped up and looked around.

*Were those hoof beats? No.* She put a hand over her racing heart and calmed her breathing. *Where is Star? Alright, good, he's by the stream eating grass. Everything is fine now.*

How was she going to explain all of this to Judd? Her foster father was not going to be happy about her running off like that. And poor, dear Flora would be worried sick. She sighed and walked over to her horse.

"You know, Star," she mused out loud as she stroked the white blaze between the eyes of the otherwise solid black stallion, "I turn nineteen soon. I could get married and never have to hear about how I live in *Judd's* house under *Judd's* rules. Lots of girls my age are already married. Or at least engaged."

She scratched under his mane and then mounted, knowing that she had no intentions of marriage. At least not yet. Maybe someday she would find the right man. More than one man had already shown interest in her, but unlike many Airissian girls her age, she had chosen to wait. She was young. Though why she had made that choice, she was not entirely sure.

But now more than ever, marriage wasn't a priority. Yesterday's events gave her plenty of stranger things to worry about.

She turned Star toward home and let him choose his own pace. She let her thoughts drift. She was in no hurry.

Wynn whispered in her thoughts, *He who has ears, let him hear.*

She stopped. Her eyebrows drew together. *Where did that come from?*

Then, as the unheard voice prompted her, she remembered the stranger's words.

*What did he say?* Her mind scrambled to remember. She gnawed on her nails, a nervous habit she had given up trying to break, *Something about going north or maybe west? Oh! And something about a mountain stream and … what was it? A tree! Some kind of mysterious tree that twisted around.* She looked back.

"Good!" said Wynn. "Follow the stream."

*Why would I want to follow the stream? So I can find this magic tree?* she shook her head and pushed Star into a swift trot. *I better hurry so I can get home before dark.*

"No! You have to turn around!"

But she had already unknowingly pushed Wynn's words from her mind.

She pushed Star faster. She was not sure how far she was from home and she wanted to get back before dark if at all possible.

Wynn just shook his head. If only she knew. If only she would listen!

☙❧

"You *what?*"

The two kneeling figures shrank at his words.

"Surely, you're not telling me that you let an untrained, unarmed, *and* unaware girl escape?" the man leaned forward and pounded the arm of his chair with his fist. "Well?"

The pretty blond girl didn't dare lift her eyes or face as she answered shakily, "My lord, I would not say she has escaped. She is still unaware and has nowhere to—"

"So you *have* lost her!" he grabbed each one of their jaws in a crushing grip and forced their faces toward his. He liked to see the fear in their eyes, though there was not as much as he had expected. Both were feisty and rebellious.

*Finally. Two people with backbones. A nice change from the usual groveling. They may yet prove useful.* "Give me one reason why I shouldn't kill you." He threw them back to the floor. "Or will you blunder that as well?"

The young man masked his anger as he answered, "My lord, she has nowhere to go. She will have to return home and we will be waiting." He dared to look up. Straight into the eyes of Nazar himself.

*Into the eyes of god.*

The lord liked the young man's defiance. He reminded him of himself at that age. For that reason alone, he would require careful watching.

He backhanded him. "Go! You have two days to bring her to me alive!" He leaned forward, inches from the defying eyes. "Don't disappoint me. I am not a forgiving man."

The young man nodded. The hatred in Nazar's eyes proved his suspicions.

To fail was to die.

༄ঙ্গ

Andrea travelled through the night. She had left the river at noon and was approaching the house at the break of dawn. Star plodded wearily to the stables, eager for his stall and a meal.

After Andrea had bedded Star down, she headed to her own bed. She had not eaten since she had left two days ago. Well, it was more like four if you counted the nights she traveled through. Her stomach definitely did. She stepped out of the barn and into the darkness toward the house.

She never heard her approaching captors. All she remembered was fighting. Clawing at the arm squeezing her throat. Fighting for every painful breath. But she could do nothing as darkness overwhelmed her and she fell. Right into the arms of her captor.

Wynn could only watch. He hated it, but she had been warned. She had brought this upon herself.

Throughout the ride from Cresso to Reed, if she started to stir, her captor would drip some bitter liquid extracted from the naxer plant's roots into her mouth. Nature's sedative would put her out for a little while longer.

෴

Musa sat in the large, ancient room of adobe. It was not quiet; there were training sessions and all the other business of their typical day just beyond the lantern-lit room. In fact, if she looked just beyond the high archway that served as an entrance, she could see people milling about the rest of the massive palace ruins.

She breathed in deeply and let out a long, contented sigh as her slender white fingers brushed a stray strand of black hair behind her ear. Her gray eyes turned back to the empty, but soon to be filled, room. Twenty-five colorful mats lined the stone floor. At each woven mat, there was a bottle of ink, a writing utensil, and a partially filled—though mostly empty—Book.

This is where she spent a large portion of her day five days a week. Of course, every Salmday, being the first day of the week, everyone had a day of rest and worship. She got another break midweek every Nevivday when Janelle oversaw the copying for her. Other than that, this is where she spent six hours each day. Only four of those hours were spent making copies of the precious Book with the groups that moved in and out of rotation. The other two she spent making sure each copy matched the original word for word.

The first rotation of people came in and sat down. Musa watched them silently, remaining cross-legged on her mat facing the others. Every eye was soon on her.

She had a moment of amazement that she, Musa of the Third Mountain, quiet natured Musa, had come all the way from Lidian and had ended up where she was now.

An outlaw in a foreign land.

A mentor. A student.

A leader. A servant.

A Lover.

Chosen.

She had been chosen by Holy Maker Himself and now served a purpose she could have never imagined. It was a humbling thought—one that inspired her to walk the path she had been given and never turn back.

Her voice carried a soft strength and was heard clearly. "Today, we shall begin to copy the next section. For the next few days we will focus on this passage."

Everyone set to work.

Musa breathed a prayer. *Elnai, please bless these people for serving Your purpose. If it be Your will, help us to stay hidden here for a little longer so we may reach Your Lovers with Your Word.*

She looked at the open Book in her lap.

> *Light soon overcame; all who had rebelled*
> *Were forevermore from Light's Courts expelled;*
> *Beneath Light's Courts lies Void in the Shadow,*
> *Though joy above you—smothered by sorrow.*
>
> *All of the fallen—as they were since known,*
> *Were forever cast away from Light's Throne;*
> *From the Courts of Light into the Shadow*
> *Where darkness consumes all joy you may know.*
>
> *Tortured with knowledge of all they had been,*
> *Cast into the Void because of their sin,*
> *This was their judgment, their sentence remains*
> *As warning to all—stay true to Light's Name!*

శ్రీ

Andrea woke slowly, feeling sore and heavy. Her groggy head was pounding.

Throat throbbing, she sat up. She heard a clinking sound. It sounded like … *chains!* Each of her wrists and ankles had a chain that was attached to the wall. She heard a scream, then realized it was her own. *What is going on?*

"Hello?" she cried. "Somebody, please! Help me!"

An angry looking guard with arms as big as she was and a sword hanging at his side hit the bars that caged her. "Quiet!" he snarled.

"No, please! You don't understand." She got as close to the bars as her heavy chains would let her. "I'm not supposed to be here!"

A scratchy cackle interrupted her. Andrea turned to see a woman in the same chains in the seven- by seven-foot cell next to hers. She looked unhealthily underweight and had scars on her hands and face. She had several missing teeth and a raspy, sardonic voice.

"None of us are supposed to be here, girl." She leaned, her back to Andrea, against the bars that separated them and cackled again, "We're all just as innocent as you."

Andrea scrambled for words. "But I didn't do anything." Her voice cracked and she hated herself for it.

"Really?" the woman said. "They don't mark you for nothing."

"*Mark?*" she practically screamed, earning her another glare from the guard. She tried to calm down, to no avail. "I can't be marked!"

"Come on, girl, this prison." She shook her chains and faced her. "These chains. This is where they drag the marked." She spat, "Still don't believe me, do you? Check your shoulder." The glaring eyes challenged her.

Andrea tried to swallow, but the rising lump in her throat would not budge. People only got marked for things like treason, murder, and stealing from Lord Nazar. Or, if you committed a less serious crime and ran for it, you were marked for the trouble of hunting you down. Every marked person had one of two penalties. Death, or the rest of your life doing hard labor in prison. She would be gnawing at her nails, but the heavy chains made it too much work.

She finally got the courage to look at her left shoulder and found that her farmer's dress sleeve had been torn off at the seam. There, staring back at her, was the tattoo of the marked. It was red and stinging. Recently applied, but there none the less. It was a big X with a circle around it, and under it, an identification number and the reason she was marked.

Her eyes widened as she read the ugly black words. *Andrea of Cresso, marked by the order of Lord Nazar for treason against Airiss.*

No, this could not be happening. She tried to blink back the tears but they spilled over anyway.

"Treason? *Treason!*" Her voice shook as she cried, "I don't even know what it's talking about—I'm not a traitor!"

The woman laughed her hateful cackle and said, "Treason. You're not so innocent after all. Don't cry, girl. Treason does not deserve prison."

Andrea looked up suspiciously.

"Of course not. Treason deserves *death*." Hate danced in the woman's eyes as she laughed her way into a coughing fit.

Andrea scrambled into the corner, as far away as she could get from the horrible cackle and hateful eyes.

It all made sense now. Her neighbors Lisa and Mark acted the way they did because they had known she was to be marked. She would be willing to bet that the fire was no accident either. Lord Nazar probably put some of his own men up to it. It would be just like him.

But why? *Why*? She could not think of one single thing she had done to deserve this. Why her? She was just an orphaned farm girl. What had she done to get Lord Nazar's attention? She hugged her knees and cried.

~☙~

Wynn was right there in that filthy little cell with her. Again, he sang the song in a language unknown to man that quieted her spirit. And again, Andrea slept deeply in the middle of chaos.

Wynn touched her mind. "Oh Elnai, remind her of the Name she was once taught to love. The only Name that has power to save her."

He received orders to give her a dream; a dream to help her remember who she was and to Whom she belonged.

~☙~

Andrea awakened to a rough boot planted firmly in her ribs.

"Give me your hands," the guard growled.

She obediently lifted the heavy chains to be unlocked. She rubbed her aching wrists and ankles as the chains were undone.

The guard jerked her to her feet and pulled her face close to his. "Don't try anything."

Even if she wanted to, the bruising grip he had on her arm and the drawn sword in his other hand banished all thoughts of escape or freedom from her mind.

He dragged her through the dark prison and out into one of the prisoner's courtyards, a place where prisoners were forced to make heavy stone bricks and mortar to be brought to the servants, builders, and other prisoners who were constantly adding to the ever-growing castle.

He didn't slow down and she stumbled behind him. He finally stopped at the other side of the courtyard at the metal portcullis that guarded every entrance between the prison and the rest of the castle grounds.

Between the portcullis's gates there was a wall of chains and a guard. She was really getting tired of chains. Once there, the guard inspected her mark and put chains on her hands and feet. They were long enough that she could walk, but heavy enough to slow her down if she tried to run. She was then handed to another guard. He dragged her through a servant's entrance and into a finely decorated hallway which led into a huge, breathtaking room where she was presented to Lord Nazar himself.

ॐ

*This cannot be her*, thought Nazar.

It was true that Andrea was not exactly what you would consider a threat to his kingdom. She was only around five foot four inches, and though she had worked hard since she could walk, she was petite and definitely not fighter material. She stood picking at her fingernails. Her brown hair was long and wavy, and she had a few freckles scattered across her cheeks and the bridge of her nose—nine if someone counted. Long black lashes framed her big green eyes. Surely this pretty girl was not—wait. Those *eyes*.

He shuddered and blinked away the image of a different face with those same eyes. She was smaller than Andrea but the emerald gaze was the same: Bright. Full of life. Stunningly beautiful.

Yes. This was the one. He could never forget those eyes. The eyes of Tisha and Andrea.

*Her* eyes.

He felt rage churning deep within his gut and pushed all other thoughts away.

Whether Andrea looked like it or not, she was a threat. A major threat that would have to be dealt with.

The guard approached and forced the girl to kneel. Then the guard knelt as well, although he did keep his hand on her shoulder. It was obvious from the stiffness of her posture and the defiant look in her eyes that if the heavy hand of the guard was not pressing down on her shoulder, she would not be on her knees.

*Yes, she is most definitely the one.*

"Speak," Lord Nazar ordered.

The guard looked up but remained on his knees. "My sovereign lord, we bring to you," he looked at her mark, "the marked Andrea of Cresso for treason against your most glorious kingdom of Airiss, as well as his majesty, Lord Nazar of the grand capital of our land, which is known as Reed …"

ॐॐ

Andrea felt like spitting as the man, with unnecessary flattery and formality, told Nazar about things she knew she didn't do. According to the guard, she had been selling secrets, smuggling spies, stealing from the castle's armory to aid Nazar's enemies—the list went on. Apparently, she had been busy. Funny how it had slipped her mind.

She nervously chewed her bottom lip.

"On this Third Biasday of Medivmonth, we ask …"

As the guard stated the date, she was a bit surprised. Her nineteenth birthday. She was not shocked, considering her situation, that this didn't mean much to her at the moment. Her overwhelming emotions manifested themselves in a slight, visible shiver.

Her thoughts took a very sudden turn. Before she realized it, her eyes were staring blankly ahead, not seeing what was in front of them, but replaying the dream she had last night about her parents. What had happened to them? She caught a glimpse of smiling faces, but could not remember what they were smiling about. She remembered sitting captivated as her mother told her stories, and strangely, she remembered her father's sword.

She didn't realize this at the moment, but she was on to something, and it was slowly changing her. The feeling of utter despair left first: she stopped chewing her lip, and then she felt an unexplainable calm wash over her spirit.

She was suddenly returned to the scene before her by the sharp tip of the guard's sword. "Answer the question," he growled.

"I-I'm sorry. What did you say?" she stammered, feeling sick again.

"Do you deny these accusations?" he asked in an almost dignified manner, but the sword threatening to pierce her side more than represented his true feelings.

Andrea still didn't quite see what was before her. Her eyes darted back and forth, her heartbeat pounding in her head. The dream—the memories—it was all falling together.

Anger swelled in her chest. She straightened her back, lifted her chin, and stared right into the eyes of Nazar.

"Nazar, I don't know what I have to do with any of this, but apparently I've frightened you enough to lie about me. The way that I see it, you are going to kill me no matter what I do—" she took a deep breath, "so I have something to say—"

Her words were cut off by cold steel, hovering anxiously at her throat. "I wait for your command, my lord." Andrea knew this bloodthirsty guard would be only too glad to finish her.

Andrea closed her eyes. Not in fear, but in an effort to focus. Anger in its purest form throbbed in her veins. She was not entirely sure where this anger had come from, but it was right. It was justified. She was only just beginning to discover it for herself.

Nazar let out a savage laugh, and his eyes burned with hatred as he said, "Let her talk." He looked like a hungry predator. "They are seldom this feisty at the end."

"Good girl!" Wynn encouraged. "The truth will set you free!"

Her heart pounded, but she carried on, the blade still close to her throat. "Someday, someone is going to see through you. You cannot oppress us forever. You *will* fall. I am tired of you forcing people to worship either you, or else nothing. You rule this land by fear, hate, and darkness. But the light is stronger than darkness." Her heart pounded faster as holy anger was stirred anew. Her voice rose and grew stronger. "And I will *not* bow before a *pig* like you!"

She struggled to her feet. The guard was too surprised to force her down. "I hope you feel guilty for all the lives you have destroyed. They will be rewarded for their valor. And I have two names that I hope will haunt you."

His face drained of all color. *No ... She cannot possibly know.*

"Ross and Tisha of Valrine! I know what you did to them!"

"Get her *out!*" he screamed.

She shouted even as two guards rushed to take her away. She struggled and fought until they were forced to pick her up under her arms and by the legs to carry her out.

This didn't silence her. She was now breathing heavily. Her whole body seemed to expand with each breath. "That's what this is all about, is it not? You're afraid I will be like my parents! And you are wise to cower! I will fight for the truth! Thank you for bringing me here, because of you, I remember the name I was taught to love!"

"Don't let her speak that name!" Nazar shrieked.

A guard clamped a hand over her mouth but she bit down until she tasted blood. She managed to work her mouth free long enough to scream, "The Maker is the True Lord!"

The hand came down so hard she could barely breathe. She fought as hard as she could against the crushing grip all the way back to the prisons.

She was whipped and thrown into her cell. Her body felt broken, but her spirit was strangely renewed. A marvelous peace consumed her entire being, draining the anger.

Lying on her stomach in the cold dirt in a tiny cell, chained and wounded, she whispered, "You are the True Maker." And she laughed.

She had won. Though her body was bound, her soul was free! There was nothing they could do to her now. The pains of this world were only for a season. For the rest of the night, through the physical pain, she sang the name of the Maker and laughed.

The prisoners around her thought she had gone mad, did she not know she was sentenced to be burned the next day?

Maybe she was—she didn't understand it herself. Yet she knew she had won. No, that was not right, the Maker had won. And this was only the beginning.

## CHAPTER THREE

# FREE

Her hands were bound behind her so tightly that it was painful. She was actually surprised. Not even twenty-four hours ago she would have been hysterical. Here she was, tied to a stake as the executioner piled wood around her.

Nazar had assembled a crowd of thousands to watch, and those in the prisoner's courtyard were allowed to peek over the wall.

But she felt at peace. Was she scared? Yes. Of course, if it was up to her, she would not be bound to a stake that rubbed her striped back with every move. In fact, she would do away with the fire that was about to be lit all together. But in that very moment, she felt strangely at peace. Because it was not up to her whether she lived or died. Did she want to die? No! Of course not! But she could accept it.

But just because she understood that she might die, didn't mean she would go without a fight. She had been praying furiously, calling out to the Name that had enveloped her with these strange feelings.

She had also left a fist-sized bruise on a guard's face—for which she got a split lip and a bigger fist-sized bruise.

A man dressed in stately purple robes and an elaborate white headdress appeared. The heavy headdress almost seemed too large, and pulled the withered old man's wrinkled face painfully smooth. The Royal High Priest. The priest opened his arms wide, palms facing the sky, and spoke in a strong voice.

"Children of our lord, reverence yourselves as we are about to be privileged with the very presence of his sovereign majesty."

Andrea's skin crawled. She closed her eyes and focused on her breathing as the man droned on.

"And now, it is with wonderstruck awe and holy silence, that we receive our beloved lord unto ourselves."

She was removed from the stake and pushed to her knees. She looked to her left over the crowd of bowed heads and palms upturned in honor, and her heart skipped a beat. Some were also on bended knee. The priest now stood facing the direction from which Nazar would come, with his back to Andrea. Arms still spread, he bent at the waist until his upper body was parallel to the wood platform beneath them. Andrea was surprised that his headdress remained in its proper place.

Nazar finally made his appearance. To the priest he said, "You find favor with your lord, High Priest and honored servant. Rise, unless your heart bids you to linger in worship." The man stayed only a moment longer before straightening to become his lord's shadow.

All the nobles, whom Andrea recognized from yesterday's mockery of a trial, then rose to bow in the same manner as the priest and kiss Nazar's hand. After returning to their seats, they remained standing.

Nazar then turned to the crowd. "Beloved of the lord, you find favor with myself. Rise, unless your hearts bid you to linger in worship." Finally, he faced Andrea, and said, "And you, my daughter, stay still, that you might listen to the cries of your heart, and return to the adoration of your lord. Whether you are humbled or hardened, may your eternal soul find the mercy of divine favor in whatever is to come."

Andrea turned her head aside; she had never been present for such a ceremony. Nothing could have prepared her for something as twisted as this lord and his priest. Much less what was to follow these sickening events.

The ceremony completed, the priest and nobles were now seated, and the crowd waited patiently for Nazar's address.

Hate flickered in his eyes and laced his words. "This woman is a perfect example of why I simply cannot allow the fine people of my kingdom to worship false gods. This woman committed treason in the service of her so-called Lord."

The crowd murmured and Andrea breathed a silent prayer as Nazar spilled lie after lie.

He spoke as if talking to a wayward child. "You see," he said, pacing and pressing his fingertips together, "our beloved nation would be divided and therefore vulnerable. Eventually, we would destroy ourselves if we were allowed to behave the way she does in the name of religion." He shook his head as if it were a true shame. "I realize that my rulings may seem a bit harsh at times. But, good people, I only have your very best interests in mind."

His true colors began to show as he glared at Andrea with tangible hatred. "This woman wished to divide us so she must be punished!" He discreetly smirked. "Now tell me, woman. Where is your Lord of Lords now? Where is your precious Maker? I don't see Him! Do you?" He looked to the crowd. "If I was going to die in the service of religion, I would want to have a living lord that I could see. Would you go to war for an imaginary king?" He looked as if he was in deep thought. Then, with exaggerated passion said, "I'm a truly compassionate lord, beloved servants! To prove this to you, I will offer even the lowest of the low a final chance!"

*So, this is what the speech is all about,* Andrea thought with sorrow. *He is going to make an example out of me and make himself look good while doing it.*

Facing her, he extended his arms toward her dramatically and cried, "Dear child!"

If she didn't know better he would have fooled her. He was personable and very good with words—which was why so many people welcomed his oppression. Because this oppression came with promises of freedom and of justice. Andrea's stomach twisted at the thought.

"If you will only give up your false beliefs and bow before a present, *living* lord for the betterment of yourself and all of Airiss, I shall let you live."

He knew she would never willingly bow. She could see it in his eyes.

"I will only bow to the True Maker—the True Lord!" She spun on her heel and faced the crowd. "People, don't be deceived! It is time to rise against this oppression. This is not freedom! The Maker is—"

The crowd cut her off with wild, almost incoherent screams.

"She is trying to divide us against our brothers!"

"Burn her!"

"She blasphemes against our lord!"

"Silence, witch!"

Nazar spoke with exaggerated sorrow. "Why? Why do you still choose to harm the kingdom?"

He discreetly nodded and the executioner tied her back onto the pole. The ropes seemed to cut into her and her wounds felt stretched.

"My children," said the heroic Nazar, "it saddens me that we have stubborn people like this woman who ultimately end up harming themselves and everyone around them. Show your devotion to me! Bow and worship the true lord!"

"No!" Andrea cried, "Be strong! Take your freedom!"

But everyone dropped to their knees. Andrea shivered as deep-throated screams rose from a group of men. A few women cried, children were encouraged to dance.

The executioner piled the wood up around her knees and lit it. An eerie, unintelligible chant was rising from the masses. A ground-shaking boom erupted, but the people barely paused for breath.

*It couldn't be*, Andrea glanced up. *Thunder!* She looked across the once clear skies to see the biggest, darkest storm clouds she had ever seen moving toward them at an incredible speed.

ॐॐ

Nazar watched as the flames spread. He fought the urge to laugh. He had an image to uphold in front of the crowd. His eyes swept over the assembly, then back to the girl at the stake. Her lips moved in prayer, her eyes lifted to the skies.

Her big jade eyes …

Another face with those same eyes burned in his mind once.

*No!* he looked away a little too quickly, and steadied his breathing. His pulse soon raced with anger. *Pray, witch. It will do nothing. Your so-called "Lover" does not care—not even for His own.*

ॐॐ

Deafening thunder and blinding lightning shook the skies.

The flames were getting closer to Andrea's feet. The nearness of the hot flame was starting to burn her flesh.

*Maker*, she prayed, *if You are doing something here, and I know You are, can You please hurry? This is starting to hurt!*

She pulled against the ropes. Her heart was beating so fast she was sure the crowd could hear it.

She squeezed her eyes shut and stood on her tip toes. Her back protested with hot pain. She gritted her teeth against a cry. The flames were inching closer.

Suddenly, the heavens opened and rain poured down. Oh, the rain!

The fire was put out and mass chaos ensued as thunder exploded and lighting flashed rapidly among the people. The water came down.

She jerked against her bindings to no avail.

"You're a witch!" cried a nearby guard, eyes wide. "Please make it stop!"

"I can't. I'm not—"

"Please, if I cut you loose, do you promise not to hurt me? I just want this to stop!"

Andrea blinked. "I promise not to hurt you if you cut the ropes."

He cut them with trembling hands.

"I'm not a witch, but I'm definitely grateful!" she cried after the man, who was fleeing in terror.

Shoving the piled wood before her, she managed to climb out and jump off what should have been her funeral pyre and into the chaos of the crowd. She hopped back and forth on her bare feet, trying to soothe the slight burns from the proximity of the fire. She glanced at the frenzied scene around her and took off running. She threw her unbound arms out and lifted her face to the heavens. The rain washed the tears from her face.

"I love You, Maker! I know You found me, now I will find You. I don't fully understand, but I will not forget Your name."

Soaking wet and unable to tell which direction she was heading because of the storm, she ran blindly, trusting Him for direction. She ran, then walked, praising as she went, for hours. The rain gradually stopped and she finally realized it was dark. She wondered how late it was.

Putting all thoughts from her spinning mind, she finally found somewhat dry ground and slipped from consciousness. She would wake as early as possible. She should not stay out in the open, but now exhaustion left her no other choice. She physically could not go on any longer. She was not sure whether she chose to sleep or if her body simply shut down.

꙳

Musa was excited about the progress that they were making.

Maybe now they could start having a bigger influence on the many deceived souls out there and make more than a little difference. Maybe now they could *really* anger Nazar and all the other leaders that had put a price on their heads.

As she invited the first group of the day in and started copying the precious text, she ran the numbers in her head. If they stayed on schedule—which they had managed to do thus far—and each of the four groups of twenty-five managed to get a hundred copies of the day's section, they would have four hundred copies by the time they worked through the entire Book! Think of what they could do with that!

Musa breathed a prayer of thanks and marveled at how much their little band of Lovers had grown. It all started with a few people with a burning desire to always love the Maker's name and had grown to almost three hundred people.

A drop of ink dripped from her pen onto the empty page before her. With renewed focus, she dipped the pen back into the inkwell and began making up for lost time.

> *Light soon longed for intimacy*
> *With a creation, with someone like He,*
> *"Let Us make creatures," He said to His Son,*
> *"In Our Own image for companions."*

> *With His mighty breath Light made galaxies*
> *And a special world with both land and seas,*
> *He assigned a star to be warmth and light*
> *And a moon and stars were made for the night.*

*He brought forth plant life to grow and to spread—*
*Everything was done through the words He said,*
*He then made creatures to fly and to crawl*
*To climb and to walk—He created all.*

જ⚬ફ

Nazar paced in front of the two assassins who had captured Andrea.

From their kneeling position, they discreetly smiled at each other. They enjoyed seeing him so worked up.

Nazar picked up the nearest breakable thing, a piece of ancient pottery, and threw it across the room. It shattered and the nearby servants flinched.

"Somebody clean that up!" he roared.

He continued to pace and throw his fit. "She's a witch! That would explain the storm. Sorcery!" He threw his head back and let loose a maddened laugh. He quickly turned to the kneeling figures.

"She knows too much!" his expression changed from maddened to nervous as he chewed on his fingernails.

"What *does* she know?" His face changed again as red rage spread. "She knows about *Him*, and that is enough." He spat, then screamed, "Find her! Kill her! Bring me her head!"

He thought for a moment, then said, "No. Bring her here for *questioning*. Even lovers of Him feel pain." His crazed laugh sent chills up the assassins' spines. "But no. She might use witchcraft. Or worse, *He* could help her."

The girl spoke up. "My lord, I don't see what her being a Lover of the so-called Maker has to do with—"

He backhanded her so hard she saw spots. She wiped blood from her split lip with a shaking hand.

"If anyone ever says that—that *name*—I will execute them personally. Is that understood?" He turned to a servant and threw up his right hand in a frenzied motion. "Write it! I am passing a new law."

He sat on his throne deep in thought, the two waited patiently to either be given new orders or dismissed. His face was now hard and stern, but otherwise unreadable.

Finally, he looked at them and said, "I have changed my mind. Don't bring her here immediately. Follow her. Find out everything she knows. Let her betray herself, her allies, and every scrap of information she has. After she has given you what you need, bring her here. I want her to beg for mercy as I kill her. She will wish that her death was as easy as it would have been at the stake."

"How do you propose we go about this?" asked the young man.

"Use your *imagination*." His face twisted into a cruel smile.

Nazar took off one of his many rings and gave it to the assassin kneeling before him. "Do whatever needs to be done. I will double—no—triple your wages when this is over. I want her dead and I want to witness every second of her journey to death. You are dismissed."

They bowed, and started to leave, but were stopped by Nazar's next words.

"Just remember," he said slowly, "if you fail me and live, you will wish for death long before it comes for you."

They bowed again and left, seemingly unshaken.

Once they were clear of any unwanted ears, they conferred.

"I say we watch from a distance. After we get what we need, we turn her in. We do this quickly, quietly, and we get out from under Nazar's thumb," said the girl as they walked swiftly.

"I would have taken care of Nazar right then and there if I could have." He traced the hilt of his sword and smiled at the feel of it on his fingertips. "And yes, I agree that we need to get away from him. As soon as he's done with us, we'll probably end up marked ourselves. I think your suggestion will work well, but I don't want to give him too much information. I couldn't care less about *Lord* Nazar and his interests."

He smiled and looked at the ring. "Before we leave, I think our lord's treasury would be willing to fund our journey."

She smiled too. "There is no telling how expensive this trip might be. We will need a generous amount."

৵৽৽৻

Andrea stirred. *How long did I sleep?* She sat up. *Oh no … Where am I this time?* She was in a bed in a small room. No chains, no guards, no locked doors. That was a good sign.

She started to get up to creep over to the cracked door, but got so dizzy she was forced to lie back down. Her head hurt unbearably.

Her stomach had given up on food and was eating itself. Her ripped back hated every movement.

Footsteps.

She panicked. She forced herself to sit up and looked around for a weapon. She grabbed a heavy vase.

"Why do you have Mommy's vase?"

She was so startled she nearly dropped it. A little girl, no older than five, peeked out from the doorway.

She put it back down. "Um, I don't know," she said.

"You don't look mean," said the little girl with a perfectly straight face.

"Mean?"

"Mommy said I cannot come in because you might be a mean person."

"Well, your mommy sounds like a wise woman," she answered carefully. "Do you know where your mommy is?"

Andrea heard a door open and the little girl ran off.

"Mommy, she does not look mean."

"I told you not to go in there."

"I just talked to her by the door. I didn't go in the room."

"You *talked* to her? Go outside right now!"

She heard quick little footsteps and the front door open and close. Then heavier footsteps her way and a woman's voice muttering about going outside for half a second and "that one already getting into trouble."

She lay down on her stomach. There was nothing she could really do. She was in no shape for a fight. Even if she was, the woman had a little girl. If she turned her in, well, she couldn't blame her. Andrea was marked, and to help someone who was marked would earn yourself a matching tattoo.

A tall woman—by Airissian standards—walked in, crossed her arms, and looked straight into Andrea's eyes.

"I would like to know exactly what you said to my daughter." Her voice was hard and emotionless.

"Well, nothing really," she shrugged. "She told me that you said she was not supposed to talk to me and that I didn't look mean. And, honestly, I told her you were wise for it."

That got her an arched eyebrow from the older woman.

"You probably know that I am marked," Andrea stated simply.

"Yes," the woman replied dryly, "I did know that. Your mark says treason. Would you like to elaborate on that?"

Andrea sighed. "I might as well tell you the truth." *Alright, Maker, here it goes.* "I have been an orphan since I was four. I was raised on a farm in Cresso by a family that took me in, but I am originally from Valrine."

Andrea sighed deeply. Who knew that even talking could hurt? "I had no idea that I was to be marked until they grabbed me from the farm and I woke up with the tattoo."

The woman didn't seem to believe her story so far. Andrea didn't blame her.

"When they brought me before Nazar the pieces began to fall into place. I had some memories of my parents, but nothing much. But as I was held on my knees I remembered something crystal clear—the True Maker."

That brought up the woman's other eyebrow.

"My parents had raised me to love the name of my Maker, but over the years I had buried the memory. As I think back now, I remember the day I had tried so hard to forget."

She closed her eyes tight and tried to keep her voice from shaking. "Nazar is the reason I am an orphan. My parents hid me in a secret place in our house that I was not even aware of, and Nazar himself was there when they took my parents. They set the house on fire but somebody—I still don't know who, all I remember was that he was very tall—rescued me. I wandered around for a while. The stranger walked with me and held my hand until the woman who raised me, Flora, saw me when she and her husband, Judd, were riding down the road in a buggy. They picked me up—and now that I think about it, I'm not sure where the man who rescued me went at this point—and took me to the farm where I lived for the next fifteen years."

Andrea paused for a breath, her head throbbing. She had to struggle to make coherent sentences. "I remember now how people used to come to our house a lot and talk to my parents. I think that my parents were a part of some sort of resistance against Nazar. But they were ultimately taken because they bowed only to the Maker, the true Lord of Lords. Somehow Nazar found out about me. And because of my parents, I was marked for treason. And because I would not kneel, and stood against Nazar in the name of the Maker,

I was sentenced to burn. But the Maker preserved me and here I am today."

The woman looked at her no differently than when she had started.

"I'm not even entirely sure who the Maker is, all I know is that He is the Lord and He found me and He rescued me. I promised Him I would find Him too."

Andrea sat, deep in thought for a moment.

"I know you must take care of your daughter and I will not blame you for turning me in. But with the true Maker as my witness, I tell you only truth."

"Are you aware that Nazar issued a law this very morning that the penalty for speaking that Name is death?"

"No," Andrea answered honestly, "but I am afraid they will have to add another offense to my ever-growing list because I will never again forget the name of my Maker." A surreal wonder warmed her stomach. "I still don't quite understand it, but this is real. My 'execution' turned miracle is evidence enough."

To her surprise, the woman's face broke into a glowing smile. "Honey, there are few enough people like you left." She laughed softly as she uncrossed her arms and shook her head. "I don't plan on turning you in."

Andrea was shocked. "Really?"

"I was going to turn you in if your story didn't check out," she winked, "but I thought it was you. You could be your mother's younger twin."

Andrea put on a confused smile at the statement.

"I know that is not exactly possible," the woman said, "but with the way you look and act I cannot help but see Tisha. And you have her beautiful green eyes."

"You knew my mother?" a bewildered Andrea asked.

"Yes, but I have not seen her since I stopped fighting with the Resistance when I had Dory."

"What do you mean?" She shot up, then grimaced at her back's protests. "My parents were executed fifteen years ago."

"I will tell you all about it in a minute." She went to the closet and pulled out some clothing. "Right now I am going to dish you up some hot soup while you get out of those muddy things. I have a dress you can use. It will be a bit big and long on you, but you can manage." And with that, she left.

Andrea got out of her battered, muddy clothing and into the stiff, clean clothes. It hurt her raw back but she bit her lip and did it anyway. The dress had buttons all the way down past the waist of the dress and she would have to ask her hostess to help her—Andrea didn't want to even attempt it with her back. It hurt to move around too much so she would just take it easy until it was time to go. She lay down on her stomach.

With a gentle knock, her hostess soon reappeared.

"I'm Rhoda," she said as she closed the door behind her. "I know I didn't tell you earlier. Oh, Maker!" Rhoda set the bowl of soup down on the table beside the bed and gaped at Andrea's wounds. "I didn't know they had whipped you! Those are deep, how did you walk?"

"It was not pleasant," Andrea admitted.

Rhoda was angry. "One day they are going to go too far and somebody big enough to do something will stop them!" She handed her the bowl of soup. "Eat it slowly, honey." She left the room with an angry, purposeful stride.

Andrea had not eaten in days; it was hard to eat slowly. She was about halfway through the bowl when Rhoda returned with some rags, a bucket of water, and small jar of what appeared to be ointment.

"You can finish this in a minute," she said gently. "I need to take care of your poor back."

Taking the bowl from Andrea, Rhoda went to work immediately. She wet the rag and carefully dabbed at the younger woman's torn flesh, then gently applied the cold ointment. Even though Rhoda barely touched her with the rag, and was gentle with the ointment, it still was painful.

Andrea kept her eyes closed and her teeth clenched.

Rhoda talked as she worked. "You see, there have always been people who didn't agree with Nazar, but it was your parents who really brought us together. When more and more people joined the Resistance, we were getting big enough to make a difference, and Nazar knew that.

"So Nazar began passing laws and making a god out of himself to stop the Resistance. One day, he went so far that he gathered up the people of the capital city, and surrounding places like Cresso and Valrine to come bow before him. And this wasn't just a respectful tip of the head, this was becoming worship. Nazar announced that he had appointed a 'royal high priest, to guide the people of Airiss in the worship of the divine, and to intercede to the lord for his children.' After ordaining the Royal High Priest, they began a twisted ceremony—likely much like the one you had to experience at your execution."

At Andrea's shocked look, Rhoda was quick to say, "Oh, I wasn't there, dear. I just know how things have been. I may not be off with the Resistance, but I still keep an eye on the Capitol. You'll find there's still some—not many, but some—who stay simply to keep the Resistance updated on what's happening here.

"But as I was saying, after the priest went through his twisted speech, we were called to 'Bow! Bow in worship and adoration to our lord—his sovereign majesty, Lord Nazar!'

"First the nobles on the platform went through their rituals. All but two. Nazar's brother and sister-in-law refused to bow, and they were executed on the spot. We have more reason than that to believe Boaz and Katrine were Lovers of the Maker. Their bodies weren't even removed before the blasphemous call was made to the rest of us.

"He used the fear of death to drive people to their knees. He had killed his own brother and everyone knew he would not hesitate to execute anyone else who defied him. It worked on many of us. Most were scared enough to abandon the Resistance and bow down with everyone else. Of the original five hundred, only one hundred fifty didn't bow."

*That is amazing*, Andrea thought. *They persevered through all of that. Maker, bless those faithful few.*

"I was there." Rhoda's voice grew softer, betraying her emotion. The memories were painted so deeply in her mind that it seemed like yesterday. Every detail was clearly relived as the story was told. "My husband and I were some of the faithful, with Ross and Tisha leading us on. We suspected what was going to happen. Nazar's men followed us to our homes.

"They hauled all of us to prison and burned our houses. They didn't mark us or even ask our names. There were just too many people. We were all going to be executed the next morning.

"But the Maker was with us, and we knew it. We sang through the night. Our Maker really is amazing. He touched the guard's heart, who, in turn, set us free. Now that guard—his name is Jay—is one of the Resistance's top fighters."

Rhoda's face softened further and a single tear traced her cheek as she resumed her story. "The early morning light had barely begun to dawn by the time we reached the portcullis. This portcullis led outside the castle and they trapped us in between the two gates. About one hundred and ten people, including your mother, were past it, about fifteen of us were trapped in between the two portcullises, and the other twenty-five, including your father, were still in the courtyard. Ross and three other men stayed behind and worked the cranks so the rest of us could escape. They … didn't make it in time."

Andrea thought, feeling emotional, *Those four men were heroes. My father was a hero. The Maker will reward and honor those men for their valor.*

"There you are, honey," Rhoda said with a sigh as she finished up. She wiped her eyes on her sleeve and her voice returned to normal. "I know it is painful, but it will help you heal faster. We will just leave the back of the dress unbuttoned. We don't want any needless rubbing and irritation. My husband is away on business so it is just us women."

Andrea read between the lines. Rhoda's husband was with the Resistance.

"So does my mother know I am alive?"

Rhoda pursed her lips and shook her head. "She thought they lost you in the fire."

And with that, Rhoda left Andrea to finish her soup. Andrea ate a second bowl of soup and could have eaten a third, but Rhoda insisted that she rest. And she did. She fell asleep before dark and slept well into the next morning.

Once again, Rhoda tended her wounds and filled her full of delicious soup. Little Dory also came and visited her; Andrea kept the sheet over her back so Dory would not see her wounds.

That night Andrea got up and went to talk to Rhoda.

The two women whispered so they would not disturb the sleeping Dory. "Rhoda, thank you for your kindness, but I cannot endanger you and Dory any longer. I am leaving now."

"But you need to heal," Rhoda argued softly. "You are in no condition to travel."

Andrea put a hand on the taller woman's shoulder. "Thank you, Rhoda, but you know what they will do to you and Dory if they find out you helped me. I have to go. I know of a place." *He who has ears, let him hear*, played in the back of her mind.

"You're right," Rhoda admitted reluctantly. "I'm sorry I cannot tell you where your mother is. I always worked from here. My husband will know, but I am not sure when he will be back."

"Thank you so much!"

The women embraced, and Andrea turned to go.

"Wait! Let me send you off with some things." Without waiting for an answer, Rhoda quickly gathered supplies. "Here, slip into the bedroom and change."

Andrea did as she was told. She emerged from the little bedroom moments later in a good pair of boots and a dark brown tunic made of thick, heavy, durable material with a belt around the waist. From the belt hung a canteen on the right and a hunting sword in its sheath on the left. The sword was around two feet long, with its single edge sharp and deadly. Its hilt was nothing special, but it was efficient.

Andrea was surprised that the tunic and boots fit her perfectly. She had wondered why Rhoda had made so many trips to town. She only wished she could repay her.

Rhoda handed her a satchel with a small amount of dried venison, the ointment that was used to treat her back, a flint, an extra set of clothes, a heavy hooded cloak, and five gold coins.

"No, I am taking enough already," Andrea insisted. "Keep the money."

"Take the money." Rhoda smiled. "We'll be fine. Tell my husband that we are well if you see him. His name is Timius, but he is called Tim."

"Tim. I will." Andrea paused before closing the door. "I only wish I could repay you."

"Stay true to the Maker and show Nazar who the true Lord is. That will be payment enough."

Andrea smiled at her one last time before disappearing into the night.

"Oh, Maker," she whispered out loud, "don't let this blessed family be harmed because of me."

## CHAPTER FOUR

# LET HIM HEAR

A ndrea walked under the stars for two hours before she finally reached the farm. This was where people were kind enough to take her in, feed her, clothe her, and educate her. Judd had his flaws, but he had provided for her for fifteen years. Sometimes they would hardly earn enough to live on, but they still took care of her even though she was not really theirs. And Flora had always been kind to her. Andrea loved her dearly.

She took a deep breath as she stopped at the door. It was about three in the morning.

She knocked gently. "Flora?" No answer. She would just sneak into her room and get what she needed. But the door would not open.

Strange, they didn't usually bar the door. But she was not usually marked either.

She sighed deeply. Judd and Flora knew that if anyone was seen with her they would be marked as well. She didn't want to cause them any trouble so she turned to leave.

"Andrea!" came the hushed voice.

Andrea turned to see the kitchen window open with Flora waving.

Andrea smiled. "Flora, thank you—"

"Shh!" The dear woman nearly panicked. "Judd would have my head if he knew!"

"I'll go. I can't cause you any trouble."

"No! I can help you. I have been waiting for you." She hurried to explain. "Take Star and whichever saddle you need."

"Oh, Flora, I can't." Andrea was touched—she was in need of a good horse—but also cautious. "Judd will be suspicious. Besides, I have only five pieces of gold and Star would be worth twenty and the saddle at least another three. Just let me get some things from my room and—"

"No," Flora interrupted. "If your things go missing then Judd and Lord Nazar will know without doubt that you were here." A sly smile eased across her face. "But silly me, you know how I always forget to shut the gates."

"You are too kind."

Leaning through the low window, Andrea hugged the woman who had done her best to be her mother.

"Here," said the younger woman as she pulled away, "take what I have; I know it is not nearly enough, but—"

"Don't mention it, dear." Flora took the five coins and reached into her pocket. She produced a small key looped through a gold chain. "You were wearing this when I found you." She let it fall into Andrea's open palm. "Your mother must have slipped it onto your neck before they took her."

"You knew my mother?" Andrea had trouble controlling the volume of her voice. She slipped the chain around her neck, feeling a little angry and no small amount of surprise. "I cannot believe you knew her." She shook her head and breathed in slowly. There was no time for this. She made an effort to hide her emotions. "What is the key for?"

"I'm afraid I don't know what it is for." Flora's voice quavered. "And yes, I knew Tisha but I failed her, her and the Maker."

Andrea's eyes grew wide, as shock completely replaced any feelings of anger. "You were?"

"Yes." Flora squeezed her eyes closed in an attempt at keeping the tears from spilling over, but her quivering voice betrayed her. "I was one of the many that bowed down to Nazar the day that we were forced to make a stand or betray the true Lord. It is something that I have had to live with." Her wet brown eyes refused to meet Andrea's. "Something I cannot hope to be forgiven for."

"There is still hope for you." Andrea felt compassion that surprised her. She hardly recognized her own voice. Were these words really hers? "The True Maker has not given up on you. He is waiting for you to return. His forgiveness and compassion are limitless. He only waits for you to let Him in. He found me, I know He can find you." Andrea understood and believed this with everything in her. The realization came as a shock to her.

She was scared. She was confused. She had no idea what would happen. She didn't understand everything.

But ever since that dream, in the middle of the prison, she felt like forgotten coals of a once roaring fire were being fanned into flame once more. Like she was ankle deep in an ocean of water and about to go deeper. She felt as though something unseen was directing her back to a path she had once known long ago. A path that would lead to greater things—and greater troubles.

Who was she? A small and unimportant farm girl who never knew her parents? Who was she to be talking like this? Did she even fully understand it herself?

Yet she felt a peace. And a hunger. She didn't have all the answers. But she had a start. And she had a longing to know this Maker for Who He was. To understand what would drive her parents to risk losing everything. Even to die. She had only scratched the surface.

She longed for the truth her parents had known.

The truth she was only beginning to discover but was already seeping into her very being, making her into so much more than just a farm girl.

Truth that *sought her out* with a fierce passion.

Truth she would uncover.

"Go," Flora urged, "before the morning light betrays you." Andrea started to leave. "And thank you. Thank you for remaining strong in our Maker."

"You can too," Andrea said gently. "He truly loves you and nothing you or anyone else does can change that."

Flora only smiled through watery eyes. "Hurry, the night is almost gone." As the two women hugged one last time, Flora discreetly dropped the five gold pieces back into Andrea's satchel.

Flora too was filled with wonder at this farm girl who sought for Truth.

The same Truth she had once known.

Truth that still called to her after she had spit in the face of the Holy Maker.

෨෧

No matter how many times it happened, Wynn was always amazed at the fact that the Maker of the universe even remembered people like Flora. People who had publicly disowned Him and fallen away from His path. But He not only remembered them, He willingly forgave them and touched their broken souls.

Wynn had seen the very face of the Maker, had worshiped at His feet, had fulfilled His works, but still could not begin to comprehend the compassion He faithfully showed these sinful rebels that took His mercy for granted. Yes, the Maker would be overjoyed to welcome back this woman with open arms if only she would ask.

෨෧

Andrea was careful to leave all the gates open so Flora's story would be believable. She even released the old mare, but she knew that the horse had lived on the farm her whole life and would not go anywhere.

*Holy Maker*, she prayed silently, *please don't let Flora catch any grief for this.*

෨෧

The two assassins rode toward the farm. She would likely show up there. Even if she was not there they would search the house. They hoped to surprise them, search the house, and question them. Their midnight visit would hardly be expected and would make it harder for Judd and Flora to hide anyone or anything and get their lies straight, assuming they were helping her.

Suddenly, their horses squealed and reared, throwing both riders to the ground, unharmed but shaken.

The poor animals allowed their furious riders to mount, but refused to take another step even though their seething masters beat them and screamed. The poor beasts just stood there, paralyzed with fear, showing no sign of noticing their riders' tantrums.

៛∽๑

Baros Yosim stood, unmoving, and watched the two throw their fit. They may not have known about his presence, but their mounts did, and they were well aware of his flaming sword.

He heard the swish of wings and the soft crunch of grass as a messenger's feet met the ground.

"Hello, friend," Yosim said, never turning away from the horses, "is she well on her way?"

"Yes, Baros," the smaller warrior answered, "Andrea is riding for the Tree of Promise as we speak."

"Good," he said, unfolding his wings and sheathing his now cold sword. "Then I shall let them pass. I will report our progress to the Maker. He will surely be pleased."

៛∽๑

As if released from a trance, the horses suddenly continued on, much to the surprise of their young riders.

"I could already hear Nazar ranting about how we could not even get to Cresso without incident," said the blond girl, touching her split lip.

"I don't want to hear that name," her partner snapped. "We are rid of him for this journey, however short it may be." He smiled. "I guess we can thank our little marked witch for giving us relief from him during this pointless little game."

"It is always more fun when they put up a fight."

៛∽๑

"*He who has ears, let him hear,*" rang in Andrea's mind as she rode toward the river, toward the tree. She didn't know what she was looking for, but she kept heading northwest toward the mountains. *Alright, Maker, I guess I am going to find this tree. I don't know why, but it just feels right.*

Andrea mused about the fact that she was talking in her head to Someone she could not see. Yet Andrea knew she wasn't mad.

Somehow, she was far from it. Somehow, He heard her. She could feel it.

She found the stream at dawn, and stopped to dip into her provisions. After she had eaten, Andrea let Star graze as she dozed on her stomach in the shade for about an hour. Her back was getting unbearable. She tried to apply some more of the ointment that Rhoda had sent with her, but her entire back was striped with ripped flesh and she could not reach it all. The ointment itself hurt too.

She finally forced herself back into the saddle after splashing her face with the cold stream water in an attempt to wake up.

∂∽∾

Musa was looking over the day's passage when there was a knock at the doorway. She looked up to see Riven, Timius, and some others at the archway.

"We will try to be finished in time for your session," Timius said.

"Thank you," Musa answered.

About a dozen people set to work right away. The place that they called home was an ancient adobe palace ruin. When they had found it, it had been in fairly good shape. They had restored it well, but occasional patching was required.

The patchwork was finished quickly and Musa helped them sweep the place clean. Then the workers went to the next room in need and the first group came in to copy the precious Book.

> *Light stirred up the dust and stooped to the ground,*
> *He formed eight people—what great joy He found!*
> *Four pairs He made them—Four male, four female,*
> *Some had features dark, others He made pale.*

> *Some hair was tight curls, some was very straight,*
> *Each color varied, His delight was great!*
> *Each made different, a gift He gave each,*
> *Some passion to build, for music, to teach.*

> *He gave others spirits of strength, of meekness,*
> *The love of nature—He loves uniqueness!*

*Perfect innocence—to all He gave this;*
*They knew not wrong, pain, shame—but only bliss.*

*Created only to love and be loved,*
*They praised Holy Light on His Throne above;*
*In the cool morning, Light and Son came down*
*And walked with Their people to Their great renown.*

*He gave them each names and said they would be*
*The start of nations and be blessed greatly;*
*They called Light Maker, on Him love they cast,*
*He called them Lovers—but it would not last.*

⤫⤫

Andrea rode until noon before she finally saw the tree. It looked like an ancient weeping willow, but she knew it was not. It was about forty feet tall with a huge knotted trunk that was a little less than two feet in diameter. Its branches stretched as far as the bank on both sides of the narrow stream and the tips of its leafy curtain hovered just above the surface of the slow-moving water. Its trunk split a third of the way up, twisted into a large oval, then merged back into one tree for the remaining third. It was majestic and mysterious; it seemed as if it hid the secrets of nations.

Andrea quietly dismounted and painfully unsaddled her faithful horse. She patted him and he nickered before turning to drink and graze, grateful for a break. She was grateful too. He was smoothly gaited and she was an experienced rider, but her back protested every step and movement.

She put her canteen in the saddle bag along with her other supplies, laid her hunting sword in the grass, and stepped out of her boots. The soft mud squished between her toes as she waded in the ankle-deep water. She gently pushed through the thick, swaying curtain that encircled the tree. Splashes of green sunlight peeked through and the cold water tickled her ankles. She stopped in front of the tree and ran a hand down the bark.

"Alright, Maker, I did what the stranger said," she prayed out loud. "I don't know why I did, do You?" A new thought flashed across her mind. "Did you send him there?"

She thought about her encounter with the stranger. He had said her life was in danger and to come here. He seemed to have known that if she talked to her neighbor it would put her in danger and had even helped her escape. Then she had felt this need to come here ever since.

"Well, whether I am foolish to come or not, I am here. Holy Maker, what is so important about this tree?"

Suddenly, the sunlight reflected, catching her eye. Andrea noticed for the first time how there was a large hole in the center of the tree, at the bottom of the loop where it first split off. You would only notice it if you looked straight down, almost from directly above it. Andrea did a double take. The sunlight was hitting something just right.

Driven by curiosity, she brushed aside the dead leaves and, to her surprise, found a box. She looked over her shoulder and then pulled it out. The heavy wooden box was sturdy, with rusted metal hinges and an equally rusted lock. She nearly dropped it at first, surprised at its weight.

She brought the box to the shore and wiped it clean of all the dust and dirt it had accumulated over time.

On top, someone had carved the words, "*The Maker is the Lord of Lords. Stand strong in His Promise.*"

Andrea pulled at the chain around her neck and the little key slipped out from behind the neck of her tunic.

*What if?*

She slipped off the chain and looked at the key. It was worth a try. She put the key into the lock. It fit, but the rust made it hard to tell whether it was supposed to or not. She tried turning the key, it slowly complied. Andrea's stomach turned flips as she slowly opened the lid. The hinges squeaked and complained, but allowed her to open the heavy box. Inside was a book, a few inches thick, with no title and a faded yellow letter.

Andrea picked up the letter with trembling fingers and carefully unfolded the yellowed pages. In some places the words were faded or smudged, but they were readable. Tears filled her eyes as she read.

*Dear Andrea,*

*At the time that I am writing this letter, we are living in Valrine and you have recently passed your third year. We have taken you here before and you have* always loved it. So because of that, as well as the meaning of the Tree itself, we have hidden this here in hopes of your finding it.

*Yes,* it was all coming back to her, *we would have picnics, Mother would tell me stories, and Papa would let me splash in the water on these very banks.* She remembered for a moment, then turned back to the letter.

*Since you are reading this letter, it means that neither your father nor I are able to tell you this ourselves, because something happened to us before you were old enough. We cannot give away too much information, for fear of this letter falling into the wrong hands, but we will tell you enough so that, were anything to happen to us, you would not be pulled into Nazar's web of lies. I assure you that we would never break the laws of our land unless it would mean breaking the teachings of the Maker, The One True and Reigning Lord.*

*Since you read this now, it means that Nazar or some other evil ruler has forced the people of the nation to choose a master. Him, whose reign will die away, or the Maker, who is the rightful and just Ruler. We will always stand for the Maker, and this is the reason why you must hear this from a letter. Your father and I pray that it will never come to this, but we fear that it shall. But no matter what is done to us, it is only temporary, and we will still have something they can never take away. The love of the Maker and the promise of justice through Elnai. So if we are gone, it is because evil feared Truth.*

*I know you have a lot of questions, and I could fill hundreds of pages, but we cannot tell you everything in this letter. But don't worry, every important question will find its answer in this Book.*

*It was inspired by the Maker Himself and written by faithful men and woman that lived in different ages and generations, yet it all matches up. It all makes sense when you compare their words.*

*Believe it. Hide it in your heart. Nothing, Andrea, is more important than truth, and this Book was breathed by Truth.*

*If you believe nothing else, believe the Book. For the Book will show you the Maker, and the Maker will show you life. True life. Not the season of existence we call living, but real, everlasting life in His presence built on His love and mercy.*

*Always stand for the Maker. You cannot serve two masters. You cannot be loyal to both. There is a line that was drawn countless ages ago. You, Andrea, must choose between right and wrong, light and darkness, mercy and condemnation. You cannot avoid this choice. No one can. If you choose to serve no one but yourself, you have chosen. And you have chosen a path that leads you into darkness. Remember, the pain of this world is only for a moment, but the reward for faithfulness lasts even beyond this universe.*

*We pray that we can tell you this in person, but there are no certainties in a once perfect, but now fading world that is slowly destroying itself.*

*But, Andrea, never lose hope. Never forget the love of the Maker. Never give in to this seemingly hopeless situation. For there is yet hope. There is the Promise. The Maker is Lord of Mercy, and Elnai is Prince of Peace. There will be justice in the end. When will that be? No one knows. Only the Maker knows the day that every knee of every power and person will bend before the true Lord of Lords. Be ready, but continue on His path. Even in your darkest hour, watch. For He is coming. And He is bringing judgment.*

*Remember the Promise! Stay true to the Lord of Lords!*

*With all our love,*

*Ross of Valrine, Lover of Elnai*

*Tisha of Valrine, Lover of Elnai*

Andrea read the letter over and over again, but the same questions still lingered in her mind. *What did they mean by the "meaning of the tree?" Who is Elnai? What is this Promise? What did her parents mean by "every power?"* Her eyes finally shifted to the Book. *What is so special about this Book?*

She carefully folded the letter and put it back into the box. This letter seemed to have left her with more questions than answers.

She picked up the heavy book, and dusted the brown cover. Wait, it did have a title. She looked at the strange symbols but could not even begin to decipher their meaning. It was not Ancient Tongue, but from her very limited knowledge on the subject, she thought there may be a vague resemblance. She blew on the Book and dusted it again. Looking closer, she saw that it read: *Writhrial Tose Ra Lindrene.* What that meant, she had no idea.

Her mother's words interrupted her train of thought, *Every important question will find its answer in this Book.* Andrea's fingers traced the strange characters on the cover, *Well, Maker, my parents thought it was important, and I guess it won't hurt to try it. I just hope it's in my language. I can't read this writing on the front.*

The pages were yellow and stiff from its idle years. The words were carefully penned in ink. Andrea knew it would have taken months, maybe even years, to write this book. She read the first page.

*This sacred book contains the truths of all things, given to His Lovers by Elnai, to show he who has ears to hear what has, what is, and what will soon take place. This is the living word, the testimony, and the very heart of the Maker and Elnai. Blessed is the one who has ears to hear the words of this record of history, wisdom, prophecy, and truth. Blessed are those who hear it and write upon the tablet of their hearts what is written in it.*

*For one who seeks truth seeks life, and one who seeks life finds the Maker, Who is the Author of life. May these words never fall to deaf ears and cold hearts, but instead cause life to spring anew. Blessed is the one who never lets these truths stray far from his lips.*

Andrea started to flip through the pages. It was filled with passages of poetry. Some were words of wisdom, others told stories, and still more held prophesies. Then something caught her eye. It was about the Tree of Promise.

She mouthed the words as she read,

*The Tree of Promise forever stands*
*Promising justice throughout the lands;*
*It watches the ages pass away;*
*Like His promise, it is here to stay.*

*Three Trees are scattered across this land*
*Proclaiming the Maker's healing hand,*
*Few know where one of the three Trees dwells—*
*Even fewer know the promise as well.*

*It stands to remind all that will hear*
*That Elnai's reign is still drawing near;*
*Just as the trunk has broken apart,*
*All of the world has hardened its heart.*

*Cannot serve two lords, nor walk two paths;*
*Divided, we all suffer His wrath.*
*But just as the Tree is whole again,*
*Elnai will free this world from its sin.*

> *The Tree and His promise will never fade,*
> *Remaining untouched by sword or spade;*
> *Evil may try to destroy the light,*
> *But the Tree and His promise stand bright.*

> *The darkness will try to smother you out—*
> *But stay strong in Him and never doubt;*
> *They shall be punished for all your grief,*
> *Pain you bear will find His relief.*

*That is amazing, Lord Maker,* Andrea thought in awe, *I don't deserve this promise … Now Who is this Elnai?*

She flipped through the pages. Finally, near the end of the book, she found an entry about Elnai. She flipped a couple of pages ahead to see how long it was. *That is a lot!* She kept turning page after page, *Elnai must be pretty important. Look at all these pages! I am definitely not going to finish reading about Him today.*

She started to read some more, but decided to save it for later and ride further away. She put the Book and the letter into the saddlebag and slowly saddled Star. Her back was hurting worse. She started to mount but could not stand the pain and slipped to the ground. She reached up from her kneeling position beside the horse and undid the buckle underneath his belly. The saddle slid off and Star walked away, confused.

She slowly crawled over to the stream, fighting tears. "Oh, Maker!" she cried aloud. "I cannot keep traveling like this!" Trying to find relief, she lay on her stomach. The water was deep enough to put a shallow cover of water over her damaged flesh. The water felt cool and, after the initial stinging from contact, felt good. She had pushed herself too hard, but what other choice did she have?

❧❦

Wynn hurt with her. If she would have listened in the first place she would not have been whipped, and she would have been far enough ahead of the assassins on her trail.

He placed a glowing hand on her shoulder. "Come on, Andrea," he urged gently, "they will be here soon. I know it is painful, but you must ride."

He turned to greet the messenger who had just arrived silently behind him. Messengers, though slightly smaller than warriors, were still beautiful and capable in battle.

"Hello, friend," he said warmly. "What brings you here?"

The messenger smiled back. "The Maker sends me with a message."

"I'm listening," he replied, hoping for good news.

"The Maker has heard her prayers and realizes that she is in no condition to travel. He said He grants you power to stir the waters. If she truly loves the Name of her Maker, the stirred water will restore her."

Wynn could already feel the healing power of the Maker coursing through his body. "Thank you. It will be done."

The messenger, his task completed, unfolded huge shimmering wings and flew to his next destination.

Wynn, with the Maker's power, stirred the waters of the shallow stream.

つ◆つ

Andrea lay stomach-down with her cheek on the dirt bank. The nonstop travel was catching up to her. Exhaustion, weary muscles, and burning wounds all hit her in full force. She was sinking into an overwhelming pit of absolute despair in her hopeless situation. She tried not to cry. Her thoughts scattered in a thousand directions.

Suddenly, the words of her mother flicked across her mind, *Remember, the pain of this world is only for a moment, but the reward for faithfulness lasts even beyond this universe.* Andrea thought that sounded familiar. *Where have I heard that before? Oh, right! In the Book's section about the Tree of Promise it said something like that.* The thoughts flowed. *The darkness will try to smother you out, but stay strong in Him and never doubt. They shall be punished for all your grief. Pain you bear will find His relief.*

Andrea realized how fast the once-trickling water around her was moving. She stood up painfully.

She was close to the center of the stream. Well, it was getting to be more like a raging river now. The water seemed to circle around her as if she was in the center of an ever-growing whirlpool.

Fear rose in her racing heart. "Maker——" As soon as the word escaped her lips, the water twisted up, enclosing her in a giant tube. She screamed just as the water came crashing down on her.

&#8253;&#8253;

The pair looked down on Andrea from behind a large rock farther up the mountain. They could hear her voice as she spoke, but could not make out what she was saying. From where they were, it would be difficult for her to spot them, but they could see every move she made as long as she stayed in the open.

They had taken a different path up the mountain than she and had not even seen her until they were ahead of her. They had spotted her about the time she was crawling into the water.

The blond girl squinted down at her. "After the lashes she received in prison I am surprised she was able to ride at all."

"The water."

"What?"

"The water," he said. "It's moving faster."

The young woman nodded.

Andrea stood up. She seemed to be causing the water to act this way. They saw her mouth move, then, without warning, the water encircled and engulfed her.

Both of them had seen and done terrible things, but they both bolted completely behind the boulder and cowered.

Each saw fear in the other's eyes.

Her voice quavered. "Do you think she really *is* a witch? You saw what she did to that water."

He tried to act as though he was not affected, but was not very successful. "Calm down," he snapped. "She is *not* a witch!"

They cautiously peeked around.

&#8253;&#8253;

As quickly as the water covered her, it washed away. She stood in the middle of the now gently flowing stream. It was like nothing had happened. But, she was soaked to the bone and still shocked.

*Maker, I am getting out of here. Just please* … she was going to say help her ride through the pain. But there was no pain. She carefully reached her hand down the back of her wet tunic as far as she could reach. Instead of feeling torn flesh, her fingers felt smooth skin that was as soft as a baby's.

She could only stand there and beam, *Holy Maker! You healed me!* She happened to glance down at her shoulder. Her mark, it was gone! "I guess You didn't want that ugly black ink telling everyone where I belong. I belong to You, not in one of Nazar's prisons!" she threw her head back and laughed. And for a moment, she danced, jumped, and laughed with the utter joy of a child. The Maker had made her whole.

৵৽

Two pairs of eyes widened and eyebrows shot up into hairlines.

The blond trembled. "She *is* a witch! She healed herself! And look at her! She is obviously *mad*. What do we do?"

Both were completely terrified for the first time in years.

The white-faced man tried to regain his composure. "Well." He swallowed. "She is *not* a witch! It must have been some sort of trick. Well, I will not be fooled." He started looking like his old self again. "We stick to the plan."

৵৽

Flora finished up the breakfast dishes. She had had a lot on her mind lately. *Where is Andrea? Is she okay? Is she still running? Did she find somewhere safe to stay? Has she found what the key was for?*

But the thought that refused to go away was: *Could Andrea be right? Could the Maker forgive me? After what I have done, would He take me back?*

Flora felt a pang of guilt as she remembered that day. The day she gave in to fear and bowed before a man. The day she betrayed the true Lord. The last day she ever prayed to the Maker.

*I cannot hope to be forgiven.* A silent tear slid down her plump, red cheek. *I don't deserve it.*

*Does anyone really deserve the goodness of their Maker?* a warrior asked, whispering into her thoughts.

*I had my chance. There is no hope for me.*

*Then there is no hope for anyone.*

*But I did the unforgivable.*

*Who told you that it was unforgivable? Where in the Maker's Book does it say that? Does the Maker not forgive through the blood of Elnai?*

Flora was weeping now. She was thankful that Judd was gone.

The warrior continued to speak into her thoughts.

*All fall short of the glory of the Maker. People make mistakes. You have. Andrea has. Tisha has. What matters is what you do after you realize what you have done wrong.*

*There is nothing I can do!*

*You are right. There is nothing you can do. That is why the Holy Maker sent Elnai. Ask. Elnai already made the way. Ask and you will be forgiven.*

Flora shakily rose from the kitchen chair and looked at her clean kitchen.

"Righteous Maker, I don't know if you are listening to me after what I did—" her voice broke and she struggled to compose herself. "But I am going try to get some answers. I am going to try to make it right."

She knew it was still early in the morning.

She bit her lip, *Judd is still in Reed selling and buying what he can after the fire. He said to expect him in five days. That's enough time.*

Judd had ridden to Reed with their neighbor Mark in Mark's wagon, so the old mare and saddle were still in the barn.

After about an hour, she had the house in order, the mare saddled, and the saddle bag packed with some homemade bread and jelly, some dried rabbit, a canteen, a shawl, an extra dress, and two blankets—one to lie on and one to cover up with.

*I have five days,* she thought. *I can do it in four.*

On noon of the second day of riding, almost two full days after Andrea left, Flora could see the mountain stream.

*I was afraid I had forgotten where it was,* she thought to herself.

She let her horse free to graze, then took off her shoes and hoisted up her skirts, *Alright, here we go.* Flora stepped into the cold water and waded to the tree. She ducked through the green curtain of leaves.

She looked at the ancient tree. She remembered Tisha and Ross bringing her and a few other people to this very tree. They had explained its Promise and showed them the passage. Flora knew that Tisha and Ross had taken little Andrea here many times.

She ran a hand down its old twisted trunk.

A leaf drifted down. Flora allowed her eyes to follow it. Then she noticed the hole where Andrea had found the Book and letter.

*I didn't realize this was here.*

She saw something. She reached down and her fingers felt something smooth and hard. She pulled it out. A book. It looked old. It had been there a while.

She turned to the first page.

*First Salmday, Tahsoarivmonth, 100 Fifth Age*

*Ross and I are finally married!*

Flora gasped. This was Tisha's journal!

*Mother gave me this journal to start along with my life with Ross. We are now living in the Outskirts. It is nothing like I imagined our first house would be, and I have to admit I gave Ross a terrible time when he told me he had taken a job in the castle. But I know I will learn to be happy.*

*But I will do my best to not complain. After all, Ross is doing his best and just could not think to move his wife in with his parents or he move in with mine. Ross made sure that we had a bedroom separate from the living area. And it is ours. Ours. I still cannot believe that I am married. And to Ross! I know I will be so happy—no matter where we live. I simply could not be more joyful! I am truly blessed …*

*First Biasday, Tahsoarivmonth, 100 Fifth Age*

*It is only our second day of marriage, but I have some sad news. Lord Nathaniel, who ruled Airiss honorably for almost forty years, died today. He was a good man who feared the Maker, and Ross and I are saddened to hear of his death. Lord Nathaniel's wife died two years before he did and they had no children.*

*They did have three nephews and the oldest, whose name is Nazar, was given the throne. I pray that he will fear his Maker like his uncle before him …*

*First Tahecday, Tahsoarivmonth, 100 Fifth Age*

*Well it has been quite a day. Only three days since our wedding and I am ashamed to say that I acted terribly. It was not even about the awful outhouse or the fact that I have to walk a little ways to the community pump for water or even that our mattress is on the floor because the bed frame would not fit in our small room. I am blushing even just writing this alone at the table. It was over rain. Well a lot of things—but poor Ross could not help any of it.*

*It rained and the roof leaked in a few places. I had to set out pots and cups to catch the water. I opened the door to empty a pot and one of the dirty stray dogs dashed in. Before I managed to chase it from the house it trampled the bed, tore my skirt—my favorite that my grandmother made me, and knocked the woodpile by the stove on to my foot. Then as I chased it through the door, I tripped on my torn skirt and fell to my hands and knees in the pouring rain.*

*By the time the dog was gone and I was back in the house, I was covered in mud and simply fuming. I tossed my skirt into the corner and threw myself into my muddy bed. After sulking for a few minutes I went about trying to put things back in order. My foot was bruised and terribly sore so I hobbled around barefoot. Ross came home from work just as I was restacking the woodpile. He startled me so that I dropped a log on my other foot. I yelled at him about my terrible day and would not even let him help me to a chair. I buried my head in my arms and refused to even talk about it …*

The entry went on, but Flora continued to skim through the entries,

*First Salmday, Fewivmonth, 101 Fifth Age*

*Today should be a special day. It's our eight month anniversary and my nine-teenth birthday. But we are worried. Lord Nazar does not seem to fear the Maker and is nothing like his uncle …*

*Second Nevivday, Soarivmonth, 101 Fifth Age*

*This has gone too far! Nazar is starting to put restrictions on Lovers! If this does not stop, something will have to be done …*

Flora pried herself away from the thick binder of yellowing pages. *I need to get home.*

## CHAPTER FIVE

# DAMON AND RAYA

Flora was sitting at her kitchen table, home again, reading through the journal late one evening. She skimmed through many entries and started reading after Ross and Tisha had founded the Resistance.

*Fourth Davday, Lilivmonth, 101 Fifth Age*

*Gathering in the Name of the Maker is officially against the law and people are becoming too afraid to sell the Maker's Holy Book. Ross and I just pulled together all the money we could find and bought as many as we could. We worry they will be outlawed soon too. Airiss is losing its freedoms quickly under Nazar's cruel leadership. Darrion and Lidian have completely banned loving the Maker and even quiet, laid back Kimble is beginning to restrict it. If Airiss bans it too, I don't know what Lovers will do …*

Several entries later,

*Third Tahecday, Tahsoarivmonth, 101 Fifth Age*

*Ross, Musa, Rhoda, Tim, and I, along with a few others, have been making copies of the Book. It is long, tiring work and the penalty for copying and distributing the illegal Books is severe, but our Maker is with us. We are ready for whatever Nazar can do. We know that no matter how big our problem, the Maker is bigger …*

Andrea rode without direction. She kept Star at an easy pace for both horse and rider. She started late, stopped early, and took frequent breaks. Andrea knew it would do more harm than good to completely exhaust all of her and Star's strength. But she was worried because she knew she had to get more distance between her and Grand Capitol Reed, as it was formally known. She sensed that the grandness of the massive castles and paved streets were hiding an evil that she didn't even begin to fully understand. She had no idea where to go so she had just ridden *away*. Wherever that may lead her. But for now, she felt that she was far enough away to take it easy.

She was cautious, but untrained, inexperienced, and unaware of the duo that had tailed her ever since the Tree.

She was no longer physically marked—the Maker had taken care of that—but Nazar, all the judges and nobles of Reed, and many of the officers and guards knew her face. To make matters worse, she began to notice posters offering one thousand pieces of gold for anyone who would turn her in, dead, alive, beaten or broken. Nazar didn't care as long as it was her. It even had a complete description of her and information on her background.

She had sold the chain her mother's key had hung from and she still had the five gold coins Flora had secretly slipped into her satchel, so she had some money to spend on provisions. But as the weeks passed, and her money and provisions dwindled, fear began to grow. In every town guards and posters awaited her, only adding to her paranoia.

She started avoiding even the smallest of farm towns. Stopping only when she needed provisions, and keeping even those visits short. It seemed like no matter how far she went or where she was Nazar already had guards and posters everywhere.

Panic set in. She was down to nine sallas—and as it took two hundred sallas to get one gold coin, nine was very little. It would buy her little more in terms of food. She was feeling smaller and more helplessly out of control each day as her money and spirits ran low.

Her faith was wavering when she needed it most, and all thoughts of the Holy Maker and His Book were drifting farther from her mind. No longer was she tirelessly searching the Book to find the Maker and this Elnai. Fear, desperation, loneliness, helplessness, hopelessness, and weariness quickly replaced all thoughts of them. She was sinking further away from her Righteous Maker and even dared to wonder if she should just give up.

෨෬

It angered them that Nazar had put those signs up. They could handle this. It was under control. They always got results. Their pride screamed one thing, but reality another. They had been following her for weeks. She didn't seem to know where she was going any more than they did. She had stopped reading that book, and no other acts of sorcery had been seen. She seemed to be losing hope. They could see it in the way her shoulders sagged in the saddle and feet dragged as she walked.

"We cannot keep wandering around like this," the young man said as they watched Andrea barter with a merchant. "It is obvious she does not know anything."

"Do you think Nazar would accept that?" came his partner's dry reply. They both knew the answer.

He took a swig from his canteen. "Well if she gives up we won't get an answer anyway."

"We need to get a better plan. At this rate, we are getting nowhere and Nazar is going to be breathing down our necks for information."

He carefully weighed their options.

෨෬

Musa was on her last rotation. It brought such joy to be counted worthy to serve the way she did. Showing everyone the correct passage, they set to work.

> *As an accuser, jealous Lavin came,*
> *Saying Light's people did not love Light's name.*
> *For how could they love for they did not choose?*
> *If given a choice, their praise, Light would lose.*

*Light said to Lavin "If My people give*
*Themselves to your fate, then they cannot live;*
*Though you may tempt them, I will punish you,*
*They give you their world if they are not true."*

*Light took from His Courts a great golden tree,*
*Placed it in a pool and made a decree,*
*"Listen or die, do not be a fool!*
*This tree witnessed sin, do not touch this pool!*

*"You will not be pure, you will taste decay,*
*You cannot see Me if you disobey,*
*For I Am Holy, therefore by My side*
*Nothing imperfect can ever abide."*

༄

Andrea walked away with very little. She had been shortchanged and she knew it. But the merchant had said it was that price or nothing. When she pushed him, he threatened to turn her in to a nearby guard if she didn't make her purchases or leave.

She was out of money and had very little to show for her last purchase. It would hardly last her two days, but she was completely out of food and the next town was two days of hard riding away. It added to her growing feeling of defeat. She untied Star from his hitching post and loaded her dried berries and now empty money sack into the saddlebag. She was more than ready to leave this little town halfway up the mountain. She was not sure where she would go, just that she wanted to leave.

"You! Girl!"

Andrea stiffened. *Please don't be talking to me.*

She heard approaching footsteps as the gruff voice drew closer. She turned to see a farmer coming her way. Her heart sank. He was not a scary looking fellow, but she still was not his match. Her heart skipped at beat when she saw that he carried one of Nazar's fliers.

She tried to swing into the saddle, but a calloused hand grabbed her by the back of the tunic.

She coughed and grabbed her throat.

"Since you are trying to run I guess you are the girl on the paper. You match the description." He spat, "You're going to make me some money."

Before he realized what she was doing, she drew her hunting sword and jerked a pace away. Her sword shook in her hand and she tried to steady it.

The farmer studied her a moment, then, without giving her time to react, he tackled her and wrestled the sword from her hand. He had a small cut on his left arm from brushing against the sword. It didn't faze him. He was skinny from the hardships of Nazar's rule, but he was also strong from the labor of a farmer.

Red faced, he yanked Andrea up by the arm. She swallowed a yelp.

"This sign says, 'dead or alive.' That means I have a choice." He leaned close. "If you try anything like that again, you will not be too pleased with my choice, understand?"

He put the sword in the saddlebag and grabbed Star's reigns with his freed hand. Andrea clawed and pulled against the hand that held her wrist, but he had an iron grip.

"This horse should bring me a nice price too."

He paraded her down the streets, and no matter how much she struggled, she could not free herself.

He glared at her and the scratches she left on his arm. "Stop all of that, now. Remember that other option we talked about?"

Andrea noticed a young man and woman walking straight toward them. The girl wore a short tunic of durable, thick material and leggings that were much like Andrea's and the boy wore a shirt and long pants made of the same material. Over that they wore a cloak that would protect against sun, wind, cold, and rain. Both wore heavy boots much like her own.

The girl looked to be about twenty with blond hair bobbed halfway between her shoulders and chin. Her icy blue eyes were cold and calculating. She had two throwing knives sheathed in the belt around her waist, as well as a quiver of arrows and a bow strapped to her back.

The man looked about twenty-five and had brown eyes and hair, a strong build, and muscles that revealed years of training. There was no doubt that he knew how to use the sword he drew from the sheath that hung at his left side. The girl's slim, toned arms also showed that she was more than familiar with her bow and daggers.

They looked alike in some ways, even though they seemed so different at first. Andrea thought they might be related.

"We will take her off your hands," said the girl in a cool voice.

"We will reimburse you with five gold coins for your trouble," said the man.

The farmer spit and laughed, never loosening his grip. "What? You think I'm stupid? You say you are going to give me five pieces of gold to give up a thousand?"

Their expressions tensed. The girl pulled a dagger from the strap on her thigh. The already quiet street was now all but empty. Anyone who had not already scurried away now moved back.

"I don't think he understands us very well, Damon." She twirled the dagger between her fingers.

Damon ran his hand across the flat of his sword. His voice was threatening. "If five pieces is not good enough, fine. Let us raise the price." With quick, purposeful strides, he closed the gap between him and the farmer until he was only a pace or two away. "Give us the girl, and, in return, you will be paid with your life." His eyes challenged the farmer.

The farmer swallowed. He looked from Damon and his sword, to the girl and her knife. He didn't doubt their abilities.

His voice was weaker and you could see his fear, but he was not quite ready to give her up. "And what if I turn the whole lot of you in?"

The cold steel was at his throat in the blink of an eye. "I don't think you will find that necessary."

Andrea felt the grip of one hand loosen from one arm and the grip of another tighten around her other arm. She liked her odds better without her "rescuers." They had come to her aid, but they were well armed and could easily be working for Nazar. Besides, if she had any chance to fight, two well-armed warriors that each outmatched her alone were not helping her chances of escape.

Damon lifted her up onto his horse as if she weighed nothing and then mounted in front of her as the girl led Star by the reigns from her own mount.

Andrea could not think clearly. She felt like she should fight, but they *had* rescued her. Then again, if they were really helping her, they would have let her on her own horse. And if she started fighting, the farmer—or worse, a guard—might come after her. Her kidnapping was going from bad to worse.

As they were riding away, Andrea saw the farmer scurrying towards the house where the guard was staying. After a moment, the guard opened the door with a bottle in hand. Andrea could tell by the guard's exaggerated, unstable body language that he was drunk. Whether or not having the guard intervene would have been better or worse than her present situation no longer mattered. It was obvious that the guard was more interested in the contents of his bottle than the ravings of the farmer. She was not sure whether to feel relieved or alarmed.

She tried to form a plan as they continued to ride further up the towering mountain.

Andrea noticed that Damon's posture had loosened and relaxed a little. She decided to take a chance. Once out of sight from the town, as hard and fast as she could, she grabbed his shoulder with both hands and shoved him. She surprised him enough that he tumbled off his horse. She quickly moved up in the saddle and grabbed the reins.

"Get up!" she screamed, giving her dark brown mount a sharp kick in the side and leaning forward.

Damon scrambled to his feet and yelled, "Rogue rider!"

The steed stopped so fast that he nearly threw Andrea over his head.

"Get up!" she kicked him again.

Getting nowhere, she slid off of the horse and ran. Andrea knew the girl would catch her on her horse, but it was all she could do.

Sure enough, the girl had her horse in front of Andrea before she could even figure out any sort of a plan.

Andrea turned around and ran—right into the furious Damon. She stumbled a little, slamming into him full force, but managed to stay on her feet. He had not moved. She might as well have run into a wall.

"That was not smart."

Andrea felt her face turn white at the sound of his voice. It was deep, angry, and even more terrifying than it had been with the farmer. He had both of her shaking wrists in one of his hands in a quick, rough motion.

All she could do was stand there wide-eyed, mouth agape.

"Raya, throw me some rope."

Raya produced a short rope from her saddle bag and tossed it to Damon.

Damon quickly wound it around her wrists through all of her useless struggling. It was uncomfortably tight, but not painful. He left a little at the end hanging loose. He put her back on the horse and mounted in front of her again, then tied the other end of the rope to the belt around his waist that held a long dagger and his sword's sheath—both of which he made sure were out of her reach.

Hot, angry tears silently traced Andrea's cheek.

They rode for a few more hours and Damon never let his guard down. Andrea could not stand the silence anymore. She needed some idea of what they were planning to do with her.

"How does it feel to grab a girl off the street to hand her over to a terrible fate?" she tried her best to lace her voice with as much icy venom as Damon had. "And all for a little gold? I don't know how you sleep at night."

Damon never turned around as he spoke. His voice was not as harsh as it had been, but it still had a hard, cool edge to it. "We are not turning you in."

Andrea was not sure what to think about that answer. "Well, then, why did you kidnap me?"

The girl glared at her with her piercing blue eyes. "Kidnapping? Try *helping*." Her cutting voice was a little raspy. "We could have let that farmer haul you in."

"So, if I am free to go, can I have my horse back?" said Andrea, sarcastically optimistic. "Can I be untied?"

"No." Damon still didn't look at her.

"Then you are kidnapping me!" Andrea knew she was not helping her situation any, but she was mad, scared, and out of options. "You must really think I'm stupid."

Damon jerked around. His voice was laced with cold anger. "Look, you obviously don't know anything about this kind of situation." He took a deep breath and calmed down as he once again faced forward. "Trust us, we have experience."

"Oh, so you've been kidnapped too?"

"*We are not kidnapping you!*" they both shouted at once.

Damon took another deep breath. "If anyone sees us, we don't want them to think that we are helping you escape. That farmer could send guards after us and we would have to get them to believe that we are on their side. Besides, after that little stunt you pulled, you're lucky that I don't tie your hands to the saddle and make you *walk*! You can ride your own horse when you give us a reason to trust you, so you don't get yourself killed."

Andrea still wasn't convinced, but she was quiet. As the farmer had been so careful to point out, the sign had said alive or dead. As long as she was still breathing, there was a chance of escape. However slim that chance may be.

By the time they stopped to make camp, the sun was setting.

"We will stay here for the night," Damon said.

Raya dismounted and led both horses to a pitiful little stream.

Damon left Andrea's hands tied, but released her from his belt. He dismounted, then lifted her from the horse and set her on the parched grass.

"Don't move."

She nodded, refusing to look at him. As if that would hurt him.

Andrea would have taken her chance if she could have, but either Damon or Raya were near her at all times. If she so much as readjusted her seating all eyes were on her.

Soon they had a fire and the horses taken care of. Everyone sat around the fire and Raya finally untied Andrea's hands.

"If you try anything, this is coming back on for good." Her voice was hard and unnerving, but not to the spine-chilling extent that Damon's could be.

Raya handed her some dried venison and the three of them ate in silence. After they had eaten, Damon and Raya went through her saddlebag and talked in hushed tones.

After a minute, they came back and dropped the Book into her lap.

Andrea felt a pang of guilt. *Holy Maker,* she thought, *how could I have forgotten You?*

"What is this?" Damon demanded.

"A book. You see, people write words on the pages and you read it," Andrea said sweetly. She then cocked her head to the side and feigned confusion. "I thought you two knew everything."

Raya crossed her arms. "Don't be smart." She touched the characters on the front page. "What is this? Some secret code?"

Andrea smiled, shrugged, and told them the truth. "To be honest, I have no idea."

Damon picked it up. "Where did you get this?"

"I can't remember," she said with exaggerated innocence. "Being kidnapped does that sometimes."

They both rolled their eyes.

Andrea counted it as a small victory. At least she was not crying. And, if nothing else, she could get on their nerves.

Raya looked at her and softened, left hand on her hip. "Look, you may not believe us, but we are on your side."

"That is amazing," Andrea said. "How did you guess I would not believe that? You must be psychic kidnappers."

Damon also softened, if only a bit. His voice was almost civil. "Look, we were there for your 'execution' and you got through to us. We have heard about the Resistance and have been trying to find you so maybe we could join."

Andrea cocked an eyebrow and looked up at them. "Then why did you bow?" She could not hide the anger in her voice as she spit out the next words. "Do what you want with me, but how dare you take the name of the Righteous Maker and pretend to call yourself His Lover."

They were surprised by the sudden fire in her voice and eyes. They could almost see her standing up to Nazar on the day of her execution.

Raya knelt in front of her. "We bowed, yes. But when we got home, we realized our mistake. We have done many horrible things in the service of Nazar, but believe me, bowing to him is our biggest regret." Her voice was soft and sincere.

Andrea felt like spitting. She was glad that she was too angry to cry. She didn't want to give them the satisfaction of seeing how scared she was.

Raya stood up and looked at Damon, who nodded.

"We're sorry we were so rough," Damon said, sounding sincere. "But at the rate you were going, you would be on your way to Reed by now. We were only trying to protect you until we could get to a safer place to talk." He paused and searched her face, then continued. "I can see you don't believe us, but we have proof of our sincerity."

He knelt in front of her and pulled up the left sleeve of his tunic.

Andrea gasped; she could hardly believe what she was seeing.

*Damon of Reed, marked by the order of Lord Nazar for treason against Airiss in service of the Forbidden Name.*

She looked at Raya, who nodded and pulled up her left sleeve as well.

*Raya of Reed, marked by the order of Lord Nazar for treason against Airiss in service of the Forbidden Name.*

"You caused a lot of trouble," Raya said simply. "The Name of the Maker is forbidden and anyone who speaks it will be marked because of you."

Andrea looked from one to the other.

"We still have plenty of rough edges," Damon said. "You cannot walk away from Nazar without scars. But the Maker has been smoothing us out."

"You can walk away right now," Raya said, "but we have told you the truth."

Damon held the Book out.

Andrea stood up. She took the Book and looked at it for a minute. "I ... I'm sorry."

## CHAPTER SIX

# FINDING DIRECTION

Flora kept Tisha's journal hidden from Judd. She knew he agreed with most of Nazar's views and if he ever saw Andrea again he would turn her in. He had never loved her. The only reason he allowed her to stay at all was because Flora had begged.

She read the journal whenever she had a moment alone and she could read without fear of getting caught. This late hour was one of those rare moments.

*Fourth Medivday, Lilivmonth, 102 Fifth Age*

*They found all our work and burned it! We were flogged, spent the night in prison, and they destroyed all our work! A whole year of work, gone!*

*They ransacked our houses, but luckily, I hid this book well enough …*

*First Davday, Salmmonth, 103 Fifth Age*

*Our small band of rebels is growing quickly. We have almost one hundred men and women who choose to serve the Maker of All Things! We have spent almost all of our time trying to find people willing to follow the True Lord. We have secret meetings to worship the Maker and all of the Lovers of Elnai share three Books. We take turns with them and pass each copy around. The real crime is that we don't have access to more …*

*Fourth Biasday, Salmmonth, 103 Fifth Age*

*We are growing bolder. We are teaching in the streets, having more meetings, and we have started making copies of the Books again …*

*First Salmday, Drayivmonth, 103 Fifth Age*

*I'm pregnant! I'm thrilled and terrified at the same time. Ross and I want a child, but this present evil age is not safe to be born into. Especially not with us being a part of the Resistance—as we have been dubbed.*

*Ross has forbidden me to do any work with the Resistance except writing. He says it's too dangerous for me now that I carry our baby. And he's right.*

*We are praying that the Maker will watch over our child …*

❧❦

Raya and Damon waited patiently for her answer. Andrea was uneasy about this. Could she really trust them?

"I don't know," she said hesitantly. *Don't do it!*

Damon stepped forward. He almost looked hurt. "You still don't trust us?"

Andrea hugged the Book to her chest and caught herself gnawing at her jagged nails.

Raya sighed. "We helped you, we showed you our marks, what more do you need?"

Andrea searched their faces; she tried to keep her voice even. "Why do you need to see my Mother's book so badly?" She inwardly winced, *I didn't mean to say that much.*

Maybe she imagined this, but Andrea thought she saw their eyes light up at the mention of her mother.

They seemed to be thinking about that.

"We don't," Raya said after a second. "We just thought that, being your mother's book, it could help us find people we could trust."

Andrea hugged the Book tighter and took a step back. She felt herself press against a tree. "You didn't know it was my Mother's book until I said that it was just a moment ago."

It was dark; the fire cast an orange tint across their faces. Andrea was nervous and jumped at every shadow.

Andrea could tell that they saw her nervousness.

"Look, Andrea, we didn't mean anything. If you don't want to show it to us, fine. If there is anything you think we should see to help us get in contact with the Resistance, let us know." Damon turned to Raya. "Are the horses taken care of for the night?"

She nodded.

"Good." He looked at Andrea. He wasn't smiling, but he wore a relaxed expression. "Do you have a bed roll?"

Andrea refused to relax. She nodded.

"Good. The mountains get cold at night the higher you go even though it is already Davmonth."

"We are going further up?"

"That is where you were going right?"

*I don't know where I was going.* "I was heading in that direction." Well, that was true.

"Do you have a better idea?" Raya asked dryly.

*Yes. Get away from you.* "I guess not."

"It is settled then," Damon said.

After a few minutes, Damon and Raya were in their bed rolls next to the fire. The three horses were staked a little ways behind them and Andrea lay on top of her bedroll shivering slightly a few feet away on the opposite side of the fire. Even though it was summer, the mountain night air was a bit cooler than she was used too.

She refused to allow herself the comfort of burrowing into the warm blanket beneath her. She was cold, but being wrapped up in a blanket would make it hard to jump up and run if she needed to.

Andrea's back was to the yellow flames. Her eyes were wide open and she was listening, determined to keep her heavy eyes from closing, no matter how much her aching exhaustion begged her too.

∽∾

Damon and Raya were listening too. And soon they heard Andrea stop tossing and turning. They cautiously opened their eyes. She was curled up, back to the fire, and they could see her small form rising and falling with heavy, slow breathing.

They cautiously sat up.

"Does she still have the Book?" Raya's voice was hushed.

Damon nodded.

"We should kill her and take the book. She doesn't know any-thing and she doesn't trust us. The Book should have the informa-tion we need."

"No," Damon whispered back. "Nazar said to bring her back alive."

"But," his sister reminded him, "he obviously changed his mind. Those posters he put up everywhere read 'dead *or* alive.'"

Damon nodded. "Yes, but she may know more. We will get the Book, but not now. We need to earn her trust if we can."

With that, Raya reapplied the staining ink to Damon's upper left arm. Then turned to have him do the same to hers. This would have to be done in secret every few days to make sure their "tattoos" stayed in place.

☞⋅⋙

Tisha could not sleep that night. She tossed and turned in her bed, hoping she would not disturb the others. She just could not get her daughter out of her mind.

*How long has it been?* She thought as she threw off her blanket, *It has been fifteen years. I thought I had found peace about this. Why is this coming back now? I have thought about Andrea and Ross countless times.*

"Maker." She switched from thought to prayer. Over the years it had gotten as effortless as breathing. Sometimes they were so inter-twined that she could not do one without the other. Her whisper was so faint she could hardly hear it herself. "I thought I had accepted this, found peace about this." She rolled over for the hundredth time. "Why have I not been able to get Andrea off my mind lately?"

She pulled the blanket around her again as she drifted back to her thoughts, *And it is mainly Andrea. Oh, I have thought about Ross, but my daughter's name has filled every quiet second. What if she is alive? No, I cannot let myself think that. I would not be able to stand it. I saw them torch the house.*

*You didn't see it burn down.*

*She was only four.*

*But she was never alone. The Holy Maker was always there.*

"Is it true?" She kicked her blanket off again and readjusted. She made sure she had not disturbed the other two sleeping women in the room and lowered her voice below a whisper. "Could she be alive?" *Am I getting my hopes up just to fall down again? It has been so long, is it possible? They would have revisited the house to make sure I didn't try to show up. They would have found her.*

*Unless she got out before then.*

*She was four. She would not have known what to do.*

*She was not alone. She was never alone.*

She lay on her back and covered her face with her hands. She was thirty-nine now. Almost forty. *My little girl would be nineteen. She could have been married by now. I was when I was her age.*

She sat up and sighed. "Maker, I know that she didn't make it."

*Do you?*

"It is just not possible."

*Are you limiting Me?*

"I need Your peace. I have not stopped thinking about her lately. I want to believe, but I am scared to. I know better."

*You know better? Than the Holy Maker? Do you really?*

"Just hold her tight for me. She is safe with You. No one can hurt her—not Nazar, not anybody—she is in Your arms. Ross is too. Give me peace."

The warrior thought about the prayer as he watched her wrap up in the blanket and try to get some sleep. He spoke words of comfort. Yes, her Maker had Andrea, but not the way Tisha was thinking. Andrea still had trouble to face in this world.

Tisha finally drifted off to sleep.

৵৽

Musa awakened and went quietly about her morning preparations in the room she shared with the leader of the Resistance and one other woman.

She stole a glance at the sleeping figure in the bed directly across from hers. She was worried about Tisha. Musa had heard her toss and turn all night and she was usually the first one up.

Musa breathed a prayer for her dear friend and decided to talk to her about it later.

*But now,* she thought as walked into the room where they made the copies, *I need to prepare for the copying sessions.*

It was Third Salmday, the first day of the new week. The day they set aside for a huge Gathering devoted to the study of the Book, the worship of the Holy Maker of All Things, and rest.

Even though there would be no copying today, she wanted to go ahead and read over the section they would cover Biasday.

*But that is all I will do today in preparation for tomorrow.* She told herself.

> *Once Maker had left, Lavin tempted them,*
> *He twisted Light's words 'til truth became dim;*
> *The waters looked sweet, refreshing and cool—*
> *At last, one Lover stooped to touch the pool*
>
> *Convincing the others, they each waded in,*
> *The Great Tree withered—each at once knew sin;*
> *They rushed from the pool, the ground now quivered,*
> *Ashamed and afraid, each Lover shivered.*
>
> *The small pool bubbled, the waters burst forth*
> *Into four rivers—East, West, South, and North;*
> *The Maker and Son with great sorrow wept,*
> *Holy Maker knew His law must be kept.*

৵৽

Andrea felt a heavy hand on her shoulder. She jumped up.

"I'm sorry," Damon said, taking his hand back and standing up. It was just past dawn. "I didn't mean to startle you." His voice was softer than it had been. More civil.

Andrea hugged her Book and looked up at him. From her sitting position he looked bigger than usual.

He was big enough already, especially from her unimpressive height. Just less than six foot one inch tall, which was tall for an Airissian, and well-toned with experienced muscles. The sword at his side was not new to blood.

She stood up just so she would stop shrinking and asked, "What do you want?" Her voice was a little higher and she hated it for it.

"It is time to go. Raya is getting the horses ready."

"So you are in charge now?" *Yes. He could take me with him and there would be nothing I could do about it.*

His voice—unlike hers—was even and controlled. "Well, we are not going to stop you from leaving, but if you stay in one place too long, they will find you. Nazar is ruthless. He is not going to let us go.

Especially not you. You publicly humiliated him and he wants people to think he has full control. He wants them to think he is a god."

Andrea was listening. Skeptical, but listening.

"Raya and I have experience in battle strategy. We know how to stay one step ahead of Nazar and his men. We are marked— like you—and have nowhere to go. You can get us to the Resistance where we make a difference. Where we can fight for our Holy Maker and make up for what we have done." He studied her a minute. "You know where to go; we know how to get us there safely." He turned, walked to the horses and said, "It is up to you."

Andrea was still cautious, *He does have a point. I am going to get myself killed just wandering around. They have had more than one chance to kill me and they didn't take the Book either.* "What if I don't know where to go?"

He looked at her over his shoulder, his voice full of confidence. "The Maker will guide us. He has brought us this far."

She looked at the Book and ran her fingers over the characters on the cover.

She looked up. "Alright."

They rode hard all day. The vegetation was getting scarcer as the mountainous terrain turned rockier. The air seemed to be getting thinner and cooler as they went higher.

As it began to get dark, the temperature began to drop rapidly.

Andrea was beginning to wonder if they were going to ride all night when Raya finally said, "We should probably look for a place to make camp."

Damon nodded and pointed a little ways up the mountain to the right. "See that little cave up there?"

Both of the girls nodded.

"We will stop there."

Andrea inwardly moaned. It seemed terribly far.

About half an hour later, they all dismounted in front of the cave. It was more of an overhang upon closer inspection. Its opening was only about twenty feet wide and ten feet deep. But it would keep them out of the wind and they were grateful.

Andrea tended to the horses while Damon made a fire and cut a scrawny sapling up for firewood with a small hatchet he had in his saddle bag.

Raya had disappeared.

*Not that I care,* Andrea thought as she stroked Star under his mane. *She makes me nervous.*

"Who? Raya?"

She jumped at the sound of Damon's voice. "I said that out loud …" she murmured.

"What?" he dropped his armful of firewood and sat down beside the fire.

"Nothing." She left the horses tied to a small tree and sat by the fire, opposite from Damon. Not because she wanted to be around him, but because it was chilly in the dark mountain air.

"Raya has always been quiet."

Andrea didn't say anything. His voice didn't seem so deep and chilling. It was warmer and lighter. Civil and maybe even friendly.

Almost.

"She still has a lot to work through. She is nervous and tense about everything that has been going on lately. I am sure you know how that feels. She will warm up to you."

Andrea thought of those cold blue eyes staring holes through her. It was more than that. *I doubt it.*

"How do you know each other?" Andrea surprised herself a little with the question.

Damon looked up from the flames. His shadow danced on the wall. "We are twins."

Andrea felt her mouth drop. Was that a smile teasing at the corner of his mouth? *I didn't know these people smiled.*

Damon laughed. It sounded friendly and light. Andrea felt her cheeks turning red, *I have got to stop thinking out loud.*

"You don't even look alike!" she said, recovering from her embarrassment.

Damon let an easy crooked smile play at the corners of his mouth. Looking at him, Andrea could see similarities in the shape of their faces and noses. Same high cheekbones, hard jawline, only Raya's was a bit softer. His deep brown eyes were stunning in the orange glow of the fire. He was handsome. There was no denying it.

Andrea cleared her thoughts, *Why do I care what he looks like? Raya is beautiful and she is scary. He was* really *terrifying yesterday.*

"How old are you?"

He pulled off his boots and unrolled his mat. "Twenty-one."

"I'm nineteen."

He nodded. "You are from Cresso, right?"

"Well, I grew up there with the woman who raised me, but my parents were from Valrine. I just found out that my mother is still alive." *I need to watch myself. I still don't feel I can trust him.*

"What happened? How did you get separated?" he sounded casual.

She looked away. "I was four."

He sensed the stiffness in her voice and knew he had pushed too far. He changed the subject. "Raya and I were brought up by a widow in the outskirts of Reed."

Andrea relaxed a little, but not completely. "Where were your parents?"

"I don't know." That was the truth. "I assume they are dead."

*Sounds similar to my story in some ways.* "The widow didn't know?"

"She said they were dead. No details about their death or even about them. She was very elusive." Again, that was the truth. "Did you go to school in the Capitol?"

Raya stopped. Still out of sight, she listened, unnoticed. It had been raining lightly while she was on her way back to the cave, now it was beginning to pick up.

"The people that raised me never had much money." Andrea was surprised at this conversation, but it felt comfortable. She still needed to watch herself. "But we had a few books and Flora taught me the best she could. I can read, write a little, and know enough about numbers to work with money."

He nodded. "The widow was not wealthy, but managed to send us to school. When we were six, Nazar started sending men to the schools. Anyone who showed potential of any kind was given access to a library and an education which included numbers, reading, writing, history, and the study of the stars. We were trained with the sword and bow. They also taught us battle strategy, navigation, basic medicine, how to ride and handle horses, and the languages of Darroon, Lideen, and the primary Kimim dialect. We got to the castle at dawn, and were sent home at dusk.

"This continued until we were fourteen, when we were taken from our homes completely to live in the castle barracks where we continued our education and training daily until we were eighteen."

That didn't sound like something Nazar would just give away. Only the wealthy were able to afford such an education. The only thing that would be available for people like the widow would be a very basic—and expensive—grasp on numbers, reading, history, and, if you were fortunate enough, writing.

"For free?"

"That is what we thought." He looked her in the eyes. "After we turned eighteen we realized the price that Nazar had forgotten to mention."

Andrea waited.

He sighed. It was all truth. "Nazar owns us now. Everyone who took that education was at his disposal. We could not refuse the education or evade the hidden price. He assigned tasks. We were given additional special training to suit that task. We did whatever he said. No questions asked. We had no choice." His eyes drifted back to the flames.

Raya had heard enough. Damon was telling her too much. Besides, it was raining quite hard now and she wanted to get out of it. She started stomping louder than necessary toward the others.

Andrea was dying to ask what kind of tasks they had been assigned to do. She opened her mouth to satisfy her curiosity when Damon lifted his eyes to the cave entrance. Andrea followed his gaze to see a very wet Raya coming with two ground squirrels and a pica— each with an arrow through its head. If Andrea wasn't convinced of Raya's efficiency with a bow before—she was now.

Raya removed the arrows and cleaned the squirrels while Andrea, who was no stranger to cleaning animals, took care of the pica. Damon took three sticks, shaved off their bark, sharpened the ends to a point, then got the horses situated out of the rain on the opposite end of the cave. After he finished with his tasks, Damon threw another piece of wood on the fire.

Damon could tell that Raya was upset. To anyone else, she looked as cool and collected as usual, but Damon knew her too well. She must have been listening.

"I thought you were just getting water," he said casually.

"I was getting tired of dried meat." She made her last cut with enough force that Damon's suspicions were confirmed. She was angry. "If you are thirsty, my hands are bloody, help yourself."

Damon took the canteen from the belt around her waist and drank a sip.

Raya skewered her portion of squirrel with the same quick and jerky motion. At least she would not yell at him with Andrea here.

They roasted their dinner on their sticks and ate in silence. Soon, after a little bit of cleanup and discussing tomorrow's plans, they all settled in for the night. Raya and Damon, seemingly asleep, on one side of the fire. Andrea on the other in her sleeping roll. She still didn't like the idea of being wrapped in a blanket, in case she needed to run, but she could not stand the thought of another cold night. Exhaustion claimed her quickly.

&ofthe;

"Have you lost your mind?" Raya hissed, inches from Damon's face.

"I had to help her trust me," Damon said calmly and quietly. "She was talking."

"Then what did she tell you? Did you see the Book?"

"No."

"Then what did you find out?" she demanded.

"Raya, calm down."

"No!" she glanced over at Andrea and lowered her voice back to a whisper. "You didn't have to tell her all our secrets!"

"I didn't." He crossed his arms. "She knows very little and even fewer details. I needed her to trust me. Besides, she will be dead soon anyway."

She glared at him for a minute. "Fine."

"Now let us be quiet and get some sleep before she wakes up."

Without another word, they both lay back down.

&ofthe;

Big green eyes looked up at her.

"Mommy, I need help."

Tisha smiled, picked her daughter up, and kissed her little head. "Andrea, you are perfectly safe."

Andrea squirmed in her mother's arms. "I'm not a baby anymore! I need you to help me!"

Tisha put the little girl down and smiled again. "Oh, yes. You are a big girl now. Four years old."

Tears spilled over little red cheeks. "No!"

Tisha was confused. "Well then how old is Mommy's big girl?"

"I'm nineteen!"

Tisha's mouth dropped open, and then she smiled and laughed again. "Sweetheart, Mommy is only twenty-four, so how can you be nineteen?"

"No, you're not!" A little foot stomped. "You're thirty-nine! And if you don't help me I am going to die!"

Tisha sat up, breathing hard. Tears streaming down her face and her heart racing.

"Elnai!" her shaky whisper was hardly audible.

But He heard it.

She put a hand over her heart. Her daughter's words from the dream echoed: "*If you don't help me I am going to die!*"

Was Andrea not already dead?

Tisha was only sure of one thing. She was not going to sleep tonight.

"Oh, Elnai, help me!"

⤜⤝

Andrea woke up slowly, savoring the moment halfway between sleep and awareness.

"Ooh …" she groaned as her body started to complain about spending hours on the hard cave floor.

She sat up and rubbed her eyes. She was up before Damon and Raya. That was a first. Her eyes wandered past the cave entrance.

The sun was just beginning to peek out, stretching little rays of multicolored light over the wet, sleeping land.

Damon and Raya would be up any minute.

Andrea pulled the Book from its hiding place under the blanket beside her feet.

She still didn't feel completely comfortable around the other two, but, for now, they were helping her. They were her best chance for food, for staying hidden, for survival.

For now.

She flipped open the Book, took the letter from between the cover and first page. Maybe there was a clue or something—*anything*—that she missed. Anything would be helpful at this point. She needed to find the Resistance. She needed to find Tisha.

Then she noticed something at the bottom of one of the pages of the letter. Andrea squinted at the tiny black markings. They were so small and faded that she had not even noticed them before.

*sbGtlgOwsrEfejAdfbySfbueTg*

*hbFvgehRfddOdfbeuM*

Andrea looked at the next page. Just as she thought. There were two more coded rows.

*bnAnhShnyAbjbCbjgRmlhbOcbWfgFbLdsagIjdtmeEbjS*

*sjSbjdwwefvfVdyuwEbbjeNfhyj*

*How am I supposed to understand this?* Andrea held them side by side and studied them carefully. *What are you trying to tell me, Mother?*

"What are you looking at?"

Andrea nearly jumped out of her skin. She looked up and saw Damon waiting for an answer and Raya waking up as well.

*Run! Hide! Don't let them see it!* Andrea tried to stay composed. "Nothing."

Raya was up now.

"Mind if I look?" Damon's voice held a curious tone.

*What if he can figure this out?* She hesitated, *It is coded for a reason. Should I trust him?*

Without another word, Damon took her silence as an invitation and looked over her shoulder.

Andrea felt uneasy. Like she had just eaten something terrible and it didn't want to stay eaten. But she didn't pull away.

He looked at the letters for a minute. "Where did you get this?"

Andrea didn't say anything.

"Is it from your Mother?"

Silence.

*Great. Now he knows it is from her.*

"There is a pretty big space between the lines." he noticed. Damon took the corner between his thumb and index finger. "Pretty thin paper."

Raya was looking over her other shoulder now.

*Well, Andrea,* she thought, still unable to shake her nervousness, *you have done it now.*

Damon stood up to stir the fire.

"Can I have it?" he asked.

Raya stood up and said, "We'll give it back. We need to look at it in the light."

Andrea sighed. *They have already seen it, I guess.*

She surrendered the papers to Damon.

He studied them for a second, then asked, "Which one is the first page?"

She showed him and he knelt in front of the fire and held them up, one over the other and the first page just a little higher.

Andrea gasped. When in the light of the fire and held correctly, the letters lined up.

*sbGtlgOwsrEfejAdfbySfbueTg*

*bnAnhShnyAbjbCbjgRmlhbOcbWfgFbLdsagIjdtmeEbjS*

*hbFvgehRfddOdfbeuM*

*SjbjVdyuwEbbjeNfhyj*

"Look for a pattern," Raya said.

Andrea couldn't see anything.

"Look at the capital letters," Damon said.

Raya read them off.

"Go east as a crow flies from Sven!" Andrea could not help but get excited.

Damon handed the pages back and stood up. He was wearing a rare smile. "Sven is on the other side of the mountain. Ladies, I believe we know where we are going."

"I will get the horses." And with that, Raya left.

Damon started gathering up the few things that they had in the cave.

Andrea still felt nervous, *We finally found a little bit of direction. Why do I feel like I have made a mistake?*

᷄᷄᷄

"Tisha?"

She looked up from the Book. "Yes, Tim?"

"I'm going home to see Rhoda and Dory. I can get there in about fifteen to twenty days. I'll stay about a month or two and then come back."

She nodded. "That's fine, Tim."

"I'm leaving tomorrow at dawn." He turned to leave.

"Wait, Tim."

He turned to face her.

She hesitated. "I'm going with you."

"But, Tisha," he said, concerned. "Somebody has been stirring up trouble in the Capitol. Nazar's men will all be on guard. If you go down there, everyone knows your face. You'll be captured."

Her voice shook with tension. "Tim, please. I'll be careful. I promise."

He put a heavy hand on her shoulder. "Tisha, we've been friends for years. As your friend, I've been worried about you. We've all noticed that you've been acting strange lately. Musa says you haven't been sleeping well—she hears you tossing and turning all night"

She sighed. "Tim, I need to do this." He took his hand back. "I will be fine. I just need a break."

He hesitated. "Promise me you will be careful."

"I promise."

His brows remained furrowed, creasing deep lines in his forehead. Tisha wasn't the same person she was fifteen years ago. Losing her family and struggling with the Resistance had affected her deeply. Much of her youthful vibrancy had been lost with Ross and Andrea. Yes, she had moved on, but something so traumatic has a profound effect on every aspect of a person.

They had all changed, he supposed.

"When will you be ready?"

"You said dawn," Tisha replied. "I will be ready."

He nodded. "Good. We leave at dawn then."

## CHAPTER SEVEN

# SEARCHING FOR ANSWERS

*Third Davday, Medivmonth, 104 Fifth Age*
    *Our child arrived safely; thank the Holy Maker of All Things! She is a beautiful little girl called Andrea. I still have to stay home and write copies of the Book until she gets older, but at least now I have some company while Ross is away.*

    *The Resistance is also thriving. Nazar's attempts to tear us down have only strengthened our faith in Elnai …*

❧

Nazar was getting nervous. The voices were relentless. *What is taking Vincent's assassins so long? I must have her. She must not meet her mother. She must be stopped.*

"Is everything alright, my lord?"

Nazar looked up from his plate of untouched food. "Why would I not be?" he snapped.

The servant dipped his head respectfully. "It's just that you haven't touched your meal, my lord. Would His Sovereignty have me fetch you something different to dine on? Or perhaps you would like to speak with the cook personally"

"No," Nazar snapped. "I'm fine."

The servant replied, "Yes, Your Excellency," and bowed low.

Nazar swept his arm across the table sending all food and dishes in his reach to the floor. "Get me Vincent and clean that up!" he roared.

The servant scurried to do his seething master's wishes.

૭∙૭

Musa presented fifty leather-bound Books to Riven, Jay, Tisha, and Tim. The five leaders that made up the Inner Circle of the Counsel stood beaming at the neat stack of fresh copies. Praise the Holy Maker.

Tisha and Tim were leaving first thing in the morning and were glad to be here for the joyous moment.

"This many in such a short time?" Tisha smiled. "How did you ever manage it, Musa?"

Musa's deep, dark eyes expressed much more than her quiet words did. "It was not me. The Lover of Our Souls has given us passion." Her smooth white skin practically glowed with excitement and her eyes shone with a hot fire that her quiet and reserved nature didn't otherwise show. "I have four groups of twenty-five willing Lovers who pour themselves into Elnai's work for an hour each day, six days a week."

"Thank Elnai we have even that many!" Riven exclaimed in his deep, powerful voice. When this young Darrionite spoke, his voice and words held maturity and wisdom beyond his twenty-three years. "The Lovers around the world are hungry." He proudly held up one of the precious Books. "And, for most, we are their only hope of getting to taste and see Elnai's very Heart."

Tim nodded and said, "The harvest is great."

"And the harvesters are few," said the other four in grave unison.

Jay placed his strong hands on the shoulders of those on either side of him. Everyone followed suit to begin the customary prayer. Everyone spoke in turn.

"Let us bless those who heeded the Lover's call."

"Let us pray for those who didn't."

"Let us sow love."

"So we may reap love."

"May Elnai send harvesters."

"May the harvest be great."

"May we live in love."

"May we die in love."

"May we worship Love."

"We are His Lovers."

"And He is ours."

There they stood. Encircled by each other. Lovers. In love with Love Himself.

After starting with the traditional blessing, they each poured their hearts out to the Holy Maker. They asked for protection and blessings for every hand that these Books touched. That those delivering them would be safe in their travels. That those who would read the very heart of their Maker would have understanding.

Finally every bowed head was lifted and every face held a smile. Some big and beaming, others faint but still wholly sincere. Some cheeks were wet. Some eyes were brimming with tears. Every heart was filled.

They finally pulled themselves from the group embrace. They could hear the other Lovers roaming the ancient rooms just beyond the archway of the Yipoc Raj.

Jay noisily cleared his throat and blinked quickly. "We have much to discuss, but we need to let Musa attend to her work."

Tisha nodded and dismissed the meeting with the greeting of the Resistance. The others gave the traditional answer in unison.

"We are His Lovers."

"And He is ours."

Musa was soon left alone to look over the next day's copies.

> *He asked His Lovers "Oh, what have you done?"*
> *No one would confess, they each blamed someone;*
> *He told them that now few would be their days,*
> *They had to work hard just to make their ways.*

> *"A pure sacrifice covers up your sin,*
> *But it will not make you perfect again;*
> *No longer will I walk here beside you,*
> *Through sacrifice—I will forgive anew.*

> *"I knew from the start you would turn away,*
> *Because I love you—I have planned a Way:*

*When time is fulfilled I will send Elnai,*
*He will walk in flesh, though only to die."*

☙❧

General Vincent stood before Nazar, who was pacing around the room.

"I need her dead *now!*" Nazar screamed. "Have you posted soldiers and papers in every town ordering that she be brought to me?"

*So, the little wench still has Nazar all worked up.* "Yes, my lord."

Nazar picked up a vase and threw it across the room. A servant hurriedly swept it up. "General, the assassins that *you* recommended have not produced results. I want to know why!"

"My lord, I assure you they are very capable." Vincent had to be careful to keep his tone of voice in check. "I'm certain that they are tailing her as we speak. If she has information, they will get it. Once they have what they need they will be more than able to escort her back to you, my lord."

Nazar thought for a moment. "General, I need results. Time is something that we don't have. If she contacts the Resistance …"

He threw a glass and it shattered across the floor.

"Which brings us to our next subject, my dear general." Nazar enjoyed watching his words anger the man in front of him, but at the moment he himself was too enraged to get much satisfaction. "*Where is the Resistance?*"

"We have reason to believe that they are cowering in Darrion, my Lord."

Nazar threw his head back and loosed a noise that could not be identified with a human. Maybe not even an animal. It sent chills down the spine of the great general himself.

"Then we send our army to Darrion." Nazar's words were followed by a string of curses. "Which district? We march at dawn!"

"My lord, I would advise against it." Vincent was concerned, to say the least. "We don't even know which district and the Darrionites would not stand for it. Our relationship with them is already strained. If we sent troops over or even near the border it would be war."

"Tell me then, *General,*" Nazar hissed. "What would you suggest we do about this?"

"If the girl from Cresso knows anything about the Resistance, my assassins will find them. May I remind you that these are the same assassins that two years ago discovered their last base, set fire to their store of evil Books, killed seven of their number, and escaped unscathed, before the fools could find their wits. In fact, they are the very two that got the journal from which you learned there was a daughter."

Nazar stopped pacing for a moment and looked at Vincent. Nazar's dark blond hair fell about his eyes and sweat poured down his face, but he was much more composed. "And once they discover the location of the Resistance, they will take care of her."

"Yes, my lord."

"Make ready your forces, General."

"How many men shall I prepare?"

"Prepare twelve hundred of your best men. Put them through additional, specialized training until we are ready to take the Resistance."

"Twelve hundred, my lord?" Vincent was shocked. "The enemy's number cannot exceed three hundred. Six hundred men would be double, if not triple, their number. In fact, I highly doubt they number that high."

Nazar stood toe to toe with the General. The evil swimming in his eyes sent had a sickening affect, even on Vincent. "I want them dead. *Dead!* No prisoners. No mercy." Nazar leaned within inches of Vincent's face and lowered his voice. "Once we have the location of the Resistance, no man, nor their God, can save them from my wrath." Nazar spit on the floor and stalked away. "*Love. Blood.* They claim that blood is their salvation. *Ha!* Will they lift up their voices in praise as their own blood spills by my swords? Will they rejoice as my arrows pierce them? They shall die in their beloved *blood*. They shall *die* in *love!*"

❧

Raya returned from her scouting mission only ten minutes after leaving.

"Well?" asked Damon, who was returning from his own scouting trip along another path.

"The path is too narrow and has many loose rocks. Our horses would not be able to take that path. We could attempt it on foot, but it would be dangerous."

Damon nodded in the direction he had scouted. "That way dead-ends into a sheer cliff face."

Andrea, who had ridden up on Star, said, "I thought you had been to Sven before."

"We have," Damon said. "We just never got there from this high up the mountain."

"So, we are lost?"

"No," said Raya. "We were just trying to find a faster path."

"Well, since we cannot go around the mountain, now what?" Andrea could see that all her questions were aggravating Raya, as usual, but Damon was patient.

"Now we have two options. Up or down," he said.

"So, what is the plan?"

Damon and Raya looked at each other. "Going down and around would be easier," Raya said.

"But going up would be faster. If we go down, we would have to head around toward the bottom and then go back half-way up the mountain." Damon thought for a minute. "I say we go a little further up, and then loop around and down. I have heard that there is a pathway. I have not personally traveled on it, but it should be easy enough to find and navigate."

Raya nodded.

"Well ..." Andrea was hesitant.

"Something wrong?" Damon asked.

"I have just never been that high before," Andrea admitted sheepishly. "I have never been much further than Cresso, much less up a mountain."

Raya rolled her eyes.

"You will be fine," Damon said with his crooked smile hinting at his lips. "Just be sure to drink plenty of water."

After working their way up the mountain for several hours, Andrea felt lightheaded. Dusk was fast approaching, and the steepening terrain forced them to walk their horses.

"I feel like I cannot breathe," Andrea panted.

"The air gets thinner the higher you go," Damon said. "Have you been drinking?"

Andrea stopped and took a sip of water. "My head hurts," she mumbled as she hurried to catch up with Damon and Raya, who had not slowed their brisk pace.

After a moment, Damon finally stopped. "Whoa, boy." He looked up at their path. "The horses are having trouble and it still gets a little steeper. I must have been mistaken about the path. We have to backtrack and go the long way."

Andrea could not help feeling disappointed. A whole day wasted and they would have to go around the bottom of the mountain and then back up.

"I was afraid this might happen," Raya muttered.

Damon nodded. "I thought we could make it or find a different, easier way. I should have just taken us down and around the mountain in the first place. It would have saved time."

And with that, everyone turned around and started to retrace their steps.

"Can—" Andrea said breathlessly, "can we slow down?"

Damon glanced back at her. "We need to hurry if we want to find a good place to make camp before dark. I know the thinner air can be hard, but as long as you drink plenty of water you'll be fine. How much water have you had today?"

"Um," she said, head throbbing, her vision blurred. "I've finished one canteen. I think."

"That's not nearly enough. You need to drink."

"I don't—" she stopped and put her hand on her forehead. "I don't feel well at all."

"Andrea?" Damon's voice echoed from somewhere far away.

ॐ∙ॐ

"Great," Raya grumbled. "She's dehydrated."

"We'll fill her full of water when she wakes up and she'll be fine," Damon said, ignoring the edge to her voice. "Don't be so hard on her. She's never been this far from home."

"Don't be so hard on her?" Raya spat back. "Have you forgotten that she's an assignment? An assignment, Damon, not a person."

Damon ignored her, led his horse over to his sister, and handed her the reins. Then went for Star.

"I don't want her horse."

"You can have the horses or her." Damon held the reins out.

Raya scowled and grabbed the reigns. "I don't see how she has Nazar so worried."

"Knowledge is power," Damon answered promptly. "And she has information about one of Nazar's biggest threats. The Resistance."

"I feel like there is something more as well. Something more personal." Raya looked at her brother. "Do you think she really knows anything? Did she even know where they were hiding until we found that hidden message?"

"She is smart," Damon said. "And she was headed in that direction. Maybe she knew all along and was playing dumb until she thought she could trust us."

"Then she's a good actor."

∞⌒⊚

Everyone was gathered, hand in hand, around Tim and Tisha.

The nightly meeting had gone well. They had presented the Books and all had lifted up prayers for the mission—but that was not the highlight.

Elnai had shown up. Every heart was filled and every eye wet— all trembled in bliss from the kiss of His presence.

Now the Lovers were preparing to send off two of their leaders.

Tisha and Tim were hugged or patted on the back as everyone wished them a safe trip and prayed for their safety.

In a few days, Riven would lead a group of brave Lovers in a dangerous mission of love. They were going to deliver the forbidden Books into the grateful hands of Lovers in Northern Darrion.

Jay waited until everyone else had left. "Tisha, is there anything you need me to do while you are gone?"

Tisha smiled. "I'm going to leave everything up to you. You know what to do."

Jay nodded.

She said, "Will you help Riven organize the hunting parties and supply runs? He'll need to assign people to fill his many roles while he's delivering Books, and everyone's already so busy. Especially since Tristan and Carson are also leaving with him."

"Of course, Tisha. But the boy has probably already worked it out with the others. I'll offer any help I can, but he's very capable."

"Yes, the Maker has blessed him with a good head on his shoulders, and strong instincts with a sword. Even so, he is still young." Tisha smiled with pride as she thought of the twenty-three year old man. "You, Musa, and Riven will do fine. You three, along with the others in the Counsel, have made my job so easy that you don't even need me anymore."

Jay laughed and hugged her. "The Resistance would fall apart if you were not here to order us around."

Tisha laughed with him.

"Be safe, Tisha."

"We will," she promised.

As the words left her mouth, the tall, strong looking young Darrionite with short, curly black hair walked in.

"Hello, Riven," Tisha said. "Need something?"

"Yes," he replied. "I just wanted to know if we should stay on schedule as usual in your absence."

"Of course," Tisha responded, noting his respectful voice. "I was just discussing that with Jay. The Book studies, hunting and supply trips, Book copying, and archery and sword training will continue as usual. Musa will take care of Book study and copying, and Jay will keep training sessions running smoothly. Can you take care of organizing leaders for the hunting parties and supply runs? I also assumed you could distribute the latest batch of Holy Books."

"Jay is usually over that," Riven said.

"I believe you can handle it," Jay replied.

"Then I would be happy to."

"Good," Tisha said. "If you need anything, you can talk to Jay. Which reminds me, will you and Jay speak about organizing the watches and scouts? I usually see to that. Oh! And—"

The young man's smile cut her off.

"I'm sorry," she said, smiling as well. "You know that I tend to worry. But the Resistance is in capable hands."

Riven's eyes sparkled and the corner of his mouth twitched, amused. "Sorry I wasn't here for the meeting. I hated to miss it. I just got back from District Thirteen with the hunting party. We have enough meat to last us a while."

"Good," Tisha said, sighing deeply.

"Safe travels. We are His Lovers."

"Thank you, Riven. And He is ours."

Riven nodded respectfully to Tisha and Jay and went about his day.

"He's a quiet young man," Tisha commented thoughtfully after Riven had left.

"He is very quiet," Jay agreed. "But he surprises me when he does speak. He's wise beyond his years."

"He has a confidence about him. He's a natural leader."

Jay nodded. "Now, I'll let you finish getting ready."

"Thank you, Jay."

Tisha and Tim finished up with their preparations and went to bed early. Tisha still could not stop thinking about Andrea.

෴

Andrea vaguely remembered falling into darkness. *Where am I now?* She was still in the heavy black, but now she felt something cool and hard beneath her.

*Am I conscious?* It seemed like such a ridiculous question to have to ask.

A horse stomped its foot on something hard.

*That sounded real.*

Someone moaned. *Was that me?* she shivered. *I think I am awake.* She tried to open her eyes. They refused. *At least to some extent.*

"Andrea?" Damon's voice. His hand was on her shoulder. "Are you all right?"

"Eh ant pen es …" *That didn't sound right.* She was trying to say, "I cannot open my eyes."

"What?"

Her eyes fluttered and finally opened. Everything was blurry. Her vision cleared after a moment. Damon was sitting next to her. Raya was next to them with all three of the horses.

"What happened?" her words still sounded slow and slurred and she was not quite awake yet.

He helped her sit up and handed her a full canteen. "Drink all of it."

"Now?"

He nodded and she obeyed.

"You blacked out," he said in response to her question. "Your body was not used to the thin air and it was more vulnerable when you added the exhaustion and dehydration. You were not even out for five minutes."

Andrea took another long drink. Her throat was burning.

"That is why I kept telling you to drink."

Andrea nodded as she looked at him over the canteen.

She handed him the now empty canteen and he helped her stand up.

"We have to turn around now, right?" she asked.

At his nod, the trio rode their horses back down the trail they had just traveled. Finally, well after dark, they reached the little cave.

"I'll refill the canteens," Raya said. "There's a clean spring about half a mile down, if you remember from the first time we came this way. Go ahead and bed down my horse."

"Here," Damon offered, "I'll get the water."

"No," she said, irritated. "I want to get it. It's no problem."

Damon knew that, for whatever reason, Andrea rubbed Raya the wrong way. His sister just needed to be alone for a moment. As she dismounted, he noticed she had kept her bow and quiver on her back. They would likely be eating fresh meat tonight. She loved the twang of the bowstring as she let fly an arrow. When she was upset, she would often practice shooting her bow. After emptying her quiver, she often came back in a better mood.

Soon the canteens were gathered up and sent with Raya.

"Where's my Book?" Andrea asked after they had attended the horses and made camp.

"I don't know," Damon said, stretching out his bedroll. "Where did you have it?"

"My saddle bag."

"Then I would assume it's there."

The saddles were against the wall next to the small cave mouth. She looked in the pocket where she had stored the Book and found the little scrap of paper still in place. No one could remove the Book without the scrap falling, so she would know if it had been tampered with. No one had. She breathed a sigh of relief and took it back to the fire.

*Now, let us see who this Elnai is*, she started flipping through inches of pages, skimming for any mention of Elnai. It was time to fulfill her promise that she would find her Maker. *Here's something.*

*A false savior for the lost,*
*Proclaiming himself the lord,*
*With cunning, he brings them death—*
*No one thinks to raise a sword.*

*They stumble around blinded—*
*Guided by his charming lies;*
*The Truth calls them to the light,*
*They have closed their ears and eyes.*

*The True Lord still calls them His*
*If they say for all to hear,*
*"Elnai is the True Savior!"*
*He saves them from death and fear.*

*We must choose which path we walk—*
*Selfish desires or life;*
*Choosing darkness leads to death,*
*And serving yourself brings strife.*

*There is one path to life,*
*You must listen to the Voice—*
*This Voice offers living Peace*
*But lets you make your own choice.*

"That almost sounds like Nazar and the Maker," she mumbled.

"What did you say?" Damon asked.

Andrea started to say "nothing" but then thought, *Well, he hasn't pushed me for information, and whenever he realized I wasn't comfortable with a question he would drop it. He's had more than enough chances to hurt me if he was going to do that. And no one's touched my Book.* Maybe her heart fluttered nervously simply because it had belonged to her mother. "I was just reading something from my Book." She cleared her throat. "You can look if you'd like."

He knelt behind her and read over her shoulder. "What does it mean?"

"I'm not sure."

"Could it be talking about Nazar? Who is Elnai?"

"I was trying to find out who Elnai was."

Footsteps.

Raya was back. Andrea slammed the Book shut quickly. A little too quickly.

Damon noticed. "What's wrong?"

"Raya's back," she stood. "I think she brought us some dinner. We should go help her."

Damon nodded and went to meet Raya. If he was suspicious he didn't show it.

Andrea hid her Book safely back in its place in Star's saddle bag.

"I thought you were only getting water," Damon said, seeing the rabbit Raya carried by the ears.

"I saw him on the way," she answered. "I wanted some fresh meat."

Damon saw that he was right. She had come back with food, and a better mood.

Raya set to work skinning the rabbit. "He does not have much meat on him, but he will do. We can eat some dried berries with him."

The rest of the night went much like the one before it. They prepared dinner, ate, cleaned up, and went to bed.

৯৽৽৻

Tisha and Tim left before dawn, before Andrea, Damon, and Raya were even awake. They had a long way to go. They guided their horses past the early morning watch toward the ocean of sand.

৯৽৽৻

Andrea awakened around the same time as Damon and Raya the next morning.

The three of them discussed the day's plans while they ate a quick breakfast of dried berries. They decided to try to make it to the bottom of the mountain and to drink *plenty* of water.

After breakfast, Damon and Raya saddled the horses while Andrea repacked everything. Then they mounted their horses and started a long day of riding.

෨⊷ৡ

Little girl's laughter broke the silence of the peaceful mountain stream.

Her papa chased her down and swept the squealing girl up.

"I got her, Mama." He hauled his squirming little daughter over his shoulder out of the ankle-deep water.

"Good." Tisha laughed. "Are you hungry, Andrea?"

"No!" she said, grinning ear to ear. "Papa, take me back to the water!"

"It is time to eat, Sweetheart," Ross said as he kissed her little wet forehead.

"I'm not hungry yet!" she protested.

"Maybe this will help." Ross tickled her mercilessly. "Are you getting hungry?" he asked, laughing as hard as she was.

"No!" she insisted through her laughter.

"Are you hungry now?" he kept tickling.

"Yes, Papa, yes!" she giggled. "Just stop!"

He set her down and Tisha handed them each a sandwich. "Ross, you are as bad as she is," Tisha said with a laugh.

He just laughed and sat down to enjoy his sandwich.

After lunch was eaten and cleaned up, Ross said, "I guess we had better head home. We have a long ride."

"Aw," Andrea whined, hugging his legs. "Do we have to? I like the tree." She looked over her shoulder at the tree in the middle of the stream.

"Yes, baby," Tisha said. "We want to get home before dark."

Andrea stuck out her lower lip and sulked over to the horse and buggy.

Andrea sat on her mother's lap on the way home.

"I love the tree, Mommy," said the happy little girl.

"So do I," Tisha responded. "Do you remember the story we told you?"

"Yes," came Andrea's reply. "It has a hole in it because we have a hole in our hearts where Elnai is supposed to be."

"That's right," Ross said, a twinkle in his eyes and a smile playing at the corner of his lips. "But it won't always be that way. We have the Promise."

"That's why the Tree of Promise is here," Tisha chimed in. "Elnai promised that whenever the time is right, He will clean the world of all evil and His true Lovers can be with Him forever. The Tree reminds us of the Promise. The Tree starts out strong and whole, just like we did when we were with the Maker. But when we did bad things, it separated us from Him, just as the Tree is divided. But, just like the Tree is made whole again, Elnai is going to come back and make everything perfect once more."

"Is this the only Tree?" Andrea asked.

"No," her mother answered, smiling down at the little girl cuddled up against her. "There are three."

"You see, Andrea," Ross explained, "there are three trees because of many reasons. There are three parts of the Maker."

"Creator, Savior and Lover!" Andrea piped up.

"There are also the three Great Wars," Tisha said. "The War for Light's Throne, in which Lavin and the fallen tried to take over the Courts of Light; the War for Man's Love—which we are in now, where man must decide whether they will be lovers of Elnai or Lavin; the War of the End Times, where Maker will defeat Lavin and judge every person, good warrior, and fallen warrior once and for all."

"There are also three kingdoms, the Kingdom of Light, the Kingdom of Darkness, and the Kingdom of Man," her father continued. "And when Elnai came to save us, He was dead for three days and three hours before He rose again."

"And I am three years old!" Andrea said excitedly.

Her parents laughed.

"Tisha?"

Tim's voice jolted her back into the present.

"Yes?"

"Are you about ready to stop for the night?"

"I'm ready when you are."

෯෯෯

After a long day of riding, Andrea, Damon and Raya finally stopped for the night. Raya immediately went hunting, and Damon rode about half a mile further to get water. Andrea bedded Star down, gathered enough wood to last the night, rolled out their bedrolls, and started a fire. Damon soon returned and tended to his horse, then sat beside the fire and shaved the bark off of sticks to roast their supper on. Andrea, her tasks completed, was reading the Book like they had done the previous night.

"Damon," Andrea said as she studied the passage, "listen to what this says about Elnai:

> "Man was corrupted with evil ways,
> Plotting and scheming filled all their days;
> Apart from the Maker's perfection,
> Laughing at His righteous correction.
>
> "Doomed forever, apart from His love,
> Elnai descended from high above;
> He came to save us from judgment's death,
> He redeemed us with His final breath.
>
> "He was human in body and mind,
> He never did wrong of any kind;
> He handed Himself to evil hands,
> They bound Him in a sinner's bands.
>
> "He surrendered and they took His life—
> He died to provide a sacrifice;
> But on day three in the third hour,
> He reclaimed the keys to death's power.
>
> "Three days, three hours, three Trees the same,
> With the three Trees a Promise then came:
> Debtor's payment, a sinner's ransom—
> These are the things for which He had come.
>
> "He showed us the path to His presence,
> He makes rich the lowest of peasants;
> If you will ask to be forgiven,
> To you, life in death is given."

This sounded familiar to Andrea as if she had heard it before.

"So who is this Elnai?" Damon asked, sincerely curious.

Excitement rose within her as she skimmed through additional pages. "Look!"

"What?"

"This passage has our answer! It says:

> *"The Son of the Lord, in mortal skin*
> *Came into this world to conquer our sin;*
> *He made the way, in Him we have won!*
> *We praise Lord Elnai, the Maker's Son!"*

"Wait," Damon said, reading the passage himself, "so, Elnai is the Maker's son?"

Andrea laughed. "It all makes sense now! Elnai is the Savior! Elnai is the Maker's son!"

Damon leaned back on one hand and ran the other through his thick, brown hair. "I don't know what to think."

Andrea felt an excitement like never before. She hurriedly flipped through the Book. "In the poem about the Tree of Promise it says: '*It stands to remind all that will hear, That Elnai's reign is still drawing near, Just as the trunk has broken apart, All of the world has hardened its heart.*'" She scrambled for her mother's letter. "And this is what my mother said about Him: '*we will still have the one thing they can never take away. The love of the Maker, and the promise of justice through Elnai.*' And a little later she writes: '*The Righteous Maker is Lord of Mercy, and Elnai is Prince of Peace.*'" She grabbed her Book again. "I also read about Him right here!" she exclaimed, finding what she was looking for. "*The true Lord still calls them His, If they say for all to hear, 'Elnai is the true Savior,' He saves them from death and fear.*" Her voice trailed off as she got lost in the passage.

❧

Andrea's face was a picture of awestruck wander. She was almost childlike in her amazement. She was not sitting across from Damon in the glow of the fire. She no longer saw the brilliant canopy of stars or felt the chill in the mountain air. She was lost in the yellowing pages. She sat, legs crossed, with the Book in her lap. Her eyes were bright and her lips hinted at a peaceful smile. She turned the pages daintily, as if they were fragile and precious.

Damon could see that she was *real*. Her beliefs, her faith, was real.

He cocked his head. She had lost so much and it only looked to be getting worse. Yet, she was real. She was transparent, but in no way shallow. Her emotions showed in everything she did. He could read right through her. He knew she was stumbling. Trying to survive. Even so, she stayed true. She refused to sell out even under penalty of death.

She didn't know much, but was hungry to know more and to discover Truth. She knew that the Maker is the True Lord and Elnai is His righteous Son. She was desperate for the truth and fought to find it. Would even die for it.

That was one thing he could not understand. She was young. She belonged in a quiet little town somewhere with a nice, hardworking husband. Andrea was the type to settle down and start a family. She didn't belong out here.

*She is young, beautiful, and smart,* he thought. *It would not be hard for her to make a life for herself and start a family.*

But Andrea was so passionate about her Maker. Damon knew that, if he were in her situation, he would have forsaken his beliefs long ago. He would have betrayed everything to keep his life. He had never known someone who was so … real.

He almost envied her. Because, if he was honest with himself, he was not real. He *had* betrayed everything to keep his own life. But what was the use? What had he saved? He had stopped feeling. All he was now was an empty, lifeless shell.

## CHAPTER EIGHT

# DISCOVERING ELNAI

*T*hird Biasday, Medivmonth, 107 Fifth Age

*Today is Andrea's third birthday! She is so smart and talkative already!*

*Ross and I have been careful to teach her the Truth and keep her covered in prayer even while she is young. She asks countless questions.*

*It is upsetting, to say the least, that if we are not careful to always tell her the Truth about the Maker of All Things and Elnai that the world we live in will teach her lies. Even as young as she is. But I don't want to talk about this right now. Not on such a special day …*

* ❧ *

Andrea's green eyes met Damon's and he realized he had been staring. He looked away, shaking his head to clear his thoughts.

Damon yawned. "It's late; Raya should be back by now."

Andrea pried herself away from the pages and tenderly closed the cover. "You're right. Should we go look for her?"

"No, she can take care of herself. Besides, we don't want her to come back while we're gone."

Andrea nodded.

Damon stretched out on his bedroll, exhausted.

"Damon?" Andrea said, hugging her knees

"Hmm?"

"We know that Elnai is the Savior that the Tree of Promise, well, promises. And we know that He is the Maker's Son."

"Yes?" he rolled on his side to face the girl on the other side of the fire.

Her face was orange in the glow of the flames. Her brows were slightly furrowed. "So what do we do now?"

"What do you mean?"

She thought for a second. "Well, are we supposed to do something? Or is believing enough?"

*If only she knew who she was asking.* "I guess you just have to believe it."

She was quiet for a moment. "But what did it mean whenever it said, *'The true Lord still calls them His, If they say for all to hear, "Elnai is the true Savior," He saves them from death and fear,'*" she said, putting emphasis on "if."

Damon thought for a second. "So you think you have to do something?"

"I don't know." She sighed. "That seems to be all I know anymore."

"What?"

"That I don't know anything," she said resignedly.

He smiled at that, then flopped back over on his back and closed his eyes.

Andrea lay on her back and looked at the countless stars. "Damon?" she whispered after a moment. "Are you asleep?"

Damon rubbed his face, *Not anymore.* "Hmm?"

"How much farther do we have to go before we reach Sven?"

"We will start heading around the mountain first thing tomorrow. Maybe about a day and a half of hard riding."

"We are getting close," she thought out loud. "I can't believe we're actually going to find my mother."

"Well," he said, "we don't know how far we have to go from Sven. The Resistance is hidden well. After all, it hasn't been discovered by Nazar yet. It could still be a while."

"You're right," she sighed. "Well, good night, Damon."

"Good night."

"Do you want me to wake you up when Raya gets here?"

"Yes."

"Alright."

෨⊷ఌ

It was not much longer until Andrea saw Raya coming. She was dragging a nice sized umpha behind her horse. The goat-like creature would last them a few days if they preserved it properly.

Andrea shook Damon by the shoulder and he immediately sat up.

"That will make several nice meals. Nice job, Raya."

The corner of her mouth ever so slightly tilted upward at her brother's comment.

*Whoa!* Andrea thought. *Was that a smile?*

"Sorry I took so long," Raya said dryly. "I wounded it and had to chase it to the top of the mountain and back before it finally bled out." She rolled her eyes. "I was lucky to find it."

"Well we had better get this thing cleaned and cooked before it spoils," said Damon.

Damon dug a hole and started a fire in it. He covered the fire pit with a semi-flat stone and rolled some fairly large rocks around it, but left a gap in the little wall. He covered the top of the enclosure with another large rock and black smoke billowed out through the opening in the side. After surveying and approving his work, he went to help the girls finish cleaning the animal.

"Are we going to cook it in there?" Andrea asked.

Damon nodded. "We are going to smoke the meat there overnight. That will keep it from spoiling."

"Are we going to need to watch the fire?"

"No. I used lagner wood. It is perfect for this. It burns thick smoke for a long time. I put enough in there to last the rest of the night."

"He put it down wind of us, too. For *once*," Raya said in her raspy, sarcastic way. When she glanced up at her brother, her eyes almost had a playful sparkle, and both eyebrows were raised.

"Really, Raya?" he asked, shaking his head. "Once, I put it *upwind* of us and we had to remake camp in the middle of the night because the smoke was so thick," he explained to Andrea. "But that was the *first* and *last* time it happened." He looked from one to the other with his crooked smile.

After a final laugh, they took the animal's remains away from camp and washed off thoroughly to avoid attracting scavengers. They returned and fell into their sleeping rolls.

At dawn the following day, the preserved meat was packed into saddlebags. The day's plans were discussed over a light, quick breakfast. Then, the twins saddled the horses while Andrea broke camp.

They rode hard. Even though they were all experienced riders, Andrea was beginning to feel the heavy hand of weariness weighing upon her. She could see that Damon and Raya's straight, proud postures were sagging a bit after hours in the saddle. Even though they were tired, stops were few and far between. Andrea was happy to dismount at the occasional stream for a drink before once again swinging into the saddle.

At noon they had some of the freshly smoked umpha. She had never eaten it before and it had a strange, rubbery texture, but she enjoyed it. It was filling and she was thankful for that. They didn't stop again until an hour or two before summer's dusk, when they finally made camp. Raya went for water, Damon started a fire and gathered wood, and Andrea tended to the horses. Bone tired, Andrea stroked Star, wishing she had a good brush.

By the time that Damon sat down by the now pleasantly crackling fire, Andrea was already buried in the pages of the Book. As the stars began to twinkle overhead, Andrea and Damon discussed a few passages. Andrea was a bit surprised at how much more relaxed they both seemed as they read. Maybe it was weariness and the night's stillness that put her at ease.

Soon the steady beat of hooves was heard in the darkness to announce Raya's return. Andrea tucked the Book away, not yet willing to expose the secrets of the precious pages to the sharp, icy eyes and still sharper tongue. Their meal of umpha was mostly silent, but Andrea didn't mind. She was ready to fall into her bed roll, knowing sleep would claim her in seconds.

The following days were much like the previous. Though they were unchanging, and uneventful, Andrea was thankful for the routine that had developed. It was the only thing consistent in the chaos she was living through. Even though her days were tiring and there was no guarantee of what tomorrow held, the routine helped her keep her sanity. And she enjoyed the time spent buried in the pages of her precious Book.

Andrea was excited when they finally arrived at Sven, though they only stopped briefly. She felt as if she could have ridden from there all night, sure that they would reach the Resistance base very soon. But, as Damon had said, it could be days, even weeks, before they actually found them. Sven was only a place to *start*. Even so, she was ecstatic to turn Star east and ride out from Sven as if the Resistance was almost within sight. Much of her excitement turned to patient expectancy over the next six days of riding, but her spirits were still high.

Another routine day came and went. They were resting for their noon break a little longer than usual today. Everyone was tired.

Raya leaned against a tree in the shade sharpening her daggers, as Damon cleaned his sword. Andrea was resting quietly in the shade watching the horses graze.

Andrea shifted her attention to Raya and watched her masterfully go about her task. Raya noticed and looked at Andrea as if she was imagining throwing the knives at her.

Andrea only sighed and looked over at Damon. She watched as he cleaned and sharpened his sword as if it were a delicate art.

"Do you enjoy doing that?" Andrea asked, noting how the corners of his mouth hinted at a smile.

Damon nodded. "This sword has saved my life many times. Take care of your sword and it will take care of you." He held it out and inspected it thoroughly. Standing up, he smiled as he slid the sword into its sheath. "I love that sound." He patted the hilt and looked at Andrea. "The sound of the sword sliding back into its place at your side. It means that the fight is finally over."

The musical twang of a bowstring rang through the moment of silence.

"That is the sound that I love," Raya said. Her voice had a slight softness that Andrea had never noticed before. "When you have a good bow, a straight arrow, and true aim, you know you can take care of yourself. Nothing can ever touch you."

"Damon," Andrea asked, "you can shoot a bow, correct?"

"Yes."

"Why do you never use a bow? I mean, obviously, you bring yours when you go hunting, but you don't seem to like it much."

Damon shrugged. "I'm just more comfortable with a sword."

"That," said Raya with a playful smirk, "is because archery requires a more skillful touch. You have to find your mark." She pulled the string to her ear and lined up a shot with an invisible arrow and target. "Account for distance, wind, the target's movements. It is an art, really."

Damon looked over at her and crossed his arms, brow arched. "Are you saying that it takes less skill to fight with a sword? You have a split-second to anticipate and react to your opponent's attacks! You have to be aware of your entire body at all times and it takes a lot of skill—footwork, speed, strength—to defend yourself and set the other up for a strike at the same time." An easy smirk played across his lips. "But I can see how it might be hard for an archer to understand."

Raya's icy glare shot up to meet his cocky, playful eyes.

She softened and matched his crooked smile. "Of course I am not saying *anyone* could face just *anyone* in a duel." Raya was enjoying this playful banter. For a minute she forgot about Andrea. "Of course it requires some skill and ability. But, it is really more about the strength of the swordsman than skill."

Damon shook his head with a slight chuckle. "Spoken like a true *archer*."

Andrea could tell they were both very passionate about this— and very competitive.

Damon walked up to where Raya was seated and looked down at her. "An *archer* fights the battle from a distance. If an *archer* makes a mistake, an *archer* can line up another shot. An *archer* does not put herself in the middle of battle. A *swordsman* does. A *swordsman* does not always get a second chance. A *swordsman* rarely can retreat."

By now Raya was standing, trying to stare her brother down with her cocky blue glare.

His eyes daring, eyebrows raised, a sly smile played across his face.

"You doubt I can swing a sword, brother?"

"You doubt I can shoot a bow?"

"Let us see."

"Give me a mark," Damon challenged as he turned to retrieve the bow and arrows he kept secured to his saddle.

Raya pointed to a slender sapling a few dozen yards away.

Damon studied his target a moment then carefully readied an arrow. He brought the bow up and pulled the string back, his posture and toned muscles showed his practice. He held steady for a moment.

"Your target would have overtaken you by now." His sister smirked. "Are you afraid that your words will outdo your aim, Damon?"

Damon let fly the arrow. It whistled through the air and sank deep into its mark.

He turned to the blond beside him. "Satisfied?"

In response, Raya, with surprising purpose and speed, retrieved from her quiver an arrow, readied it, aimed, and let it fly. As soon as her first arrow began to whistle through the air, she readied another. The second arrow was loosed almost immediately after the first met its mark with a thud, and she did the same with a third.

*Twang, thud. Twang, thud. Twang, thud.*

Andrea blinked and felt her jaw drop as Raya sent three arrows whistling to their mark in slightly less time than it had taken Damon to shoot one.

Damon's arrow was slightly right of the center about six feet up the sapling. Raya's first arrow was dead center about a foot below Damon's, her second a few inches above and slightly to the right of the first, the third was a good foot below her other two and dangerously to the left—it barely managed to sink shallowly into the edge of the sapling.

"Third was a little sloppy," Damon said.

"I can do better." Raya looked disgustedly at the arrow. Her voice held its familiar, icy edge.

"I was only teasing," Her brother said softly. "You bested me."

Raya nodded. "You don't always have as much time as you took."

Andrea realized that Raya's criticism came from concern for Damon.

"Of course," Damon assured her. "I can shoot faster, but we are not in a battle."

Raya and Damon went to retrieve the arrows and Andrea wondered if they truly ever stopped fighting. Was this all they knew? Who were they outside of the battle? Did they themselves even know?

Andrea had seen them as emotionless fighters, but rarely did she see them as family or even relaxed.

Of course there were moments of rest, but even then, their eyes always scanned for unseen enemies, their posture ready to jump to action at the slightest hint it was called for. Their weapons never left their sides.

Words that were not related to their situation were seldom spoken, and even then, their voices were never light and carefree. Laughter was almost unheard of.

Even in softer moments, such as Raya saying she was afraid Damon needed to be faster with the bow, it was laced with anticipation of trouble.

Andrea could understand to some extent. The situation she found herself in was not to be taken lightly. But there was something different about the pair walking toward her. There was a cold hardness about them. It was unnerving.

Andrea shook the thoughts from her mind and blamed it on the seriousness of their situation.

Damon was speaking to Raya as they walked back. "—cannot best me."

"We shall see," Raya replied.

Raya retrieved from her saddle a sword like Damon's.

The sound of two blades leaving their sheaths reached Andrea's ears.

One second they stood facing each other, idle swords loose at their sides, about ten paces apart, the next metal clashed as they sparred.

Andrea gasped at the incredible speed and precision with which they fought. Their bodies moved with fluid skill to match their speed. Feet never missed a step, determined clashes of metal on metal, eyes that took in everything about the opponent.

Raya's jaw was set, eyes blazing with fiery determination. With Raya on the offensive, Damon was confident, but careful. He met every blow.

Raya grunted and put her whole body into a well-aimed swing to the right toward his exposed torso. Having just blocked a jab to the left, Damon quickly recognized his weakness and swiftly moved to intercept the blow.

Raya leaned into the swing and Andrea held her breath.

Damon's experienced eyes saw that the swing left her off balance and her side exposed.

"You over committed, Raya!" Damon cried as he blocked her blow.

She was off balance. Seeing her error too late, Raya was sent to the ground by Damon's swift right knee to her left side.

Stunned and slightly winded, Raya gasped, fell back, and lost her grip on her sword. On her back, she heard her sword clatter just out of reach of her fingertips.

She rolled for it, but Damon kicked it away.

Raya rolled to her feet. Damon stood between her and her sword, about five paces away from her. Both breathed hard as sweat ran down their faces.

"I have you, Raya," Damon said. That cocky, crooked smile of his played across his face. "You cannot win."

Raya saw him relax a bit and took advantage of it. With a cry, she closed the gap between them and ran left last second. A shocked Damon whipped around to see her drop into a roll to the right and come up with her sword.

"Don't let your cockiness get you hurt." Raya smiled, panting.

This time Damon went on the offensive. He put more strength into his blows this time as he forced her to back away as she blocked.

Raya attempted a counter jab, but Damon met it and kept the upper hand.

Andrea knew they would not purposefully hurt each other, and they both had incredible skill, but still she was nervous. What if one didn't block before the other pulled back?

But it seemed as though they were physically incapable of making a mistake. Each movement was executed with such a precise mastery that Andrea was completely amazed. It was almost as if it were a dance.

Finally Damon jumped at the opportunity he had been waiting for. Their blades met and he expertly twisted his in such a way that Raya's sword was ripped from her grip. Before she had a chance to react, Damon had the tip of his blade at her throat. She stiffened and froze. Neither moved, breathing heavily.

"Well fought, sister," he said as he sheathed his sword, "but I have killed you."

Raya took her sword from the ground and sheathed it as well. "Well done."

"Remember don't over commit."

"It seems we have both proven our point," she said as she reached for her canteen. "It takes skill for both arts."

Once more, everyone was seated in the shade resting.

"So, Andrea," Damon asked, never taking his eyes from the small stream ahead. "Do you prefer sword or bow?"

"I'm just a farm girl," Andrea replied. "I don't even know how to use this sword that I have. Before now, I have never had to fight for anything. I had my chores and my routine. That was life." Andrea felt a little homesick for her simple, but safe world. "I would consider myself a good rider though. Star was my escape. I spent countless hours in his saddle."

All was quiet for a moment.

"What about you two? Who are you outside of this fight? Without the weapons?"

To Andrea it was an idle question, but Raya's expression darkened. Damon just sat there, deep in thought.

"I don't know," he said in a tired voice. "I don't know any different."

"Do you ever think you will go home? What is waiting for you there?"

∂°∾

*Nothing,* Damon thought. *A castle. A tyrant. Another mission. Another fight. Another kill.*

"Nothing," he said with a sigh. *Who am I beyond the battle? Beyond the constant fight?* He didn't know. He was numb in many ways.

Don't ask questions. Don't feel. They are targets, missions—not people.

Andrea was a target. An assignment. But she was just as much of a person as he was. In fact she was more of a person. Because, unlike him, she felt the emotions that separated humans from animals. That made her human. Ignoring the fact would not change it.

So if he was numb to the emotions that made Andrea human, what did that make him?

*An animal.*

Damon was shocked, but not as much as he would have thought.

His world was kill or be killed. His world was numb to taking another's life. His world knew no other way. His world was that of an animal.

*But there is still hope,* he thought, *at least I understand it.*

But did he? What was hope? What did it mean to him?

There had been nights where he was haunted by his own actions, but what did that mean? He knew it was wrong, but what was right? Did right exist?

"We had better get moving," he said.

"What's the hurry?" Raya asked.

"There is no hurry," he snapped. "But we are leaving now."

He was shocked at his own voice. It was more of a growl really. Barbaric. It just made him boil all the more.

They rode in heavy silence. At camp the mood was not much better. Damon went to bed early.

అంఉ

After another long day of riding, while Raya was out for fresh meat and Damon was gathering wood, Andrea was once again searching the Book for anything that might tell her more about Elnai. She had already given Star a rubdown and refilled the canteens, so she was eager to relax. But she was a bit distracted. Damon had informed her that tomorrow they would cross the Darrionite border. She would have officially left Airiss. Damon said they would be in District Ten once they crossed the border. It made sense that the Resistance would be there, he had explained, because District Ten was mostly desert, with few small cities and only the capital city fortified. The border of this district was not closely watched. It would have been fairly simple for the fleeing Lovers to escape Airiss and avoid Darrionite attention.

It was exciting to think of leaving Airiss, yet terrifying. She was very far away from everything she had ever known.

Andrea pushed those thoughts aside. She shifted her focus back to the task at hand. She had to see if there was something additional she needed to do. Was simply believing that Elnai was the Son of the Maker and Promised Savior of the World enough?

"Holy Maker," she whispered. "If there is something that I need to do, I want to do it. Please help me read what I need to and give me understanding."

She skimmed through page after page before she finally found something.

*You believe that Elnai is Savior,*

*That alone will not save you—*
*For even the powers of darkness*
*Believe that these things are true.*

*It takes a commitment from your heart*
*To walk on the path of light,*
*Repent of sin and declare your faith,*
*You will be clean in His sight.*

*You were separated from Him once*
*But will never be again;*
*When you confessed Him Savior and Lord*
*He cleansed you of stains and sin.*

Andrea put her face in her hands and let that sink in.

She traced her fingers over the passage.

Suddenly, she heard something. It almost sounded like a cry.

"Damon?" Andrea stood up and looked in the direction she had heard the noise. "Raya?"

She thought she heard hoof beats, *That sounded like more than one horse. Did Damon and Raya meet up and come back together?*

She squinted into the darkness. Then she saw Damon's silhouette. "Oh, Damon, where is your horse? I thought I heard someone yelling and was getting worried."

The figure kept walking towards her. Finally, the firelight showed her it was not Damon.

"Hello?" her voice was high with nerves.

He was tall and muscular. His eyes were black like his short, tightly curled hair. His skin was a deep, dark brown. She recognized him as a man from Darrion.

She had been close with a Darrionite family back in Cresso. They were kind people, but something told her that this man was not.

"Who are you?"

He showed no signs of hearing her; he just kept walking towards her.

Andrea glanced at Star. Her hunting sword was in the saddlebag next to him. She took a timid step back, her heart racing.

The man noticed that she was about to make a run for it. Without giving her time to react, he drew his sword and rushed her.

Andrea turned and tried to run. He grabbed her arm and jerked her back. She screamed. That earned her a hard slap in the face.

He had a sword at her throat and a bruising grip on her arm. When he spoke, he had a thick accent. "No trouble. Make easy. Go better for you."

❧❦

Janelle sat alone in Yipoc Raj. She had already looked over the copies that had been made under her supervision today, and she now looked over the passage Musa would be working on tomorrow.

> *To Lavin He said, "Your image be scorned!*
> *For you appeared to them in serpent's form;*
> *Your cursed flesh shall rot and sag from your frame,*
> *You shall be looked at by all with disdain.*

> *You will strike Elnai, He will fall three days,*
> *When I raise Him, nations will sing His praise;*
> *Your judgment shall come when I make all right,*
> *Once Elnai returns, He shall end this fight.*

❧❦

Without warning, Tisha's thoughts were suddenly consumed with Andrea. It was almost as when Elnai would put Ross on her mind and she would pray for him. Later, she would find out that he had been in trouble.

"Tisha?" Tim looked worried as he stopped his horse. "Are you all right? You look sick?"

Tisha didn't respond.

"Tisha!"

He startled her. "Yes?"

"What is going on?"

"I ... I don't know."

"Tisha, please." He searched her face. "Don't tell me that. You can trust me."

Tisha looked at him. "Tim, it's not that I don't trust you. I just … I don't know what to do. I don't know what's going on. Where do I even start?"

"Try the beginning."

They both slid off their horses and sat down. Tisha, through tears, told him everything. She told him how, for months now, she had not been able to stop thinking of Andrea. About the dreams. All of it.

"I don't know what is happening, Tim," she finished. "Do you think I am going mad?"

"No, I don't think you are." He thought for a minute. "Do you believe that Andrea is still alive?"

Tisha shook her head. "No. Maybe? I have no idea anymore. Is there any chance?"

"Well, Tisha, I guess there is always a chance." Tim hesitated. "But I don't believe she would have made it. You know that some of us went back and searched for her."

Tisha nodded and wiped her eyes. "I have prayed and prayed. I just don't understand."

Tim didn't know what to say. "Tisha, I will not say that I know what you are going through, because I don't. The only thing I know to do is pray."

They held hands and cried out to their Maker. They cried for understanding, but most of all for peace.

After both of them had composed themselves, they resumed their long ride. Tisha felt better, but Andrea's name never left her thoughts.

෨~ල

Andrea's hands were tied to Star's saddle, who was led by her captor, also on a horse. Her cheek still hurt and she tasted blood on her lip from the futile fight she had managed to put up. She refused to show any signs of discomfort or fear even though the ropes cut into her wrists and her heart practically pounded out of her rib cage. She would not give this man the satisfaction.

They had gone less than a mile when they stopped at a camp. Andrea counted fifteen men, all of whom spoke in a foreign tongue and looked as strong as her captor.

Some of the men were starting a fire and tending to the horses. She noticed that three others were wounded, one severely.

One man had just removed an arrow from his shoulder and someone was tending to the wound. Another had blood-soaked rags tied tightly around his upper arm. The last was unconscious, and had taken a severe blow to the side from what Andrea guessed was a sword. Two others were trying to stop the bleeding.

Andrea's captor and another man spoke sharply and Andrea felt even more helpless not being able to understand what was being said. She swallowed the lump in her throat.

Finally the fire was giving out a good bit of light and she saw Raya, hands bound tightly, leaning against a tree. Icy gaze carefully taking in every detail of her surroundings.

Damon lay bound and motionless beside her.

"Damon!" she cried out before she could catch herself.

A heavy hand struck her face so hard that she felt lightheaded. "Don't speak!" he barked.

She was roughly untied from the saddle and put on the ground. Still feeling dizzy, when the rough hands snatched her from the saddle she tripped and, being unable to catch herself with her hands tied, landed on her stomach.

Both men began yelling at her and one started to clench his fist.

"Please!" She flinched, hoping they would not hit her. Her cheek still throbbed. "I cannot understand you!"

"Stand!" he demanded, reaching for her with a giant, calloused hand.

"I don't need help," she said calmly, hoping that she would not provoke him. She blinked back tears. She got up and was shoved down beside Raya.

She didn't allow herself to yelp. *I could have sat down just fine by myself, thank you. I didn't need to be shoved,* she complained inwardly.

Once the men walked off, Andrea whispered to Raya, "Is Damon okay?" Blood matted his hair on the back of his head and his shoulder was cut.

She nodded. "They cut his shoulder but it is not deep. They hit him on the head and knocked him out, but not before he got one guy in the arm and the other in the side. Damon will be fine. He has survived worse."

"The man who was cut in the side, will he survive?"

Raya looked at the large man lying limp in a growing puddle of his own blood. "He will most likely die. They have given him naxer root extract to keep him unconscious. They also gave him some crushed moy-moy." Before Andrea could ask, Raya continued, "That's a plant that grows in northern Darrion. It slowed his bleeding, but they have not stopped it. Even with the moy-moy, I would not give him more than a few hours."

The man already looked lifeless.

Andrea was scared to even ask. "If he dies, what will happen to Damon?"

Raya thought for a moment. "I don't know. They may want to punish him or decide he is not worth the trouble. If they do he could be killed. For that reason alone, I hope the dog stays alive until we can escape." For a moment her stern expression softened as she looked over at her brother.

"What about you? Are you okay?"

"I'm not hurt. I had tied my horse and was on foot. I had just killed a nice goat and was walking down to get it when six of them jumped out at once. I barely had enough time to react. I grabbed an arrow and stabbed one guy in the shoulder before they hit me in the back of the head with the handle of a sword and I woke up here. Damon and the man he wounded were dragged in here by five men, just before you were brought here." She turned to face Andrea for the first time. Raya's face had some bruises and her eyebrow and lip were cut. Her voice was flat. "Did you put up a fight at all?"

Andrea ignored the slight sarcastic edge in Raya's voice and told her what had happened.

"Do you think they will kill us?"

"No," Raya answered. "They are taking us across the border to Darrion to sell us as slaves. They will not do any real damage. They want us to be healthy and strong to impress the buyers."

"How long will it take them to get us across the border?"

"A day if they travel quickly. If they get us into Darrion we have no chance."

"I don't see how it matters," Andrea sighed. "It is not like being in Nazar's country is going to help us any."

Raya cursed under her breath.

"What?"

Raya spat the words out. "That is *my* goat. They are eating the goat that I killed."

Damon rolled onto his back and slowly began to sit up. Raya helped him the best she could with her tied hands.

"Are you alright?" Andrea whispered.

Damon, now sitting up, shook his head trying to clear his mind. Head throbbing, he assessed the situation.

"I will be fine." His voice was deep and firm, but a bit groggy. His deep brown eyes took in every detail. "Illegal slave traders?" it was more of a statement than a question.

Raya nodded.

"What are we going to do?" Andrea asked.

He said nothing for a moment. "Are either of you hurt?"

"Nothing worth mentioning," Andrea said.

"Do they have our horses?"

"They are tied with the others," Raya replied. "Our weapons were brought to the one they call Jodai. He seems to be the leader." Raya pointed, hands still in her lap, to Jodai.

Damon nodded.

The man who had cooked the goat walked over to them. He was slightly taller than Damon, with a few days' growth of beard, and appeared muscular and capable with the curved sword that hung at his side. Even so, he was small for a Darrionite. Darrionite men often averaged six foot five inches. "Eat." He dropped three small pieces of meat in the dirt by their feet.

Damon spat.

The man began to yell something in the Darrionite tongue that Andrea could not understand, but, before he had time to hit Damon, Jodai yelled at the man.

"*Ert gi mage hev ene anni ne bar les kaziim wa yain ingo hiv mayahx!*"

The man glared at Damon, apparently considering the words carefully, before stomping away.

"Why does he want us to eat so badly?" Andrea asked.

"If we don't eat," Damon explained quietly, "we will not look as healthy and strong and when they go to sell us, they will not get as much money. That is why the leader told that man not to hit me." Everyone was quiet as Jodai approached.

Jodai was much larger than Damon, who was definitely not small. He had long dreadlocks tied in the back. His voice was deep and his accent not as thick as the others'. He was built like a warrior and no one doubted his abilities.

"I give you clean meat," Jodai said. "You will eat."

Raya, hatred dripping from her words, spoke in Darrionite. "*Nai ne gi dyrt um so jaix elihim anni.*"

He backhanded her and she was almost knocked down on her side, but she caught herself.

Jodai yelled something in return.

Damon, in a deep but calm voice, said something that earned him a cold stare. "*Bree anni ne evice aw odo ree anni ogg ilt tiv ain.*"

"*Ina ne cahn annis widnai,*" Jodai said, anger edging in his voice. He switched back to Common Tongue, and Andrea could finally understand. "This is a fight you cannot win."

"*Nai ne yas, Jodai,*" Damon said. "We will see."

Jodai looked at Andrea. "*Anni ce dray. Ujayun broh annis xaiv.*"

Raya smirked and rolled her eyes at whatever he said.

Andrea felt very aware of her small stature as Jodai stared down at her. "I cannot understand you," she said timidly.

Jodai studied her a moment before speaking in Common Tongue. "You are wise not to speak. Your companions could learn from you.

"If you behave and bring a good price I will be sure that you are sold to someone who treats their slaves well. You're a beautiful, strong girl who knows how to act. It should not be hard." Jodai almost spoke in a friendly way with Andrea. The way he looked at her was unnerving. Andrea tried to hide the shiver running down her spine.

Andrea bit her tongue before she retorted, "I suppose you want me to thank you" in a way that would have made Raya proud. Although she wanted to say many things, she realized the wisdom of staying silent.

Instead, she stared back at him defiantly until he finally returned to his place by the fire.

"What did you say?" Andrea asked Damon.

"Raya told him that we would not eat food from pigs like him, and he said that we could starve. That is when I said that he would not do that because he wants a good price."

☙❧

Damon and Raya slept in shifts. Damon took the first shift and Andrea said she would sit up with him. Damon tried to convince her to sleep since she could not understand Daroon, but she was determined.

After Raya had gone to sleep and they had been sitting in silence for a few minutes, Andrea asked, "Damon, do you remember how we were wondering whether or not we were supposed to do anything now that we understand who Elnai really is?"

He turned to face her. "Yes. What of it?"

"I think I figured it out."

Damon had to admit that he was curious.

"I was reading the Book and I found a passage. I don't remember exactly what it said, but basically it said that knowing the truth is not enough, you have to act on it."

"What does that mean?"

"It said something about a commitment in your heart. And in the other passage it said, '*If you say for all to hear, "Elnai is the True Savior," He will save you from death and fear.*' It also talks about Him sacrificing Himself to save us. I think that we need to tell Him that we know he is real, believe that He sacrificed Himself to save us, and that we accept His sacrifice so that we can be forgiven for everything that we have done wrong." She looked into his eyes. "Do you understand?"

"I think so," he said. *I only wish that it could be true. That I could start over. That I could be real.*

"Will you pray? With me?"

"Andrea," he hesitated. His gaze dropped to the ground.

"If you don't want to, I understand. This is personal. A commitment. I am going to pray. If you want to you can, if not, that is alright too." She closed her eyes and prayed quietly and earnestly. "Elnai, I think I understand now. Thank You for helping me find Your Book so I could find You. I know that you are real and that you died for me. Thank you for taking the punishment that I deserve for the things that I have done when you were perfect and innocent. Forgive me for everything I have done wrong. I am committing my heart—my life—to You right now. Help me to live a life that will make You proud and bring honor to Your name." She looked up with tears in her eyes and smiled. "I feel clean, new. I know that I

have done wrong in many ways, but now I know that I'm forgiven."
She swatted at the tears that traced her cheeks.

Damon was overwhelmed, *This is real. This kind of peace, of con-tentment, of assurance. This is what I've been searching for—what I want.*
"Andrea—"

## CHAPTER NINE

# THE ESCAPE

*Second Davday, Biziwmonth, 108 Fifth Age*

*Something is not right. Everyone in Valrine, Cresso, and other nearby towns has been ordered by Nazar to bring their families to Reed in one week's time. I can't explain it, but I feel like something terrible is going to happen and Ross feels the same way. Tomorrow we're leaving. Where, I have no idea. It scares me to think of having to go on the run with Andrea. She is only four, and it terrifies me. But we have to run. We cannot let our daughter bend knee to Nazar. I cannot stand the thought of Andrea not knowing the name of her Maker.*

*Ross even said to me earlier, "I would rather die than see my beautiful little girl grow up serving anyone other than the True Lord. I would rather her die. Because this ... denying the name of Elnai ... this is more than a physical death."*

*I shivered at his face and tone. Ross spoke with such intensity, such conviction. I never doubted that he would indeed die before seeing our baby deceived, but if I was not convinced before—I am certain now. I agree wholeheartedly. My daughter belongs to the True Lord. To Light and Love Himself. And no one—no man, no deceiver, no darkness—will have her. Not while there is breath in my lungs.*

*Third Salmday, Biziwmonth, 108 Fifth Age*

*Ross cannot come home. I'm not even allowed to visit him. They won't let him leave the gates. He wanted me to take Andrea and run, but I can't. Our house is under surveillance. With the help of Rhoda, I was able to sneak into Reed and speak with Ross. I could not stay long because Tristan's shift was almost over and he warned me not to let the man replacing him at the gate catch me.*

*We have decided to get everything that has to do with the Resistance's work to locations B and C. We are also putting my journal in location A along with the box for Andrea if anything happens to us. We will just tuck the diary under the heavy box. Maybe if the box is found, this journal will not be. We should probably burn it, but I want Andrea to know the Truth if anything happens to us. I will trust Elnai that this and the box and journal will only be found by the right person.*

*We have six days to do all of these things and get to Reed. We are even think-ing about hiding Andrea in the secret room Ross dug under the loose floorboard under the stove. We don't want to take Andrea. It's so hard to trust Elnai with my baby when I have no idea what will happen. I know He will take care of her, but I cannot help but worry so …*

Flora's heart fluttered. She checked around the dark room. Her husband was still asleep. Good.

She could hardly believe what she had just read. All those years of work that Ross and Tisha had done for the Resistance may not have burned with their house! Location A had been the Tree of Promise, now if she could only remember where locations B and C were.

"Elnai," she whispered shakily, "if you will help me find their work, I would be able to finally do some good again. I will try to make up for all those years I spent in fear and regret. I can finally do something for Your worthy name again."

She was quiet for a moment. Waiting. Listening. Once again sur-rendering herself to her Lord and Savior. And He answered. She heard no audible voice, but she remembered. And she knew Elnai had welcomed her into His grace and, for the first time in years, she entered in His loving grace and perfect will. Tears ran down her face. No more running. No more fear. No more regret. She was safe. She was where she belonged.

A savage cry pierced the night's silence. Andrea and Raya were sitting up, wide awake and alert in an instant. Damon's eyebrows were drawn together and his jaw was set. The whole camp was alive with activity. Foreign words were screamed into the night.

An all too familiar fear tingled through every nerve in Andrea's body. "What is happening?" her voice was barely audible amid the frenzied cries.

Her companions, seated on either side of her, only focused on the scene in front of them.

Jodai's sharp, booming voice could be heard above the others'. Whatever he said silenced all but one man.

The man had thrown himself to the ground beside the man Damon had injured. He jumped up, still screaming. He was throwing his arms around and making maddened gestures in their direction.

"*Qui payryl! Nylra savine cahnus qui payryl!*"

"Damon, what are they saying?" Andrea's voice was high and frantic. "What is going on?" her voice broke.

Raya looked her in the eye; her voice held more concern than Andrea had ever heard before. "The man Damon injured is dead. The dead man's brother is talking to Jodai."

Andrea's heart dropped into her stomach.

Jodai turned a steely gaze on Damon.

"What is he saying?" Andrea asked shakily.

The man still stood over the dead Darrionite, yelling in near frenzy.

"*Hiv kogh fain lene cahndnn qui payryl!*"

"He keeps saying '*qui payryl*,' what does that mean?"

"My brother," Raya answered sharply and continued staring ahead and straining to listen.

Jodai held up a hand and barked a sharp order.

"*Dreyund!*"

The man was silent.

Jodai turned to the men beside him and spoke to them quietly. They hurried to comply with his instructions.

"Damon!" Andrea cried. "What are they saying?"

"The brother wants me dead." Damon's voice was low.

Andrea didn't realize how shrill her voice had gotten. "No! They cannot do that! Damon—"

Damon's eyes were hard. "Don't speak," he growled. "Pull yourself together!"

"*Drayund! Mayuh hev ilt quil,*" Jodai barked. Four men approached with their weapons drawn. Damon was jerked to his feet; his efforts to resist the four massive men were futile.

Damon and Raya exchanged grave glances.

Andrea prayed with every ounce of her being.

Damon was thrown before Jodai. He jumped to his feet, only to be forced to his knees as his four escorts held each arm and shoulder.

"We have to do something!" came Andrea's panicked whisper. Looking to Raya gave her no comfort or hope. For once, Andrea could see almost completely through Raya's cold, angry exterior. Andrea saw fear, anger, helplessness, and a desperation that mirrored her own.

Jodai took a dagger from his belt and walked over to Damon. The leader's eyes were arrogant and his posture rigid as he glared down at Damon, who struggled to no avail. Damon was breathing hard. His face was still defiant and his eyes glowed with anger and hate that matched Jodai's.

Jodai bent his massive frame and yanked Damon's head back by his hair. He brought the dagger to his throat. The brother of the dead man waited in anticipation.

"You shall die like the dog you are," Jodai hissed.

"Elnai, please!" Andrea's voice cracked. She could not see through her tears.

࿇

Raya jumped to her feet and screamed in the Darrionite tongue, "Stop, Jodai! If you kill him you will lose a great fortune!"

Some of his men started to move towards her, but Jodai stopped them. "Speak quickly. Your companion does not have long." The knife never left Damon's throat.

Still speaking only Daroon, she spoke quickly and clearly. "We serve Lord Nazar himself. He would not be pleased if we were killed."

"Why would I care about Nazar's wishes?" he turned back to Damon.

"Would you care about Lord Nazar's treasury?" Raya asked confidently. "If we were to return safely and tell him of your fair treatment towards us, your reward would be far greater than what you could dream to receive from selling us like cattle."

Jodai laughed savagely. "You lie, wretch! Nazar would not give me a salla from his treasury! Now you shall both die!"

"She speaks the truth," Damon said, also speaking in the Darrionite tongue. "We have a ring from Lord Nazar's finger. We could retrieve the money ourselves."

"We have searched you and your saddles and found no rings. Now tell me, dog. Where is the ring?"

"It is hidden well. I can show you where it is. We can also pay you eighty gold pieces before we start the journey."

"We have already found your gold," Jodai said. "Show me the ring."

Jodai threw Damon to the ground and ordered his men to escort Damon and Raya to the horses, leaving two to guard Andrea.

"Wait, where are you going?" Andrea asked, as calmly as she could manage.

Damon shot her a stern look and Jodai snapped "silence" so she was quiet. All she could do was wait and pray.

❧

Raya looked back at Andrea, knowing that she had not understood a word that was just said. Soon, she could no longer see her through the darkness. The last thing Raya saw before turning away was Andrea's lips moving silently. She was probably praying. Raya rolled her eyes.

*It is foolish to even think He could hear or care if He existed. He has done nothing for Andrea so far.*

❧

Nazar was feeling much older than his forty-six years. His ever-present scowl had left lines in his otherwise handsome face. His dark blond hair, now speckled with silver, was still thick. He was tall with a thick and strong build. And though his muscles had lost the battle-hardened tautness of his youth, he was still as strong as he was when he earned fear and respect for his abilities on the battle field. If Airiss were to go to war again, he would still be able to fight like the skilled warrior he was. But today, he felt old and weighed down. In his younger years—and even now—he was considered handsome. But his demeanor was far too stern. His brows were always creased in a frown. Even as a very young man, there was always an underlying anger just beneath the surface. Many could sense it, even if they could not quite place it.

As Nazar retreated to his private quarters everyone scrambled to stay out of his way. He was obviously in one of his moods again. Everyone in the massive castle dreaded it when he got this way.

He sat on his enormous bed in solitude.

*The voices* ... he thought as he hugged himself and rocked back and forth, *Why will you not just leave me alone!*

An unseen serpent-like creature squeezed Nazar tighter.

It was not from this world. It had a scale covered body like a wingless dragon with a long tail and four legs. Its head was like that of a snake and was triangular in shape. The creature had two rows of spines from head to tail and long talons. Its eyes were solid black like the rest of its body. Its skin, filthy and rotted with disease, hung loosely from its bony frame. Acidic saliva dripped off of two large and two small fangs.

Wrapped around Nazar's back, the creature dug its talons into Nazar's neck and hissed into his thoughts, *I want that girl dead. Why have you not done this? She must not find the Resistance.*

Nazar felt a burning sensation in his throat and began to whimper, *I will kill her! She will die! I am trying—*

It dug its talon's deeper, *That is not good enough. I am growing weary of your incompetence. I don't have to use you. I can find another if you are no longer useful to me. If she does not die,* someone *must.*

"Please!" Nazar shrieked, throwing himself to the ground sobbing. "She will die!"

ॐॐ

"Why won't you tell me where you're going?" Judd was red in the face, trying to keep his temper in check—and hardly succeeding.

"Please just let me go," Flora pleaded softly. "I will try to be back by the week's end."

Judd took a deep breath and rubbed his face, his eyes still red from being awakened at this late hour. "That is a good five days, Flora. If you would just tell me what you are doing I might be alright with it!"

Flora would not meet his gaze. She nervously tugged at the shawl that was wrapped around her shoulders. "Judd, I must know that I can trust you with this," she whispered timidly, her voice barely audible. "I need you to trust me."

Their eyes met and she could tell that her husband was finally beginning to understand.

"Flora." He cursed under his breath. "I thought you forgot about all this nonsense years ago." He rubbed his face and grabbed her by the shoulders, shaking her gently. "You know what almost happened to you last time you got into this. Now it is even worse! If you do this, Nazar will have you marked before you can even say the Forbidden Name!" He crossed his arms and searched her face. "I cannot let you do this."

She straightened up to her full height. "Judd, this is something I have to do. With or without your approval."

"What if I report you?" he screamed.

"I'm sorry, and I love you," she said through watery vision. "I have lost so many years already. You do what you think is right and I will too."

He was furious, but she could also see the painful worry and sadness he was trying to hide.

"Then go!" he shouted, shaking his head in disgust. He cursed all the way to the barn and slammed the heavy door.

Flora swatted at the tears on her plump wet cheeks. Then, taking a deep breath, she took her small bag and headed to the horse she had tied to the fence by the road.

☙❧

A young woman sat against a tree in the dark, with hands bound. She looked worried and as if she was watching for someone.

Tisha walked up to her, but the girl obviously didn't know Tisha was there. Tisha could see a few large men that seemed to be guarding her.

*They look like Darrionites,* she thought. "Hello?" she called, kneeling beside the girl and placing her hand on her shoulder. The girl acted as though Tisha was not even there. "I feel like I know you from somewhere," she said, and her voice sounded dreamy. She cocked her head as she studied the girl. "You look much as I did when I was young."

Tisha turned around to see a massive figure that seemed to light up the night.

Tisha felt no fear. In fact, she felt nothing. "You are a warrior of the Holy Maker." She was not sure if she spoke out loud, but he understood.

"Yes." His lips never moved, but his strong voice reached her with astounding clarity. "I am called Wynn."

"Who is that girl? Is she alive?"

"Yes. She is alive. Her name is Andrea."

"My daughter."

"Yes."

"She was lost in the fire."

"Man cannot hinder the will of his Maker. He has great plans for Andrea. I pulled her from the flames, and your faithfulness and prayers have enabled me to watch over her all her life."

"Where is she? Can I help her?"

"I'm not permitted to say more. But know this, Tisha: your daughter is alive."

She blinked and he was gone.

"Wait!" Tisha woke, breathing heavily. The warrior's words echoed clearly through her racing mind.

"Tisha?" Tim called from outside her tent.

"Come in, Tim," she said.

He ducked inside. "Are you alright?"

"I had a dream. Andrea is alive."

❧

Damon and Raya watched as all three of their horses were brought to them.

"The ring is in the saddlebag of the brown gelding," Raya nodded toward her horse.

One of the men emptied the bags and produced a dagger with a thick, rounded handle, and a small canteen among other things.

"Well?" Jodai asked expectantly.

"It's in the knife's handle," Damon said. "Hold the blade and the end of the handle and twist. No, the other way."

The handle came unscrewed and a ring fell from the small hollow place.

"Pick it up," Jodai ordered.

Another man bent to retrieve it.

Jodai examined it closely. It was heavy, thick, and made of pure gold. There were two large rubies with an even larger Ephrite, the King's Jewel, in the center. Nazar's seal was inscribed on both sides of the gems. Engraved around the inside of the ring were words so small that you almost could not read them: *Lord Nazar's authority*

Jodai glared at Damon and Raya for a moment, then nodded to the men holding them. They were immediately released and the ropes that bound them were cut.

"Jodai," said the dead man's brother through clenched teeth, "what are you doing?"

"We are going to Reed," he replied coolly.

The brother now visibly shook with rage. "He must die for what he has done! He killed my brother!"

"Nazar's treasury is more valuable to me than revenge for one man!" Jodai yelled. "They will not allow access to a foreigner. Even if we presented Nazar's ring!"

The trembling man glared at Damon.

"Damon—" Raya's words were cut off by the brother's savage cry.

The brother pulled out a dagger and dove for Damon. Damon managed to grab the man's hand before the knife found its mark, but he was knocked off his feet, sending both men to the ground.

Everyone was still shocked. "Stop! Now!" Jodai screamed. "*Avitom! Avitom!*"

Damon was slightly winded from landing on his back under the weight of his attacker but his opponent was not even dazed. The brother, screaming savagely, had his knife free from Damon's grip again almost immediately.

Raya acted fast. She grabbed a dagger from the belt of a man beside her before he had time to react.

The brother raised the knife over his head and brought it down with all his might.

Damon rolled to the right as Raya threw her dagger. The brother's knife had nicked Damon a little above the elbow. Raya's blade pierced the man in his shoulder, just missing the heart. The brother fell screaming to the ground beside Damon.

Jodai and his men were in a frenzy. Everyone was shouting but no one was heard. As one, they raced toward Raya.

Raya had already removed the blade from the man beside Damon and she threw it at Jodai. The knife sank into his stomach and he cried out, falling to the ground.

The leader's cry made all heads turn, giving Damon the moment he needed. He dodged the one man standing between him and Jodai and retrieved the knife from his trembling body. He brought the red blade to Jodai's throat.

Everyone froze.

"Tell your dogs to listen to me or I will end you," Damon hissed.

"I'm already a dead man," Jodai coughed out.

"You cannot be sure you will die. Moy-moy works wonders. Shall I make it certain?" he watched Raya hurriedly retrieve all three horses.

"Let us kill them!" his men screamed.

"No!" Jodai cried weakly. "Do as he says."

"Drop your weapons and back off!" Damon commanded.

They hesitated.

Damon slowly increased pressure on their fallen leader's neck.

"Do it!" Jodai screamed.

Finally, they dropped their weapons and slowly stepped back.

Damon allowed them to stop about forty feet away.

Raya picked up two swords and two daggers. Damon lept on his horse. Raya was right behind him. The Darrionites sprinted towards them.

"I loosed their horses!" Raya cried, speaking in Common Tongue again, as she tossed him a sword.

Damon threw the dripping scarlet dagger straight for the heart of the fallen leader as he kicked his steed. It found its mark. Jodai was dead and the two were gone by the time the others got to their leader's body.

ҩҽҩ

It was Nevivday. That meant that it was Musa's midweek break. All she had to do that morning was show Janelle which passage was being copied today.

Musa had a lot of respect for the young woman. Janelle was just barely fifteen and already a big part of the Resistance. Musa really wasn't surprised though. Jay—a hardworking leader who led by example—was the girl's father.

Musa prayed a silent blessing over Janelle as she looked over the passage copies that had been made under Janelle's supervision that morning.

Musa knew it was late and her day of rest, but she could not tear herself away from the words straight from Elnai's Heart.

> *Elnai the ancient prophesies fulfilled,*
> *It was done just as the Maker had willed*
> *To make atonement for every man's sin,*
> *So that through Him even in death we win.*
>
> *Elnai lowered Himself to a man—*
> *He was fully God yet fully human;*
> *In His mother's arms as a child came He,*
> *Only she knew all that He would be.*
>
> *He grew in wisdom, in love and in truth,*
> *He never sinned once as man or as youth;*
> *He healed many sick, the deaf and the lame,*
> *He traveled afar, widespread was His fame.*

ҩҽҩ

Something was definitely happening.

Andrea's two guards looked up from their conversation toward the commotion. Crazed screams pierced the air. They rushed into the darkness to aid the others.

Andrea saw her chance. She bolted for the dagger that one of her guards had dropped in his hurry. After sweeping it up she frantically worked to cut herself free with tied hands.

"Praise You, Elnai!" she sighed as the ropes slipped from her wrists. She escaped her bindings with only a small cut on her arm.

She knew she needed her horse. She too slipped away from the warm light of the fire towards the commotion. Maybe, just maybe, she could get to her horse without being discovered through the chaos.

కలా

Damon rode directly beside Raya, Andrea's horse in tow. They separated and wove in and out of the group of horses, scattering the petrified creatures in all directions.

"We have to get Andrea!" he cried. He turned his horse back towards the enemy's camp, where the furious slave traders scrambled after their horses.

Raya stopped. "Damon!" she screamed. Getting no response, she raced her mount beside his. Whipping around in front of him, she forced all three horses to stop, nearly throwing both riders off in the process. "You cannot go after her!" she cried.

"They will kill her," he answered.

"It is time *someone* did," she spat back, venom dripping from her words. "We don't need her!"

"She has information!"

"She has nothing. *She is nothing.*"

కలా

Tisha had not been able to sleep at all. For hours she had just been listening to Tim snore from the tent beside hers as she thought and prayed about her dreams.

She quietly sang the words to the song playing in her mind. *"He is watching me, He will give me strength to stand, He gives peace in pain, Nothing moves me from His hand ..."* Then she went back to the chorus. *"I will fix my eyes, upon the one who saves, upon the one who gave, His life for me, And I gladly give, my life to Him, If that be the case, I will take my stand ..."*

She opened her Book to a passage she had been studying more and more recently.

> *To man and woman, to young and old,*
> *The Maker sends from on-high,*
> *Visions and dreams to his faithful ones,*
> *That teach, warn, or prophesy.*

*That teach, warn, or prophesy*, Tisha thought. Andrea was once again on her mind. A burning desire to pray for her daughter consumed her. She believed her dreams were indeed from on-high. That meant, Andrea was not only alive, but in trouble. Tisha knew of only one thing to do.

"Tim," Tisha said, now standing outside his tent in the cool desert air, "get up. We need to pray."

❧

Andrea arrived just in time to see Damon and Raya scatter the horses. Thinking they would look for her by the fire, she turned to run that way.

"*Avitom*! Stop!"

Andrea glanced over her shoulder to see a man easily twice her size in pure muscle sprinting after her.

A shrill scream escaped her lips as the man grabbed her left shoulder, causing her to spin towards him.

She kicked at his shins and flailed her fists at his face. He quickly caught her hands with his left and his right encircled her throat.

*Pain.*

❧

A high-pitched cry echoed in the night.

Damon's heart sank. "That was her!" he cried, searching for her amid the commotion.

"Damon!" Raya screamed. "We are outnumbered six to one!"

But he was already racing away. They had covered a lot of ground and she was a good ways off.

Raya cursed and raced after him. Their only hope was that they were on horses and most of the Darrionites were on foot without a weapon.

As he rode, Damon only saw Andrea struggling and clawing at the brute that held her a few inches off the ground.

☙❧

Pain screamed throughout her entire body. She kicked for ground and desperately clawed at the massive arm holding her.

Black spots. *Pain.* Cannot find the ground. *Pain.* Cannot breathe. *Pain.* Her soundless cries. Panic. *Pain.* Darkness. Slipping, fighting, sliding, struggling, falling … *embracing* the darkness. Finally. Sweet, sweet darkness swallowed her. No more struggling. No more pain. Then light.

CHAPTER TEN

# FIGHT

Flora wasted no time. She had left well after dark, but was making excellent time. She would make it to Reed around noon.

As she traveled, she poured her heart out to Elnai. She prayed for Judd, Andrea, and every member of the Resistance that she could remember. She prayed that she would have strength, wisdom, and guidance as she worked for the Maker's cause.

⤜⤙

Damon kicked his horse faster and faster. He watched Andrea fight, kick, and struggle, and then, gradually stop. She slowly loosened her grip on the man and her limp arms slipped to her sides. Her already tiny frame seemed to shrink next to the man who held her over a foot from the ground.

"Andrea!" he screamed, sword drawn. "Keep fighting!"

Her captor turned to see Damon. He released Andrea. She crumpled to the ground, completely limp and motionless.

From his horse, Damon easily destroyed the man. Hardly allowing the poor animal time to slow down, he leaped off his panting horse and rushed to Andrea.

Her tanned skin bore a bruised red handprint.

He swiped her hair out of her blue face and was frustrated to leave scarlet smears along her forehead from his battle-stained hands. No time to waste over that, he felt her neck with the tips of his fingers.

"Elnai," he whispered fiercely, "if You're real, if You're the Great Lover she professes You to be, how could You let this happen?" His sticky red fingers flew from her neck to her slender wrist. "She was real. She has done nothing to deserve this. She gave up everything because she refused to deny You! I deserve this! She doesn't."

❧❧

Rayas was close behind Damon as he rushed for Andrea. Even after going limp, her attacker held her in his crushing grip. By the time Damon got there, she had not been able to breathe for a while.

Too long.

If Raya would have been the one to kill Andrea, she would have done it as quickly and painlessly as possible. No need to make her suffer. But it had to happen eventually. Even though what Andrea had experienced was painful, it was better than turning her over to Nazar. That would mean a much crueler death than what Raya or the Darrionite would ever do.

*Maybe it would be merciful if she died tonight.* Raya thought. *Maybe now we can move on.*

She saw Damon quickly defeat the attacker and check for Andrea's pulse.

The Darrionites finally spotted them and began to regroup. Raya pulled a sharp left and stopped near the fire. Jumping down, she quickly retrieved her confiscated bow and arrows.

Spinning on her heel and taking aim in one swift motion, she ended one of the now armed slave traders. His body fell mere feet from Damon. Only nine more to go.

She again took aim.

❧❧

Blinding white light banished the darkness. A massive white robed figure stood over her.

Andrea lifted her hand to shield her face. She could only see the glowing silhouette in the midst of a flood of light. There was a certain warmth about its peaceful glow.

The voice came, smooth and compassionate: "Stay still, child. Peace. Receive your rest in this moment."

She breathed in the light. Warm bliss filled her lungs. Even though her eyes gently closed, the comforting light was still there. She was weightless. Floating. Relaxed beyond what is humanly possible and oblivious to everything but bliss, she surrendered herself to a light so thick that she could *feel* its radiance. She remembered nothing from the distant world full of endless hardships.

It seeped into her very being. She was ushered into a state of conscious sleep where all five senses experienced the light. Andrea was completely and beautifully consumed by the light. By the flowing, weightless waters of pure bliss.

ᢒᢒᡐᢙ

Damon still found no pulse. He cursed. His hand went to hold her nose. He prepared to attempt to breathe air into her lungs, but before he put his mouth over hers, he noticed the color returning to her face.

His fingers gently caressed her cheek. There was a very faint warmth to her skin.

He finally noticed her faintly inhale. She gradually breathed deeper until it was slow and deep as if in a perfect, dreamless sleep. After a moment he was able to feel it. His heart was racing far faster than hers was.

*If I had just calmed down for a second I would have felt it and realized she was fine.* He scolded himself, surprised and a bit angry at his own emotions.

This had been a very long thirty seconds.

An arrow whizzed by him. Damon snatched up his sword and got to his feet. The arrow left its mortally wounded target only a few feet away from Damon.

He looked to Raya, who was about thirty-five feet away, already taking aim once again. "You shoot left, I'll go right!"

Raya turned quickly, targeting a man to the far left.

Damon bolted right, evaluating the situation as he ran.

Three men were coming for Damon, one with his upper right arm bandaged and a two foot long, single edged blade. Another with a dagger, and one with a curved sword identical to the one Damon held. Four others were sprinting, weapons drawn, towards Raya. The remaining two were hurriedly grabbing swords from the pile they had been forced to surrender.

Damon threw his dagger at the man in the middle of the three proceeding towards him. Meeting its mark, the dagger brought its target to the ground with a final scream.

A battle cry escaped from deep inside Damon as he rushed the Darrionite with the sword. Switching targets at the last second, he hurled his body shoulder first into the wounded man with the dagger.

Damon felt the knife rip into his outer thigh as the stunned man fell, groaning into his teeth but without missing a step, he dodged left to avoid the standing attacker's sword. Before the attacking swordsman could raise his weapon again, Damon dealt the fatal blow, then turned and finished off the man at his feet.

The adrenalin of battle kept him hyper-alert. His years of training and experience were evident in his every move. All his senses were alive. The smell of the slick, sticky redness on him and his weapons, the sound of horses stampeding, and arrows whizzing through the air. His sight and reflexes were exaggerated.

This was why he was one of the best at what he did. His mind was able to channel the adrenalin and heightened senses that overwhelmed most in his situation. Instead of making him go mad, his mind used this to make split-second, and often life saving, calculations. He refused to allow himself to think of the odds. After a while he was almost numb to it. Almost as if everything but the moment he was in ceased to exist as his battle-driven mind took over.

৵৵

Musa was unable to sleep. Something didn't feel right. She prayed for a while before deciding to delve into the Book. She picked up where she had left off when planning the morning's session earlier.

> *The Maker's own Lovers began to rage;*
> *Out of jealousy, war they would soon wage*
> *Against the very Savior they longed for,*
> *Against the One Who would save and restore.*

*He poured out His heart, they poured out His blood,*
*Yet over them still His mercy would flood;*
*He was drowned in front of the Holy Tree,*
*Naked, He was left there in mockery.*

*The Courts of Light quaked at the Maker's cries,*
*Rumbling lightening shook now darkened skies;*
*Down into the Void then was sent Elnai—*
*The Maker's own Son brought down from on high.*

❧❧

Raya paused for a moment after eliminating all but two of her targets. Damon had killed all but two of his men. He was fighting one and the other was retreating.

She brought her attention back to her own battle. The two remaining Darrionites were too close for her to take both down before they reached her. Leaping onto her faithful horse behind her, she dropped her bow and pulled the sword from her belt. Riding between them, she ended one, but the other man's dagger ripped into her mount's left thigh.

The horse screamed and bucked, tossing Raya to the ground and wrenching the sword from her grasp in one violent motion. She landed hard and was left dizzy, disoriented, and in pain.

She stood shakily as her vision cleared. The Darrionite was rushing towards her with his dagger. She glanced around for her sword. It was out of reach and she was out of time.

Taking her only weapon from her belt, she aimed the dagger carefully. The man was only a few strides away. She could not miss. Closer, still. Finally, she sent the knife flying through the air. Though her dagger killed the man and she tried to dodge to the right, the falling man's knife cut her left arm from the shoulder to the elbow.

Crying out, she allowed herself to slip to the ground. Her body begged her to slow down and actually take time to recover from being thrown from a horse and cut.

❧❧

After Damon defeated his opponent, he glanced back at Raya. She was holding her own from her horse. He turned to pursue the fleeing Darrionite. But the short shrill yelp had him sprinting toward Raya in an instant. The sight of his sister on the ground with her damaged arm made Damon all the more frantic. Reaching her, he literally fell at her side.

"Raya—" his voice was thick with worry. His heart pounding.

"I'm alright, Damon." She grimaced as she sat up.

"Your arm—"

"Is fine!" she snapped. Her tone softened. "Sorry. But, really, it is not as bad as it looks. It is not deep."

Damon helped her stand. "Let me help you to the fire."

"I can walk, brother," she insisted, her voice just above a whisper. "It is my arm that is hurt, not my legs."

After watching her for a few steps to be sure she *could* walk, he went to see about Andrea.

Seeing she was breathing, though still unconscious, he washed the blood off of himself.

Feeling a little cleaner, he scooped Andrea up, surprised at how light she felt. She stirred a bit. That was a good sign. He carried her over by the fire and set her down.

Raya was sitting on the other side.

"Let me help you." Damon took some crushed moy-moy, a cloth, clean water, and some bandages from the saddlebag on Raya's horse and brought it over to fire.

"My horse is hurt," Raya said. "Unsaddle him before you tend to me."

Because Raya insisted, Damon quickly unsaddled the gelding.

Damon inspected the deep wound in the horse's leg. He was afraid that Raya would have to take one of the Darrionite horses. Her horse was not going to be able to handle the long hours of riding with his wounded leg.

Damon quickly finished with the horse and turned to Raya.

Raya looked away and clenched her teeth as Damon cleaned and dressed the wound.

"It cut you from the shoulder to just above the elbow," he said as he finished wrapping the damaged arm. "The cut is long but shallow. You were lucky."

"Yes. It could have been much worse. For both of us. If they had all been armed and we didn't have the horses we would have stood no chance." Raya turned her cold stare toward Andrea. "We got lucky this time. But we could have easily been killed." Her blue eyes now bore into Damon, but her voice showed the exhaustion that came after the adrenalin rush of battle. "Why did you go back for her? What does it matter if she dies here or we hand her to Nazar?"

Damon sighed heavily as he slumped forward. He felt like he was twice as heavy as he was as the adrenalin drained. "She has information." He rubbed his face with both hands.

Raya's icy anger seeped through every syllable. "You do understand that Nazar will have her put to death, do you not?" She leaned forward and Damon refused to look her in the eye. "All of this was to save a dead girl."

৵৽

"Have no fear, Andrea." A voice like music spoke clearly into her mind. "Your time has not yet come. For your task has not been completed."

"Who are you?" she didn't speak with her voice, yet she was heard.

"I am Wynn," the warrior replied. "I am the Maker's humble servant and He has sent me to you."

"Why?"

"Quiet your heart to receive the Maker's words. For it is written: *'To man and woman, to young and old, The Maker sends from on-high, Visions and dreams to his faithful ones, That teach, warn, or prophesy.'* He who has ears let him hear.

"For the Holy Maker says unto you: 'Get up from this place and travel deep into the desert at the foot of this mountain. You will meet my beloved vessel. But beware. Beware those who would deceive you. Guard your heart and mind. For trial, temptation, and hardship is fast coming. If you don't guard your heart, I shall still use you to fulfill my purpose, but the battle will be hard won. The cost will be great. Remain strong in Me and I will show Myself strong through you. Write upon your heart these words. He who has ears, let him hear.'"

Andrea opened her eyes to the light and squinted at the radiance of the massive warrior before her. "Please, what does this mean? Who am I to meet in the desert? Who would deceive me?"

"He who has ears let him her."

"But I don't understand. I need to know more! I cannot run into the desert with so little information."

"Do you question or defy the Holy Maker of all Things? He Who calls you chosen and beloved? He Who has delivered you from harm many times?"

"No …"

"He who has ears, let him hear."

Andrea felt humbled and ashamed, *Holy Maker, I will do as You have said. I ask that I may be worthy to walk this path You have set before me. Forgive me for not fully trusting You. I surrender my life to You. Whatever that may mean, wherever that may lead, however short it may be, I am Yours.*

She breathed in the radiance one last time as she closed her eyes. The light began to fade away. Her entire being begged to drown in the light again.

ॐ∽ঔ

"Raya, I believe we are close to finding the Resistance. She can take us there."

Raya glared at him skeptically. "Nazar will have our heads if we don't hurry. If we don't find them soon, we must take the girl back."

Damon picked up a wet cloth and wearily knelt next to Andrea instead of answering Raya.

He gently wiped the blood from her face and hands where he had touched her with his scarlet stained hands. She weakly stirred. The firelight's orange glow danced over her face. He dropped the rag. Andrea didn't seem hurt anymore; it now appeared as if she was in a deep sleep.

He picked up her small hand to check her pulse. It had the calluses of farm work and was tanned from their months of constant exposure to the sun as they traveled. Her pulse was strong and steady. He also noticed a strange warmth to her skin.

"Mmmm …" Andrea was beginning to wake.

She turned her head and a wavy strand of brown hair fell across her face. She wrinkled her nose and Damon gently brushed the stray strands away. Andrea's eyes fluttered open.

"Damon?" her voice sounded thick. Her hand went to her throat.

"Careful." Fatigue showed through Damon's voice. "It is bruised."

She let her hand drop to her side. "Are you hurt?" her words slurred together a bit. She blinked rapidly and furrowed her brow, visibly trying to make sense of her spinning world.

"I was cut in the thigh, but it's not bad. I'm fine."

"What about Raya?" she asked, shakily sitting up.

Damon helped Andrea sit up and glanced at his twin. Raya was sleeping.

"She has a long cut on her arm. Luckily it is not deep. We will need to keep it clean, but she will be fine."

Andrea raked her wild mane of waves out of her face with shaky fingers. "What happened?"

Damon told her of the fight, which had lasted only fifteen minutes, though it seemed like hours, and that she had been out for around twenty minutes.

"Thank Elnai that we're all alive," she muttered, staring into the fire. She looked back at Damon, her head now clear. "I need something to write with and on."

"What?"

"Do we have anything?"

"Well, yes." He started to get up, but she stopped him.

"Just tell me where it is and I can get it."

A few minutes later, she had written out, in vivid detail, her dream and tucked it within the Book.

After Damon had read it, he asked, "What does this mean?"

"I'm not completely sure of all the details," she said confidently. "But I know we have to trust Him. And that means going into the desert."

## CHAPTER ELEVEN

# RED

Flora nibbled at her bread with a song in her heart. She would reach Reed soon and felt encouraged and bold after hours of talking to her Lord.

She hummed the song she had once sung with the Lovers of the Resistance, *He is watching me, He will give me strength to stand, He gives peace in pain, nothing moves me from His hand.*

৵৵

Andrea was up before Damon and Raya. Not surprising, considering all they had been through last night. Though Andrea was weary herself and her bruised throat was sore, she had a new fire burning within her. She had already known that she was on a mission, but now she had direction.

Careful to avoid the scenes from last night's battle, she went about getting ready to leave. The saddlebags were already packed for the most part, as they had been too exhausted to even spread their sleeping mats. She packed the remaining few things scattered about and saddled their two horses—she knew Raya would have to choose one of the Darrionite horses to replace the injured gelding.

The sun was now finally beginning to rise. She started toward the freshwater spring not far from camp to water the horses and refill their canteens.

She then changed out of her bloodied garments from last night and gathered up Damon and Raya's as well to wash. As she scrubbed at the scarlet stains, she was sickened and could hardly finish her task. She was thankful that she had been unconscious during the battle and even more careful to avoid the aftermath just a short distance over the hill from where they had spent the night.

As she went about her sickening task, her mind traveled to Damon. She remembered his face in that moment where she was waking up.

His brow slightly furrowed, dark hair falling about his face, covered in sweat and blood, and his eyes betraying the feelings he had tried to hide. She had looked into his brown eyes and seen such fear and compassion.

As he had helped her sit up, the same hands that had ruthlessly wielded a sword just moments before, were so gentle and tender, they treated her as if she were made of glass. Her hand had felt so small and delicate as he had taken it in his strong one and helped her up.

His voice had held a softness that she had never heard before. Maybe from anyone.

Andrea's heart skipped a beat. Not sure what to think about these thoughts, she pushed them aside and continued her work.

Even after she returned a few minutes later, her companions were still sleeping.

Now that she had a bit of light and a moment of peace, she decided to study the Book.

She found the passage about the Maker sending dreams and visions that the warrior had mentioned and, after reading it, continued to flip through.

At last, one passage caught her eye.

> *Given to you is a choice to make,*
> *Here before you is a path to take,*
> *You can now choose to live or to die:*
> *Trust in the world, or trust in Elnai.*
>
> *Those who seek the riches of this world*
> *Find their treasures a fading reward;*

*Worldly splendor lasts but a season,*
*No matter how you fight or reason.*

*Those who forsake the worldly delight—*
*No matter the loss, heartache, or fight,*
*Receive more than the foolish faker—*
*For they will abide with the Maker.*

*I'm sorry I questioned You, Holy Maker,* Andrea breathed in the peace she always found when reading Elnai's Book. *I could never begin to deserve what You've done for me. I choose Your path. I know that though I give everything, maybe even my life, to walk in Your footsteps, I'll receive an eternal reward in the end. Thank you, Elnai.*

Andrea allowed the others to sleep a little while longer.

෨‒෬

Tisha woke with the sun the next morning. Even though she and Tim had spent much of the night in prayer for Andrea, she felt refreshed because she was finally at peace. She had to find her daughter, but she was trusting Elnai for direction. For now, she felt at peace with the decision to continue on to Valrine to meet Rhoda and Dory, as originally planned.

෨‒෬

Flora nervously tied her old mare to the fence. With Tisha's journal in her hands and a prayer in her heart, she raised her hand to knock, but froze right before her knuckles touched the door.

*What will dear Rhoda think of me?* she thought. *After all these years? After what I did? After how I betrayed her, the Resistance, and Elnai in a single moment of fear?*

Then an entirely new thought entered her mind, *Elnai has stood before the Maker and called me redeemed. I am forgiven. I cannot miss my chance to make things right because I am afraid of what others think. Elnai has made me new.*

With renewed confidence, she boldly rapped on the door.

"One moment!" Rhoda called from inside.

Flora waited patiently. She heard Rhoda inside talking to Dory. "Get out of my bread dough! Now you have flour all over you. Run along before you get into anymore trouble."

The door opened. "Yes?" Rhoda's jaw dropped when she saw Flora standing there. The look of shock was immediately replaced with a glowing smile.

Before Flora knew what was happening, she was pulled into a warm hug. Rhoda held her for a moment before pulling her inside and shutting the door.

Flora could not even speak. She was overwhelmed with the joy of being welcomed in such a way by this woman who had been her very close friend.

"Come! Sit down and tell me how you are." Rhoda pulled out a chair for Flora, then barred the door, and closed all windows and curtains.

A few moments, a lot of tears, apologies, and a few hugs later, Rhoda was brought up to date.

"This is amazing!" Rhoda said as she poured over Tisha's journal. "We thought that all that work had gone to waste, but this tells us that they managed to hide it!"

"Yes!" Flora exclaimed. "I have lost so many years that after discovering this I knew I could wait no longer!"

"If I remember correctly," Rhoda said, leaping to her feet, "location B was the secret compartment under Ross and Tisha's old house and C was in the woods behind the church!"

"We should leave right away!" Flora exclaimed, also getting to her feet.

"Dory!" Rhoda called.

The little girl appeared from behind the door to her room.

"Go put on your shoes," her mother instructed. "You are going to go play with Saj."

A smile lit up Dory's face as she hurried to find her shoes.

Rhoda grabbed a basket, placed a knife and hammer in it, and covered it with a table cloth.

"I have a bit of bread we can put in there as well. You can see that I was making a new batch, but I have a little already made."

In went the bread and a few cookies.

"There you are, sweetheart," Rhoda said as her daughter finally came back with her shoes on. "Your shoes are on the wrong feet. Let Mommy fix it."

Once Dory's shoes were on correctly, the three headed out. After about an hour's buggy ride, they reached a little house on the outskirts of Valrine. Two large dogs ran barking from behind the horse stables. The chickens pecking in the vegetable garden fussed noisily at the dogs. Before the women could knock, a Darrionite woman appeared at the door to see what the commotion was about.

"Hello, Rhoda!" the tall woman beamed. Her eyes lingered on the basket Rhoda held. "Where are you going this fine day?"

"Hello, Zania. Flora and I are going on a picnic," Rhoda answered. "I was wondering if you could watch Dory."

"Of course."

Rhoda turned to Dory. "Go find Saj and you two may play together."

Dory ran to the backyard with her friend as the three women sat in the kitchen after closing windows and curtains.

Rhoda waited until the giggling little girls disappeared from sight.

"Zania," Rhoda said, looking into the taller woman's eyes, "let me tell you quickly. With this exciting news, we have not much time to lose."

❧

As they rode in silence, Damon's thoughts ran wild.

Damon knew Raya was angry. The only reason she had even agreed to go to the desert was because she refused to discuss it in front of Andrea. He left her no choice but go with him. But he could tell from her icy glares that Raya wanted this to be over. She was ready to turn Andrea in and get out from under Nazar once and for all.

But there in lay the problem. There was no end to this. Not really. They had two options, be Nazar's puppets, or never stop running. Both seemed to be dead ends.

Or no end.

He glanced to his right where Andrea rode beside him. She seemed lost in the world of her thoughts as well.

Damon blushed slightly as he remembered the events of last night. He still didn't understand the feelings that had gripped his heart. The panic that had been aroused. The fight itself didn't cause his heart to constrict. The fight was nothing compared to things he had been through. But then he saw Andrea. And for a moment, he had thought she was gone.

He quickly shook his head. Angry. Why? He didn't know. That girl was a target. Nothing more. Andrea was already dead as far as he was concerned.

*Then why do I feel like she is far more alive than I could ever be?*

Damon glanced at Andrea. She had lost a little weight. Weight she didn't have to lose. Her brown waves of hair were wild. Her skin tan and her posture tired from long days of riding.

Yet her green eyes were bright with life. Many in her position would be broken … yet he felt as though he was more broken than she …

*She likely has Kimim blood.* He speculated. *She is a bit small for an Airissian, and the curly texture of her hair and vivid green of her eyes are characteristic of the Kimim as well. Not to mention the diehard stubbornness. The Kimim are known for being hardy and stubborn. And look at Andrea. Through all that she has been through, she has stubbornly stood firm. She refuses to accept her fate and full heartedly rejects any notion of a lost cause. Even now as she rides, you can see it.*

He noted the determined square of her small shoulders, the slight lift of her chin, and the vibrancy of her emerald gaze as it remained fixed solely on the trail before her. Perhaps what amazed him most about her was not that this same stubborn resolution didn't waver in the greatest of odds. Perhaps it was not even that it emboldened her to stand for her beliefs and drove her to courageous actions in the face of danger. But maybe it was that she herself didn't see it. The determination straightening her small posture was as subconscious as breathing. Perhaps that is what was to be admired most of all.

Could this inward strength be pulled not from her Kimim blood, but her faith? Or perhaps it was this same faith that magnified the admirable qualities of the vivacious Kimim in her veins.

Damon caught himself, *What is happening to me? I am a battle hardened warrior! Yet a short time around this, this girl, and suddenly I'm questioning everything I once knew.*

ॐ•ॐ

Flora and Rhoda made good time reaching the old property that had once belonged to Ross and Tisha. They excitedly began to search what was left of the old house.

It had been burned to the ground and anything that survived the flames had been destroyed or taken by Nazar's men. Grass and weeds grew wild where the scorched floor didn't cover. No one had dared to touch this property after that day.

Rhoda found the area that had once been the kitchen and dropped down on all fours. After moving some unrecognizable pieces of debris, she finally smiled.

"Flora." She beamed. "I think I found it!"

The two women worked to get what was left of the blackened floor up. After a final pull on the hammer, they removed the board to reveal the secret compartment.

"Praise Elnai!" the women embraced as they lifted up thanksgiving.

Light poured into the small opening, revealing a dirt room. It was about six feet from floor to ceiling, six feet wide, and ten feet long. A large, dusty chest was pushed against the wall and a ladder lay on the ground below the entrance to the little hidden room.

Without hesitation, Rhoda dropped into the room.

Flora was content to stay above ground.

The heavy chest's lid complained as Rhoda forced it open. "Flora, it's Books!"

Rhoda produced one from the chest and held it up for Flora to see, beaming. "There must be at least twenty, maybe more!"

Flora and Rhoda took one of the twenty-three Books and, after carefully hiding the entrance once more, hurried to the next location. The old meeting place had also been burned.

Rhoda closed her eyes to think as they stood behind the burnt building that had once served as their meeting place.

"We start at the door," she said, trying to remember.

Flora stood at the charred remains of the door and asked, "Twenty paces straight ahead, correct?"

Rhoda's eyes flew open. "Yes!"

They walked twenty paces from the door and found themselves just a few steps into the woods. There was hardly any evidence that where they stood had once been a series of trails and paths worn down by heavy traffic. The years of neglect had left it overgrown and wild—almost unrecognizable.

Rhoda looked around, feet glued to their spot.

"East," she whispered—for whispering seemed appropriate. "Ten? Ten paces east?"

The two women turned on their heels to their right—east—and as soon as they saw what stood in that direction they remembered.

"That tree!" they both cried in excitement. Knee high grass and thorns pulled at their dresses as they hurried over to the old tree.

It was not unlike the other trees, but under its massive roots was a hidden secret. Some creature had long ago burrowed a home underneath the roots near the base of the tree. Its home had been re-purposed to house some of the Resistance's biggest secrets.

Without hesitation, Rhoda quickly cleared the dead leaves and sticks that filled the small tunnel. Bugs scattered, causing Flora to gasp and keep her distance. But Rhoda simply brushed away the tiny spider that scurried up her arm.

The little hole was hardly large enough for a human arm to reach through.

Flora felt a bit unsure. "Rhoda, are you certain that this is it? What if it has a snake living in it?"

Rhoda, still on her knees in front of the little tunnel, turned her attention to the woman standing beside her.

"This must be it. The Holy Maker has not brought us this far for nothing."

Rhoda reached through the tunnel. Once her arm was swallowed up to the shoulder, she beamed.

"I feel something!"

Rhoda proudly produced a little package. It was a tube sealed with tar to protect it from moisture. Removing the lid, she pulled out dozens of quills.

Rhoda once more reached into the little tunnel. Soon the two women sat cross-legged on the ground going through dozens of little tubes.

Besides things such as quills and ink for making copies of the Holy Book, there were maps and lists of names.

There were lists of safe houses scattered throughout Airiss and Darrion, members of the Resistance, trusted printers, locations of the different Resistance camps and secret store houses, people inside the Palace of Nazar himself who were secret Lovers, plans for dangerous missions for Book distribution—things that, in the wrong hands, could have been the end of the Resistance. Even now it would cause a lot of trouble.

Some things were no longer relevant of course. A lot had changed after that terrible day when Lovers were forced to make a stand. A lot had changed since Nazar's persecution had intensified.

Rhoda didn't know much, as Tim didn't keep her informed of every detail for her own protection, but she knew that many of these names were no longer involved in the Resistance. Some had decided to lay low to take care of family as she had, others had bent their knee to Nazar and never looked back, still others had taken up new roles—such as those in Nazar's castle who had been discovered, and sadly there were those who had given their lives for the Resistance and the love of the Maker.

Gathering the ink, quills, maps of old Resistance stashes, and any other usable information, they destroyed the rest.

It was almost completely dark by the time they hurried back to Zania's house with a much heavier basket. Rhoda threw her shawl over it to conceal its contents and they avoided the busier parts of Valrine—which was not hard considering that it was a small town.

Zania opened the door and hurried them in before they had time to knock. The children were sent to a different room to play as Rhoda and Flora brought Zania up to date.

"This is incredible!" Zania whispered excitedly. "Using these maps, we can probably find more hidden stashes of Books. We could do something big here."

Rhoda beamed and leaned in closer. "Tim will be home soon, he told me to expect him sometime this month. We could gather any copies we can get from these locations—maybe even make more!— and send them back with him so the Resistance can distribute them!"

Flora's heart fluttered. The thought of being a part of the Resistance again excited her, but there was also a little fear. She knew the consequences if she got caught, and what would Judd do?

The three excitedly whispered plans far into the night.

৯৽৽৻

After a long ride, Andrea, Damon, and Raya finally stopped. Cuts were once again checked, cleaned, and bandaged. After camp was made, and the horses were taken care of, Damon grabbed his bow and arrows and went hunting.

After a short time, Damon returned with some meat. After they had cooked and eaten, the weary trio finally just rested in silence.

They all huddled close to the fire. The stars were brilliant, seemingly just out of reach, but they were too exhausted to appreciate them.

Andrea lay on her back on top of her blanket, her sword at her side. She had intended to clean it, but would finish it in the morning.

৯৽৽৻

Musa was very happy with the progress they had made that day. They had managed to get two days' worth of copying in!

Musa was so thankful and blessed. Although it was tiring and consumed about six hours of her day, she was amazed to be considered worthy to serve the Holy Maker in such a way.

With a happy sigh of contentment and awe, she sat at her desk and planned tomorrow's session by the light of a lantern.

> *Three days and three hours Elnai fought the Grave,*
> *Elnai fought to set free all of sin's slaves.*
> *Soon He rose in victorious splendor—*
> *All He asks is for us to surrender.*
>
> *To accept the gift He gave so freely,*
> *He asks that we declare His victory;*
> *Through faith we are called Elnai's very own—*
> *Soon we will worship Elnai at His Throne.*
>
> *For coming is the day of His return—*
> *A day for which all Lovers deeply yearn;*
> *For He will come to heal and restore,*
> *Elnai will make all clean and new once more.*

☙❧

Andrea was not sure what awakened her. But she fought to stay asleep. The horses became restless, to her further annoyance.

*Just be still so I can sleep.*

Andrea was on her side, face towards the fire. A shadow crossed over her.

She forced her heavy eyes open. Her heart dropped. There, with a dagger and standing over Damon, was one of the Darrionites.

Andrea moved in a blur, completely numb. Her body seemed to move on its own. It was as if she was watching through someone else's eyes.

Screaming, from fright as much as anything, she swung her sword—which had apparently found its way into her hand—with all her might from the man's right. Her eyes forced themselves shut, the sound of her shrill scream and pounding heart was all that filled her ears.

Andrea felt her blade sink into flesh. The man's furious scream shook the night. Her eyes flew open to see the damaged, bleeding arm in front of her.

Her scream mixed with his before being cut off by a wave of nausea and terror. Shaking hands dropped the sword as a sob got caught in her throat. She tried to keep her last meal down. The realization that she had caused the gory damage was as overwhelming as the terror of the moment and blood itself.

The Darrionite pulled a dagger with his left hand and wildly threw it.

Andrea lunged to the left, but felt the blade rip into her right side. The clumsily thrown knife, grazing her as it passed, fell to the ground a few feet behind her.

Like a wounded animal, the man swung a frenzied left fist at her. Frozen with fear and shaking with nausea, Andrea could do nothing as the man's fist pounded into her right ear.

Pain racked her body as she fell through the swimming darkness to the ground.

☙❧

Raya shot straight up at the sound of Andrea's shrill scream. She looked up just as Andrea's sword ripped into the Darrionite's arm.

Grabbing her bow and leaping to her feet in one quick motion, she watched as Damon rolled out of the attacker's way and to his feet.

Damon didn't have his sword.

In one moment, in which time seemed to stop, Raya readied an arrow and took aim, as the Darrionite swung wildly at Andrea. Raya barely had time to stop herself from releasing an arrow as Andrea dropped limply to the ground and Damon rammed into the raging Darrionite. Raya saw that Andrea was bleeding but could not tell the extent of the damage.

Raya could not risk an arrow hitting Damon. She spun around and frantically grabbed for a sword.

ॐ⸱ॐ

Andrea struggled to regain consciousness. She shakily tried to sit up just as Damon seemed to fly into the screaming Darrionite.

Damon stumbled and the Darrionite nearly fell onto Andrea.

Andrea weakly tried to stand and get out of the way—her side spilling scarlet liquid in protest. She felt her feet fly out from under her as a strong hand grabbed her ankle.

Her scream was cut off as she smacked to the ground, and gasped for the air that was forced from her lungs. Black spots filled her dizzied vision.

The hand released her and she flipped over in time to see a dagger, red with her blood, plunging toward her abdomen.

ॐ⸱ॐ

Damon watched as Andrea was pulled to the ground. As he dove for the Darrionite he saw the man grab his dagger from behind Andrea.

An animal like scream escaped Damon's open throat as he tried to save Andrea.

He collided with the man, successfully knocking the knife from his hand. But not before it tore into Andrea.

Damon heard Andrea's scream as he wrestled with the struggling man, but he could not turn away. Even though the larger man's arm was injured badly, he was a strong opponent.

Damon managed a quick glance back through the darkness to see red shimmering in fire's glow. The color of blood. Andrea's blood.

"Andr—"

He allowed himself to be distracted for a second too long. Damon's cry was cut short by a solid left hook to his temple. He helplessly fought in vain as his body went limp. As darkness consumed him, he felt himself being thrown aside like a rag doll.

Damon fought against the dizzying pain and confusion as a cry jerked him back into consciousness.

"Raya." His slurred words were barely audible.

As he sat up—the swimming world around him making it difficult—he forced his heavy eyes to open.

Squinting to try to bring the blurry scene before him into focus, everything in him screamed for him to get to his feet and do something.

As his vision cleared, he saw that the smaller blur of movement a few feet in front of him was Raya.

As he struggled to his feet, he watched Raya, sword in hand and a cry in her throat, finish the unarmed attacker in one, precise motion.

Sword pierced into flesh with blood thirsty wrath.

Damon watched the lifeless body drop to the ground as Raya stood panting over it.

Dropping her stained sword, Raya turned to Damon.

"Your arm," Damon mumbled weakly, noticing that her previous wound was once again bleeding.

"It will be fine," she said. "Are you hurt?"

Damon shook his head. His heart tightened within his chest as he came fully to his senses. "Andrea!"

∽✄

Andrea felt as if raging fire was consuming her entire being. Ripped, jagged flesh screamed in urgency as hot pain trembled through her entire body. She was not entirely sure where she was hurt.

She gasped and tried to hold back the sobs and cries ready in her throat—it would only make it worse. Tears squeezed through closed eyes as a weak whimper—from confusion and fear as much as pain—escaped trembling lips. She didn't know how to handle the adrenalin—the heart pounding in her ears, the heavy breathing that she discovered to be her own, the hot pain, the incoherent thoughts racing through her mind as the sounds of the fight nearly on top of her rang in her ears.

Andrea realized that she had curled up, lying on her left side with her knees pulled up close to her chest.

Her eyes opened to blood. Her blood.

Although she heard the fight around her, she was basically oblivious to it.

Her entire right side was wracked with searing pain that pulsed through the rest of her body.

Unable to see past her blurred vision and fear, she rolled to her stomach with a yelp and pulled herself away—as best as she could tell—from the fight.

*Elnai.* Even her thoughts sounded urgent and pained, as a sob shook her body.

She struggled to her hands and knees. *Pain.* The pain screamed through her and pulled her back to the ground with a cry. She could feel the warm fluid flowing from her.

She closed her eyes. *Please, Elnai, help me.*

"Andrea!"

"Damon," she cried softly, through clenched teeth. She tried to push herself up but fell back to the dirt with a cry.

"Just lie still." His voice sounded calm and soothing, but she detected a trace of worry ebbing at the quiet confidence behind his words.

❧

"Raya, get the moy-moy," Damon said.

Panic wrapped its unrelenting fingers around his pounding heart. He tried to calm himself. He had to think straight and be strong for Andrea.

Andrea opened her eyes to meet his. Her words quivered. "How bad is it?"

Damon's breath caught. He could not see the damage well, not with all the blood. Blood was pouring from her right leg and side.

"Where exactly are you hurt?" his voice sounded much stronger than he felt. He had seen death, injury, and battle, but this time it made his stomach turn.

Raya and he had been hurt before, but never this badly. This time he cared about the person staring back up at him with eyes pleading for relief.

The thought caused his heart to skip a beat. Care. Did he even know what that was? He cared deeply for his sister, yes. But did he even know what it meant?

"I don't know," Andrea answered shakily, breathing heavy. "I remember my side got cut. But my leg—" without thinking, she moved the injured leg, sending waves of pain stained scarlet.

"Can you lie on your back?"

Damon gently helped her.

"Damon." Raya's voice was soft in both tone and volume as she gave him water, bandages, and crushed moy-moy. "I'm going for more water. We can patch my arm later. Do you need something?"

"Put on some moy-moy tea before you go," her brother responded. "I will take it from there."

Damon identified the wounds. Andrea's right outer thigh had a jagged rip. It was deep.

Damon knew that when he had tackled the Darrionite, he had successfully kept the man from plunging the knife into her abdomen and killing her, but the man had still managed to tear deeply into her leg.

Andrea also had a much shallower and less serious cut on her side from the Darrionite's thrown knife. Luckily the dagger had barely grazed her side and didn't sink into her.

Damon set to work. He calmly spoke to her, reassuring her as he worked quickly. He had to cut away her tunic and leggings about a foot above the knee so he could get to the wounds.

Damon used his belt as a tourniquet on her leg, and then gently rinsed the wounds with a little water. Saving a small bit of crushed moy-moy for her side, he put all that he had left on her leg.

"Give me your hands, Andrea," he said, placing a bandage over the wound on her side. He took her small, shaky hands in his and guided them to the bandage. "Keep pressure here. Very good. You're doing well, Andrea," he soothed, his hand covering hers.

Andrea's wide green eyes met Damon's. He could see pain and fear in them, but also trust. Trust that was being placed in him.

"You will be fine. Stay strong, you are doing well."

As he held her gaze for a half second more, his heart felt uneasy. How sure was he of his own words?

Damon placed a bandage over her leg and applied pressure.

Periodically loosening the tourniquet, Damon calmly talked Andrea through everything he was doing and made sure that she would respond to what he was saying. He had to keep her conscious and responsive.

The blood had long ago soaked through the bandages, but he kept applying pressure and encouraging Andrea.

Raya soon returned with more water. "Do you need anything? Do you want me to finish the moy-moy tea?"

"Thank you, Raya," Damon said, never losing focus on the task at hand. Andrea's side had stopped bleeding a few minutes ago, but he would wait and bandage it properly after Andrea's leg stopped bleeding.

"Finishing the tea would be helpful," Damon said. "Andrea? Andrea, look at me please."

❧•❧

Andrea lay perfectly still. Her steady breathing was strong, and she stared at the stars, whispering silent prayers and occasionally responding to Damon's calm voice. It seemed as if she had been there for ages. She had no idea how long it had actually been.

She was in pain, but between prayer and Damon's reassurance, she was calm. Even at peace.

Ever since Andrea first remembered her Great Lover and called upon His saving grace, she had experienced many things. Both good and bad. But perhaps the most astounding of all was the peace in the storm. The Holy Maker was always faithful in washing her soul with a peace that passes all human understanding in otherwise hopeless situations.

Andrea focused on Damon's calm voice as he talked her through everything he was doing.

Andrea was lightheaded. She knew that she had lost a lot of blood. She breathed a prayer.

She thought she heard Damon say the bleeding finally showed signs of stopping.

"Andrea? Andrea, look at me please."

She took a deep, shaky breath, blinking rapidly. She focused on what seemed like a faraway echo.

"Yes?" Andrea saw a glimpse of worry flash through the deep brown eyes that held her gaze captive.

"How do you feel?" Damon's voice was now clear.

"I feel very lightheaded … dizzy." Her words sounded stronger than she felt, but Damon had successfully helped clear her mind again.

"The bleeding has almost stopped." A faint, tired—but relieved—smile hinted at the corner of his mouth. "You are doing great." His eyes held hers for a moment more before he finally looked back down.

She could tell he was tired, but she was surprised as well as thankful for the gentle, encouraging strength he had shown that night.

His thick, dark hair was tousled, and she saw the slight sag in his shoulders. As strong as he was, she had seen the hint of worry behind his deep brown eyes. But now, as he carefully bandaged her wounds, the same hands that so masterfully swung a sword, were gentle.

His relief was visible in his careful movements. The stress of a moment ago seemed to physically drain away.

Andrea breathed a prayer of thanks for him.

Damon helped her sit up, and kept a strong hand on her back as he tended her side. Soon both her wounds were bandaged.

Andrea looked down at herself. Her clothing was a mess. The right leg of her leggings had been cut off several inches above the knee and her tunic had been cut off just above the belly button so that Damon could care for her wounds. She was still covered in blood—as was Damon by now—and her entire abdomen and thigh were wrapped in bandages.

❧

Damon sighed with relief. Andrea would need time to heal. But she would be fine.

"We need to move from … all this. Raya has set up camp by the river," he said, nodding toward the fire a short distance away. "Stay still. You are in no condition to walk even that short distance."

Andrea looked up at Damon.

Without another word, he gently lifted her up, being especially careful with her leg. He was surprised at how light she was. He heard her quiet gasp as he scooped her up and her arms encircled his neck. She held tight and closed her eyes.

"I'm sorry," he said softly. "I know I hurt you."

"It's not your fault," came her whispered reply. "Go ahead. I'm fine."

As Damon turned toward their camp, Andrea caught a glimpse of the dead Darrionite.

With a short, startled cry she buried her face on Damon's shoulder.

Damon felt his breath catch. He should have been more careful and protected her from seeing that. Andrea wasn't used to this.

He hurried past. "I'm sorry, Andrea. We're past it."

"Sorry," she whispered as she pulled away, her grip around him loosening.

He saw traces of silent tears on her pale cheeks. He should have protected her.

*Why do I feel so protective of her?*

She seemed so delicate and weightless in his arms, as if she'd break if he dropped her.

*She did save my life. I'm only repaying her for that,* he reasoned. *She nearly lost her life for me, yet she still took that risk. Why?*

Damon forced the thoughts from his head. He was mindful to be as gentle as he could as he carried her the short distance. He wanted to jostle her as little as possible.

Soon, Andrea was settled safe and sound by the fire. After she had washed up as much as her limited mobility allowed, Damon brought her a cup of moy-moy tea and something to eat from the rations in the saddle bag.

Then, he went looking for Raya.

"What is the body count?" he asked as he rode up to Raya. She was also mounted, doing a precautionary perimeter search around their camp. He slipped off his horse.

"That was the last one." Raya cursed. "If we would have done a body count before making camp, we would have known that one had gotten away. We knew how many men were in that camp."

She spat. "So are you finished playing nursemaid with Andrea?"

"She could have lost her life trying to save me!" Damon felt the red anger that dripped from his words color his face. "I was only hoping to save her in return. Show some respect."

Raya's blue eyes cut into him with icy rage to oppose his red-hot anger. "You were hoping to save her? Show some respect?" She dismounted and spat again. "Since when do we try to save the *dead*? Or show respect to a *target*? Have you forgotten why we are out here? She is on borrowed time as it is and my patience is growing very thin, Damon."

Damon ground his teeth and clenched his fists.

"Get it through your skull that she is already *dead*!" Raya shook her head with disgust. "She knows nothing! She is nothing! We need to bring her to Nazar now. She has served her purpose and can no longer lead us to the Resistance. Now is the time to take what we have, turn her in, and get out from under Nazar while we still have a chance."

Raya softened a bit—but not much. "I would not believe it if I was not a witness to it myself, but Damon, I do believe that you are letting a pretty face and innocent words confuse you. She is getting in your head. Remember what we are doing here." She swung herself back into the saddle. "Go clean yourself up."

Damon fought desperately to find something, anything to say. To defend himself or Andrea, to deny everything and prove Raya wrong. But he had nothing. He was confused himself. He had to figure out whatever he was struggling with for himself before he could combat his sister's sharp tongue.

The worst part was, did he honestly want to show Raya that she was wrong? Did he *want* her to be wrong? Because he had a sinking feeling that her words rang true. Andrea had somehow become more than a target to him—much more.

He thought of her voice, how it was filled with such emotion and wonder as she read from the Book. Of her face, a picture of serenity as she poured over the Book, the fire's orange glow dancing across her. Of how he felt as he had searched desperately for a pulse not so long ago. How he had taken care of her after she could have lost her life saving his. Her big green eyes had searched out his, completely trusting, and etched themselves into his mind. As he carried her, his heart had skipped a beat simply because she was so close to him. That protectiveness that he had felt. As though he would break her if he wasn't careful. And as she held onto him when he didn't shield her from the sight of the Darrionite.

She was no longer a target. Her name was Andrea. She was much more than an assignment. She was a person and Damon knew that. Which was a very big problem.

Right?

Andrea was just a girl, an innocent girl full of life. He couldn't just turn her in, but what other choice did he have?

Damon was attracted—even drawn—to her for a reason he couldn't fully comprehend. Yes, she was beautiful. Yes, he loved the way the glow of the fire danced in her bright green eyes. But there was something much deeper. She had some unseen quality—whether she was aware of it or not—that made his very soul cry out.

He sensed something in her. Something that his very being had been searching for without his knowledge of ever having such a void to fill. She had answers to questions he hadn't even known to ask.

How could one person make him feel so fulfilled and real, yet so empty and meaningless at the same time? How could his heart beat with both exhilaration and terror, clarity and confusion, fulfillment and emptiness at the sound of her sweet voice reading the enchanted words of her Book?

He stood there in the dark, confused and alone. What was happening to him?

*That Book,* he thought. *There is something about that Book. I have to talk to Andrea.* His heart beat faster as he felt the confusion slipping away. All the passages that she had read aloud to him flooded through his mind.

Could it be possible that there was hope? That he could find a way to escape his past? Could it be that Elnai really was calling him, begging to bring fulfillment to Damon's broken spirit?

Damon was bursting with excitement—this is what he was looking for!

He put his hand on the saddle to swing himself up and ride back to camp.

Red.

His heart constricted. He stepped back, hardly daring to breathe. He stared at his trembling hands. All he could see was red.

The color of blood. The color that stained his past.

Damon's throat thickened as all his previous excitement was

drowned in hopelessness. He could never escape his past. Everything in him screamed as it broke and tore apart. He dropped to his knees moaning. Eyes closed, red still filled his vision. How could he even think of mercy? Of happiness? Of real? After all he had done? He didn't deserve it. He could never hope for the bliss that seemed just within reach only moments before.

His soul shattered.

A ragged sob, dragged from his most inward self, shook him. Tears ran down his cheeks unchecked.

He jumped on his horse and rode for well over a mile. Going nowhere but away. But he could not escape the red memories. The emptiness. The pain.

He finally slipped off his horse, wearily closed his eyes, and just breathed. He was hurting in a way he had never experienced. No sword or arrow could pierce this deep, could literally make him feel as if his inner self was being ripped away, fiber by fiber, by despair. By a longing for something Damon knew he would never deserve. Could never have.

All he could do was stand. And breathe.

He could not take it any longer. He looked up to the stars—utterly alone—and screamed at the night sky with his entire being until his voice broke.

Finally, his tears were wept dry, his voice was screamed gone, and his soul was shattered numb.

He silently got back on his horse and rode back. It would be dawn in a few hours.

Damon rode into camp, his face hard, saw both women were asleep, and fell to restless sleep. Still haunted by red.

## CHAPTER TWELVE

# TRIAL AND TEMPTATION

Flora was filled with joy unspeakable as she watched from the window. Two little girls were playing in the sunshine. She had agreed to watch them so their mothers could spread the wonderful news.

She knew that this was the start of something big.

Zania and Rhoda had left early that morning on a mission to get the word out to the nearby Lovers. They were going to meet back here in two days to pray about and discuss what they should do with this turn of events. This was the start of something amazing. This could help the Resistance and show others the very heart of their Maker.

Flora prayed, beaming as the warm feeling of joy and excitement fluttered within her.

*Thank You, Holy Maker,* she sang within, *for giving me another chance to feel Your heart and share Your love with others. Please guide our decisions, direct our steps, protect us, and bless our efforts so we may wholly serve You with all we have to give.*

ॐ∾ઙ

Musa stood, blessed and pleased, before the third group of the day.

"Today," she said, "we have made quick progress. We have met the day's number of copies, so with you and the last rotation, we will do what would have been tomorrow's section."

Everyone clapped and cheered. Musa could only sigh with blissful happiness as a slight smile hinted at her lips. What joy they found in the service of the Holy Name!

Ink was put to paper with flowing strokes. Passion for the Name they loved and the very heart of Elnai which they were so privileged to copy was evident in each fluid movement.

Musa adored this passage. It brought a hope, a consuming desire. This is what they risked it all for. This was what they lived and what they died for. This was the Promise.

*Proclaim Elnai's coming from the rooftop*
*Even through persecution—do not stop!*
*For the day is coming and souls are lost,*
*Tell all of the Promise through any cost*

*In the final days there shall be great grief—*
*Lovers and sinners will cry for relief*
*When the world is finally broken and torn,*
*Ravaged by sin, hatred, fury, and scorn.*

*The days when evil runs wild and is praised*
*When a generation of sin is raised;*
*When all hope is blackened by sin's great stain,*
*Elnai will come to establish His reign.*

༺༻

Around noon, Raya and Damon woke. They walked a short distance away from camp to talk. Today's discussion was much less harsh. They both kept their cool and remained halfway civil as they talked through their options.

"Andrea can still lead us to the Resistance," Damon insisted.

"She cannot travel in the state she is in. The longer you wait … Damon, you are only making this harder. For both of you."

"Please, Raya, I know what I am doing. It is fourth Bizivday. I can have her ready to travel by first Salmday. That is three days. If not …"

Raya arched her eyebrow and crossed her arms. "If not?"

"We'll turn her in."

Damon felt as though half of him died as those words left his mouth. He wished he could be numb again. But yet, even with the pain of feeling came a freedom. Something had come alive. Something that would not be silenced. A burning feeling of emptiness and yearning because he was so very close.

But close to what?

"Good. Now that your head is in the right place again, I am going hunting," Raya said, swinging herself onto her horse.

She started to leave, then paused. She didn't look at him, but said, "Damon, I want you to know that this time is different for me too. I do feel. I hate that it has to be this way." She sighed; her voice was still soft as she looked down at him. "Just remember that no one is innocent. Not even her. And even if this is not what she deserves, we have no choice. Once this is over we can get out."

Damon watched Raya leave. On the way back, he noticed the dead Darrionite and immediately looked over at Andrea. He remembered the pain she had felt when she had seen the corpse last night. How she had hidden from it and held him as if he could protect her.

Damon set his jaw and walked to the Darrionite camp. The recent battle was evident. He took a blanket from the Darrionite men's supplies and walked back. Andrea would not see the other battle scenes, and he covered the Darrionite with a blanket from the trader's camp. He would protect her if they went back this way.

He walked back to their camp and tossed a log on the fire. He wanted to cook as soon as Raya got back.

Damon sank down on his sleeping roll and sighed. As he sat there he glanced at Andrea. She was still sleeping. She was safe. He had to find out how to keep her that way. She had to be able to travel. He could not stall forever, but he had to. He had to think of something and buy any time that he could.

ও্≈

Andrea awakened after noon. She tried to sit up, but was reminded of the cut on her side.

"Ow."

"Are you alright?" Damon asked as he came to her side.

"Yes," Andrea replied as she sat up, "I'm fine."

"Are you in pain?"

Andrea was in pain, but no more than to be expected. She could manage. "I'm fine," she repeated.

"Just take it easy," he said, brows slightly furrowed in concern. "Do you need something?"

"Water?"

Damon handed her a canteen.

"Thank you," she said, handing it back.

Damon searched her face.

"What is it?" Andrea asked quietly.

He tenderly brushed her hair from her face. She was surprised at the flutter of emotions that came as he gently touched her face.

He was looking at the bruise that the Darrionite had left with his fist. "He left a bruise."

"Yes," she responded weakly, confused by the mix of emotions.

Damon blinked and finally pulled his hand back.

"Thank you, Andrea," he said. His voice was barely above a whisper. "You saved me. You could have been—nearly were—killed."

Andrea looked up into his deep brown eyes. Her heart skipped a beat. Her emotions seemed to contradict themselves.

"Why would you risk everything for me?" he asked.

Andrea could not think over the pounding of her heart. "Why would I not? You saved me too."

Something flashed across his eyes. It looked almost like pain.

"I didn't think I could," he said, looking away. "I thought I had lost you."

Andrea's heart beat harder. "But you didn't. You saved me, Damon."

Their eyes met once more.

"Thank you."

Andrea could not look away. A strand of hair fell in front of her eyes.

Andrea's heart pounded as Damon brushed her hair aside and gently pulled her into a kiss. Her eyes drifted closed. She didn't pull away. Her cheeks flooded with the warmth she felt all over as her hand reached his shoulder. She wanted to pull him closer.

Then fear overwhelmed her. Her hand moved from behind his neck to his chest and she pushed him away firmly. She pulled away with a gasp.

"I'm sorry," she whispered, her voice thick with emotion that she could not understand. She closed her eyes and looked away. "Just … please."

In the short second when their lips had met, Andrea had gone from the overwhelming desire to kiss him back, to drowning in fear.

Without a word, he stood. She heard his footsteps get farther away and waited.

Silent tears spilled over and a few minutes past before she dared to open her eyes.

She was hurting and confused.

Andrea loved Damon.

When? How?

Somehow, she had fallen in love with him.

But something was not right. She knew nothing about love, but she knew it wasn't supposed to feel like this. Her heart was beating for Damon, but her spirit was filled with fear, and she had no idea why.

How could a kiss that had barely lasted a second feel so *right*, yet so very wrong?

స్తం

Damon rushed away. Confused. Hurt. And angry with himself because of it. He couldn't think—didn't even know where to start to think.

He had never felt *that* way about anyone. He knew she had wanted to kiss him back, yet something was wrong. Very wrong. He had felt it. Andrea had felt it. That's why she had pushed him away.

The only thing he was sure of was that he was not turning her in. If that was all he knew, he knew that.

స్తం

Raya was having a hard time focusing. She could not help thinking about the situation with Andrea.

If she was honest with herself, she was starting to see her as more than just an assignment as well—which scared her.

Raya knew that Andrea didn't do what Nazar claimed she did. Anyone with half a brain could see that she simply was not that kind of person.

And there was something about her. Damon saw it as well. It made Raya want more of that feeling, whatever it was. Yet it terrified her. Her soul seemed to burn for more understanding, but everything else shuddered.

Peace. Contentment.

Confusion. Fear.

A perfect contradiction.

Maybe it was not the peace and contentment itself that scared Raya the most, but the fact that she couldn't understand it. Maybe she was scared because in order to get to that place she would have to move past the numb shell she had wrapped herself in. Maybe she feared that Andrea and the words of her Book could be right.

If that was true, she was in trouble.

Raya never chose this life which was thrust upon her. She hadn't chosen to become a mindless weapon, to be numb to all feeling. Maybe she was terrified because believing the message Andrea brought would force her to deal with herself. With her past. Her broken soul that had long ago been hardened by a wall of ice.

*But if this is truth I see,* Raya thought, surprised at her own acknowledgment, *why should I fear it? Shouldn't I want freedom from this lie? From this prison I exist in? I'm ignoring all things right and true so I won't feel guilty after doing Nazar's work. I know this. It's always been this way. I've just always ignored it, pretending to live in ignorance. Why, now that I may have found a way to escape this, am I afraid?*

*That wretch is poisoning both of you,* something hissed from the back of her mind.

Raya felt a shiver travel through her spine as that thought seemed to come from nowhere. The words seemed to pierce through her mind. Raya was shocked. Where had this come from? Her skin crawled as the words echoed.

*You don't need her so-called Maker to tell you what is right. Where has He been your entire life? Why would He care now? We don't need Him.*

Raya set her jaw as a hardness enveloped her.

She immediately turned her horse back towards camp. She had told Damon that she would give Andrea more time, but she could wait no longer. Raya felt an urgency to deal with this before Andrea could further poison them.

As she rode, she remembered her own thoughts just before she had gotten so angry and once again, she softened. What was wrong with her? What had possessed her to think in such a way?

*I will tell Damon we can give Andrea more time,* she thought, tying her horse with the others. *Maybe she can tell me more about this Book. Maybe there is a way out of this. For all of us.*

As she trudged up the hill, she gasped. Raya refused to believe it. *It can't be real.*

But there was no denying it.

Looking down at the camp a short distance off, she had seen it.

Damon had kissed Andrea.

He had leaned close and pulled her in. She had reached a hand around him.

Raya turned and ran for her horse as the words from a moment ago hissed through her mind.

*That wretch is poisoning both of you.*

Fear gripped her. Damon would never turn Andrea in. She'd poisoned his mind and turned him against his own sister. He had nearly gotten himself killed already trying to save that girl.

That girl.

*She is trying to take him from you.* Raya threw herself on her horse and pushed him to the nearest town. *This was the last straw. She knows she is dead and is trying to take Damon down with her. I will not let that happen.*

A shrill, inhuman screech. Twisted laughter?

Raya jumped and looked frantically around. Nothing. She shook her head clear.

❧❦

Tisha was at camp alone. Timius had just left on a supply run to a nearby town and would be back in a day or two. Tisha had stayed behind; her face was too well known by Nazar's followers to risk any unnecessary trips to town.

It would be different in Valrine. They knew the place well and there were many Lovers there—besides that it was very small with basically no soldiers. They would disguise her as an old peasant and sneak her in where no one would see her. Tisha would stay with

Zania and Tim would bring Rhoda and Dory from Reed to see Tisha. Tisha would not leave Valrine and would not go to Reed under any circumstances.

Tisha had already traveled several miles on her own from where they had camped the previous night. They had agreed to meet here.

She had just led her horse to some nearby grass when she noticed something in the distance.

She staked the horse so he could graze and squinted toward the horizon. Smoke. Was there a fire? It would have to be a camp fire— which meant that people were nearby. No one from the Resistance had made plans to be this way right now, which worried her.

She carefully started walking in that direction. Trying to keep out of sight, she finally spotted a fire with a girl beside it. The girl was hurt, but had been bandaged up well.

Tisha carefully looked around. The young woman's back was to her. No one else was there and she saw no sign of horses, but the girl was not traveling alone. Tisha saw three bedrolls and two swords.

Then she saw the young woman reach for something. It looked like the Book! The young woman must be a Lover!

Tisha stood up and walked closer. This was a risk, yes, but she wanted to reach out to the girl if she didn't understand the Book, and talk with her if she was a Lover.

৵৽৽

Andrea reached for the precious Book with a confused and heavy heart.

As she opened it, she heard a woman's voice behind her.

"Hello."

Startled, she nearly jumped out of her skin. She turned, heart pounding, to see a woman.

"Hello?" Andrea answered, unsure. *Who is this woman?*

The woman froze. Andrea felt the woman's eyes piercing hers and searching every inch of her face. The woman's face a picture of sur- prise, her lips parted to say the words that she could not seem to form.

*I almost feel as if I've seen her before. She looks familiar,* Andrea thought.

The woman blinked rapidly and shook her head as though in disbelief, shock, or both.

"Do I—" Andrea cleared her throat. "Do I know you?"

"Andrea?" the woman spoke her name in a whisper heavy with emotion.

Andrea gasped, her eyes widening. *There is no way.* "I—yes," she stuttered. "Tisha?"

Tisha melted into tears as a huge smile crossed her face.

Before Andrea could react, she found herself wrapped in the arms of her mother. She embraced her, silent tears running down her own cheeks.

They finally pulled away and sat there, just looking at each other.

"How?" Andrea asked, too dumbstruck to say anything more intelligent.

"I—I don't know, I believed you had been killed in the fire, or by Nazar's men." Tisha spoke quickly, her words tumbling over each other. "We looked for you for so long and there was only so much we could do. We were being hunted and the house was—"

"Elnai saved me. He sent someone to get me out and then Flora found me—"

"Flora? But—"

"I know. She turned away. I thought that Nazar had … I know that Papa." Andrea bit her lip. "Rhoda told me everything."

The two women could do nothing but stare at one another, dumbstruck. There was so much to say, so many questions—but where to start?

"Rhoda?" Tisha finally managed. "You met Rhoda? When? She would have gotten word to me."

"Well, it was after I had escaped from Nazar," Andrea said, not sure how much her mother knew.

"What? What happened?"

Andrea started from the very beginning and told Tisha everything.

∽⌒∾

Damon finally started walking back to camp. He had not really gone anywhere—just away.

As he drew nearer, he heard two female voices. One was Andrea, and he didn't know who the other was. It definitely was not Raya.

As camp came into view, he saw them both sitting by the fire.

He recognized the older woman with a gasp.

Tisha. Andrea's mother. Leader of the Resistance. Nazar's most hated enemy. Sitting in his camp.

Damon quickly dropped to his knees in the brush. What could he do? Tisha might recognize him. Raya and he had been the ones to find a Resistance base, kill some of them, and destroy much of their work.

Tisha had been there. He could not be sure that she had seen him well enough to recognize him, but what if she had?

He quickly set out and found her camp and horse nearby. From the looks of things, she had just made camp here not long ago today. There was no evidence that she was traveling with anyone else.

Leaving everything undisturbed the way he had found it, he headed back toward camp.

From a distance, he watched them talk until it was close to dark.

Finally, Damon watched carefully as Tisha got up and left in the direction of her camp. He watched for a moment more to be sure that she had really left before finally standing up and walking to camp.

Andrea sat with the precious Book that her mother and she had pored over for the past hour. She was reading it in the light of the fire as Damon had seen her do so many times before.

At the sound of his approaching footsteps, Andrea looked up and greeted him with an excited smile.

"Damon! You will not believe this!"

He claimed his seat by the fire and played along. "What? Did you find something in the Book?" His voice held curiosity and interest as he pretended to be clueless as to what Andrea was about to tell him.

He had to admit that it brought him no joy to further deceive the excited girl that so desperately confused his emotions and completely turned everything he thought he knew upside down. But he had no choice. She could never know about the truth, his past.

Was it really his *past*?

*It is not your past. Don't lie to yourself as though you are a foolish child. It is not the past if you still live in its chains. Do you really think that there is hope? A way out? Your hands are stained red with the stains of the past—the present—that you can never escape.*

Damon's heart pounded within him. As Andrea bubbled on about her mother, Damon hoped he was responding appropriately.

His mind was far from her words, but consumed by his thoughts. By the hiss that haunted his mind. That *battled* for his mind.

" ... and I just cannot believe it!" Andrea exclaimed. Her eyes wandered past him and her smile spread broader. "And now you can meet her."

That jerked Damon back into focus immediately.

Feeling himself tense up, he turned to see Tisha herself riding towards their camp.

His hand habitually found the hilt of his sword as he stood.

*Relax*, he scolded himself, *first see if she recognizes me. It is dark and I cannot be certain she would know me even if the light was good.*

"Hello," Tisha said in a friendly manner as she swung down from her horse. "You must be Damon."

"Yes," he said, relaxing a bit, but keeping his guard up.

"I'm Tisha. Andrea's mother." She approached him with a smile.

Before he knew what to do, he found himself wrapped in a hug. He honestly wished he could run. His back went stiff and his muscles tensed up.

"I'm sorry." Tisha laughed as she pulled away. She kept both hands on his shoulders. Her sharp green eyes searched his face.

Damon's discomfort grew. Perspiration slicked his skin.

"I didn't mean to make you uncomfortable," Tisha said pleasantly, finally turning back to her horse. "I just wanted to thank you."

Damon relaxed a little as she released him from her gaze. He felt as though she had looked into his very soul. But if she had, she would not be thanking him.

"Thank me?"

"Andrea told me that you have taken excellent care of her."

He glanced down at Andrea, who was sitting beside him. She blushed and looked away. Now that some of the excitement had died down, both remembered the events from earlier. He felt his own face growing hot.

And now Tisha—*Tisha* of all people—was thanking him. He didn't know what to say. All he'd done was hurt and deceive Andrea.

"I should thank *her*." This was the truth. "She saved my life and nearly lost hers in the process."

Tisha looked at Andrea with surprise. "I'm afraid you failed to mention that, Andrea."

Andrea only smiled shyly. "How can I tell you everything in so little time?"

Damon noticed that Tisha was unsaddling her horse.

"Andrea said no one would mind if I stayed with you tonight," Tisha said.

*Is she ever wrong,* Damon thought nervously.

What if Tisha recognized him or Raya in the morning light? What would Raya do?

*Relax. I have to relax.*

࿐

Andrea could tell Damon was a little nervous. She assumed it was from earlier. *I don't want to think about this right now.*

"Tisha, um, Mother." Andrea didn't know how to address her. Yes, Tisha was her mother, but she had not been in her life since she was four. Now they were both grown women and in many ways, it was almost as if they were meeting for the first time.

"Tisha or Mother is fine, Andrea," Tisha said, understanding her position. "Call me whatever feels natural."

Andrea knew that this must be difficult for Tisha. After all, she remembered Andrea—even though she was young then—perfectly.

Andrea returned the smile and asked, "Since this Book was yours, and they are difficult to find now that they are illegal, did you need this one back?"

Tisha happily pulled one from her saddle bag. Andrea could tell that her mother was passionate about the Book that she handed to her. "Part of what we do at the Resistance is make copies to distribute to the Lovers."

Andrea was relieved that she would not need to part with her precious copy.

"So the rumors are true?" Damon looked interested. "The Resistance is behind the illegal copies?"

Tisha nodded. "Every Lover deserves to taste and see the very heart of their Maker and His Holy Son. But I would rather not discuss it in detail. It is for your own protection. Once we get to Haavene we can show you everything."

"You would show us the Resistance camp?" Damon could not hide the shock from his voice.

"Of course," Andrea laughed. "This is where we have been going this whole journey, was it not?"

"Andrea tells me that you and your sister are both Lovers and were Marked for it," Tisha said. "Even if you don't want to participate in Resistance missions, we would offer a place of refuge."

Damon simply nodded and said, for he knew not what else to say, "Thank you."

The sound of the fire reaching for the stars above was all that pierced the night's silence for a moment.

Andrea's thoughts drifted to the Book in her lap. She caressed the letters engraved in the front of the Book.

"Tisha," she asked, "do you know what this means?"

Tisha breathed in deeply as an easy smile lit up her face. "That, Andrea, is read '*Writhrial Tose Ra Lindrene*.'"

There was something hauntingly beautiful about the musical words. They seemed to fill the night with warmth that permeated the very soul.

Damon spoke in a low respectful voice that matched the mysterious, serene mood that had fallen so heavily. "That is unlike any tongue I have heard, it is not the Ancient Tongue."

"No," Tisha said just above a whisper, "it is *Lythrainial.*"

Andrea felt as though her soul was reaching to grasp the words that hung in the air. These words held a deep meaning.

"It is the Tongue of the Courts."

The night itself seemed to tremble at the words.

"*Writhrial Tose Ra Lindrene* is translated 'Holy Heart of Light.'"

Tisha gently took her Book from Andrea and held it with tender care, running her hand over the words.

"When the Holy Maker of All Things gave us the Book, He gave us His heart."

Tisha looked up. She looked into Damon's eyes and handed him her Book. "And with His heart, we were given the Promise."

"Promise?" Damon asked as he took the Book. When he touched the cover, he felt a tremble travel through his entire being. A tremble of both awe and fear. His heart beat faster as he pulled the Book to his chest. He dared not look at the engraving on the front.

"The Promise of the Tree?" Andrea asked.

"Yes," Tisha responded, finally turning away from Damon. "The Promise of the Tree. The Promise of the Coming Reign."

Andrea could not stop—nor would she want to stop—the smile that came. Her entire being seemed to sing as a spirit of boldness and joy overwhelmed her. "Elnai will rescue His lovers, bring righteous judgment, and establish his reign."

"Yes!" Tisha was now beaming. "And we will be ushered into His presence forever."

Andrea could not contain the joy that bubbled from deep within her. It overflowed into laughter.

Tisha and Andrea both laughed from the pure joy bubbling within them. Joy. Light, pure, unchecked. Bliss.

Andrea finally noticed Damon. He seemed to be deep in thought. He stared, brow slightly furrowed, at the Book in his trembling hands.

Damon looked up and their eyes met. He finally presented his crooked smile, which seemed a little unsure.

"Tisha," came his humble words, "may I keep this?"

Tisha searched his face and smiled. "Of course. I gave it to you to keep."

Andrea saw something flash in his eyes. Whether it was shock, awe, joy, confusion, fear—she didn't know.

"Thank you." Damon cleared his throat and stood abruptly. "I'm going to put it in my saddlebag."

Tisha showed them the passages explaining the Lythrainial writing on the front. The two women studied the book and talked long into the night, as Damon listened.

Andrea found Damon very difficult to read. She could tell he was interested, but there was something different than when it was just Andrea reading. He seemed to have much on his mind.

Finally, at well past midnight, they closed the precious Book and settled in for the night.

Andrea stared at the stars, overwhelmed with all that had happened that day. It was so much to take in. Maybe that would explain the uneasiness in her spirit.

Finally she pushed all the racing thoughts from her mind and went to sleep with a final prayer.

*Your will be done, Holy Maker. Guide and direct me. Thank You for giving us Your Heart. Thank You for the Promise. Your will be done in me.*

৯•৩

Throughout the night, Damon worried about Raya. He had a sickening feeling in his gut. She was not one to disappear without reason. The *reason* for her extended absence, rather than her absence itself, troubled him.

What is she doing? Damon pushed down the nagging possibilities. It really was not much of a question. He knew the answer.

Andrea didn't think to even ask about Raya until they were ready to sleep. She had been so caught up in the excitement of finding her mother.

He shrugged it off with, "I guess she lost track of time. I would not worry," and it satisfied her.

Damon stared at the stars. Tisha and Andrea both slept soundly. Damon could not. He knew it was coming.

Yet he did nothing.

Maybe that is what bothered him the most.

## CHAPTER THIRTEEN

# HARDSHIPS

It was still night, hours before dawn. Tim was staying in Sven at the home of the owner of the horse stables. The little home was on the main road through the tiny mountain town. The single window in his room looked into the street.

He sat straight up in bed, awakened by the thundering hoof beats outside his window.

He peered through the shutters. A young woman. He could tell she was a warrior by her apparel and the weapons on her back and belt. She was riding hard, in spite of a heavily bandaged arm.

Hardly letting her poor mount stop, she leaped to the ground and pounded on the door of the small home that housed Sven's two guards. Even the smallest of towns had at least two of Nazar's men posted now.

Tim watched cautiously through his cracked shutters, near enough to hear their voices but not near enough to understand them, and saw the warrior point off in the distance.

Tim's heart skipped a beat, *Oh dear Elnai, that's one of Nazar's assassins. They're after Tisha! Her camp was discovered!*

The woman finished her animated conversation with the guards and immediately swung herself back up on her sweating horse. The two guards quickly emerged armed and went about making preparations.

Praying earnestly as he threw on his clothes and gathered his things, he quietly left the house. Careful to stay hidden and quiet, he went around the back of the stables to get his horse. Before entering, he listened. Voices.

"Can you believe that we finally found her?"

"Prepare quickly. We have no time to waste."

"Is all they say of her true? Is she truly a witch?"

"Shut up and finish readying the saddles! As soon as you finish, get the bird. We are sending word to Nazar immediately."

Tim's heart was racing. From the sound of it, they were sending their fastest riders to nearby towns for reinforcements as well as sending a messenger bird to Reed. Knowing Nazar, he would send his best warriors to escort Tisha.

He turned to leave, when he heard something that made his hand reach for the hilt of the sword at his side.

"Do you really think that the Resistance base is so near to us?"

*Holy Maker, they cannot possibly know where we are.*

Tim slipped further into the safety of the shadows as the two men hurried out to continue their tasks. As soon as they had rounded the corner, he rushed into the stables and hurriedly saddled his horse.

As he led his horse out the back, he saw the assassin and two guards riding hard in the direction of Tisha's camp. Others were hurrying about other tasks and sending out swift riders to nearby towns.

Tim managed to slip out unnoticed and followed the three riders from a distance, careful to remain unseen.

It was difficult to follow them without drawing attention to himself. They were wasting no time. And why would they? This was Tisha. Leader of the Resistance and Nazar's most hated enemy.

*Lover of my soul,* his heart screamed, *they cannot take Tisha! They cannot find Haavene! There will be war!*

Tim felt in his spirit that there would be no way around it. He was afraid that the time they had been preparing for—and dreading—was here. The time where the Resistance would be forced to fight. To save Tisha, themselves, and everything they worked for.

*Elnai, please. Have mercy.*

৯৯

Flora woke up early on First Davday. It was the last day of the week and that meant, she realized with a sigh, that today Judd would expect her home.

While Rhoda, Zania, and the two little girls slept, she quietly left. When the two women had returned late last night, Flora had discussed this with them. Before they had gotten some much-needed sleep, they had shared stories of the eventful day, plans, hugs, a few tears, and plenty of prayers.

Flora thought and prayed about what to do when she got home. She knew that she wanted to stay and help Rhoda, but she was still a wife and loved Judd. Even with all his flaws.

*Please show him Your love. Let his heart be open to receive it.*

❧❧

Damon woke first. It was a few hours before noon. They had slept in today after spending most of the night pouring over Andrea's Book.

He sat up, and his worried eyes swept the area.

*Where is Raya?*

Damon looked over at Andrea and Tisha. Wait. Where was Tisha?

Damon jumped up and quickly took in every detail. Tisha's bed-roll was neatly rolled up beside Andrea. Her horse was still with the other two. Her sword was gone.

Both Tisha and Raya were missing—and he could not say which he was more concerned about. His training scolded him for not being aware of everything at all times—especially when it was something as important as why someone like *Tisha* has disappeared with her sword.

Raya was one thing. Yes, he was concerned about her being gone, but she could take care of herself.

Tisha, on the other hand, was different. She seemed sincere, but could he trust her? She was smart—too smart. And from what he had heard, a capable fighter. Her deep green eyes seemed to see right through him as she had searched his face, and that scared him. For a man like him, with secrets like his, that was dangerous. He lied for a reason. And when that lie was discovered, it was guaranteed to compromise the mission.

Was it the mission he was worried about? Was he worried that the mission would be compromised or was he too ashamed to let others even glimpse his past?

"Good morning, Damon," said Tisha's soft voice behind him. "Finally up, I see."

Damon jumped. "Where were you?" *Easy*, he scolded himself. His voice came across much harder than he had intended.

They both kept their voices down to prevent disturbing Andrea.

Tisha's sharp eyes searched his. "I went to get water."

Damon felt a little stupid as he noticed both of her hands full with their canteens. He never felt this way, but something about Tisha put him on edge. Maybe it was just the knowledge of who she was.

"I'm sorry." He didn't know quite what to say. "I didn't mean to say it like that. I am a little worried about Raya. She should be back."

Tisha immediately looked concerned. "I stumbled upon the—" she hesitated "—the aftermath of the fight. Are you sure one of them didn't escape?"

"We evaluated the situation and got a headcount upon capture. We did a body count yesterday. We are positive that they were all taken care of." Damon felt a little defensive. "Andrea got hurt because we neglected to do a body count the night of the fight. One had slipped away."

Tisha only nodded thoughtfully before saying, "You and your sister must have had considerable training. You can see it in the way you speak and even walk—not to mention the fact that the two of you killed all of those men."

She put the canteens with their supplies and stood straight, looking him in the eye. Damon wanted to look away. He felt as though her gaze was piercing into his very soul.

"You never let your guard down. Your hand is always at the hilt of your sword. You are always evaluating your surroundings. Your posture is always ready and strong." She furrowed her brow and cocked her head a bit. "What are you looking for?"

Damon was at a loss. "What are you saying?"

"You're looking for something." She took a step closer. "You're hurting."

Damon looked away and busied himself with tending the fire. Tisha was far too sharp. He couldn't look her in the eye. He felt as if she knew him better than he knew himself.

"Are you implying that I am not who I say I am?"

"I'm saying that I don't think *you* know who you are."

The silence lingered heavy in the air for a moment before Tisha continued. Her voice was soft in both tone and volume. Damon felt as though his pounding heart would burst or melt—or both—at her words.

"I know you're hurting. I could see it as we read the Book. And you're searching. Yet something holds you back. You're scared. What are you so afraid of?"

He continued to poke at the fire. "I don't know what you're talking about."

"You don't have to hide, Damon, Elnai gave us all that we need. You cannot outrun your past. Your hurt. But the Lover can bring healing and wash you clean of all stains. All you have to do is surrender. He loves you, Damon. He wants to heal you."

Everything in him was breaking.

A hot, sudden anger rose up in him. It was not his own, yet it claimed him.

*No,* he shoved the thoughts from his mind. *Where did that come from?* He felt trapped.

*They did this on purpose.*

*This is what they want. They want to trick you into thinking this way so you will become a brainwashed follower like them.*

The thought of Tisha's sharp gaze only enraged him more. He was not sure why. He started a little and felt a chill run down his spine. He could've sworn he'd heard something. A haunting echo, almost like twisted laughter.

He slowly stood and turned to face her. He struggled to keep his voice from showing his anger, fear, and confusion. "You are mistaken. I am not afraid. We've been running far too long, I'm only tired. Now I must go find Raya."

He saddled his horse and rode away from camp. He had to look for Raya, and he had to get away.

*What they say about her is true,* something hissed in his mind, *she is nothing more than a rebel wanting power over her followers. She preaches how unworthy we are and how gracious Elnai is so she can set herself up as His little prophet and control the so-called Lovers.*

Pushing his horse faster, he thought of Andrea.

*She was in on it.*

*No. Andrea's different.*

*You are letting her get into your head. Her beliefs, her precious Book—none of that is real. She is deceived. She is a deceiver.*

Damon was shocked at his own thoughts—if they were even his. Deceived. Funny how that word was used. It wasn't her fault. She was the one scared. She had grabbed onto a set of false beliefs and found along with it a false sense of security.

*She is gullible. After all, she did fall for you.*

Memories of the kiss that had lasted barely a second flooded him. The warmth that had overwhelmed his senses as she allowed him to pull her in.

Guilt stabbed at him. But was it guilt because of his deceit? Or guilt because he knew that for once something he had done had not been a lie?

He sighed deeply and stopped his horse. He was away from camp now. He didn't want to hurt her.

*She knew what she was doing. Do you really think she cares about you?* The thoughts raging through his mind robbed him of breath. He slipped from the saddle and began to pace. *You made your choice. You chose who you are and you cannot choose again. You are chained to your past. You don't want to change. Why would you?*

His throat tightened.

Damon fell to his knees, gasping. He could faintly hear the twisted screech taunting him.

*She made her choice. You made yours. She chose deception. She chose to suffer for a false hope. She chose death. You chose to survive. You chose to thrive. You know it is true. You love the rush of battle, the power that rushes through every fiber of your being with the sound of the sword sliding from its sheath. The feeling you get as you stand over the life you just took. You were born for this. You chose this.*

Damon grasped his constricting chest and fell to his side. His chest slowly closing in on itself.

*She chose her path. You chose yours. You will kill her. You chose this. This is you.*

Damon was desperate. He didn't know what was happening. He just knew he had to make it stop.

Not even fully realizing he was doing it, he managed a whisper from his closing throat. "Dear Elnai!"

He sat up quickly with a gasp.

*Air.*

He sat there and drank it in huge desperate gulps. He laid down, hands over his face, sweating and breathing hard, trying to comprehend what had just happened.

*I have to find Raya.*

He carefully mounted once more. Convinced that he was fine, he kicked his horse and searched for Raya.

≈∽≤

Andrea was still sleeping soundly when she felt a hand on her shoulder.

"Hmm?"

"Andrea, I need to speak with you." It was her mother.

Andrea wearily sat up and faced her mother. "Is something wrong?"

Tisha looked as though she could not decide how to approach the subject. "How sure are you that you can trust Damon?"

Andrea was shocked. "I trust him with my life. He has saved me more than once."

Tisha only nodded thoughtfully.

"Why? Do you not trust him?"

Tisha sighed. "You just cannot be too careful when there's so much at risk. When it comes to the Resistance, I have to be careful where I place my trust. And I can see that he's hurting. He knows the truth but is afraid to act on it, and that's a very dangerous place to be. A very vulnerable place. Fear opens doors to the heart that are not easily closed. And if you leave your heart open, it's an invitation to all sorts of abuse—and often by what you feared in the first place."

For a moment all was quiet. Andrea let it all sink in as her thoughts began to sort themselves out.

"Damon's saved my life—and nearly gotten himself killed in the process—more than once. And I've seen his mark," Andrea began. Her words were non-confrontational and careful—she was still sorting her thoughts herself. "You never saw that. You didn't see the nights when we sat by the fire and poured over the Book. He listened. He asked questions. He responded."

"But did he commit?" Tisha asked gently, looking into Andrea's eyes. She let that sink in a moment before continuing. "Andrea, I don't doubt your word, but you have to be careful. I can't put the Resistance at risk. He is searching. But if you stay in that place of searching too long, if you refuse to commit to the calling, it will destroy you just as if you had run the other way. It may take a little longer to catch up to you, but if you aren't chasing after truth as hard as you can, if you're just standing still, you will be overtaken by everything outside of Truth. You can't survive just standing still."

"Then he needs our help all the more!" Andrea said as she gingerly brought the precious Book from beside her and pulled it to her chest.

Tisha chose her words carefully. "I don't think you understand that the undecided friend is more dangerous than the unrelenting foe. Because your enemy knows his purpose. But the undecided swings his sword with no idea what he's fighting for, ultimately hurting himself and everyone around him.

"Damon needs our prayers, but if he stays where he is now, he will leave himself open to other influences. Elnai and His warriors are not the only ones fighting to woo our hearts. Lavin and the rest of the fallen are doing everything in their power to bring deceit and pain, and to ultimately separate us from the Maker forever.

"The Maker's love and redemption are free gifts to us, but we must take them. We must *choose* our side. And if you are not for the Lover—you are against Him."

Tisha sighed. "Which is why the place of indecision is so dangerous. Because by not choosing the Love of Elnai, you are choosing. And you have chosen the wrong side. There is no middle ground. There is right or wrong. Light or darkness. Life or death. Our sins separate us from the Maker's love and side us with death, but we can choose to accept Elnai's sacrifice for our sin's atonement and forever side with the Author of Life Himself."

Andrea considered her mother's words. She knew it was truth. And that hurt. She cared for Damon deeply.

"Then we need to pray for Damon and Raya," Andrea said quietly, "and we need to pray for wisdom."

৵৽৽

Damon finally saw Raya. She was on horseback and didn't seem to notice him.

"Raya!"

She immediately spotted him and pulled her horse to a stop. He rode up beside her.

Her expression was hard.

"What have you been doing?" he asked, aggravation lacing his words. "Where did you go?"

Her eyes flashed with an icy rage that cooled her voice. But she kept her voice low so as not to be overheard. "What have I been doing? What have you been doing? You let her get in your head!"

"What are you talking about?" he practically screamed.

"Keep your voice down!" she snapped. "Don't pretend that you don't know. I saw you kiss her, Damon."

"Raya." He lowered his voice. "It's not what you think."

Raya spat. "I was beginning to believe you. I was willing to give her more time, hoping to find a way out. For all of us." Her expression darkened further. "But I cannot allow her to play with your mind. She knows she is doomed and wants to drag you down with her!"

"Raya, a lot has happened since you have left, I need you to listen."

"A lot has happened indeed," she said. "I could not let some pretty face with a stupid Book and a death sentence make you throw your life away."

Damon followed her gaze to see two riders approaching.

"What have you done?"

"What was necessary. They have just finished scouting the area." Raya looked him in the eye. "Choose. Now. Don't be stupid."

Raya rode to meet them and Damon took a deep breath.

Both guards dipped their heads and awaited permission to speak.

Raya kept her chin high. "Report?"

"The girl was there as you said," they answered, eyes still downcast. "But someone else was with her. Another female."

"What? Who?"

"We couldn't get close enough without being seen."

Raya nodded, finally releasing them to lift their heads, then turned to Damon. "Who is it." It was more of a demand than a question. Her eyes demanding him to answer. To choose.

Damon felt his face harden as he sat straighter in his saddle. Looking right back into his sister's eyes, he spoke with purpose.

"It is Tisha. Andrea's mother. Leader of the Resistance."

Raya gasped. A twisted glee swelled within her. It thrilled her. It terrified her.

Damon felt strangely empowered. He had chosen.

"Here is what I know."

☙❧

Musa loved the feeling of the smooth strokes as she copied the heart of her Maker. It was tiring, but so very fulfilling. Especially with a passage such as this.

> *He shall come in power, glory, and might*
> *To cast all evil away from His sight!*
> *His Lovers will enter into His fame,*
> *In the light of His face, praising His name.*
>
> *Oh, be ever watching the eastern skies!*
> *For Elnai will call His Lovers to rise;*
> *Do not be found sleeping at His return—*
> *Be diligent and for His coming yearn.*
>
> *Yearn, oh Lover, for the fast-coming day*
> *Of Elnai's return and power display!*
> *Every knee will bend before Maker's Throne;*
> *This is the Promise—He will bring us Home.*

☙❧

As Flora took care of her horse—that was glad to be in its own stall—she continued to pray for wisdom and words to say. Taking the Holy Book that had been sent with her, she walked to the house.

She walked into a mess. Not much housework had been done. It looked like Judd had just finished his midday meal.

"Judd?"

"Flora?" Judd's surprised voice came from their bedroom. He appeared with a look of surprise and relief. "You are home already?"

"I told you I would return by the week's end. It is Davday."

"I'm glad you are home." He looked at the floor like a nervous schoolboy. "I'm sorry I yelled at you before you left."

Flora felt a smile ease across her face as she crossed the room to hug him. "I love you, Judd."

After a moment of awkward silence, she finally asked, "Now, would you like some tea?"

"I was just making some," he said, sitting at the kitchen table. He watched as Flora brought the dirty dishes scattered around to the sink. "I have some water on the stove."

"I'll finish it up."

After Judd finished bringing her up to date on all he had done in her absence, they both sat with their tea at the now cleared and wiped down table.

"So did you finally get all of this non-sense out of your system?" he asked after a while.

Flora was hurt. She had been hoping and praying that he would have a change of heart.

"No, Judd," she said tiredly, eyes begging him to understand, "this is not non-sense, this is life."

Judd shook his head as if he truly pitied her. "Will it be life if they kill you, Flora?" He cursed under his breath. "You do understand that they will kill you for this foolishness?"

"I'm fully aware of that," she said, letting her eyes drop.

"Flora, look at me."

He spoke with such softness that it broke her heart. Her eyes met his. The heartbreak she felt was mirrored in his eyes.

"I love you, Flora, please think about this. Don't waste your life on nothing!"

"You don't understand," she said, wiping watery eyes, "I *have* thought about this and I have *already* wasted most of my life on nothing."

Judd set his jaw and looked away.

"Judd, please try to understand," she begged softly, tears in her voice. "I finally have true purpose—true life. Life is more than breathing, Judd."

Without another word, he got up, just about knocking his chair to the floor in the process, and stormed away.

Flora let tears and prayers flow freely. Picking up her precious Book, she retreated to the comfort of its words.

കൈ

Andrea and her mother looked up from their study of the Book.

"Do you hear that?" Andrea asked.

"Sounds like horses," Tisha replied.

Both women were quiet and listened.

"From over there." Andrea nodded toward where the sound seemed to come from.

Damon and Raya rounded the rocky corner on horseback.

"Raya," Andrea asked, "did you get lost?"

Both riders let their horses graze and unloaded a nice bit of meat.

"Yes," Raya said as she set a sack of cooked meat down. "I wounded a nice mountain goat and had to chase it down. By then it was dark and I lost my sense of direction by the time I found it. Too much cloud cover to see the stars so I just made camp for the night."

"She would have come back earlier today," Damon chimed in, "but she had to finish cooking the meat. She didn't want it to spoil."

Tisha stood and smiled. "Hello, Raya."

"You must be Tisha," Raya said with a polite nod. "Damon told me that you were Andrea's mother."

"Yes. And you are his sister?"

"Yes." Raya sat and finished off her canteen of water. "Are you hungry? I'm famished."

"We only had a little from our rations yesterday," Andrea answered. "We're ready to eat as well."

Damon began gathering up canteens. "I'm going to refill our water. Will you hand me yours? I'll go ahead and fill them all and then we may rest the remainder of today."

Tisha and Andrea handed him their canteens and he went off on his horse.

A few short minutes later he returned with filled canteens. He handed Andrea and Tisha each one, then gave one to Raya and sat down with his own.

"Thank you," Andrea said before taking a drink from hers.

"I didn't mean to make you wait on me," he apologized. "You could have eaten without me."

"It's fine," Andrea assured him. "We just finished preparing the rest for travel."

They mostly made small talk as they ate.

"I was just thinking …" Andrea was having a hard time forming a complete thought.

"Are you alright?" Damon asked, concern in his voice.

Andrea tried to blink her world into focus. "I feel dizzy."

Damon came to her side, concerned. "Drink some water and lie down."

His voice echoed somewhere far away. She groggily obeyed.

As she closed her eyes and the world faded away, she heard Raya's voice. "Tisha, you don't look well either."

∽∾

Tim had to fight to keep from charging out there. He had helplessly watched as the assassin he had followed from town met with the other. They had discussed plans with the two guards before returning to camp where Tisha was with Andrea.

He could tell even from a distance that it was Andrea—she looked just like her mother.

After the four had discussed plans, the two assassins went to the camp. The tall male had filled their canteens and Tim could do nothing but watch helplessly as the assassin put naxar root extract in Tisha's and Andrea's water. Though it would not hurt them, it would put them to sleep.

And now he watched as both Andrea and Tisha succumbed to the effects. The assassins motioned to the two guards, who came from their hiding places to join them.

Tim felt as though he had failed. He had not been able to get to Tisha in time. But he must not get captured as well. That would not help anyone.

Finally, he quietly turned his horse to leave. He had to get to the Resistance. He had not been able to warn Tisha, but he may still be able to warn the others.

*Dear Elnai*, he prayed as he urged his horse faster once a safe distance away, *give us strength. Save us.*

∽∾

Andrea slowly began to wake up.

"Look." A gruff voice boomed through her head. "One of them is trying to wake up."

*What is happening?* her heart pounded within her chest. She opened her eyes to the stars above her. She started struggling to sit up, then gasped.

Her hands were tied!

"Be still!" came the sharp command.

She lay still a moment before looking around cautiously. A few feet away, bound hand and foot and unconscious, was Tisha.

Four people were seated around the fire. Two wore what looked like Nazar's standard guard uniforms, the other two were only silhouettes facing the fire. She tried to blink her vision clear.

Her words were still slightly slurred. "Who are you?"

"All right," said one of the men as he stood.

He grabbed Andrea's mouth and poured something down her throat. Her struggle only led to a death grip on her jaw and got the liquid all over her face as she choked.

She was clawing at the hand that held her to no avail.

"Stop fighting! Just drink it! Water will not kill you," he barked.

She was forced to swallow a big gulp and the man finally let go. Andrea was left coughing and trying to breathe as the man took his seat by the fire.

"Stupid wretch," he growled. "I won't let her wake up again."

"Keep them both unconscious." The other man scowled. "Less trouble that way."

As Andrea faded away from consciousness, she saw one of the men looking back over his shoulder.

Damon.

She gasped as the realization hit her with its full, crushing force.

Their eyes met. She saw nothing. His eyes looked distant, cold.

She could manage no words as darkness engulfed her.

The words of the warrior echoed through her spinning mind.

*But beware. Beware those who would deceive you. Guard your heart and mind. For trial, temptation, and hardship is fast coming. If you don't guard your heart, I shall still use you to fulfill my purpose, but the cost will be great.*

Fast coming indeed.

Trial had come in the attack of the Darrionite that left her injured.

Temptation had come with the kiss.

As a result, now the hardship had come.

Andrea had left her heart unguarded and left herself wide open to be deceived. If she had been careful and guarded her heart as she had been warned, she would not have let herself fall for Damon. She would have listened to her mother's words and escaped before this.

These swirling thoughts were the last thing she could remember.

## CHAPTER FOURTEEN

# BETRAYAL

Musa went about Salmday as usual—as did every other Lover at the Resistance base camp. They gathered together for a day of meeting, fellowship, prayer, worship, and rest to start off the new week.

No one knew that Tim was riding earnestly to reach them.

No one knew of Tisha's capture.

Flora was studying the Book with a heavy heart. Judd had kept to the fields all day yesterday after their discussion at tea. He had come in late, they had eaten a silent meal, and he had retreated to bed early while she cleaned up. Whether he had actually been asleep or not when Flora had retired for the night, he didn't stir.

She knew that she had to serve Elnai, but how could she if her husband was not a Lover and would not permit her to go back to Valrine?

With a troubled sigh, she wearily got up from her place at the table to tend to the breakfast dishes.

Judd had already left for the fields when she had gotten up early that morning. The evidence of the bread and jam breakfast he had prepared for himself was left scattered about. Flora had also eaten a quick, easy breakfast before sinking into the words of the Book.

Now, as she washed the dishes, she looked out the window above the sink. The rolling hills with rich soil that made much of Airiss perfect for farming stared back at her.

The Maker truly was a breathtaking artist. His love of beauty was evident in every aspect of His creation.

Flora breathed a silent prayer of thanks before turning back to her morning chores.

She threw a log in the stove and put the tea water on. As she swept the old wooden floors, Judd came in.

He looked as if he had aged ten years since she had first poured his tea after coming home.

"Flora, I—" he stopped mid-sentence as his eyes came to rest on the Book, which still lay open where she had left it on the table.

Judd walked over to the table, picked up the Book, and roughly flipped through a couple of the precious pages.

Flora held her breath. She had been hesitant to show him the Book.

Color spread up his neck to his face as Judd angrily slammed the Book shut and looked at the symbols on the cover.

"How could you bring this into my house, Flora?" he cried. "Do you know what they will do to you—to us—if they found out that you had *this*?"

"Judd. Judd, please." Flora's voice was barely above a shaky whisper.

"I know that you cannot seem to understand this, Flora, but I am trying to protect you!" He walked over to the stove.

Flora realized what he was doing. Her cry was thick with emotion and desperation. "Please! Judd, don't do this!"

"I'm sorry," he said, shaking his head wearily. "I really am."

Flora's hand flew to her mouth, the broom noisily clattering to the floor, and choked back a cry as she watched her husband throw her Book into the fire and slam shut the door to the stove. Hot tears ran freely down her face.

Judd looked at her as though he truly was sorry. He was hurting. He was sincerely trying to do what he thought was best for Flora.

He was deceived.

He crossed the room and took her gently by the shoulders. "I'm only doing what is best for you. Try to understand that."

"You need to understand that I will never go back," she said, hand still over her mouth as she cried. "This is what is best for me. I pray for you continually but you have hardened your heart. You refuse to hear the Maker that beckons you."

His expression hardened and he took his hands from her shoulders.

Finally, he cursed and stormed back outside.

"Oh Dear Elnai!" Flora cried, sinking to the floor and burying her face in her hands. "Let him hear You! Give me strength!"

❧

"Wake up," a gruff voice demanded.

Andrea struggled, grasping at consciousness. Her heavy eyes opened to the blurred world spinning around her.

"Sit up."

She felt a strong hand pulling on her arm. She struggled to sit up as her vision was finally blinked into focus.

The strong hand and deep voice belonged to Damon.

All confusion was banished by the stabbing pain of reality. Memory of all that had happened flooded in with the crushing emotions.

She had been betrayed. She had been drugged. She had been bound. And now she was being taken to Reed. To her death.

"Eat," Damon ordered as he held out a small bite of meat and a bit of bread.

Andrea could only stare at Damon as she tried to sort her frenzied thoughts and emotions. She hardly recognized the hard face with distant eyes that didn't seem to actually see her.

"Take it," he demanded again.

"How long, Damon?" she whispered, trying to hide the emotions that cracked through her voice. "How long did you plan this? When did the lies start?"

"Last chance for food today," he said, unwavering.

She searched his deep brown eyes, praying for some glimmer of hope. Andrea might as well have been staring into the eyes of the dead.

"Just tell me. I will be dead soon anyway. When did the lies start? You owe me at least this much."

"Ravelle." He said it as if he were stating the time of day. His hard, emotionless words never changed. "Last warning. Take the food."

Ravelle was where she had first met them. The lies had gone that far. "So none of it was real?"

Raya marched over and took the food from Damon. "You missed your chance. Maybe you will be smarter tomorrow."

Damon looked down at Andrea. "You were an assignment. You would be wise to keep your mouth shut."

Cold. Dark. Hard. Lifeless.

Did he really feel nothing? These eyes that held hers she didn't recognize ...

Could they really be the same that lit with curious interest as they poured over the Book in the light of the dancing fire? As they had for so many nights that seemed so very long ago?

The same eyes that betrayed worry and fear at the sight of Andrea when she was hurt?

The same deep brown eyes that had pierced her very heart as he pulled her in and kissed her ... It had only lasted a moment ... but it had taken her breath away ... For a moment his lips pressed against hers and she felt overwhelmed in a beautifully terrifying way. Her eyes had melted closed ... she had felt her hand slip behind his neck ... but then her heart quickened and all beauty was banished from the moment with such sudden finality. She had pushed him away ... fear screaming though her being.

Andrea shuddered. Somehow, she had known.

Dead. That's all she saw now. No more passion. Only death.

Damon finally turned and left. Andrea dropped her watery gaze to the bound hands in her lap. She felt as if two hands were tearing her heart slowly as if to make her feel every rip ... every stabbing pain of confusion and betrayal ...

Merciless. Betrayed. Broken. Torn.

*Sound familiar?* the whisper echoed through her aching heart, *You have been here before, beloved ... I have been here before. I did it for you. I did it so I could save you, Andrea.*

Tears flowed silently.

*I was blameless, yet they showed no mercy. I was betrayed by the very ones I came to save. I was broken and torn as they killed me and claimed it was for the love of my Father. But I made a Way.*

*Andrea, you let the trial and the temptation overtake you.*

Andrea crumpled to the ground. She could not breathe. She could only lay there as silent tears traced her cheeks. Her lungs were being squeezed. She was so very guilty. So very unworthy. So stained. Unclean, impure. She felt Elnai crying with her. He was not doing this to her. She was doing it to herself. She was doing it to *Him.*

*I am sorry! Please forgive me! I cannot take this!*

Andrea felt as if she were submerged in water, but not getting wet. It was a peace so real she could *breathe* it. She drew it deep into her lungs. No more tears. No more pain. For a moment, all was perfect. Beautiful. Bliss.

*Beloved, you are forgiven. The consequences of your actions will seem unbearable, but I have not forgotten you. I made a way. Stay faithful. I have overcome.*

Andrea sat up. The pain and bleakness of reality was ever present, but dulled by the blanket of peace that now covered her.

*Thank you.*

Andrea watched as Tisha was awakened and offered no food.

Soon, they were both given water to drink. This time they were not drugged. They had to be awake enough to stay in a saddle.

The two guards soon returned with two additional guards. Apparently, they had ridden to meet them.

As their six captors prepared the horses, Andrea and Tisha were left alone for a moment.

They whispered to keep from drawing the attention of any of their captors. At any given time, one of them was no more than a few yards away.

"I'm sorry," Andrea whispered. "I should have known."

"You cannot blame yourself for the evil choices of others, Andrea." Tisha's voice had a quiet confidence to it. A peace. "Stay strong. Pray continually. Have faith. Elnai sees us even now. Elnai will make a way."

"Shut up!" came an angry voice belonging to a rough-looking man who approached them. "Talking will get you hurt. Especially *that* name," he spat. "Now get to your feet!"

The man was joined by another and they jerked them to their feet.

Andrea tried to stand, but pain from her injured leg shot through her. Crying out, her knees buckled. The man never loosened his bruising grip on her arm, causing more pain.

Andrea bit her lip in an effort to fight back the cries. Tears threatened to spill over as her entire right side throbbed.

"She is injured!" Tisha cried, earning herself a quick, hard slap.

"That one is injured," Raya's hard voice said. "She cannot stand."

The man cursed, then picked her up and dropped her into a saddle in one rough motion.

Andrea grimaced, but refused to cry out. Andrea's and Tisha's hands were then roughly tied to the saddle of their horse. Their horses were led by two of the captors.

Every day for the next ten days, Andrea and Tisha were awakened and given a meager portion of food and water. They were then put on horses, where they remained tied except for the few, short breaks that were taken from the long hours of riding. Damon and Raya always rode ahead, leading the others, while the guards who were not leading the prisoners' horses followed at the back of the procession. As they rode day after day, other guards met up with the growing escort.

After camp was made for the night, Tisha and Andrea were both given water with naxer to force them to sleep until morning.

The two captives were not given any opportunities to talk. They were kept separated. There was some talk among the guards, but there was mostly silence.

Andrea hardly saw, much less spoke to, Damon and Raya.

Tisha and Andrea were given only enough food and water to survive, tied to horses to be led on for endless hours, forbidden to speak, and only spoken to in harsh commands.

*We're no more than animals to them,* Andrea thought. *How do you get to this place? Where life is considered worthless, a human is treated like an animal, and you remain cold and distant as you destroy another person as if they were nothing?*

Andrea had plenty of time to think. To sort out and pray about her hurt, betrayal, and fear.

And pray she did—and often. What else could she do? What else would she *want* to do? It brought peace in pain and grace in trial. Andrea was amazed to realize that in this moment—this place of darkness and hopelessness—she could feel the love of Elnai so near. Perhaps she felt closer and more connected to her Maker than ever before, even through the hardship. And she was truly thankful.

Andrea was not thankful for the situation—but thankful for the grace that *surpassed* the situation. The grace to know that no matter what happened—whether she lived or died—she was safe. She was loved. She was promised redemption—either in this life or the next.

࿈

Tim made really good time getting back to the Resistance. When he first came this way traveling with Tisha, it had taken ten days. Seven days after watching Tisha and Andrea be captured, he now rode through the ruins of the ancient Darrionite city.

For miles around the forgotten city you saw only desert sand. The grand palace as well as the city which encircled it was mostly buried, forgotten except for the whispered stories still told by the few that cared to remember.

Very few even remembered this place. It was well out of the way that anyone traveled. But more than the fact that it was surrounded by miles of desert were the stories told of it.

The city had once been the capitol of a tyrant of the Third Age. This tyrant had brought war, destruction, and poverty upon the Darrionite people.

A great disease suddenly struck the city. Many, including the tyrannical leader, died very soon after and the survivors fled. Soon after that, a heavy sandstorm blew in that partially buried the city.

Because disease and storm had struck the once grand city, reducing it to nothing more than a buried legend—many considered it cursed.

Even though it was now the Fifth Age, the Darrionite people were still very superstitious. The few that even remembered the ancient ruins remembered it only for the stories behind it and had no interest in finding out whether the city was cursed—and whether a trespasser would be for entering it—or not.

The fact that it was surrounded—and mostly buried—by desert in the middle of nowhere, the story behind it, and that not many knew about it all made it perfect. The palace had needed repairs, but it was spacious and now home and base of the Resistance and its many members.

But now, Haavene was in danger. Tim was fairly positive that their location had been given away, and he had to call a meeting immediately.

He tended to his horse and quickly woke the leaders. It was midnight by the time he had all the Resistance leaders in Yipoc Raj.

He told them all that had happened and they listened without interrupting. Urgency laced his voice and exaggerated his body language.

᳨

Flora rose from her knees, but continued to pray. The last few days had been hard. Ever since Judd had burned the Book, little had been said. Judd stayed in the fields from dawn until after dark, coming in only for silent meals, and Flora tended the house.

Both were hurting, but saw no way out. Judd would not back down because he thought he was protecting her, and Flora would never turn on her Maker again.

Finally, after many tears and prayers, Flora worked up the courage to address the subject that had been so carefully avoided for the past week.

When Judd sat down for the midday meal, she sat across from him at the small table, nervously pushing her food around her plate.

"Judd," she said carefully, "I need to speak with you."

He looked up from his meal. "Please don't tell me that you still refuse to come to your senses."

He didn't sound confrontational, but genuinely worried, defeated, and tired.

"Judd, you know that I cannot turn away," came her soft, but firm and unwavering response. "I pray that you will understand soon."

"Don't waste your breath, Flora," he said gruffly. "I don't want your prayers."

"Which shows how desperately you need them," Flora said, barely above a whisper. Looking him in the eye, her voice got stronger. "I need to go back to Valrine. I would like to leave today. The house is in order and I will return in a few days."

Judd cursed and hit the table. "I refuse to allow you to run off again over this, this *lie*. I cannot lose you! You know what almost happened last time."

"Judd, please, I have to do this. I know you are scared but when I am serving the Holy Maker I am in the safest place I can be."

"Do you even hear how crazy you sound?"

Flora's calm, even tone was a stark contrast to her husband's. "I know it is difficult to understand. Even as a Lover it can be. But I know Who gives me breath. I know Who holds my soul and is preparing a place for me when I no longer walk in this world. I know that the Author of Life is in control. I know that there is no better or safer place to be than where He calls me."

Flora could see the range of emotions, but Judd was listening. If he was actually *hearing* her words, she didn't know, but it was a start.

She breathed a prayer before continuing. "I know you love me and want to protect me. I love you too, Judd, and I hate to see you hurting. Please understand that this is something that I have to do. I love you, and I pray for you to see the truth."

"The truth?"

Flora could tell by his bitten off words that Judd was fighting to control his temper. She knew he didn't really want to hear it, but, taking a deep breath she told him anyway.

"The truth. The truth that you are scared to hear so you have closed your ears to it. I understand. I have been there. You are scared of what believing this Truth will mean. Because you know that choosing to remain ignorant does not require sacrifice. The sacrifice, the risk, the change, it is all difficult—but it is *worth* it. Would you spit in the face of the One who gave you life trying to save it from those who may wish to take it?"

Silence rang loud, seeming to shake the room.

Finally, Judd's enraged words shattered the ringing silence. "Then go." He stood and refused to look at her. His voice was low and grave, shaking with rage and emotion. "Go now. Before I come to my senses and forbid you from ever leaving the house at all."

"Judd."

But he was gone. The house seemed to tremble as the door slammed with angered force.

Flora arrived at Valrine that same day in the late evening.

After excited greetings from Rhoda, Flora wept as she told her all that had happened. After prayers, hugs, encouragement, and a promise to provide Flora with another Book, the conversation took a happier turn.

Rhoda told Flora that ten women—Rhoda, Zania, and Flora included—had been making excited plans. They would meet twice a week for "tea and quilting."

Of course, there may actually be tea and a little quilting at some point so they could honestly say that they *did* do those things, but they were actually gathering for different reasons entirely. They would work at making copies of the Book, and spend some time in fellowship and prayer.

The first meeting was planned for the following day—the same day that Tim would arrive at the Resistance camp to report that their leader had been captured exactly eight days ago.

෧ඁ෧

The day after both Tim and Flora had reached their respective destinations, Tim and the other leaders all looked at each other—faces heavy with the gravity of the situation.

They had spent the entire night in intense prayer—seeking wisdom, courage, guidance, and begging for the lives of all the Resistance as well as Tisha's and Andrea's. They had finally retired to a fitful two hours of sleep before waking up and calling a meeting in the Zann Raj.

The room they called the Zann Raj—where they would gather for Salmday or other meetings—had been the great court room of the ancient castle. The platform where the throne had once sat was the length of one of the narrower walls in the rectangular room. Three elaborate stone steps the length of the platform led up to it. This platform now served as the stage for the Resistance meetings.

Tim, Riven, Jay, and Musa now stood on this platform overlooking the silent crowd. This was the entirety of the main Resistance. Of course some, like Tim, had families who were Lovers but didn't live in Haavene. A few had left to visit family earlier, as well as small groups, safe-houses, and other Lovers who didn't serve the Resistance from Haavene but were scattered about the world.

Those who actually lived at and served from the Resistance Base were what was commonly referred to as "the Resistance" and numbered just under three hundred—two hundred eighty-three to be exact. Although it was estimated that there were around seven hundred Lovers who contributed to the Resistance in countless other ways from around the world.

As the four leaders looked over the members of the main Resistance, they were grave. Every soul in the room sensed something terrible had happened—especially since Tim had returned without Tisha.

As Tim's firm, clear voice told of what had happened, not a whisper of any other voice was heard. A grave silence seldom seen in this room with this crowd hung heavily in the air.

After Tim had said his piece, Jay stepped forward.

"This news reached us only in the middle of last night. We have spent the night and morning in earnest prayer. We believe that we must immediately evacuate this location and be prepared to fight."

The cries of hundreds erupted. Thousands of questions were lost in the chaos.

Jay shouted and gestured for silence. Finally order once again stilled the room.

"We have been preparing for and praying about this for years," Jay said. "There were times when The Maker Himself would call His people to fight for what is good. This is why we have trained.

"We didn't ask for this fight. We don't want it. But Nazar must be stopped. He is destroying countless lives and the rest of the world is following his example. Even leadership of the care-free Kimim has been restricting the worship of the Holy Maker.

"We shall spend today in prayer and preparation, and tomorrow at dawn we will leave. If anyone is unwilling or unable to possibly put an arrow to the string or draw a sword, see any one of us leaders."

Jay covered a few more details and then asked that everyone go to their rooms to pack and make it easier for the leaders to find them. After an hour, the leaders would divide them into groups and assign tasks. The four respective groups (one under each of the four present leaders) would meet later. The plan would be discussed in greater detail and then any necessary changes would be made.

Rough plans had already been discussed on more than one occasion with the entire main Resistance for just such a situation, so everyone already had a good idea of what to do.

Finally, Jay asked Riven to dismiss them. Jay, Riven, Musa, and Tim each put a hand on their neighbors' shoulders and the others followed suit in preparation for the Resistance's traditional dismissal prayer.

"The harvest is great," said Riven, his deep voice ringing loud and clear as it bounced from the towering ceiling over the crowd he faced.

In response, the voices of almost three hundred Lovers rang in unison: "And the harvesters are few."

"Let us bless those who heeded the Lover's call."

"Let us pray for those who didn't."

"Let us sow love."

"So we may reap love."

"May Elnai send harvesters."

"May the harvest be great."

Riven's voice grew stronger as courage swelled in every heart. "May we live in love!"

"May we die in love!"

"May we worship Love!"

"We are His Lovers!"

"And He is *ours!*" Every voice rang loud and clear as they shouted in victory over the last statement.

"We are His!" Riven shouted at the top of his voice. "We are His! This world cannot stop us! *We are His!*"

"And He is ours!" came the joyful proclamation. Every voice cried out as one.

They would not be silent. They would not be moved. They would not be shaken. They would not be afraid.

This was their proclamation. Their hope. Their future. Their Maker.

As one heart beating with love for their Maker, every knee hit the floor as reverent silence washed over them. Hands still on the shoulders of their neighbors, united in love of Elnai.

Musa, tears streaming down her face and voice thick with emotion, broke the silence. Her voice rang clear with a quiet strength that pierced every soul as she recited from heart a beloved passage from the book.

*"Do not fear, Beloved*
*When it seems all is lost,*

*For I Am your Lover*
*And I have paid the cost.*

*You, dear Lovers, are Mine,*
*I gave for You my life;*
*Be strong and courageous!*
*I hold you through the strife.*

*I breathe life, I give love,*
*My glory covers you;*
*I prepare great rewards*
*For the faithful and true."*

Every heart was stirred and every eye wet.

Janelle stood, beaming as tears streamed down her cheeks. Her sweet, pure voice carried a song of love and glory to the Maker. Emotion laced every lyric as the melody seemed to dance to the heavens. She looked up as if turning to face the Light of The Courts, eyes closed, heart abandoned, song rising sweet and clear.

A gentle breeze seemed to whisper through the room as Janelle's song grew stronger. Soon, every soul was standing as they joined their hearts with Janelle in song. Some stood beaming, others laughed, many sang, tears flowed freely. Tears of love, of hope, and of peace.

They were where they belonged. Worshiping in the presence of their Maker. They were safe. No matter what happened.

After their hearts had been poured out in song, they simply lingered. A silent prayer and a growing peace in every soul. Finally, almost as one, they silently slipped away to their rooms.

Elnai had washed them with His love and filled them with His peace. Courage and hope renewed, they were prepared for whatever may lie before them. They were ready to live—or die—for their Maker more than ever before.

The Inner Circle—save Tisha—as well as the fifteen other Council members, met to discuss and finalize plans. They had only a few details left to work out. They pulled maps and drew routes.

As they worked, Tim looked around at each face. He loved each one dearly … they had been through a lot together. Many had been there since the very beginning.

*Jay, Riven, Musa, Ryele, Bennen, Dray, Tori, Al, Darcy, Tristan, Carson, Tamar, Jiff, Aleb, Bellynne, Lana, Ardin, Rema.* As he recited each name, he lifted up a prayer for them.

Tim's heart panged as he thought of those they were missing. Some had loved ones at home, he had Rhoda and Dory. Tisha and Andrea had been captured. Ross had died. Fourteen years ago, Ross and three other brave young Lovers had given their lives. Their brothers, sisters, parents, and children now stood in this room.

Before that, they had lost many to betrayal. It took great bravery to stand as they watched their loved ones bend knee to Nazar. Lana had lost her fiancé Drew, and Ardin lost his brother Asher to betrayal that day.

Finally, two years ago, two assassins had attacked a large group of Resistance members and leaders who had gathered in Shaylo for a meeting. Seven lives and all their supplies were stolen by the time they escaped. Rema lost her parents Matthew and Ami, and Carson lost his wife Rene.

That was only naming the losses taken by the twenty members of the Resistance Counsel. There were hundreds more lost to death and betrayal. How much more loss would they have to take? Tim sighed as he turned his attention back to the task at hand.

By the end of the hour, each of the nineteen leaders had detailed instructions and maps. A plan was made and, most importantly, prayers were unceasing as they carried it out.

That night, the messenger bird was sent out to Kander, a nearby town where a Lover took care of several horses for the Resistance. The note tied to the bird's foot had instructions to prepare all available horses and ride out at dawn to meet them.

☙❧

Unbeknown to the women sitting in Rhoda's house for "tea," the Resistance base had evacuated almost six hours ago. As they sat studying the Book and excitedly discussing ideas, they were completely unaware of the danger the Resistance—and they themselves—were in. Always there was risk, but it was looming darker now than it had in years. Someone pounded on the door.

"Flora!" came a slurred yell. "Flora, I know you are in there!"

"It's Judd," she said quietly. "Hide the Books."

The danger was now becoming all too real.

Flora breathed a prayer as she opened the door.

She hardly recognized the man that stood before her as her husband. His hair was wild, his clothes rumpled as if he had slept in them, his eyes bloodshot. The smell of alcohol was so heavy that Flora almost gagged.

"Flora, Flora, please come home," he slurred loudly.

"Judd, please keep your voice down," she begged softly. "I was going to come home tomorrow. We talked about this."

"I love you, Flora," he whimpered. "Come home, please."

"Judd, you are drunk—"

"I'm not!" he yelled angrily, spitting as he did. "I try to take care of you, I work hard all my life, and this is how you treat me. You would rather die for this than let me keep you safe? Am I not good enough?"

"Judd," she whispered frantically as he rambled at the top of his voice, "please, Judd, I will come home with you right now—"

჻჻

*She does not want to come home.* The words ran through his mind and shivered down his spine, *She does not love you. She has been brainwashed! They*—He—*has turned her against you!*

"You don't mean that!" Judd wailed, vision swimming. "They brainwashed you! *He* brainwashed you!"

He stumbled to retain balance as Flora's pleas were drowned out by the voice in his mind.

*You have no other choice. You have to protect her. This will bring her to her senses. She will give up this foolishness and come back to you.* The twisted, inhuman hiss haunted him.

"I'm sorry, Flora." Judd sobbed freely now. "I'm sorry. I have to protect you."

"What? It's fine, Judd. Why are you sorry? I will come home right now. Please, Judd, look at me," she pleaded.

Judd wagged his head and nearly fell over.

*There is no other way. You are doing what is best. You are protecting her.*

"No other way to make you come to your senses," he mumbled, not really in control of his own words. "I'm protecting you. I am sorry."

❧

Fear began to grow as Flora slowly began to see what had happened. Judd refused to look at her, his eyes darted rapidly.

"Judd, what have you done?"

He just kept rambling his now incoherent apologies.

Flora finally spoke firmly. "Judd! Judd, look at me!"

He looked at her like a terrified puppy.

"What did you do?"

"Just tell them it is not true. They said they would let you go."

Flora's heart sank as the breath was pulled from her lungs.

She turned to the group of concerned women behind her.

"Where are the kids?" Flora asked frantically.

"Not here." Rhoda's voice was heavy with the seriousness of the situation. "Safe."

"And the Books?" Flora said, leaving her husband a sobbing mess and lowering her voice. "Did we bring them all here?"

"Not all of them." Zania sighed. "We have ten here."

Rhoda straightened her back at the sound of stomping feet and horses coming down the street. "They're coming."

They scrambled to hide the Books and then calmly stood in a circle in the living room.

"There is no use running. They have us." Zania sighed.

"No." Rhoda's sad, yet peaceful smile and the strength in her voice encouraged the others as much as her words did. "*He* does."

Rhoda put her hands on the shoulders of the two women standing on either side of her. The others followed suit. Encircled by each other as well as the peace of Elnai through the coming storm, Rhoda led them on.

A genuine smile graced her as the words she still cherished from years ago left Rhoda's lips.

"The harvest is great."

"And the harvesters are few," Zania responded, voice steady and strong.

"Let us bless those who heeded the Lover's call," Rhoda said, looking each woman in the eye.

"Let us pray for those who didn't." Every voice united as one.

"Let us sow love."

"So we may reap love."

"May Elnai send harvesters."

"May the harvest be great."

"May we live in love." Rhoda's voice grew stronger, louder, and clearer.

As one spirit, united by one Spirit, courage rose with their strong voices. "May we die in love!"

"May we worship Love!"

As armed guards stormed in by the dozen, the Lovers were not fazed. There they stood. Encircled by each other. Lovers. In love with Love Himself.

The guards screamed for them to get on the ground, but their barked commands and stomping feet fell to deaf ears as the Lovers lifted their voices ever stronger above the chaos.

"We are His Lovers!"

They were thrown to the ground and bound by rough hands.

"And He is ours!" Rhoda's voice was echoed by the others before they were gagged.

Flora, though she fully understood what lay ahead in the dark road before her, felt peace. She looked at the man who, with drawn sword, pushed her toward the door and felt pity for him. He was so deceived, she offered a prayer for his salvation. He had no idea that by following orders, he was arresting Lovers of the Almighty Maker—*his* Maker—and spitting in the face of Elnai.

"What of the drunk?" Flora heard a guard ask.

"Let him run. He turned them in, and we have no orders to comprehend him."

*Dear, Elnai,* Flora's breaking heart cried out, *Please, please touch my husband. He is so deceived. Show him that he needs You.*

## CHAPTER FIFTEEN

# IF THEY BIND MY HANDS

Two days after the meeting at the Resistance, one day after the capture of the Lovers at Rhoda's house, and ten days after Andrea and Tisha's capture, it was late in the evening.

Andrea was not completely sure how long it had been. As she rode, she was weary. She barely had the strength to stay on her horse. Her wounds still hurt and had been bleeding a little from the rough, unending riding.

She slowly blinked as she stared at her hands, which were tied in front of her to the saddle.

*Please, Elnai,* She prayed desperately, *Give me strength. I don't know how much longer I can take this. Help me to bear the pain and help my aching muscles. I don't think that I can stay on.*

She slowly looked around, and was surprised to see that her surroundings seemed familiar.

"Stop," ordered the man who had been sent by Nazar himself to lead what was by now almost a small army escorting the prisoners.

All stopped.

"We are close. Blindfold them. At the first sound they make, gag them."

A heavy sack that made it hard to breathe was thrown over Andrea's head. She assumed that the same was done to her mother, but she had no time to look.

After riding a little longer, Andrea heard the sounds of small running feet, gossiping tongues, and barking dogs as well as the never-ending plodding of the horses' hooves on the loose gravel. They were in the outskirts of Reed.

Only the rich, noble, or important lived within the walls of the city—where the grand castle was. Outside the walls lived the poor and commoners. The streets, lined with rows of tiny and poorly constructed houses, were so narrow that the horses could hardly walk two abreast. The houses were constructed so closely together that there was barely room left between them to walk. They were built as close to the nicer part of the Outskirts and the protection of the wall as possible.

The swarming crowds of curious onlookers posed a problem as well. The guards around Andrea swore and barked at the people to keep their distance.

Some of the poor were the direct descendants of slaves who had been freed after the Great War of the Fourth Age.

The war was fought for much more than just slavery, and had been terrible. None in all of Airiss, Kimble, Darrion, or Lidian had been left unaffected. Many—slave, servant, commoner, and wealthy alike—had lost everything and everyone had lost something. When the war ended, it was proclaimed that with it ended the Fourth Age. It was hoped that born with the Fifth Age would be new beginnings.

In many ways, the Fifth Age did bring new beginnings, though it didn't seem to be living up to the name it was given one hundred twenty-two years ago. *Age of Life, Liberty, and Peace* it had been dubbed by hopeful spirits still broken from the terrible war.

*Age of Life, Liberty, and Peace*, Andrea thought, *Elnai help us, I would hate to see hard times if this age is living up to what it was hoped to be.*

As they got closer to the walls, Andrea knew there to be larger houses, some of which were two story, and small businesses. This was where the middle class lived. The streets were wider and the houses were not stacked on one another like those of the lower class.

The horses were stopped and the leader of their procession barked an order to the gatekeeper. Andrea heard the massive gate groan as it was opened and then again as it was closed behind them.

*Strange*, Andrea thought, *they don't usually keep the gates closed until well past dark. They must have locked the city down because of my mother and me.*

Andrea knew that there was not much further to ride until they would be taken through the gates of the massive castle.

Until her first capture about three months ago, although it seemed like lifetimes, she had never been inside the walls of Reed. From what she had seen when she had been marched to her "execution" at the stake, she knew that they were passing large homes and estates belonging to the wealthy and important, as she was once again led to the castle.

Without warning, she was pulled from her horse. Still bound with a sack over her head, Andrea could not catch herself and she hit the ground with a cry.

Andrea's world spun for a moment. She could hear her mother's voice demanding to be heard then become muffled as she was gagged. Andrea struggled to sit up. Her head throbbed from the bump she had received when she was yanked from her horse. The dirt and gravel felt cool beneath her bound hands.

Andrea bit her lip to keep from crying out again as a rough hand grasped her upper arm and yanked her roughly to her feet.

The sack was ripped from her head and her vision was flooded with angry scowls that cursed and demanded her to get on her feet. The ringing in her ears made it seem as if she was hearing the hard voices under water.

A guard's crushing grip on each arm, Andrea was half dragged as she stumbled along between them. Her injured leg buckled with each step and blood oozed through the tattered bandages. Clenching her teeth, she refused to cry out again and tried her best to keep up.

Dozens of guards crowded around Andrea on all sides. She could not see Tisha, Raya, or Damon. She could not even see past the guards all around her. Her five foot four inches seemed to be shrinking.

Finally Andrea was rushed through the gates and halls until she was once more brought before Nazar.

Damon and Raya stood beside Nazar's throne.

Already in front of the throne where Nazar sat, Tisha was being held on her knees, her lip dripping scarlet. She had been struck again, but her lips still curved upward ever so slightly with the knowledge of truth. Her eyes shone defiant and unafraid.

Andrea could still not help but notice that, despite their faith and spirits, both she and Tisha were showing the effects of their treatment.

Tisha's shoulders sagged wearily and her face was bruised from the strikes she had taken for the truth she had spoken.

Andrea was practically dragged next to her mother. Injured and weary, her body's strength was all but gone. Pain accompanied every movement, refusing to be forgotten. Andrea knew that, unless Elnai provided a miracle, this was only the beginning. What awaited her and her mother would far surpass this level of pain.

Andrea's escorts shoved her to the ground. Andrea fought to remain conscious as black spots blurred her vision and her legs buckled beneath her. A stifled groan echoed in her throbbing head. It took her a moment to realize that it belonged to her. The heavy hands on her shoulders were forced to support Andrea as they held her on her knees. She was small, and had lost a little weight over the last few months, but now she felt heavy. Her body couldn't take much more.

"Well, well, well," Nazar growled as he rose from his throne. He descended the three steps from the platform on which Damon and Raya stood and paced in front of his two prisoners.

As he drew closer, a shiver ran down Andrea's spine. Nazar's eyes looked dead. Yet not empty. They almost didn't seem human, looking as if they belonged instead to a hungry predator.

Her skin crawled at his nearness. There was something more to him. Something her eyes couldn't see, but her spirit was repulsed by.

"The great Tisha and her daughter." Nazar pulled a deep laugh from somewhere darker than any man should be able to reach.

This man truly was evil.

Anger's red poison crawled up Nazar's neck and spread over his face. Wild fury glazed over his eyes. His voice hard and dark.

"Tell me, where is your precious Maker?" He threw his head straight back and raged at the ceiling, "I have them! They *will* die! Will You do nothing?"

His gaze swept over Andrea's wounds, wrapped in the same tattered and stained bandages from before Andrea's capture.

Nazar towered over Andrea. "Stand her up," came the deep command.

The rough hands dug into her arms, Andrea's head spun as she was pulled to her feet.

Nazar leaned in inches from Andrea's face. His voice low and sinister.

"Have you lost your voice now that you know that your life is mine? Now that you see that your precious Elnai is not the so-called 'Lover' you make Him out to be? That He is deaf to His own? That He is *dead*?"

Andrea stayed silent and turned her face away.

Nazar backhanded her so hard that the only reason she remained standing was because of the guards on each arm.

Tisha was struggling against the guards restraining her. Her words smothered by the hand clamped over her mouth.

"Your precious Elnai is *dead*! He has lost! Do you hear me? Dead!" he roared. "Speak!"

The room fell silent.

Andrea took a deep breath and struggled to get her legs back beneath her. She exhaled shakily and looked straight up into the eyes inches from hers.

Inhale through her nose, her lungs took a strong pull and expanded with oxygen; exhale through her mouth, her voice was now calm and quiet, but not weak or wavering.

"If Elnai is dead, why do you fear Him?"

Stronger. Bolder. Louder.

Holy anger arose in her and the words that spilled forth were not entirely her own. "You fear the Holy Maker because He is *not* dead! You fear Him because He has *defeated* death! *Elnai has won!*"

Nazar snarled, eyes flashing, and almost staggered back. His body reacting to her—His—words of Truth as if they dealt physical blows.

Andrea felt a hard knee from the guard crash into her legs and she fell to the ground.

Choking back a scream, Andrea squeezed her eyes closed as her lips parted for a hoarse wheeze, *Elnai, give me strength.*

Andrea looked up, willing her eyes to focus on the tall figure they happened to rest on. Damon. He was looking at her. His face hard and expressionless. He diverted his eyes.

Nazar, recovered and still snarling, lunged forward in a frenzied motion and grabbed her leg.

≈∾≈

Nazar could not look into her eyes. He focused on his hand, on the wound, everywhere but her eyes.

*He does not care. I will prove it. She will die and He will simply let it happen just like He did before. Love, ha! Scream, foolish wench, call out to deaf ears.*

ॐ∙∞

Andrea cried out, back arching against the guards that held her, "Elnai!"

Her fingernails dug into her palms and her leg quivered as she writhed under Nazar's ruthless grip.

Tisha was still fighting. Tears streamed down both Tisha's and Andrea's cheeks.

Andrea could not help but cry as Nazar dug his fingers into her wound. She released a hybrid between a scream and a moan through clenched teeth.

Her free leg kicked and the wounded one contracted, trying to force itself against her body. She arched her back again, screaming through sobs as she pushed up on her elbows, which were held by the guards. She was no longer touching the ground, suspended parallel to the floor. Black spots swirled in front of her. She thought, felt, heard nothing. She was only aware of searing pain.

"He cannot hear you!" Nazar screeched wildly. Releasing her and storming back a few paces, he screamed barely coherent orders.

Andrea went limp in the arms of the guards, her sobs in hoarse breathless bursts.

Andrea was then dragged away, her blood leaving a trail of scarlet, toward the prisons. She looked back, barely conscious as she was drug by her arms, to see Tisha struggling against the guards and Damon and Raya were both nowhere to be seen. Her chin dropped to her chest and she closed her eyes, focusing only on breathing, still crippled with the pain. The air rattled in her throat. Exhale. She felt as though she was floating. Then realized she was upside down. She was in too much pain to make sense of it, or even try. She had never felt the rough hands grab her under the arms and throw her over his shoulder.

ॐ∙∞

Andrea looked up at Damon. Her eyes streaming with liquid pain. A result of Nazar's cruelty. A result of his betrayal.

He diverted his gaze. He couldn't watch this.

In a few quick, unnoticed strides he found himself walking down the hallway away from the throne room. His echoing steps chasing him. Green eyes, wide and wet with pain, still burning into him.

His pace quickened, but the guilt that raged within him could not be outrun.

"Damon, where are you going?" Raya demanded as she caught up.

"To my quarters," came Damon's sharp reply.

Raya followed him down the series of extravagant halls and finally into the large room given to him by Nazar that very day.

With the doors to the elaborate room shut and locked behind them, Damon turned stiffly to face his sister. Raya stood there studying him, arms crossed, face hard but clearly exhausted.

"I couldn't watch that." The detached, emotionless words hung in the air.

"Damon, they will notice you are missing and start asking questions," came Raya's slightly nervous reply. "We want as little attention on us as we can manage if we stand the slightest chance of getting out from under Nazar's thumb. We already have enough to deal with after delivering to Nazar two of his most wanted enemies."

Raya hesitated slightly before continuing. "You knew this would happen and, Damon, you do realize that you will have to be present for her execution."

"I know, Raya," Damon said. His voice carried sharp anger. "I didn't ask for this. I never have asked for any of this. This is not what I wanted!"

"Damon, I understand how you feel." Raya's words were hard and firm. Fear of what this kind of talk could lead to was ever present behind them. "Do you think I wanted to become *this*? What we are for that beast Nazar?"

"Just say it, Raya!" Damon yelled, fury gleaming behind watery eyes. "You are a murderer! We both are! Nazar has used us to shed innocent blood. We both know this. We always have."

"Lower your voice before someone hears you!" Raya lashed back, matching his volume. "Yes! My hands are stained red from the lives I've taken! I never wanted this. But this sorry excuse for a life was forced upon us! You're just letting your feelings for that *girl* overwhelm your thoughts. We have no choice!" Her voice dropped, shaking with anger. "We never have. Which is why we couldn't afford to feel."

"Is that what you told yourself when you retrieved the guards without giving me the least bit of notice?" Damon growled, more quietly but still forceful.

"Maybe if you would have kept your head it could have been different! You kissed her! I saw you! I was looking for a way out, but I could not let you throw your lot in with hers. I had no choice. I was trying to protect you."

"I didn't need your protection!"

"You knew—as you still know—that this is what had to happen. Do you really think you loved her? I think that it was only guilt you felt after hearing the words of the Book and allowing her to soften you. You let her break your mask, knowing she was an assignment, and you felt guilty."

"And you don't?" his voice was low and trembling. "I know you haven't been sleeping either."

"Yes! I feel guilty. And not only for Andrea, but she has aroused the pain that was numbed long ago." Raya felt hot tears slide down her red cheeks, flushed with anger and conflicting feelings. Her voice was raspy and thick with the emotions of her next words. "I didn't want to become a numb, soulless weapon in Nazar's hand." Her voice broke. "I *hate* myself."

Damon was not shocked at Raya's confession. He felt the same way. He jerked around and stomped a few paces away, his back to his sister. Damon struggled to blink back tears that seemed to burn as they slowly leaked out. His thoughts raced so fast that he could not begin to process them.

Damon glanced back over his shoulder at Raya.

Her face was that of a broken and conflicted soul. Hurting. Confused. But utterly trapped. A perfect reflection of his own.

"What if what Andrea believed—what she read from the Book, what if it was true?"

Raya sighed shakily, eyes melting as they looked up into his. "Why would it matter? There is no hope. Not for us."

The whisper screamed throughout the room, causing it to shake to its foundations.

*There is no hope.*

Damon embraced the words, letting them tear their way through his heart, mind, and soul. Burning themselves in deeper than he even knew he could feel. Far deeper than he could ever reach.

The burning talons of despair tore into him with a grip no man could loose.

ঙ—ৎ

Riven's group rode ahead of the two larger groups behind them. They were making good time for such a large assembly. At this rate, they would reach Reed in eleven days.

He hoped they would have enough horses for all the west-bound Lovers in four days. They currently had only twenty-five horses, most of which were brought by the small Resistance group in Kander. Riven and his twenty scouts were each given one, and Musa's group, heading north, was given the last five as pack horses.

Lovers from Kander were riding hard to bring the horses from the various farms and ranches where they were kept for Resistance use. They would be waiting with the mounts on opposite sides of the border in the Darrionite town Cole, and Airissian town Rihff.

Riven estimated that the two hundred Lovers heading to Reed would reach Cole late that night. At dawn the next morning, they would travel a full day and spend the night just over the border on the Airissian side. They would once more rise with the sun and reach Rihff after dark. From there—Elnai willing—they would be able to all set out on horseback and push hard for eight days until they reached Reed.

Riven's thoughts continued to race over each detail of the plan. Of the two hundred eighty-three Lovers that lived in and worked from Haavene, they had two hundred fifty-nine present. The other twenty-four had left before Tisha's capture to visit family, go about various Resistance errands and missions, or—in Tisha's case—been captured.

Immediately after the meeting, twelve riders had been sent on their fastest horses to send messenger birds and recruit other Lovers to help them spread the word. There were safe-houses to be warned and secret stashes to be made ready for the precious supplies. Lovers needed to be informed of the situation and given the strictest instruc-tions: Haavene has been evacuated—stay away at all costs.

Following on foot behind Riven's mounted group Riven-Reau, was one hundred Lovers armed with swords. The largest, Jay's group Jay-Vax was divided into five subgroups with twenty each. Council members Al, Tristan, Carson, and Bennen were each over one of the subgroups. Jay was charged with the last twenty.

Also on foot, following behind Jay's group was Tim and seven-ty-nine Lovers armed with bows and quivers of arrows. Like Vax, this group, Tim-Marj, was divided into subgroups of twenty with Council members as their leaders. Tim, Ryele, Dray, and Tori each were tasked with one.

Musa's group, numbering forty-seven counting Musa and Janelle, was heading north to various safe-houses and stashes in Kimble and the northern districts of Darrion. Their job was to hide people, Books, and other important Resistance work and supplies. Since they would not be fighting, they were referred to only as "Musa's group." They had five pack-horses—everything else was carried by willing hands. Their progress was slower as they were on foot and had heavy loads, but they would gradually lessen both the load and numbers as they reached safe-houses.

Their numbers were few, but they had been preparing for this and had the Holy Maker of All Things leading them. Nazar had been slaughtering Lovers and terrorizing those he deemed traitors for too long. Enough innocent lives had been destroyed.

They didn't ask for this war. They didn't want it. But they were ready.

৵৽৶

Andrea was lifted off the man's shoulder and lowered to the ground, her legs, still quivering and useless, made no effort to support her. She was dragged behind the massive guard, her bleeding, injured leg refusing to bear her weight. Another man stood guarding a locked door that led to the dungeon beneath the prisons.

The two guards exchanged a few words that Andrea didn't catch, and a key was produced. Andrea was hauled through the door, and she heard the outside guard lock it behind them, then she was taken down a poorly lit, winding staircase. She managed to get her feet under her, but tripped down each step. Searing pain in her damaged leg prohibited any real use and her arm was nearly being wrenched out of its socket in the process.

The guard kept a steel grip on Andrea's arm. The single flickering lantern halfway down was the only light, and cast strange, dancing shadows over the stone walls and steps. Andrea moaned through clenched teeth with each jarring step. She no longer tried to fight the tears. Fighting for consciousness was hard enough. She was tired. Tired of acting tough and unaffected. She was in pain. She deserved to cry. She was past the point of caring about stifling yelps and cries and blinking away tears.

Finally, they stopped before another door and yet again a key was produced. The heavy lock complained as the key was inserted and slowly turned, but it complied.

Andrea blinked at the thick darkness that was on the other side of the door. It seemed more like a dark hole than a cell. Andrea could not see an inch in front of her eyes. She blinked to make sure that her eyes were still open.

The heavy door creaked open, and Andrea was thrown in. She fell to the ground with a sharp cry.

The dirt beneath her cheek felt cool and sent a shiver down her spine. The smothering darkness engulfed her completely as the door locked once more and the heavy footsteps carried the guard up the stairs.

Andrea took a deep, shaky breath and didn't attempt to move.

*Breathe. I cannot forget to breathe.*

Inhale.

*But breathing hurts too.*

She exhaled with a whimper.

*Unconsciousness would be a mercy*, she thought, biting her lip and quivering slightly from the pain shooting up her leg and the utter desperation. *Elnai, have mercy on me and my mother.* Nazar still had Tisha up there.

Painfully, sobs rose from deep within and shook her small frame. The smell of blood—her blood—overwhelmed her.

"Andrea?" the whisper seemed near.

Andrea gasped and struggled to sit up. Blinking swiftly and desperately willing her eyes to adjust to the black. Her movements were sluggish and painfully careful, but she finally pulled herself to a sitting position.

"How do you know me?" Andrea's voice was breathless, her pulse quickened. "Who are you?"

"Dear Elnai, it is you." The woman's voice broke with emotion.

Andrea looked around, but her eyes might as well have been closed, *That almost sounds like—but no, it can't be Flora.*

"Andrea, calm down. Your eyes will adjust," said another familiar voice. The words sounded tired, but still courage was evident. "I prayed I wouldn't see you here. It's Rhoda. Flora is here as well as eight other women. We are all here for the same reason as you, my dear. We're all here for being Lovers of the Almighty Maker."

"Holy Maker, have mercy," she said, her voice strained with emotion as the crushing reality hit Andrea all at once. She was beginning to make out faint outlines of the other woman. "Flora?" she sounded like a small girl.

She blinked rapidly. She wished that the weak glow that squeezed through the small space under the door offered a little more light.

"I'm here, Andrea."

Andrea heard shuffling. Flora's hand, feeling in the darkness for the girl she had raised as her own, rested on Andrea's wound.

Andrea jerked away and bit down hard on her lip. "Ow!"

"Dear Maker, Andrea, you are hurt badly!" Flora exclaimed as she pulled her hand away bloody. "I'm so sorry! What happened? You must tell me how this happened! Was it Nazar?"

"Let the girl rest, Flora," said a voice Andrea didn't recognize.

"You're right, Zania." Flora sighed shakily. "I'm sorry for hurting you, Andrea."

Andrea's vision was now as well adjusted as could be expected. The cell seemed to be about twenty feet long by twenty feet wide. Along the walls, nine dark outlines could be made out. Andrea could see Flora's round black figure sitting at her feet.

Andrea reached out and took Flora's hand, squeezing it tight.

Though Andrea was happy that Flora had returned to her Maker, it was devastating to have to hear the joyous news here of all places.

"How I hurt my leg is a long story." Andrea sighed. "Before I continue: Rhoda, is Dory safe?"

"Yes," Rhoda replied. "The children are safe. We had them stay with another Lover during the meetings."

"Thank Elnai, some good news." Andrea leaned back against the wall and let her gaze drift upward into the dark, seemingly empty space above her. *Breathe in. Breathe out. In, and out.* The smallest movement caused pain, making even breathing a chore. "I'm afraid I have even more bad news."

The silence rang as the women drew in a collective breath, dreading the same news they were waiting for.

"When I was captured, I wasn't alone. I had met with my mother. Tisha was captured with me."

Stunned silence.

"Nazar still has her up there."

Excited voices muttered worries, whispered prayers, and asked questions that were not necessarily directed to anyone and were not expected to be answered.

Finally, Rhoda's voice, steady and strong as always, asked the question that every heart echoed: "What do they know of the Resistance?"

Andrea answered, wincing as she tried to adjust, "They don't know the exact location of Haavene, but I fear that the little they do know puts the Lovers there at risk. I pray they are not found."

Flora didn't speak with the same steadiness that Rhoda's voice possessed or even the same calm—though tired—way that strengthened Andrea's breathless words. Though Flora's voice trembled slightly with emotion, it carried a rediscovered faith in the Name that had power over their situation—however bleak.

"Then we should pray." Her simple words were growing more confident. "For our own lives and strength as well as for Tisha's and the rest of the Resistance."

The women moved towards Andrea and Flora, and placed hands on each other's shoulders. Once again binding their souls in a united plea that Elnai's name be glorified and His Lovers be saved.

As they prayed, they poured out their souls for the protection of their children, the salvation of Judd, protection for the Resistance, and courage for themselves—but especially Tisha, the heavy boots of the guard descending the stairs reached their ears.

"It's Tisha," Andrea whispered.

They sat back against the walls once more to clear the door as the guard unlocked and opened it.

Tisha was shoved into the black cell in the same rough manner as Andrea had been, but managed to catch herself before she fell.

"Give me courage to continue bringing glory to Your Name …" Tisha whispered. "Through it all, You are high above it all."

"Keep your mouth shut!" The guard growled as he once again shut and locked the door and left them alone.

In the faint glimpse of light from the open door, Andrea had seen that her mother had been struck. Her face was bruised and swollen.

"Tisha, it's Andrea. Ten other Lovers are here as well."

"Andrea?" Tisha repeated as she felt her way to the wall and leaned against it. "Who else is there?"

"Rhoda, Andrea, Flora, Zania …" Rhoda named all ten women.

Tisha breathed an exhausted sigh. "I love all of you, and I missed you dearly, but I hate that this is where we meet again after all these years."

Silence followed Tisha's tired words.

*Inhale. And exhale.* Andrea focused on breathing, the pain in her leg still nearly unbearable. *Elani, Holy Maker, what are we going to do? What can we do?*

Finally, Andrea spoke and recited from heart a passage of the precious Heart of Elnai Himself. Slow, careful effort showed in her tired words,

> *"Given to you is a choice to make,*
> *Here before you is a path to take,*
> *You can now choose to live or to die:*
> *Trust in the world, or trust in Elnai.*
>
> *Those who seek the riches of this world*
> *Find their treasures a fading reward;*
> *Worldly splendor lasts but a season,*
> *No matter how you fight or reason.*
>
> *Those who forsake the worldly delight—*
> *No matter the loss, heartache, or fight,*
> *Receive more than the foolish faker—*
> *For they will abide with the Maker."*

Heart stirred, Rhoda followed Andrea's example and proclaimed His Promises as well,

> *"Do not fear, Beloved*
> *When it seems all is lost,*

*For I Am your Lover*
*And I have paid the cost.*

*You, dear Lovers, are Mine,*
*I gave for You my life;*
*Be strong and courageous!*
*I hold you through the strife.*

*I breathe life, I give love,*
*My glory covers you;*
*I prepare great rewards*
*For the faithful and true."*

Tisha, too tired to form the words, began to hum the melody to a song known by every Lover who had been in the Resistance.

Andrea let the tears flow freely and just let it sink deep into her spirit as the voices of the other women wove the lyrics from their deepest hearts,

*"You beat my body*
*But you cannot touch my soul,*
*Because in Elnai*
*I will again be made whole.*

*Chain me in the dark,*
*I will still look to the Light;*
*You can crush these bones—*
*This is not a worldly fight.*

*If they bind my hands,*
*I will lift my praises higher;*
*If they take my life,*
*I will sing through the fire.*

*I fix my eyes, upon the one who saves,*
*Upon the who gave His life for me;*
*And I gladly give my life to Him,*
*If that be the case, I take my stand.*

*He is watching me,*
*He will give me strength to stand,*
*He gives peace in pain,*
*Nothing moves me from his hand.*

*You can kill this flesh,*
*I still will not bow to men;*
*What you do not know,*
*Is even in death I win."*

They poured their hearts into that song long into the night. Simply singing the words, and the courage and promise they held, and hoping in their Maker.

## CHAPTER SIXTEEN

# SHOW HIM MY HEART

Damon stared at the ceiling high above his bed and listened to the ring of silence in the darkness. He could not sleep. Because when he slept, he would dream. He could not dream.

He blinked. Only for half a second, but it was long enough. Now he could not blink. He smothered a groan with a fluffy pillow. This bed was too soft. He had been sleeping outside for too long. He walked over to the sofa and stretched out. Better, but he still could not sleep. Or blink.

Because he saw her. Andrea. A perfect picture of her big green eyes staring into his dark ones. The image burned itself into his mind. Even in his dreams, her bright eyes had always seemed to look past his mask and stare into his deepest heart. But of course, if that were true, she would've seen Damon for who he was. A murderer.

*I had no choice. I have never had a choice*, he screamed inside.

Blink. Flames casting orange shadows across her face. Her green eyes, bright with wonder as they read the precious words of her Book. In that moment, the night had been peaceful and still. Her mouth had a contented, gentle curve to it that hinted at a soft smile. Her small nose had exactly nine freckles. He had counted. Her eyes met his.

Then she was on the ground, held by guards as Nazar ruthlessly crushed the wound she had taken while saving Damon, those same bright green eyes streaming with tears. Blood flowing from her wounds as the mouth that had curved into a gentle smile was now showing clenched teeth as she tried to bite back the cries of pain. Then, once again, her eyes met his.

With a gasp, Damon opened his eyes. He jumped up and threw some clothes on.

*Maybe a ride will distract me.*

Damon walked quietly down the long halls, passing guards who saluted and nodded respectfully. No one questioned him for wandering around the castle fully dressed, sword and all, in the middle of the night because they knew who he was. Nazar had thrown a feast in honor of the capture of the Resistance leader and her daughter, and Damon and Raya's part in making it happen. It sickened him. They were treating him like a hero for destroying lives. For what he had done to Andrea.

He finally reached the castle stables and made his way to his horse's stall. He reached up and stroked the head of his dark steed, sighing deeply. His heart was pounding and his thoughts racing. A nice, long ride would help him feel normal again.

*What does it mean for me to feel normal?* His own thoughts surprised him, *It's not so much feeling a certain way as it is the* lack *of feeling* all together. Is that what I really want?

He remembered the nights when Andrea and he would sit by the fire and study her Book for hours. Her eyes alight with life at each new revelation. Her lips gently turning upward in peaceful contentment as she read. Her voice filled with childlike wonder as she read the words aloud to him.

He thought of how he had felt as he had cared for Andrea's wounds after she had nearly died saving him. The cold and desperate fingers of worry that had seized his beating heart. He remembered how he had felt as she had buried her face in his chest with a small gasp as he carried her away from the gore of the scene. How he had wanted to shield her from that. How she had trusted him to take care of her in that moment. She was so small and delicate in his arms. Weightless. Vulnerable. Trusting. How he'd felt she would shatter like glass if he wasn't careful.

Finally he thought of the immense wave of relief when he knew she would be fine. How he'd looked into those big green eyes and felt. He let his guard down long enough to admit to himself that he finally felt.

Then he had kissed her. His lips gently met hers for only a moment, but in that moment the conflict of *feeling* and *knowing* were separate. Knowing who he was and his mission, but feeling the protective need to care for her. Feeling the desire to hold her as the warmth of that brief moment where her soft lips met his spread through his body and quickened his heart-rate. She seemed to melt, and he felt as though he might too. But then she'd pushed him away. She looked up at him with bright eyes, as transparent as ever, filled with fear and confusion. And she dropped her gaze.

The same green eyes that had first been full of life, wonder, and trust were soon filled with entirely different things.

He lied to her and she trusted him.

He kissed her and she sensed who he really was. Her face painted the picture of uncertainty.

He betrayed her. After she nearly gave her life for his, he delivered her to her death. She looked him in the eye and asked him how long? How long had it been a lie? He told her the truth for once, and watched the hurt darken her green gaze.

Then, as she was hurting, choking on cries of pain at Nazar's cruelty, he had only watched. When Nazar finally released her, she had looked at him once again. Her small, shaking frame hung from the guard's grip, not strong enough to support herself. Tears streamed down her cheeks as her blood flowed scarlet from her wounds. Gasping, breathless sobs trembled through her as she looked him straight in the eye. Her eyes filled with pain and resolve. She steadfastly refused to back down. She wasn't looking to him for pity or help, or even with blame. Which is what confused him most.

*She's willing to face all of it. The pain. The torture. Even death. And I'm guilty of trading the lives of others for mine.*

Damon breathed in deeply, hand finding the hilt of his sword out of sheer habit. He turned around to retrieve his saddle from the wall.

"Going somewhere, Damon?"

Damon jumped at the voice only feet away. He turned to find that it belonged to General Vincent.

❧

Vincent watched the seemingly conflicted Damon quietly for a while. He held something he'd found in Damon's saddlebag. Something that deeply disturbed him.

He watched Damon's reactions very carefully. Damon covered his initial surprise seamlessly and then turned to face Vincent.

"The gates are locked at this hour of the night, and the gatekeepers are under orders to keep them shut until morning since we have dangerous prisoners." Vincent's gaze fell to Damon's hand, which was resting on the hilt of his sword; Damon noticed and casually removed his hand. "Strange hour for a ride. And with your sword?"

"Force of habit," Damon responded, nodding at Vincent's sword, "although I dare say, I could ask the same of you, General."

"Watch your tongue, boy," Vincent snapped. "You may have performed well with your recent accomplishment, but remember your place."

Damon simply stared at the General, showing no signs of acknowledgment or even hearing.

"You best get your rest," Vincent snarled. "Nazar's little pet has a big day tomorrow."

Damon's jaw muscles twitched. His dark eyes deepening. These subtle signs the only evidence of his anger. Easy to miss.

"And Damon," Vincent said, "before you return to your quarters, I need you to clarify something for me."

"Yes?" As an afterthought, he said, "Sir?"

"We found this in your saddlebag." Vincent held up Tisha's Book. Damon showed no sign of recognition. "Why was it not reported to the officer I sent to escort the prisoners back?"

Damon didn't hesitate. His answer was sure. "I planned to personally present it to Lord Nazar myself, General."

*The boy is good. Difficult to trip up. A little too good at his job.* "I shall take care of it for you."

Damon nodded his head a single time, still standing perfectly straight.

"Next time, be sure to inform someone of interesting items such as this. You would not want to be mistaken for a traitor."

"Of course," Damon said. Vincent's hard, heedful gaze noticing the subtle movement as Damon's jaw muscles flexed.

*The boy still clenches his teeth when he is angry.* "Be sure you don't get lost on the way back to your quarters."

Damon stared into Vincent's eyes, defiant. Finally, he turned and left. Vincent watched to be sure that he entered the castle, then turned back to the reason he had come here. To prepare for battle. He would lead his men to Darrion's District Ten at dawn's first light. The Resistance could not escape.

Vincent looked with revulsion at the Book he held. The cover read *Writhrial Tose Ra Lindrene.*

*It must be code,* He spat on the words.

అ·ఎ

Baros Yosim flew with swift urgency. He had already sent messengers to spread the word and was flying in to meet Wynn inside the prisons. He finally reached the city and took on the appearance of a man. He walked through the outskirts and up to the great gates of Reed's mighty walls.

He sensed the very present evil that infested the city. In fact, at least three of the fallen perched themselves along the gate, ever watchful of the entrance to the city that Nazar had given them. Yosim resisted the urge to gag as the stench of the serpent like creatures' rotting flesh reached him. The city reeked of evil incarnate.

"The gates are closed until three hours past dawn," the guard said sleepily. "No one is allowed in or out: our Lord Nazar's orders."

*Holy Maker, help me to fulfill this mission. Help me to stay hidden.* "Sir, I have an important message to deliver to Nazar, lord of Airiss. I am acting under orders of the Lord Himself."

Raspy hisses exchanged between the fallen. The Baros hoped to avoid drawing attention. He could not storm into Reed and cast its evil into the Void alone. The fallen's hold on this city was too strong. There were simply too many. Reed would be taken back into the Light, but first, he had to wait and speak to the guardians watching their imprisoned charges. The Maker was setting all things into place and would send His armies in His perfect timing.

"Our lord has not informed me of this," the gatekeeper said skeptically.

"I assure you, friend, I am serving the Lord's mission. I must pass."

The gatekeeper studied Yosim for a moment before finally opening the gates.

"If you are not who you say you are, Nazar will not be pleased."

"My Lord would be even more displeased if I didn't run His errands."

The baros felt his skin crawl. He felt the holy light from being before Light Himself burning within him, eager to shine bright amid the suffocating darkness. Unseen by Reed's inhabitants, but ever present, all *too* present, were twisted creatures. The baros saw, smelled, felt their rotting presence as they slinked in the shadows.

He felt their dead black stares boring holes into him as he passed. They knew something was different.

Finally, he reached the castle, then appeased the guards and gatekeepers by telling them that he was on His Lord's errand. They assumed he meant Nazar, but Yosim called only the Holy Maker and His Son by such a reverent name. The Maker's blessing shined upon Baros Yosim, who had no trouble with the guards and managed to stay undetected by the fallen serpents.

As he neared the dungeons, he felt power surge through his veins. He could not contain a glowing smile.

*The Lovers are praising the Holy Name above All Names.*

A rich, warm chuckle bubbled within him.

"Who are you? State your intentions," demanded the guard who stood before the door. Beyond it was a long, dark staircase. The staircase led to another door, the door to the hole that the faithful Lovers had been thrown into.

"I'm a humble servant of the Lord. I am on His business."

The guard released an exhausted sigh, then produced a key and stepped aside.

Yosim heard the door close behind him, but his eyes were focused on two shining, robed figures guarding the way.

"Baros Yosim," said Jarab, who was charged with Zania, "what news do you bring?"

Yosim smiled and felt the light radiate through his skin. "Elnai has not forgotten His Lovers, nor their cries. Warriors are being sent to their aid." He spoke in a tongue unheard by mortal ears, and far beyond mortal understanding. "How is it?"

"We were able to stay with our charges, but it was difficult. The fallen only allowed us passage because they knew that they had no choice. Even so, they have given us much trouble."

"Yet there were none outside the door." Baros closed his eyes and breathed in the songs of praise that the women sang to their Maker. It was as sweet incense. *To You be all glory, Holy King.* "Continue to minister to them. Don't cease to remind them in Whom they find their strength. The forces of Life and death are stirring. There will be a fight. Of course, the Maker shall be victorious; even now His armies are marching with the strength of the Lovers' prayers. We will take the city."

"Baros, you know I have not a shadow of doubt that these things are true," Jarab said. "But at what cost? When the battle is fought, it will be hard won. Will the Lover's be victorious in life or in death?"

"Only the Maker knows," Yosim replied gravely, no longer smiling, but still confident. Yes, there would be cost to this war. "Decisions made—and to be made—will have a great impact on what the cost will be. Nevertheless, the Holy Maker will be glorified. The battle is already won."

࿇

Damon's steps echoed loudly as he stormed down the dark halls into his quarters. He slammed the heavy door shut behind him and kicked his shoes off. They hit the wall with an angry thud.

"I take it from your behavior that you are not happy with our beloved general." His sister's hard, sarcastic voice broke the silence. Relaxing his jaw but holding himself his rigid posture, he turned to face Raya.

"Why are you awake?" he snapped.

"I could ask the same of you," she replied, arms crossed as she leaned against his bed post. "I heard you leave and followed you. I saw General Vincent approaching the stables and stayed back. I came back and waited once I saw you storm out."

"I left quietly," Damon said, studying his sister. "You must have been awake as well to have noticed."

Raya bit the inside of her cheek. If he had not known what to watch for, he would have missed her subtle nervous habit, but he knew her too well. "You're getting off subject, Damon," she said. "I assume you were going for a ride before the General sent you stomping to bed like a child. What did he say?"

Damon told her what Vincent had said, careful to omit his thoughts of Andrea.

"Raya—" Damon hesitated, popping his knuckles in an effort to release some of the nervousness. "I want to get that Book."

"Are you crazy? Tell me you're not serious."

"Yes. I am serious."

"Serious, maybe, but you're not sane if you're truly considering this. How do you expect to get it from Vincent or Nazar? They're in possession of the two copies we had."

"I don't know," he breathed.

Both Damon and Raya sighed, deep in thought, and slowly begin to relax, exhausted. Finally, they both sank into the couch and sat staring up at the ceiling, neither looking at each other as they spoke in quiet tones. The mental and physical strain of the past few weeks settled over the pair like a heavy blanket.

"I can't do this anymore," Damon said, defeated. "I can't choose to be blind and numb to the evil we are forced to do and say we have no choice."

৯৯৯

"Damon." Raya's voice trembled slightly. Vulnerable. Confused. Conflicted.

*You have no choice. There is no hope. It's too late.*

The thoughts were not her own.

Raya shivered visibly. When had she become this monster? When had this despair sank its talons so deeply into her mind?

*I have* always *been this monster. I* chose *to* ignore it. I pretend to be blind. Deaf. Oblivious. I am hopelessly broken. I deserve this despair. I invited it in.

*Yes*, it whispered back, *you invited me here. Embrace me.*

"We have *no* choice."

Rattled exhale. A single, silent tear.

"We have already chosen," Raya continued, "and tomorrow we will ride with Vincent and his army to wipe out the Resistance. Once we have killed them, we will return to witness Andrea's murder."

৯৯৯

Damon showed no sign of surprise at her blunt statement. They were both far past that. No more rationalizing it to make it easier. They were taking *lives*, whether by death or destroying the person in other ways. No more "neutralize the target."

"We could run," Damon said without conviction.

"You know that we can't. We can't escape this."

*There is no escape.* Despair burned into Damon. Deeper still.

The creature tightened its grip.

"What were we, if we were to be honest, before Andrea?" Raya asked. "It was not like this before her."

Damon's vision blurred in and out of focus. Shrill ringing filled his ears.

Laughter?

Damon's face flushed red with rage. He rose slowly to his feet and ran all ten fingers through his thick brown hair. His chest was imploding, collapsing in on itself as his throbbing heart beat against the closing walls.

*Andrea wanted this. She knew that she was going to die, so she wanted to drag you down with her*, came the inhuman hiss.

Damon's lips twisted into a snarl, then quivered. Her green eyes looking up at him through tears and pain flashed before him. He blinked twice. Twice more.

*No. What is wrong with me? Andrea was real.*

It sank its talons deeper. Damon flinched at the sudden pain in his neck.

*You have been fooled. Before her, you never doubted your abilities. Andrea was an act. It was all an act to make you feel guilty. Think of the madness that Andrea and the Resistance have instilled in countless minds. It is madness to willingly die for a lie. This same madness almost had you. If you were weak like the others, you would have been fooled. But you alone are in power over your mind. You answer to no one.*

Damon moaned and looked Raya in the eyes. For a moment he saw Andrea's. Green. Shimmering with tears. He blinked until Raya's eyes were icy blue as always, anger boiling inside him.

*She just wanted to take me down with her. I have done nothing wrong. I have done what was necessary to protect Airiss from people like her. I am no fool. I alone am in control of my mind.*

*This is her fault.*

"This is all *her* fault!"

Damon was hardly aware of his body as it moved in a blur, seemingly without his consent. His voice, for he could only assume the distant words that echoed in his pounding skull came from his moving lips, had a sinister and twisted edge.

*Liar. Witch.*

"She—that *witch* has poisoned my mind! That evil little *seductress* with her precious *Book* has filled my head with lies!"

৵৽৹

Something that felt like a knife twisted inside Raya's gut—no—somewhere deeper. A strange energy buzzed through her. Quivering through her lungs as her breathing quickened; pulsing through her veins as her heart beat. As anger crept hot up her neck and spread through her face, Raya felt completely in the moment. She didn't think. All she felt was this *energy*. The energy strengthened and emboldened her, yet she felt almost drained. It brought upon her a ravenous glee, yet fear still lingered.

"We will end this madness!" she screamed, to the creature's twisted delight. "The Resistance and its minions can no longer destroy minds!"

She felt energized, yet in aching pain with every breath.

Freedom like she had never tasted, yet heavy and bound.

Alive, yet dead. Not numb, but experiencing every sense like never before. Painfully intoxicating. As the energy seemed to be leaving her, she felt desperate—lustful—for it.

Breathing, yet not alive.

Raya's body shuddered as she exhaled the last of the energy.

Alive, yet dead. Breathing, yet not alive.

*What is wrong with me?* she bit her quivering lip. Bile rose in her throat as she sank to her knees: head hanging, heart pounding, lungs taking deep pulls of air, and blood throbbing in her veins.

*Nothing is wrong with you. You have tasted true power.*

The hissed thought didn't terrify her, but instilled a longing hunger, a desperate lust.

She embraced it.

৵৽৽

Riven-Reau rode ahead of the other two groups as usual. It was just before dawn as they set out from Cole. Now seventy-six of them were mounted on horses. The Lovers from Kander who were gathering the horses assured Riven that they would have all of the resistance forces mounted. If they could not have enough ready at Rihff when they arrived, they would have the rest in Saxon, an additional day's ride away. It was on their route to Reed, but Riven prayed they would be ready in Rihff. They had no precious time to spare and the sooner they were all mounted the better.

"Dear Elnai, give us strength," he prayed. "Protect Your Lovers and guide us as we serve you."

৵৽৽

Searing pain shot through her entire right side and spread through the rest of her body. Andrea thrashed and woke to her own scream.

Her eyes opened to darkness, reminding her where she was. The smell of blood reached her nose as warm sticky liquid seeped through the pitiful remains of the bandages on her leg.

Andrea squeezed her eyes shut and moaned through clenched teeth. Several excited voices all muffled together in the background. Andrea could only hear her throbbing heart pounding in her head as it pumped hot pain through her body.

Unfortunately, this was not the first time she had awakened because something had happened to her wounded leg, only this time she was among friends.

Andrea felt the gentle, concerned touch of multiple hands. Blinking away the tears and darkness, she saw the dark forms of Tisha, Flora, and Rhoda leaning over her.

"I'm so sorry, Andrea!" said Rhoda tearfully.

"What happened? Are you alright, dear?" asked Tisha and Flora at the same time.

"I tripped over her injured leg," Rhoda said.

"It's fine," Andrea gasped as the pain gradually dulled.

"Don't lie, Andrea. I know you are feeling far from fine," Rhoda snapped, almost scolding. Seeming to catch herself, she said, "I'm sorry. I didn't mean to snap at you."

Andrea just nodded into the darkness. They didn't see it, but Andrea felt too exhausted and in pain to respond.

*Breathe.* Inhale. Exhale. *Just breathe.*

Andrea chewed at her fingers, the nails jagged. She bit too far into the bed and tasted blood. She didn't notice the dull aching pain in her fingers—it was nothing compared to what she felt with her wounded side and leg.

"It's worse, isn't it?" Tisha asked, exhaustion seeping through her voice. "It hasn't had a chance to heal, and then Nazar—"

"Yes," Andrea said evenly, trying to swallow the lump in her throat, "it is worse."

A few silent minutes dragged by. Then footsteps on the stone stairs.

Collectively, they held their breaths as the door creaked open. They all blinked against the dim light that blinded them.

"Everyone sit against the wall," ordered the guard. He sounded young. He nodded to Andrea. "You. Come with me."

*Breathe*, Andrea took a deep breath and slowly pushed her body up with her arms. After she managed to get her good leg under her, she exhaled. The cut on her side protested, but she knew it would soon be overwhelmed by her leg's demands to be noticed. She ran her left hand up the cold stone wall and cautiously rose. No weight was put on her right leg, but still Andrea bit her quivering lip from the pain as she stood.

Barely giving her time to get to her feet, the guard seized her right arm and pulled her into the dim light. Andrea's eyes were still trying to adjust from the thick darkness she had been exposed to for … how long had it been? It seemed like a lifetime, yet still barely a day. Maybe the darkness, and the all too short snatches of sleep she had managed to get contributed to that feeling.

*Maybe I'm still losing blood.*

As Andrea was escorted up the stairs, she was forced to lean against the guard for support, her thin right shoulder pressed against his left one. Standing straight, her chin was barely above the guard's shoulder. But as she was slumped against him, dragging her right leg and dizzy from the searing pain, she seemed even shorter. Andrea was thankful that this guard didn't just drag her behind him like the previous had. This one said nothing about her leaning against him.

Andrea knew she should be crying right now, but she was out of tears. Her throat ached for water; her breaths came in wheezy gasps as she struggled up the stairs.

Finally, they reached the top of the stairs. The sound of the key scraping inside the keyhole seemed loud in her suddenly sensitive hearing.

She was taken through the prisons, where she had first been held what seemed like years ago, although she knew that scarcely three months had passed.

An image of the woman with the scarred face and hateful cackle flashed before her mind's eye. Andrea didn't see that woman now, but she was too exhausted to look. She idly wondered what had become of her.

Her eyes lifted up to the man who held her arm. His effort in supporting her was evidenced by the beads of sweat on his face. He was young. Still a boy really. Andrea would guess about seventeen. Did he even know what he was doing? Did he choose this life? Or was it somehow forced upon him? As he dragged her along by the arm, his firm, yet not cruel, grip and her inability to support her own weight caused her shoulder to almost press against her ear. Did he understand—*truly* understand—what he was doing by simply following orders?

She looked down to see blood on both of them. Her blood.

More shocking still was the state her clothes were in. Her tunic was torn off in a jagged diagonal just above her bellybutton. This exposed a tattered, stained bandage wrapped around her abdomen and wound in her right side. The bandage was probably held to her more by caked blood than anything. After all she had been through, it was hardly recognizable.

It looked nothing like it had after the careful work Damon had put into wrapping her wound.

Around her right thigh, the bandage was still there, but in worse shape than the one around her abdomen. Over half of the wound was now exposed. The right leg of her leggings had been cut off above the wound on her thigh as well.

Andrea was not as dismayed at her clothing as she might have been three months or even three weeks ago. Her circumstances were far worse than the shape of her attire.

When the smell of her own bloodied bandages nauseated her, when she was unable to support her own weight by herself, when she knew that short of a miracle she was going to die, when she had had very little to eat and drink in days and it even hurt to draw shaky breaths ... Things like the fact that she was barely clothed didn't have such a profound effect as they might have in another situation.

Finally, after passing through several halls, they were locked inside a plain, walled cell. In the center was a table with two chairs on either side. The room was small and well lit.

Without a word, the boy pulled a chair back and helped her into it. Andrea sighed with relief, her muscles quivering.

The guard produced the spare tunic she had had in her saddle-bag and offered it to her.

Andrea looked at the boy, the tunic, and back once more, unsure of what to make of this. Finally, she timidly reached out and took it.

The guard took an unsure step back and stood by the door, avoiding eye contact with Andrea. In fact, his eyes looked everywhere but at her in the small room.

Andrea, remaining seated, struggled to pull it over her head, wincing as she pushed her arms through the sleeves, her side not appreciating the stretching movements. She would have someone help her undress and replace the old garment underneath the one she now pulled straight once she was returned to her cell.

She dropped her gaze to her trembling hands now in her lap. They looked smaller than ever and pale. Her hands trembled not from fear, but from exhaustion, pain, hunger, thirst, and blood loss. Andrea knew that it would only get worse from here.

After a moment, Andrea heard footsteps. Nazar himself, followed by two guards, walked in. He held himself royally.

"Hello, Andrea." He glanced at the boy and nodded at the door. The young guard left without a word. Nazar sat in the chair across from Andrea as the two guards who escorted Nazar locked the door.

Andrea looked up at him. A blank expression on her face.

Nazar produced her Book and set it on the table between them. She could see her mother's letter and the written account of the vision she'd had sticking out from between the pages. It sickened her to think of Nazar going through everything.

Andrea longed to reach for it and pull it close to her heart. Her eyes swept over every inch of the precious Book. She could almost feel the pages between her fingers as she turned them to new discoveries of Hope and Love.

"I see you were given your fresh tunic," Nazar observed in an almost friendly manner. "I noticed the pitiful state of your other one when you were brought in. I am sorry that you were not given proper clothing sooner."

Andrea lifted her eyes from the Book to see the man who represented the opposite of everything it stood for. His face had a civil, almost pleasant expression. His hands were folded neatly on the table in front of him.

*Does he honestly not remember the way he has been treating me?* Andrea was dumbfounded. *Does he truly not remember his cruelty? Has he deceived even himself?*

"You look parched." He turned to a guard. "Bring down some bread and water for Andrea and me."

The guard hurried to do as he was told.

Nazar opened the Book and idly flipped through the pages. Andrea inwardly cringed at the thought of him touching the precious Book. As if he would contaminate it just by touching it. Hot anger boiled inside of her.

*I died for him too, child.*

Andrea was shocked at the whisper that echoed loudly through her mind, *But, Elnai, surely You know what he's done?*

*All have sinned and fallen short of My glory. I died for all of you. From the lowest sinner to the highest saint. I love him. I want him, Andrea.*

Andrea's heart seemed to burst. She blinked back tears. She was angry and she felt justified in her anger. Elnai must not understand. There must be a mistake. Even as she thought it, she felt a twang of guilt at her foolishness.

*Show him My heart.*

*You don't know what You're asking. After all he's done to me? To Your people? You can't ask me to do that. It's too much!*

*Did I say it was too much when I died for you? When I died for him? I know. I am. You, little child, don't know what you say. Do you doubt me? Do you doubt my Love for you and even Nazar? I created you. I love you. I am Holy. Yet you question me?*

The gentle chide crushed her. Her heart pounded in against itself, crushing itself until it would surely burst. Andrea felt her face twist into a grimace as a hot tear escaped from tightly closed eyes and ran down her cheek, *I'm sorry! I'm so sorry. You are holy. You're perfect. But I'm weak. I'm scared. Angry. I can't understand Your love. But I thank You for it, Holy Elnai. Please help me because I can't do it. Not alone.*

*Beloved, you are never alone.*

The words reverberated through her entire being, growing stronger and giving her strength.

*Breathe.*

Inhale.

*Beloved,*

Exhale.

*You are never alone.*

Inhale.

*Show him My heart.*

Exhale.

Eyes wide open, sitting straight. Strengthened. Encouraged. Loved by Love Himself. Peace fell heavy upon her like a blanket, yet she felt lighter than air.

*He calls me beloved.*

A subtle smile gently tugged at the corners of her mouth.

Nazar was studying her. Their eyes met. She still looked into the eyes of a monster, but this time she could see the man beneath it. A man with fears, emotions, a heart and soul. A glimpse of what Elnai saw. Andrea felt pity.

Nazar was a man. Broken. Hurting. Drowning in his own sins. In need of Love. Just like anyone else. Yes, he had done terrible things, but beneath it all he was a man created by the Holy Maker Himself to love and be loved. Elnai still died for him. In this way, he was not so very different from Damon or even Andrea herself. He needed a Savior.

*Show him My Heart.*

"This is quite a Book, Andrea," Nazar commented, shifted his eyes and running a hand over a page of the open Book. "It is precious to you?"

"Yes. It's one of the greatest gifts."

"I understand your mother gave it to you."

"Yes," Andrea was surprised at both the absence of anger and the ease of her words.

*I love You, Elnai. You are holy.* "It was from my mother, but that is not what I was implying." She reached out her hand and let her fingertips tenderly rest on the open page. A gentle smile graced her lips. "This is Elnai's gift to us. This is His heart. He's given us His very heart. He's given *you* His heart."

Nazar pulled the Book back, looking disgusted. He roughly turned pages, anger evident in his eyes and heavy breathing, until he recovered.

He made a show of sighing wearily. "You truly are deceived … Surely such an intelligent girl could see that." He seemed to consider that, or perhaps his next words, carefully. "Or perhaps you believe me to be a fool."

Andrea's words were not her own.

*Show Him my heart.*

"No, Nazar, you are not a fool. But you are deceived." She held her hand out for the Book. "Let me show you His deepest heart."

Nazar's chest rose and fell with rapid breaths. He lost his careful composure. "This is some kind of code!" he cried.

He slammed the Book, then his palms on the table and leaned across, his breath hot in her face. "You will tell me what this means."

Andrea set her jaw and prayed for guidance.

Nazar sat down and slowly began to compose himself.

The guard returned with a pitcher of water, two cups, and a plate with warm bread. The sweet aroma was tantalizing and her aching throat screamed for water. The guard set the plate down in front of Nazar, then, at Nazar's nod, put a cup in front of each of them and ever so terribly slowly poured Andrea's cup full of beautiful, clear water. The sound of the pouring water in the silent room echoed through her. Every cell cried for it.

Andrea sucked in her bottom lip. It was rough and cracking but her mouth was too dry to wet it.

Nazar's eyes never left Andrea. His gaze seemed to drill into her very soul.

Andrea's fingers anxiously tugged at the hem of her fresh tunic, which was bunched in her lap in the front since she was unable to stand up and put it on properly.

Nazar continued to stare her down as he slowly reached for his cup and lifted it to his lips. He emptied it in three long pulls. Andrea imagined the way it would feel. The sweet water wetting her dry lips and tongue. The cool liquid life sliding down her throat. Her stomach was empty, so she would be able to feel it all the way down.

Nazar noisily set the cup back on the table. "Are you not thirsty? Drink."

*Well, if there was some kind of poison I doubt Nazar would have had his poured from the same pitcher,* she reasoned. *Besides, if I don't get water soon, I will die anyway.*

She tried not to seem too eager as both of her trembling hands grasped the cup. Her fingers wrapped around it, feeling the coolness. She brought the life-giving liquid up to her mouth and it was better than she had imagined. It stung her cracked lips a bit, then slid cool and sweet down her aching throat. She drank every drop. Her lungs started asking for oxygen, but that could wait. She needed water. She emptied it in one long drink.

Andrea put the cup down and caught her breath. Her eyes found the bottom of the cup, longing for more, then drifted up to meet Nazar's unwavering stare.

"Now I hope that you have been refreshed," he said, composed once more. "We have work to do. You said that this was El—" he seemed to stumble on the Name, but quickly recovered, "—that it's your Lover's heart?"

*Show him My heart.*

"Yes." She cautiously reached over and pulled the Book towards her so she could see it as well. "The Maker's love letter to me—" she looked into his hazel eyes, "—and you."

She delicately flipped through the beautiful passages until her eyes rested on one. *This is it. This is what I will use to show him Your heart.*

"I know it is some kind of code." Nazar demanded with growing impatience, "Tell me the meaning of it!"

Andrea smiled softly. "That is what I intend to do."

And she began to read the passage, feeling the Love of Elnai seeping through every syllable,

> *"You are My Beloved!*
> *I made for you the Way;*
> *I give to you freedom.*
> *Claim your blessings this day."*

"This is not what I said!" Nazar screamed.

> *"I love you, I want you;*
> *For you I gave My life.*
> *My burden is easy,*
> *Lay down your pain and strife."*

Nazar lunged for the Book and wretched it away, throwing it across the room.

Andrea felt as if she had been punched in the gut, *Do you see what he did, Elnai? He just spit in Your face! You cannot possibly—*

*Show him My heart.*

*But—*

*Show him My heart.*

"He loves you, Nazar."

"He does not love me!" he screeched, jumping from his chair and sending it across the floor.

Andrea stayed calm, feeling pity and strangely sad. Maybe because her—his—Creator was sad.

"He wants you, Nazar. He died for you."

"He is not real! He is *dead*!"

"He is *risen*!" she cried back. "He wants to show you His heart! Lay your burdens down and let Him love you before it is too late! He wants you!"

"*Get her out*!" he screamed, flailing his fists. He threw the plate with the bread at the wall. The plate shattered. He stormed over to where the Book lay face down on the floor and stamped on it.

The boy that had escorted her came in and took her back to her cell in the same way which they had come.

The guard delivered Andrea back to the dungeon, then nodded to Tisha. It was her turn.

తోజ

The next morning just before dawn, around the time that Riven, Jay, and Tim set out with their groups, Damon and Raya rode side by side just behind Vincent. In front of an army of twelve hundred men.

*This is the end. They cannot be allowed to deceive another soul into giving their lives to a lie,* Damon thought. *If they had not deceived Andrea, she would see the truth and not be doomed. But she is too far gone. And it's their fault. El*—His ... *fault.*

৵৽৽

"Wake up." The voice sounded young.

Andrea blinked against the light from the open door of her cell. It felt early in the morning. Or perhaps late at night? She had lost track of the days already.

A lean figure stood in the doorway. It was the same guard from yesterday. He helped Andrea to her feet and took her right arm. His grip was firm, but not harsh.

She was even thankful for his firm grip as they went up the stairs and she was once again forced to lean against him. She noticed that he had purposefully gotten on her right side to support her injured leg, and even slowed down on the stairs. She was escorted to the same small room as yesterday.

*At least I'm fully clothed this time,* she thought. *Well, I don't have fresh leggings, but the tunic is long enough and these torn ones are better than nothing.*

Once they were locked in the little room, he once again pulled out the chair and helped her into it.

She could tell he had a good heart, and he was so young. What was he doing here?

*Show him My heart.*

"Thank you." Her voice was not intended to be a whisper, but it came soft and weak. Her leg throbbed and she was out of breath.

The boy looked confused. "Thank you?"

"For supporting me and not just dragging me along."

He blinked twice, then recovered. "I was simply doing my job."

"Yes, but you're not cruel and heartless like some of the other guards," she said, studying him. "What are you doing here? You don't belong in this place. I doubt you even want to be here."

His eyes widened. "I'm not supposed to talk to you. They say you're a witch."

A heavy, tired smile turned the corners of her mouth up just a bit. "They say. What do you say?" Andrea sighed shakily. "Do I look like a witch?"

She looked into his eyes. They were deep and dark, yet alight with youth and life. He had shaggy light brown hair and a tall lean stature. His hands looked as if they would sooner hold a book than the heavy sword at his side.

"Ask yourself what you're doing. Even more importantly—*why*. *Why* you're doing what you're doing. Don't blindly follow orders. You have more to offer than they—Nazar or whoever has you here—would allow you to be. Is this really what you want?"

His deep eyes betrayed his efforts to hide the confusion, the questions, the hurt. "You know nothing about me."

Those eyes. Andrea looked away, blinking tears and chewing her lip. They looked like Damon's. Was this how Damon had been? Young and confused. Trapped. Being forced into a mold, a prison. Being made into what he is today. Forced to lose himself. To become numb, a mindless, soulless shell. Something he never wanted to be. Something he was never created to be.

Andrea could not bring herself to believe that it had all been a lie. She had seen the light behind his mask when he had let his guard down.

When he was leaned over the Book with her, brows furrowed together in wonder at the words.

When he had leaned over her, calloused hands gentle as they brushed her hair from her face and worked for hours to tend her wounds.

When he had leaned in to kiss her, she had not looked into the eyes of a cold calculating man, numb to all feeling.

In each instance, and in others, she had seen *life*. Yes, she had seen pain, fear, questions, but there was *life*. She had seen it in his wonder, compassion, emotion. Maybe there was hope.

Then Damon's eyes flashed before her mind again. Dark, as always, but in a different way. Hard. Distant. Dead. Dead, yet living. Living but not *alive*.

Andrea tasted blood as she bit too hard into her bottom lip.

"You're right." She twisted in her chair to face the boy standing guard at the door. "I don't know anything about you. But, please," her voice thickened with emotion, "I feel like I understand. You feel trapped. It's not too late. Get out while you can."

"I chose to come here," he said, surprise at her emotion evident by his shocked expression.

"*Why* did you choose to come here? Think about it. The decisions you make can make the difference between life and death. Just because you're breathing doesn't mean you're alive. Think about Nazar. Look into his eyes. There's no light behind them. He breathes, yet he is dead."

The boy's gaze dropped.

Andrea didn't fully understand where the words—or even the strength to speak them—were coming from, but she felt strengthened. She prayed that her words would take root before another life and mind was bound.

She felt as if she was pleading with Damon, and very nearly addressed the boy as Damon by mistake. He reminded her of who she believed a younger, innocent Damon would be. A boy who was scared of becoming a monster but didn't know how to escape it. Not in appearance, there the similarities ended with the dark eyes, but in other ways.

"What's your name?" she asked.

"Ezra," he answered nervously.

"Ezra." Andrea took a deep breath. "I'm sure that Nazar or whoever he would send will be coming soon, but please don't forget my words. Do you know who I am? Why I'm here?"

He seemed to have forgotten that he was not supposed to be conversing with her. He shook his head.

"My name is Andrea. I'm here because I'm not afraid to speak the truth and that terrifies Nazar."

Ezra glanced nervously at the cell door. There were footsteps.

"I don't want to get you in trouble, don't worry," Andrea said quietly, lowering her eyes.

Nazar walked in with his two escorts and Ezra left the room. Nazar sat down and made himself comfortable.

"Tell me everything you know about the Resistance." Nazar spoke with surprising civility, considering yesterday's fit of rage. Andrea had assumed he would drop this little act by now. "If you are cooperative, then I can allow you, as well as anyone else who is cooperative, to live."

Andrea set her jaw and dropped her gaze to the tabletop. She knew that best case scenario would be life in terrible prison cells for all of them. And even that was best case scenario.

"We know that the Resistance camp in Darrion is the main base. It is only a matter of time before we take it, and find other large groups. Please make it easier on yourself; it would be better."

He sounded so genuine. As if he honestly believed the lies that he presented as truth.

"Are you not tired of running? Of fighting? *You* can make it all end here and now. *You* can restore peace to our great land."

He sighed as if he solely carried the cares of the world on his shoulders. He spoke to her as if gently pleading with her to see reason. "I know you, as well as many others in the Resistance, have the best intentions but you are only tearing this land apart rather than healing it as you claim to desire. You are misguided, deceived. If you could only realize that, we can overlook many of the charges that are being pressed upon you. You could stop running. No more fighting. You would be given a new life. A new start. You could even pride yourself in playing an instrumental part of restoring peace to our broken land."

Even with all Andrea knew of this man, she was taken aback at how convincing and genuine, even comforting, Nazar's words sounded. Part of her almost longed to embrace them. To swallow the lie that she was simply deceived and could stop running. That she could truly find peace in this life.

Almost.

She remembered the true Nazar. She remembered the True Peace. She remembered the True Lord.

*Show him My heart.*

Andrea shook her head. Her words were gentle—soft, but sure. "I pity you, Nazar. You even have yourself deceived. If you had even a taste of the true peace I've come to love, perhaps you could see past your own deception. It isn't too late. *You* can bring healing and peace to this land but first you must let healing and peace work in your heart."

His lips twisted into a snarl. He backhanded her.

Everything went black as she felt herself hit the ground. Her own moan vibrating through her skull. She blinked the black spots away and pushed herself to a sitting position. The two guards grabbed her upper arms and lifted her back into her seat. Nazar stood, glaring angrily down at her.

He slammed his hands onto the table and dug into it with his fingers. He leaned in close to her face. She looked into his eyes. Living, yet dead. Breathing, yet not alive. Empty, yet filled with darkness. Perfect contradictions—or maybe conflict. Wars waged behind the windows of deepest heart and soul.

"You think that death is the worst I can give you?" he snarled. "I can make it painful and slow, drag it out so you feel every torturous minute of it. Make it easy on yourself. Answer my questions. Tell me the truth."

"The truth?" she asked.

He found his seat again and nodded.

Andrea took a deep breath.

*"The Truth is, Truth was, Truth is yet to come.*
*Truth's words remain unaltered and true—"*

Nazar struck her mouth. Andrea blinked back tears and spit blood from her split lip. These words empowered her.

*"Truth is steadfast, not bowing man's will.*
*In Truth, take heart—find hope anew."*

"Shut up!" Nazar screamed, throwing his chair across the room. "This is not what I asked for!"

Andrea was silent once more.

"That *Book* is full of lies! Not truth!" he screamed. "Answer my question!"

*Show him My heart.*
*"He who searches for answers not in Truth,*
*Shall find his struggles fruitless, vain."*

Her soft, steady voice was a great contrast to his enraged screams.

He grabbed her shoulders and shoved her sideways from her chair to the ground.

Her hands grasped for anything they could find. She found the ground. Hard.

Her world spun, loud ringing filled her ears.

"Just deny Him!" Nazar said, sounding bewildered. "That is all I now ask. Simply deny His Name. Say He is not Truth, is not Love, is not Life, and I will end this interrogation. I will even allow you to eat and consider moving you to a better cell."

*To those who love Truth, Elnai is life, youth;*
*But the blinded see only death's stain.*

Head throbbing. She had hit it hard. She could feel blood pulsing in the rising lump.

"I can't."

Andrea felt a sharp kick to her right side, forcing the air from her lungs. She pulled herself into a ball. Her fingers felt sticky. Blood oozed from the cut on her side. She gasped to recover her breath. Her eyes refused to open and the world still spun.

"Get her up!"

Once again, Andrea was pulled to her feet. Her head felt impossibly heavy.

She felt his rough fingers scrape against the blood seeping through her tunic from the wound in her right side. He rubbed the scarlet substance between his fingers. "Does that feel like love? Truth? Life? Why won't you just deny Him? Make it easy?"

Nazar wrapped a crushing hand around her jaw and forced her to face him. "Do you want to die?" he hissed.

Andrea shook her head against his hand, breathing heavily. "I don't want to die. But I am ready. I know Who holds my soul. Who holds yours?"

"*I* do." he wrenched his hand away and proudly drew himself up to his full height. "If you refuse to deny His Name, you will die."

"To deny His name is to die. To deny Elnai is to deny Life."

He studied her, breathing heavily, fists clenched, before growling, "Get her out of my sight."

Andrea sighed with relief at the thought of her dark cell.

She was handed to Ezra, who was waiting at the door, and then marched back through the long halls, past the prisons, and down the stairs. This time, Ezra had to basically drag her, even though he held her right arm. Her left knee buckled every other step and her right leg would not lift enough to get her foot off the floor so it was dragged behind her. Andrea tried to support herself the best she could and keep pace with Ezra. She didn't want him to slow down and as much as could be helped didn't lean against him. She didn't want him to get in trouble. Even simple kindness could be taken as "Resistance sympathy."

Finally they stood at the top of the stairs leading down to her dungeon. The thick door locked securely behind them. Ezra still had not looked at her. He started down the stairs, slowly, for her benefit.

Andrea gritted her teeth and focused on breathing and each individual step. Even though she had once again leaned her shoulder into his for support, she was unable to make it. She stumbled and cried out. The stone steps bruised her. She managed to avoid hitting her already throbbing head and finally pushed herself into a sitting position.

Ezra stood there for a moment, looking down at her. It was too dimly lit to read his expression. He glanced back at the door several steps behind them.

"Why don't you just deny Him?" Ezra asked softly. "What have you gained in refusing to deny Him?"

Andrea smiled weakly, breathing heavily. "To deny Elnai would mean to deny His eternal love. His life. To deny Elnai is to deny life itself, for He's the Author of life."

"But Nazar will kill you," he said. "How is that life?"

Andrea took a deep breath as a real smile spread across her face at the sheer beauty of it all. "Our life here is a season. But *life*, true life in Elnai is eternal. When we take our last breath here, we take our first breath in eternity. We'll be taken into His Courts and stand before the Almighty Maker of All Things and give an account of our lives—the season we live in now. Then we will be taken into—or from—His presence forever."

"But I don't understand." He ran his hand through his hair. "If the Maker is so loving, then why would He push us away?"

"He doesn't push us away. He never has. *We* separated ourselves from Him. *We* pushed *Him* away."

Before Andrea could explain, she heard pounding on the door.

"I have to go," Ezra said worriedly. "Come on."

He helped Andrea to her feet, but seeing that she could not support herself enough, he scooped an arm under her knees and around her back and picked her up. Andrea held onto his shoulders and squeezed her eyes closed in an effort to block the pain. Even though Ezra was not rough, he struggled to carry her down the stairs and it was painful.

He set her down in front of the final door and produced the key.

"Thank you," Andrea said softly. He didn't acknowledge her. "Will I see you again?"

He opened the door and helped her into the cell. "I'm your assigned escort to and from your cell and interrogation"

"Ezra, don't forget what I've said," she pled. "I'll try to explain it more clearly, there is just so much to say. This is Truth. And so much more."

He only looked at her a short moment before breaking eye contact. "You," he said, nodding to Tisha. "I have to bring you next."

Tisha rose from her place in the corner and stepped around and over the others.

Ezra took her arm and left, locking the door behind him.

After they heard the door at the top of the stairs open and close again, they all turned to Andrea.

"What happened?" Rhoda asked.

Andrea told them everything. And immediately they begin praying for strength for each woman imprisoned as well as the Resistance and Ezra.

Andrea finally collapsed into a fitful sleep.

Ezra brought Tisha back and immediately called Rhoda. He continued to escort them back and forth until each woman had gone to Nazar's interrogation, and returned bruised.

Tisha was told upon her return of Andrea's conversation with Ezra and once again they united in prayer.

"If our persecution leads even one soul to freedom in the Maker's love," Zania said strongly, "it will be worth it. In even this, Elnai is calling the hurting to himself. I am blessed to serve Him even now."

Everyone let those brave words sink into their spirits, bringing courage. Every heart was united in Elnai's love.

Even in pain and death, they would not deny their Lover.

They would show all who had ears to hear and eyes to see Elnai's heart.

## CHAPTER SEVENTEEN

# GLIMPSE

Chains. The smell of metal. The obnoxious clinking. The weight dragging him down. His own labored breathing loud in his ears. Reverberating through his pounding skull. Sweat pouring, stinging his eyes, wetting his hair, and slicking his skin. Yet the chains would not move.

Would never move.

Laughter—an inhuman, twisted shriek—echoed from somewhere far away, yet all too near.

He had heard it before.

"Where are you?" Damon cried. His voice cracking with fearful panic.

The laughter came from nowhere, yet everywhere.

Damon struggled to twist about to see something, anything. All he saw was darkness. No, something more—or perhaps *less*—than darkness.

Emptiness.

He strained against the chains. Every muscle in his body rippled in vain struggle. He cried out in desperation. It sounded like a hybrid between a groan and a scream.

The laughter stopped as abruptly as it had begun. The chains tightened. He wheezed as the breath was forced from his lungs.

Hot, putrid breath billowed over him. Damon lost all sense of composure as fear swallowed him whole. He froze from sheer terror.

The words belonged to the unseen owner of the laughter. A gravely, dark hiss.

"Welcome to my truth. Welcome to my freedom."

The crazed laughter that followed nearly caused Damon to faint from sheer horror. His heart pounded in his throat. Damon was now on his hands and knees. The chains sinking hot into his flesh and pulling him to the ground.

Damon screamed. Or tried to scream. He couldn't breathe. The chains had somehow dissolved into his body. They were gone, but their weight wasn't. He still felt their crushing force. The chains had become a part of him. Were him.

"Stop!" he cried.

"Stop? No. Do you not want to be free? This is freedom. This is life."

"Damon." This voice was soft. Gentle.

He looked up, still on all fours, to see Andrea.

She was dressed in a clean white garment that ended just above the knee. She wore no shoes and her hair fell beautifully about her petite shoulders. Her bright green eyes burned with vibrant life.

She held the Book clutched tenderly to her chest.

Damon felt the owner of the laughter recoil. Damon could not move, still weighed down.

Andrea knelt in front of him. Her whisper sweet and pure.

"Let me show you the heart of Elnai."

The chains within him twisted and burned red hot.

"No!" he begged through breathless groans. "It hurts! You'll kill me!"

Her voice still gentle and soft, but sure. Strong. "Sometimes death is good."

The creature hissed from behind Damon, "She is not only trying to take your freedom, she is trying to kill you!"

Andrea's eyes never left Damon's. She in no way acknowledged the creature. Her gentle whisper never once wavered. "When the chains sink so deep that they're a part of you, sometimes it's necessary to kill the old flesh. To kill the chains, you must kill your own heart. Kill the evil desires. Kill the past." A radiant smile glowed on her face. "It will hurt. You will die. But you will find life." She leaned in close, only inches from his face. "You'll find His heart."

"But this *is* freedom. I am not bound to Elnai's will!" he screamed.

Andrea sighed deeply. "This is freedom? This is death." She cocked her head. A picture of innocence. "Yet you are afraid to die? Kill the chains, the death, the past desires. Find His heart. Find His death so you can find His life."

She stood and began to walk away, but looked over her shoulder one last time. Tears silently traced her cheeks. "He wants you. He wants to show you His Heart. He wants to show you true, living Freedom."

"This is freedom!"

"This isn't freedom. This is simply what you've chosen."

"*No!*" Damon screamed. He blinked. He was sitting up in the bedroll in his tent. Breathing heavily, heart pounding, sweat pouring, drawn sword in hand.

Trembling, he dropped his sword and ran both hands through his wet hair. His lips tasted salty.

"Dream," he gasped. "Just a dream."

*He wants you.*

"Just a dream." He swallowed the lump in his throat.

*He wants to show you His heart.*

"It was just a dream."

*Was it?*

⤫⤫

Andrea was sleeping when Ezra came for her the next morning.

*At least I assume it is morning.*

Ezra came to her right side and encircled her upper arm in his firm grip. Once again, Andrea was forced to press her thin shoulder into his for support.

Andrea winced with each step. Her leg was becoming more useless each day. Andrea worried that she would not be able to walk at all—even with someone supporting her—if this kept on for much longer.

Andrea was thankful for the short rest at the top of the stairs while they waited for the door to be unlocked. She closed her eyes and just focused on breathing. Well, panting would be a better word for it. She opened her mouth and gulped in the air. Her heart pumped wildly, the pain in her right side throbbing with each beat. She sagged, her ear pressed against her right shoulder.

*I cannot take much more, Elnai.*

Even her thoughts sounded breathlessly weary.

*I see you, child. I hurt with you.*

*How much longer? I am trying to show them Your heart, but I'm weak. I'm failing.*

*But I am strong. You are doing so well.*

*But, Elnai, I'm not doing Your heart justice. I failed to show it to Damon, I failed to show it to Nazar—I even failed to show it to Ezra.*

*You have not failed Me. You have shown them Truth. Whether or not they accept it is beyond you. You have done your part. I am proud of you. Stay strong, beloved. I have not forgotten you.*

Now her heart raced for an entirely different reason.

*Elnai—the Lover of My Soul—is proud of me. He says I am doing well. He calls me beloved.*

Now each beat of her heart pumped a peaceful bliss that drowned out the pain.

Andrea opened her eyes and stood as tall as she could manage as she was once again led along.

Finally, Andrea was seated in the little room, alone with Ezra at the door.

"I'm praying for you."

Ezra shifted his eyes to avoid hers.

A short moment of silence passed before he finally spoke. "What do you want?"

"What?"

"What do you want?" he repeated, meeting her eyes. "What do you want from me? Is this some ploy to get me to help you escape?"

"No." Andrea sighed.

"Then what could you possibly want?" he motioned extravagantly with his hands, his voice sounding strained.

"I want to show you my Lover's heart. Elnai loves you, Ezra. He wants you," came Andrea's calm reply.

Ezra started pacing and ran both hands through his shaggy mane. "I don't understand."

"I'm willing to die for His Holy Name," she said confidently. "I do not—would not—ask or expect you to try to free me. If I must die here, so be it. I'm at peace. Because even here, I'm free. I'm covered by the power of His great love. He holds my soul and promises true life after this season. He promises that my suffering here is not in vain."

She let that sink in for a moment, then continued. "He promises me that I will be rewarded greatly for the wrong that is done to me for His sake. Even now, He empowers me. In even this, He gives me a peace and strength far beyond my comprehension. He emboldens me."

She grasped the edge of the table with both hands and stood. Desperate to show this boy his Maker's heart.

Passionate. True. Zealous. Bold. Strong.

"What reasoning beyond madness would drive me to these words? This passion? This determination? And if I was mad, would I be willing to die for it? If I was mad, would I not forsake all to preserve my own life? Yet not once have I begged for it. Not once have I asked you to save me. Because this is not madness." She sat. "This is hope. This is love. This is truth. This is confidence in the One Who holds my soul."

Ezra stared, wide-eyed. His chest rising and falling with heavy breaths.

"Tell me," she said gently. Softly, yet earnestly, she asked, "Am I mad? Tell me that these words have not stirred your heart."

He blinked rapidly and looked away.

"He wants you, Ezra." Even as she said this, the realization settled in her own heart. "I believe that I am here, in part, because of you."

He whipped his head around. His eyes asking unvoiced questions.

"Elnai wants me to show you His heart, and I believe that's part of the reason I'm here. You're hurting. But He sees you. He loves you. He wants you."

"You say He sees me?" his young voice broke with emotion. Hurt. Confusion. Anger. "That He loves me? Then why am I here? You were right. I don't want to be here. I had no choice. My father is dead! My sick mother and my little sister depend on me! So I came here. Because I have to provide, after your so-called Lover has failed to. What kind of love is this?"

Andrea felt a lump rise in her own throat.

*Show him My heart.*

"Ezra," she said gently, "I know you hurt. Believe me, He sees. He knows. He hurts too." The tears she held back showed through her voice. "We live in a broken world. He never made it to be this way. We, in our sin, corrupted His perfect creation. Sometimes, as a result of choices we make or simply living in a dying world, things happen. And it grieves Him. That is why He came, lived a perfect life, and died. That in His death, His atonement for our broken-ness and imperfections, we can have life. That's why He gave us the Promise."

"What promise?"

"The Promise that He's coming back to revive and restore. To take us into His eternal life and heal our broken world."

Ezra's lips parted to speak, but the door was opened and Nazar and his two guards entered. Ezra ducked out to wait to escort Andrea back after Nazar was through with her.

"I hope you have had time to think over your situation," Nazar said, his expression hard as he took his seat. "I'm truly a patient and forgiving man. If you would only denounce that Name and answer a few simple questions, I will once again extend to you my most generous offer. I will allow you, as well as any of the other women who cooperate, to live. I can have many of your charges dropped and make sure you receive more satisfactory accommodations as we work to clear this mess up."

He laced his fingers together on the table in front of him. "This is your very last chance to make the wise and, I would say, obvious choice to accept my most generous offer."

Andrea was silent.

"Don't be foolish," he barked. "Speak!"

Silence.

"So you refuse? You would rather die than listen to reason?"

Andrea remained silent and unmoving. She was at peace.

Nazar set his jaw, a hard and hateful gleam in his eye. He spoke through clenched teeth. "So be it. You will die."

Andrea simply breathed and wondered at the peace she felt, *Thank You, Holy Maker.*

What started as a low rumble erupted into a roar as Nazar leapt to his feet. His chair clattered noisily to the ground and bounced against the wall.

He leaned across the table, inches from her face, and slammed his palms against the tabletop with each syllable.

"Just deny Him! It is lies! It is lies! It is lies! Say it!" he screamed in a frenzy.

Andrea closed her eyes and breathed, listening to the whisper in her heart. Elnai's voice was quiet, but heard clearly.

Her green eyes found his brown ones. She spoke the whispered words strong and clear.

"He still offers you His heart, Nazar."

Her mouth, His words. His vessel. His Lover.

"This is your last chance. If you harden your heart again now, it will be lost. You will harden yourself completely. This is your last chance."

Nazar threw his head all the way back, arching his back, and laughed at the ceiling. "*You* offer *me* a last chance?" He slapped the table again and stared Andrea down. "You have nothing. You *are* nothing!"

Andrea felt a strange twist of pity. What did it take to get a person to this state? He had spit in the face of Life Himself for the embrace of his mistress—Death.

"Then you have chosen."

A wicked, twisted smile contorted his face. "It seems we both have, my dear. We shall see who has chosen wisely."

"Without a doubt," she said, sadness shadowing her words. *Yes. All will see. I promise. He Promised.*

Nazar paced to the door, then swung around to face her once more. His lips twisted into a disgusted snarl. "Get the wench from my sight! I am done with her!"

Ezra came and led her away. Andrea noticed that his hand trembled as it took her arm.

৵৽

*Thank You, Holy Maker!* Riven rejoiced in his heart. They were now all on horses.

They would ride swiftly.

They would ride hard.

They would reach Reed in nine days.

৵৽

Andrea was exhausted. She heard the door lock behind her at the top of the stairs. Muscles heavy, she stood there dizzy and feeling as though she had been through a war.

And she had. Whether she realized it or not, she had been through a battle. A battle which, though unseen, was very real.

A battle in which her courage and strength in the Holy Maker empowered His warriors in their struggle against the fallen. Every time she stood for Truth, she was choosing her side. And a hard battle was fought all around her, unseen. But the effects were real.

Wynn dropped to his feet, folding his wings and sheathing his sword. The fallen were getting anxious. Something was happening beyond this dungeon that would shift the balance of Light and darkness. Whatever it was, it enraged the fallen. They were lashing out. Growing bolder. No, not bold. *Desperate.*

Wynn and the other guardian warriors were constantly fighting just to keep the fallen from the dungeon cell. Something had to shift. Darkness had dug its talons deeply into this city. The Lovers would have to remain strong and pray with great fervency if they were to retake it. The warriors would need their faith for strength.

Wynn could feel the tension mounting, like subtle vibrations over still waters before the mighty waves of the coming storm.

None of the guardians had received any news or messengers since Baros Yosim had left, so they didn't know much. All they knew was that war would be waged. And they were ready. They were on the winning side, no matter the outcome.

Wynn lifted his voice to the heavens. "Holy Maker of All Things, to You the love! To You the honor! To You the glory! To You the power! To You the victory!"

He looked at Andrea. She was so very weary. She could not take much more. Wynn was always amazed at the perseverance of the Lovers. Yes, he served the Holy Maker, but He also worshipped in His Holy Courts. He glowed with the Light of the Face of Elnai.

The Lovers—like Andrea—daily chose to serve their Elnai. Though they could not see their Maker, though it was a constant fight, though it cost them everything, though they were recklessly flawed by their own choices, still they stayed true.

In fact, the warriors gained their strength from the faith and worship of the Lovers.

The warriors—who see the Light of the Courts. The Lovers—who were flawed. Yet it was the *Lovers* who strengthened the *warriors* in the fight against Evil. The very Evil that these same Lovers in their rebellion had invited to stain their perfection. To ravage their world.

A perfect mystery.

Perhaps that is why Elnai took such delight in it. He loved mystery.

"Your humans, and Your love of them, never ceases to fascinate and surprise me, Holy Maker. To You be the praise. Now I ask You to strengthen Your beloved vessel."

And Wynn began to intercede for her.

❧❧

Andrea collapsed when she tried to descend the first step. She was too weak to cry out or attempt to catch herself. Her world went black. She was conscious, but her eyes were simply too heavy to open.

Ezra managed to catch her before she hit her head.

"Andrea?"

His arms slid under her knees and around her back. She felt herself be lifted. Her world bumped and shook as she was carried down the steps. Her hands managed to find his shoulder and she held on weakly. She was petite and had lost weight, but the lanky boy still had trouble carrying her down the stairs.

He set her down at the bottom and fumbled around for his keys to the last door. Andrea could hear the other women's hushed voices.

"I'm sorry," she whispered weakly. Andrea dug her palm into the ground and struggled to push herself into a sitting position. She leaned against the wall.

The keys stopped clanking for a moment. Andrea seemed to have caught Ezra off guard.

"Sorry?" he repeated.

"You have been so kind," she said shakily. "Thank you."

He sank down the wall opposite to her and hugged his knees. His legs were too long for the narrow passageway. Andrea couldn't even stretch out full length.

She couldn't read his expression. The light was too dim. But he expressed himself with his whole body when he spoke. His hands motioned his frustration.

"You're not supposed to thank me. I don't understand," he said, careful to speak quietly. "I'm bringing you to and from one place of torture to the next, yet you thank me?"

"That may be true," she said, "but you don't drag me around like a dog as you do your job. You have the decency to treat me more human. For lack of a better word."

"Why are you so kind? So calm? Nazar will kill you! Yet you refuse to back down for even a second, even when no one else can see you."

*I see you, child.*

"Ezra, if you knew what He did for me—what He did for you—you would understand."

He rubbed his face, ran his fingers through his hair. "But I don't understand."

The guard beat at the door at the top of the stairs.

Ezra jumped up and got the door open. Andrea was once again back in her cell and Tisha rose to leave.

"Ezra," Andrea said before he locked them back in, "He wants you. He is calling you. He wants to show you His heart. That's what you feel. You're so close! Don't lose that feeling, because there's something so much more. I know we don't have much of a chance to talk to you, but don't stop searching. He's already chasing you. You won't have to look far."

Without another word, Ezra shut and locked the door.

*He's so close. Elnai, why do I feel this way for him? I want him to see the truth so badly I can hardly stand it!*

*Because I've shown you My heart, beloved, and I want him. You feel the beating of My very heart in your chest.*

Andrea exhaled shakily as tears came at the very thought. She ached for Ezra to see the truth because the Lover wanted it.

She was seeing the heart of Elnai.

And this was only a glimpse.

A breathtaking, beautiful taste of the sweetest of Loves.

She was undone, and she wouldn't have it any other way.

*I love You, Holy Maker.*

৵৽৽৶

Raya noticed that Damon was acting strangely. Of course, he had not been himself ever since the mission with Andrea, but now even more so. He seemed distant. His mind was clearly somewhere far away.

*He's been dreaming,* she shivered at the thought.

Raya knew. She had been dreaming as well. If his dreams were anything like the ones she'd been having, she understood. She dealt with it by refusing to acknowledge it. She simply threw herself wholly into the task at hand.

But he had always been one to think. To linger over a thought until it about drove him mad. Obsessive. Many times, he used this to his advantage. It made him a brilliant strategist. He was never impulsive. Calculating. Which is why she was so shocked when he kissed Andrea. Why Raya knew she had to act immediately. It was so unlike Damon.

*Andr—that girl really had polluted his mind.*

Even as Raya turned these things over in her mind, Damon's dark eyes were not seeing the road in front of them as they rode in front of an army to Darrion. Or, more specifically, the Resistance base. True, they didn't have the exact location, but they knew that it was in District Ten. That was enough. Most of that district was desert. It would be simple enough to search. Especially since only the District's capital city was walled and fortified. They might face some Darrionite resistance, but Raya doubted that they would be too much trouble. Ten was a lightly populated District, and with the strict thinking of the Darrionite people as a whole, Raya doubted they would go to war over the Airissians roaming the desert—provided they left their people and cities alone, attended their business and left quickly.

Raya felt a strange twist in her gut.

*No!* she chided herself. *This mission is necessary. These people, these so-called "Lovers" are not innocent.* Anger churned within her once more. The tips of her fingers tingled with the energy. Yes. She was right.

*They deserve this,* came the all too familiar hiss. *They brainwash people in the name of "Love" and cause them to bring death upon their own heads. Even their children. They must die. They are a sickness. A plague. A lie.*

*Yes.* The lustful energy—painful yet exhilarating; maddening, torturous bliss—quivered down her spine. Raya's lungs spasmed. She took in a sharp gulp of air. Her pulse spiked. Her vision blurred.

*This is only the beginning.*

*Welcome to my truth.*
*Welcome to my freedom.*

❧

Peaceful waters. Blue. Clear. Cool. Beautiful. Perfect.

A hand. A hand with strange writings, the black ink nearly completely covered the skin.

The hand plunged recklessly into the still waters.

The black from the stained hand violently twisted through the clear blue. The hand withdrew, but the damage was done. The waters rolled in blackened turmoil.

A single drop.

Blood.

The crimson drop splashed silent into the waters. At first there was seemingly no effect, but slowly the waters began to change. As the scarlet began to spread, vibrations rippled through the surface of the stained waters. The single drop of blood, instead of disappearing into the raging waves, spread.

The waters raged more violent still, but at last, the scarlet swallowed the black. Slowly, the raging waves were reduced to ripples.

Finally, the blood-red waters settled.

Two slender hands reached for the crimson surface, but hesitated.

"Drink."

The Voice, both beautiful and terrifying beyond description, washed over the waters and a sweet aroma arose.

The hands Andrea realized to be her own trembled with sheer thrill, with desire for the Voice. For the waters.

"Drink."

The Voice, a sweet and thundering whisper, the sound of strength and love, banished every doubt.

Andrea dipped her hands into the waters.

Joy. Reverent fear. Bliss. Humility. Peace. Overwhelmed. Undone. Love.

In the form of thrilling, beautifully terrifying energy surging through her fingertips, into her veins, permeating every atom of her being.

She laughed. A light, girlish laugh from her deepest being. Tears streamed freely.

Andrea's hands cupped just beneath the scarlet surface. As her hands pulled free, the waters ran scarlet from around her hands.

The water she drew up in her cupped hands was clear. Perfect.

She brought it to her lips and drank.

The sweet liquid slid down her throat.

Joy. Reverent fear. Bliss. Humility. Peace. Overwhelmed. Undone. Love.

In the form of thrilling, beautifully terrifying energy permeating every atom of her being.

There was a warmth. An energy that burned hot within her.

"This is but a glimpse."

She opened her eyes. Andrea's dry throat burned, aching for water. Her empty stomach twisted in an impossible knot.

She was awake.

Yet the dream felt more real than *reality*.

Andrea groggily sat up, greeted with shooting pain and a dizzying headache that was an all too real reminder that she was indeed awake.

The others were whispering. She heard her mother's voice.

"Then I heard the same Voice. He said, 'This is but a glimpse.'"

"Wait," Andrea said, "Tisha, did you dream of this? Did you drink the waters?"

Tisha turned to face her. She had been sitting with her back to her.

"Andrea!" she said excitedly. "Yes! Did you hear the story?"

"I dreamed." Andrea's heart fluttered within her. "There were perfect blue waters. A hand with black markings reached down and the waters were stained and began to rage."

"Yes!" Tisha clapped her hands in girlish delight.

"Then a single drop of blood overcame the blackness and calmed the waters again. I reached for it, but doubted until the Voice said, 'Drink.' I dipped my hands into the red water and this feeling ... I can't begin to describe it."

"It was wonderful. Maybe even terrifying. But pure bliss."

"Yes. So I drank. The feeling intensified and the Voice said, 'This is but a glimpse.'"

"Clearly the Holy Maker has given you both the same dream,"

Flora said. "But what could it mean?"

Tisha and Andrea's eyes met in the darkness. Neither could answer.

Rhoda clapped her hands together. Many of the women jumped at the sudden loud noise. "We will know in His perfect will and timing!"

"Yes," Zania cried, "to Elnai be glory! He sees us even now! He has not forgotten us!"

"Yes!" many cries rose unified in heart and love as one.

And the Lovers lifted their hearts and voices to their Maker in song. They praised loudly, unashamed, unafraid.

After about an hour, the door opened.

Andrea jumped, startled. She had been wholeheartedly in worship and none of the women had heard the footsteps.

"Andrea," Ezra said, he sounded almost embarrassed. "I'm sorry, but Nazar wants to see you again."

Andrea struggled to her feet.

"We will not stop!" Tisha said.

"Now," agreed Rhoda's determined cry, "more than ever we will not stop! We send you on wings of prayer and praise, Andrea!"

Andrea felt courage rise in her chest. "We are His!"

"And He is ours!"

As Andrea and Ezra struggled up the stairs, Andrea could not help but beam with joy. *Joy*. In even this! Because the voices of the lovers behind her carried strong and true.

*"Elnai, our Risen King!*
*Oh death, where is your sting?*
*Maker of land and sky,*
*Our Lover, King Elnai!*

*Elnai, our Precious Lord!*
*We are called His adored!*
*To You, all honor goes,*
*Oh Lover of our souls!*

*Elnai, our Holy Love!*
*What Name could be above?*

*We praise You bold and true,*
*Nothing else will do!"*

Andrea laughed with childlike glee, tears streaming down her face as she was taken through the door at the top of the stairs.

Ezra seemed nervous and rushed her along. She strained to hear every word as the woman looped through the lyrics again.

*"Elnai, our Risen King!*
*Oh death, where is your sting?*
*Maker of earth …"*

And finally she could no longer hear their words. But she could feel them. Andrea felt herself drawing strength from them. She sighed, completely at peace. It was the strangest feeling—she was the first to admit—but she was at peace in these raging waters. Like the single drop of blood, Elnai's peace overwhelmed the dark turmoil.

*This is but a glimpse.*

৵◌৻

Wynn drew his sword. It glowed hot with the Light of the Courts. He had just received instructions from the Holy Maker of All Things Himself.

From now on, half of the ten guardians were to protect the lovers in the dungeon, while the other five—including Wynn—were to accompany Andrea when she was taken to interrogation. Since she went first, she was the only one who had a real chance to speak with Ezra.

He left Andrea for only the briefest moment as she was being led to the little room. In an instant he had flown back to the little dungeon. He told the other Guardians the mission, then left at once—now accompanied with four others.

They caught up with Andrea. She was just now reaching the interrogation cell. The guard was unlocking the door to let them in.

Dark creatures slithered suspiciously about. The fallen hissed their displeasure. They knew something was going on with the five guardians with drawn swords.

"We have to keep Nazar away from Andrea and Ezra for as long as we can," Wynn said, taking his post by the door of the cell. "I and one other shall stay here with Andrea. The rest of you must delay Nazar. Make haste! Maker's Strength!"

Solemn nods all around. "Elnai's Light!"

With that, the warriors hurried off on a rush of light and wings to heed Elnai's will.

꙰

Andrea didn't know that there was a battle being fought just beyond the closed door as she desperately presented to Ezra his Lover's heart, but she nevertheless wasted no time. She started at the very beginning.

She started with a perfect world. A perfect world for the Perfect Maker. As she spoke, an image burned ever present before her mind's eye. Clear blue water. Peaceful and pure.

She spoke earnestly. Pleading with Elnai to help her make the Truth plain and clear for Ezra. The words came easily. And Ezra was listening. Whether or not he was hearing, letting the words take root in his heart and bring him to Life Himself, she didn't know.

But he was listening. And Andrea could see the questions, the turmoil, the longing to embrace it but fear of what it might mean if he did. Perhaps he was afraid of what it might mean if he didn't. He was listening. If only he would hear!

꙰

Nazar paced nervously about his chambers. *I have the witch waiting for me. I need to go. I'll make her talk. I'll make her deny Him, and then she'll beg me for mercy.*

Nazar picked up a vase and threw it. It shattered against the wall. He could only pace about the room and rage.

*She will beg for mercy, but I will show her none.*

He carried on in this manner for half an hour. Then, he finally marched down to question the girl.

Later that day, he crawled fuming into his bed.

He had questioned each of the women for a substantial amount of time. Not a single one of them spoke. Not a word. They each remained perfectly silent. No matter how he raved, no matter what he did. Nothing.

"Witches! All of them!" he screamed. "I will kill them all!"

He leaped to his feet, determined to order every one of them to the stake.

*They will all burn this very night.*

But, no. He still needed them. He had to be sure that the Resistance base was discovered and dealt with before he killed his only link to it.

He cursed. They would have to live a little longer.

*But I will kill them. As soon as my general returns with news of my success, they will die. I will personally light the fire.*

## CHAPTER EIGHTEEN

# BLACK WATERS

Chains. The smell of metal. The obnoxious clinking. The weight dragging him down. His own labored breathing loud in his ears. Reverberating through his pounding skull. Sweat pouring, stinging his eyes, wetting his hair, and slicking his skin. Yet the chains would not move.

Would never move.

His lips parted in a hybrid between a moan and a scream.

The inhuman laughter screeched once again.

Black waters rushed in from the darkness. From the emptiness. The water looked like death. Smelled like death. Tasted like death.

*No, this isn't death. This is freedom. I'm not under the thumb of a so-called "Lover."*

"Welcome to my truth," came the wicked hiss.

The raging black waters swirled viciously. Damon choked and breathed in a burning gulp of water.

"Welcome to my freedom." It shrieked into laughter once more.

Damon stopped fighting. He let himself sink below the dark waters. He pulled the black into his lungs. *Pain.* Again. *Pain.* Damon thrashed and screamed. It was too late.

*What am I doing?*

*Embrace your freedom, Damon.* The hiss came from nowhere, yet everywhere all at once.

*This is freedom? This is death!*

*He wants you.*

Andrea?

*Let Him love you. Elnai wants to show you His very heart.*

The chains dug deeper.

*This is not freedom,* he thought.

Damon sank further still.

*This is not life.*

His lungs burned, heavy with the black liquid.

*This is not truth.*

His body convulsed with pain as his desperate lungs forced him to take another pull of water.

*This is death. I need Elnai.*

The unseen owner of the gravely hiss screeched again—not with laughter, but with fear. With pain.

Damon screamed with all his might. "*Elnai!* I need You! I am sorry! *Elnai*! *Elnai*!"

He opened his eyes. The black water stung them. He looked all the way up to the top of the thrashing waves as he continued to sink. Something caught his eye.

A single drop.

Blood.

The crimson splashed silently into the waters. At first there was seemingly no effect, but slowly, the waters began to change. As the scarlet spread, vibrations rippled through the stained waters. The single drop of blood, instead of disappearing into the raging waves, grew. The vibrations shook his entire body. The powerful current entered his veins and spread throughout his entire being. He trembled to his core.

With fear. With sorrow. With humility. With pain.

With bliss.

With peace.

With *Love*.

The waters raged more violently still, but at last, the scarlet swallowed the black. Slowly, the raging waves were reduced to ripples.

Finally, the blood-red waters settled.

Damon watched as the scarlet waters seeped into the chains that bound him. For a moment, it burned. He knew he was being rescued, but he was still drowning in the once-black waters. It still hurt as the chains were pried away by the scarlet grace.

*Elnai!* Damon sobbed. Overwhelmed by so many emotions. Relief, fear, hope, pain, love.

*It hurts! I don't want to die!*

*I know. I am. Give it all to Me. I already paid the price. I want you, Damon. I love you.*

*These chains won't release me!*

*No, child. You won't release the chains.*

Damon looked down. His hands clutched the chains with all their strength. Like they always had. It was all he knew.

This is what it felt like to die.

*Sometimes it's good to die. When the chains sink so deep that they're part of you, sometimes it's necessary to kill the old flesh. To kill the chains, you must kill your own heart. Kill the evil desires. Kill the past. It will hurt. You will die. But you will find life. You will find My Heart.*

*Andrea said that …*

*No, child, I used My precious vessel because you could not hear Me. Now, beloved, I need you to let go. Surrender to me your past, your fears, your pain. Surrender to me your hopes, your love, your life. Kill the chains, the death, the past desires. Find My heart. Find My death so you can find My life.*

Damon lay drowning beneath the waters, clutching the loosed chains to his chest.

*Find My death so you can find My Life.*

Damon fought it even as his body convulsed with pain and his lungs filled with water.

*I am tired of fighting. I surrender.*

He stretched out face down and spread his arms open wide. The chains sank without him.

*I surrender.*

Damon felt himself rising. Slowly the chains at the bottom disappeared from view as he floated towards the surface. He closed his eyes as living Peace and Love swallowed him whole.

This is what it felt like to die.

Still, he floated slowly to the top as he watched the bottom grow further and further away. Light, lungs no longer burning, free, in love with Love Himself. It seemed like he stayed there for a thousand ages. And maybe he did. Maybe it would never end. But that would be fine with Damon. He had never felt so *free*, so happy at surrendering all control.

This is what it felt like to die.

*Why did I fight this so long?*

Yes, it hurt to die. It was terrifying. It was the unknown. It was out of his control. But it was *worth it*. It was *Life*.

"Find My death so you can find My Life," Elnai had said. Yes.

Finally, he reached the surface. His back arched suddenly, rotating him upright. His feet found the ground and he stood, gasping in the beautiful air. The crimson waters dripped from his hair. He now stood firmly on solid ground. The waters only waist deep.

He desperately filled his lungs with air in frantic gasps through his nose and open mouth.

It was dark, but not an evil, heavy, or empty darkness. Dark like a cloudy night.

He stood there, simply breathing, until the red waters soaked completely into the ground. Damon fell to his knees on dry ground.

He could still feel water heavy in his burning lungs. He vomited up every drop of the dead black water from his lungs and body.

He rocked back on his haunches, closed his eyes, and breathed.

He was exhausted, but he was clean. New.

*Thank You, Holy Maker. I love You.*

*Oh beloved child! I have chased you and I have won you! How I have longed for you! This is what I always wanted! Now you are perfect in Me. Oh, are you not beautiful? Look at how perfect! I have done so well! I made you and you are Mine, beloved.*

Damon felt tears running down his face. The best kind of tears. His Maker was thrilled with him. His Lover was *delighting* in him. He was so unworthy. He was so loved.

*Welcome to true freedom, true life, true love. Now I get to show you My heart.*

Damon sat up.

He was awake.

Yet the dream felt more real than reality.

The reality that he was dressed in battle leathers in a small tent. It was night, but at dawn he would once again pack up and ride in front of an army assembled for the sole purpose of slaughtering the Resistance and all they stood for. All Elnai stood for. All his Lover stood for.

His heart beat faster. He had to find Raya.

He threw the blanket from him and jumped to his feet. Grabbing his sword, he fastened the sheath around his waist as he ran from his tent.

*Calm down,* he told himself, *If they catch you running around like this, they will know something is amiss.*

He walked as casually as he could manage to his sister's tent. The few people that were up gave him no more than a passing glance or respectful nod.

"Raya," he whispered as he swept aside the flap of her tent and cautiously ducked in, "it's Damon."

She awakened immediately and eyed him carefully. He noticed the dagger clutched in her right hand.

*Good thing I learned my lesson from last time,* he thought. The last time he had secretly crept into her tent silently in the middle of the night, she had nearly slit his throat. They didn't usually get friendly midnight visitors.

Damon felt a pang of guilt as he remembered the midnight encounter with the Darrionite—and how Andrea nearly gave her life for his.

"What is it?" she asked, worried.

He knelt beside her. "Raya," *Dear Elnai, how am I going to do this? Where do I even start?* "I know that this is going to sound mad, but I need you to listen."

"Yes?" her icy blue eyes held both skepticism and slight concern.

Damon sighed and started from the beginning. He told her everything—of the conflict ever since they betrayed Andrea, of the guilt and doubt, of the dreams.

"Raya, this is *real.*"

"Damon, please," she scoffed.

"No," he said, pleading for her to understand. "This is real. This is everything we've been searching for! Everything *I've* been searching for."

"Damon, we've discussed this. You can't let a ridiculous dream cause you to throw your life away."

"But I haven't thrown my life away. I've gained my life. His life."

"Do you not realize that you prove my point?" She stabbed her dagger into the dirt and put both hands on his shoulders. "This is why Andr—the *girl* must be stopped. Why the Resistance must be stopped." Her hard gaze pierced him. "They deceive themselves, and everyone around them. They swallow this lie so wholly that they needlessly die."

"No, Raya." He gently removed her hands. "You're deceived. I was too. I know it's hard. It hurts. But it's the truth. You say 'they swallow this lie so wholly that they needlessly die.' Do you not hear yourself? They don't 'needlessly die,' Raya, they're hunted down and murdered by those who hate the truth because of the pain it brings. Because although truth brings life, it brings death to their life, their lie, as they've always known it."

Raya's jaw was set. A steely glare glimmered in her clear blue gaze.

He rose. "Raya, I'm going back."

She jumped to her feet, fists clenched at her sides. "Damon, stop being ridiculous! You cannot go back! Andrea is already dead by now."

"You know that's not true. Nazar said he would kill them after we confirmed the success of our mission." His steady calmness was the polar opposite of his sister's rage. "I love you, Raya. Elnai loves you. He wants you."

Raya slapped him. Hard.

Damon just took it. He put a hand to his cheek. He was sure that it would bruise.

"You are not thinking clearly."

"No, Raya. I am thinking clearly for the first time. I'm going back—with or without you."

Her icy blues narrowed. "You don't mean that."

"I love you. I pray you'll allow Elnai to show you His heart."

"Don't waste your breath," she spat.

Damon turned and walked away, heart heavy. He gathered a few things from his tent, saddled his horse, and left. He refused to look back.

*Elnai … Raya …* he could manage no words. But he knew his Lover had heard them, even though unspoken. Because he felt His comfort. He recalled the words spoken from the dream and drew strength from them.

*I know. I am.*

No matter what happened.

*I know. I am.*

Elnai knew. He saw.

*I know. I am.*

He was more than enough.

❧❧

Raya tossed and turned half the night away.

*He didn't mean it. He didn't leave.*

But he did mean it. She had seen it in his eyes. He was more determined than she had possibly ever seen him. She cursed and threw off her blanket.

She found his tent empty and his horse gone just as she had feared.

She cursed again and hurriedly gathered her things. She would have to go after him. She had no choice. Once General Vincent found Damon gone, Raya would be treated no differently than Damon would be if he was caught. No one would believe that Damon was actually doing something like this without Raya. She would be guilty by association regardless of her protesting her brother's actions.

She kicked her mount hard. She could still catch Damon if she hurried.

She thought of how many nights Damon and she had spent secretly reapplying their "marks" to fool Andrea.

*Well, Damon,* she raged, *now we shall get our marks back. Real this time. That is what you wanted, right? Real? It will be real enough when it is staring back at you in black ink.*

❧❧

Vincent had the entire army spend a full hour searching for the twins. They were gone.

*I will have them marked for this,* he growled, *but first, I will destroy the Resistance.*

❧❧

The night after Damon doubled back towards Reed, Riven and two others from Reau were riding hard back to camp. Riven was leaned down on the neck of his sweating mount. The smell of wind and horse perspiration. The sound of his own breathing and racing hooves. The feel of the reins slick in his sweaty hands and his leg muscles tight against the horse. The sight of fleeting dark landscape as they rushed past, filled his senses. One urgent thought filled his mind.

*We have to get back to camp. We have to warn the others.*

They finally reached camp, and immediately went to work.

"Jac, wake everyone. We will be having an urgent meeting soon." Riven dismounted and strode purposefully to gather the Council. "Liv, care for the horses, then help Jac."

Within fifteen minutes, Riven and all present members of the Council were seated in a large tent at the center of camp. It was now only a few hours before dawn.

"As you know, Liv, Jac, and I scouted ahead tonight." He ran a weary hand over his face and dark curls. "There is an army under General Vincent camped just north of Rebber. We can only assume they are riding to meet us."

"Rebber?" Tim said, "That is only a day's ride away. We would meet them in less than a day if they ride toward us as well."

"How many?" Jay asked.

"We didn't know for sure. We couldn't get close," he replied. "We estimate anywhere from one thousand to fifteen hundred mounted swordsman."

The Council erupted into murmurs.

"So many?" Tristan voiced. "Nazar is determined! He must know we're few in number, yet he sends five or six times us!"

"We don't have much time," Jay said. "We must immediately seek wisdom. We need to tell the others."

"I already had Liv and Jac gather everyone."

The Council discussed it for another ten minutes before encircling one another in prayer. Finally they informed the rest of the Lovers.

Their options were discussed and camp was unmade. Everyone got ready to move. Everyone got ready to fight. Riven, Jay, Tim, and the other Council members discussed final details, and continued to seek the Holy Maker's guidance in prayer.

In less than a day, it seemed war would be waged.

In more ways than they fully realized.

∞∽∾

Baros Jakkiv was ready. He, along with tens of thousands of other warriors, watched over the Resistance as they prepared for battle. They were prepared themselves—as they knew the enemy was. A lot was riding on this battle. War was about to be waged on more fronts than the humans could imagine.

As the humans fought, the warriors and fallen would be hard at battle as well, unseen all about them.

Even as Damon rode to rescue Andrea, legions of the Court's fighters were preparing to retake Reed from the slimy hold of the fallen.

Nazar had long ago prostituted himself and Reed to Darkness, but now Airiss would be returned to its True Lover.

"Pray, worship, and love earnestly, oh beloved of Elnai," Baros Jakkiv said. "We will need your steadfast faithfulness to win this."

࿎

The door to the cell opened, protesting loudly as it complied. Ezra stood on the other side.

*We have already been brought to Nazar once today,* Andrea thought.

"Here," Ezra said, holding something out.

Andrea blinked against the dim torchlight from the staircase.

"It's water," he told them.

Andrea was seated next to the door, where she weakly collapsed in exhaustion each time she was brought back to the dungeon cell.

She reached for the canteen and shakily unscrewed the lid. She was careful not to spill a single drop or drink too much. They were only given one canteen to share among all of them every day. They each took a cautious drink and passed it around. Each woman was able to get a sip from the canteen two or three times, but still their aching throats begged for more.

Andrea drank the last drops—barely enough to wet her tongue—and handed the empty canteen to Ezra.

"Thank you," she said, looking up at him from her sitting position.

Ezra nodded and turned to go.

"One quick question, please?"

He looked back at her.

"How long have we been here? We lose track of time with the constant dark."

"Um." He thought for a moment. "Well, the others got here the day before you, and you have been here six days. You and Tisha have been here six days, the others a week."

Andrea simply nodded. She was not surprised. It seemed like it had been anywhere from three days to eternity.

Ezra just nodded again and turned to leave.

Andrea closed her eyes and leaned her head against the wall, just listening. She heard the door creak shut, the key slide into the keyhole and click the lock into place. Ezra's boots climbing the stone steps, and finally the last door open and close. Then silence. Just the sound of their own breathing.

"How has Ezra been?" Tisha asked. "You seem to be getting extra time with him. Is it helping?"

Andrea thought for a moment. For about six days now, she had been trying to show Ezra the Heart of Elnai. She sighed. "I know he is listening but I am not certain that he is *hearing*. He is so close. He is asking questions. You can see the longing but you can also see the fear. He longs for it to be Truth, yet is scared of what it would mean if it is."

"I don't blame him," Flora said. "He is scared because he feels trapped. He knows that both paths lead to hardships—look at where we are now, but I fear he does not understand that our struggles for Elnai's Holy Name will be justified."

"We have the Promise," Rhoda agreed. "It is the hope we cling to. The Promise that our fight is not in vain. That our Lover will make things right and we will be ushered into His very Courts."

"It is difficult. Our persecution is not to be envied," Zania said with a heavy sigh, "but it is worth it. Though there is pain in the struggle, it is worth it in the end. In His Promise."

Everyone let the words sink in. Yes, though their struggle was long and hard, they had the Promise. It was more than worth it.

After a moment of quiet, Andrea spoke. "I think I am beginning to understand the dream."

"Oh?" Tisha asked. Everyone turned toward Andrea's voice, even though all they could see was a dark outline of her form.

"As I have been talking to Ezra, starting at the very beginning of Elnai's story, images from the dream have been playing in my mind." She readjusted to soothe her injured leg, then continued. "In the beginning, Light was. He made our world and everything in it. He made it beautiful and perfect—without corruption or flaw of any form. He delighted in His perfect creation."

"The clear blue waters," Tisha said, growing excitement mounting in her voice.

"Yes." Andrea smiled. "Then we were given the gift of choice. And we chose darkness. We touched the forbidden pool, and stained His perfect world with the black hand of sin."

"We prostituted our hearts to darkness and plunged our blackened world to turmoil!" Tisha said enthusiastically. Everyone, but Tisha and Andrea especially, got swept up in excitement as the pieces fell into place. "The raging black waters represent the desperate state of our fallen world. The single drop of blood is Elnai's atoning sacrifice!"

Andrea jumped in. "After Elnai died for us, we were reconciled through Him. When our Lover sees us, He does not see our raging black sin, but the perfect life He lived and undeserved death He died in our stead. He sees the calm red waters!"

"Yes!" Tisha exclaimed.

"But what does the rest of the dream mean?" Rhoda asked. "You said that when He told you to drink and you drew up the water, it was no longer red, but clear and blue. What does that mean?"

Everyone, including Tisha, turned expectantly to Andrea.

Andrea thought for a moment. "Well, I don't know."

"I'm sure that Elnai will reveal the rest of the dream in His perfect time," Tisha said. "I'm thankful for the understanding He has brought so far. We are in awe of You, Holy Maker!"

Andrea felt an urgent pang in her heart. She felt pressured, like she was running out of time.

"Let us pray for Ezra," she said. Her tone serious. "I feel an urgency to just pray. I feel like we are running out of time."

What Andrea didn't know, was that at that very moment, Damon was only a few hours away, the Resistance was riding to face Vincent, and unseen legions were warring for—or against—the Lovers. Light and Darkness. Love and Hate. Truth and Deception. Life and Death.

❧❧

After catching a few short hours of sleep, Riven, Timius, and Jay each led Reau, Marj, and Vax in different directions not long after dawn. Riven-Reau and Tah-Vax were heading slowly west. They would frequently double back to get eyes on Vincent's army and make sure that the other two groups knew exactly where they were at all times. Tah-Marj, Nev-Marj, Nev-Vax, and Med-Vax rode northwest, while Sa-Marj, Bia-Marj, Sa-Vax, and Bia-Vax rode southwest. They would ride like this, one step ahead, until Vincent's army made camp. Once Riven-Reau and Tah-Vax gave them the word, the other eight groups would circle in on Vincent's sleeping army from the north and south, Tah-Vax would enter from the west and take care of the lookouts, and Riven Reau would slip in from the east and capture Vincent. They hoped to do this with as little spilled blood from both parties as possible.

❧❧

"Stop," Vincent ordered, dismounting his horse. Leaving just after dawn, his army had ridden almost seven hours. "You," he nodded to two of his lieutenants, "follow me."

"There was a large camp here," he said. "There were only a few small fires, but you can see by the trampled grass and prints that it was a large gathering. They were here only hours ago." He walked about, studying the area. "This might have been a Resistance meeting. We are nearing Darrion."

"There are a lot of hoof prints. It appears they are not on foot, sir," one of his lieutenants said.

"It could be as many as a few hundred. We may have stumbled upon a large Resistance group meeting. Or maybe they are going somewhere. They could be moving since we captured their leader." Vincent continued to study the campsite. "The group splits and the tracks lead in three directions."

"Sir, if there is a possibility that it could be some or all of the Resistance rebels, should we divide our forces and pursue each of the three groups?"

Vincent thought a moment, one arm crossed and holding his other elbow, and one hand holding his chin.

"We do have the numbers, sir."

"I know that," Vincent snapped.

The lieutenant dipped his head.

"I want each of you to take a group of two hundred men and take the northeast and southeast tracks. I will continue with the remaining eight hundred to Darrion."

"Should they be Resistance, sir, should we engage?"

"No," Vincent said, turning to face them. "If they are in fact Resistance, I want you to return to me as soon as possible. I want to know how many, their apparent route, if any of their leaders are there, if they are all on horseback, everything. If they are Resistance, send back five riders to tell me all you have learned and pursue them. Don't engage or be known to them until given further order. Understood?"

"Yes, sir," they both responded.

"Good. Now I will immediately appoint to each of you two hundred men and send you on your way."

೪⊸ॐ

"Alright, Damon," Raya said, "we are here."

They sat on their tired horses overlooking Reed from a nearby hill.

Damon didn't respond, just nudged his horse forward.

Raya felt her pulse quicken. He was going through with it. He was actually going to rescue Andrea, or attempt to do so. They were betraying Nazar. Why not swoop into his castle, throw it in his face, and ride away with his most hated—not to mention heavily guarded—prisoners?

Raya felt fearful, conflicted, desperate. She could not understand or compress her own raging emotions—which is perhaps what scared her the most.

Was she scared to rescue Andrea because she knew it was nearly impossible to succeed with their lives? Or was it because in doing so, she would be admitting that Andrea and what she stood for was right?

Raya knew—though perhaps refused to admit—that the reason she had so much anger toward the girl was because Andrea and her Book would force her to stop choosing to live in ignorance—to own her mistakes, her fears, her past, her lack of control, her hurt.

Pain twisted into her heart like a knife. Maybe a knife would have been easier. Then her heart would have stopped beating. Then she would be able to stop running from the pain, to stop lying to herself to make *it*—everything—easier to swallow. She had heard it said that ignorance is bliss. Maybe it was only said because it seemed easier to lie to yourself that you are ignorant than face the truth about who you are.

Who she was.

*What* she was.

*Child*, hissed the haunting voice.

*No*, she frantically tried to make it stop.

*Pawn*, it hissed louder.

*No!*

*Murderer.*

Raya gasped and she realized she had not been breathing. Still could not breathe.

The laughter from her dreams screeched madly.

She closed her eyes and clamped her hands over her ears like a small child.

The energy flooded through her once again. This time it didn't feel like power. Not her power. This time it only felt like pain. It felt like chains crushing her rib cage against her pounding heart, squeezing her desperate lungs, closing her throat, silencing her screams, weighing her down.

*This is your choice. Your destiny. You chose this. You chose me. Now you will take it. Now you are mine.*

*I don't want this! Who—what are you?*

It laughed again, *I am your truth. I am your freedom.*

*This is not freedom!*

*I am your choice. You are mine.*

Her vision went hazy as the energy died down. Her eyes seemed to look through discolored goggles.

*I accepted your invitation. You accepted my power. Now you will accept my freedom.*

As if released from a trance, Raya's vision and mind snapped back into clarity. She jerked her head up sharply. She could not clearly remember what had just happened. She remembered that she had said something to Damon, then it was all hazy and muddled. Now her senses were sharp and clear.

She kicked her mount to catch up with Damon and pulled to a sharp stop in front of him. Damon's horse nearly bumped into Raya's.

"What are you doing?" Damon demanded, his horse's front foot stamping, irritated.

"Damon." Her voice was hard. It sounded strange in her own ears. "You will not go to Reed. This is madness. That witch has toyed with your mind. I will not allow you to march to your death because this wretch has manipulated you."

"Do you not hear yourself?" Damon asked. "Andrea. Her name is Andrea. Why are you so careful to avoid her name?"

Raya felt hot rage creep up her neck. "I'm not! Stop accusing me of lies! Andr- that witch has turned you against me!"

Damon spoke softly. "I'm not against you. I'm not accusing you of anything. You're the one screaming."

"So now you're perfect? Blameless?" she spat. "You think you're better than me? Ha! Your hands are stained with a past that cannot be escaped—no matter how many lies you swallow. Don't forget *what you are.*"

His face was unreadable, but Raya knew him well enough to see past his masked eyes. But there was no mask. She saw only hurt.

"I'm not blameless. I am far from it." His words were laced with emotion, with hurt, but Raya's heart was too hard, too angry to be stirred.

"I'm a sinner. I'm broken. But I'm not running from it. I'm not excusing it anymore. I've brought it to Elnai," —her face twisted into a grimace at this— "and He's forgiven me. He's given me new life in Him. I'm not saying that I fully understand it—I'm just saying that this is real. This is what we were looking for."

"Now you speak for me as well?" she snapped. "I already have what I want!"

৵৽৽

Damon did a double take. Raya's eyes had flashed, and if he wasn't mistaken, with something more than emotion. They almost seemed to change. To darken. But now her eyes were cool blue as always.

*Maybe it was nothing,* he thought, *but something does seem different about her. Something just doesn't feel right.*

When she had pulled her horse to a stop in front of his, the hair on the back of his neck had stood on end. A strange, eerie feeling had not stopped shivering over his skin ever since.

Tired and hurt, he swallowed the growing lump in his throat.

"Can you tell me," he asked calmly, "being completely honest, that you never once felt the slightest bit of guilt about any of our missions? About Andrea?"

Raya glared, jaw clenched, but remained silent as Damon continued.

"Think about the time we spent with Andrea. From Ravelle to the day we drugged her and her mother. You never once doubted? You never once dared to hope that there was the slightest possibility that there might be truth in her beliefs? Never once was your heart stirred in the least?"

"Never," she spat vehemently without hesitation.

*Elani, help me. Help Raya.* "Even now you lie to yourself, Raya." He shook his head and looked away to hide his emotion. He faced her again. "Have you forgotten so quickly? I guess you have. I understand. I myself was where you are only days ago. Remember that night? Remember that night that we had delivered Andrea to Nazar? You wept that night."

"You lie."

He searched her eyes.

Hard. Cold. Unyielding.

Lost.

৵৽৽

"I will not warn you again," Jaav said, glowing eyes flashing. "You are no longer welcome here."

The two brother serpent creatures hissed.

"He is *mine*." The fallen beast removed its claws from Raya's heart and slinked towards Damon. "He invited me long ago. His heart and soul belong to me."

Jaav drew his sword and stepped between his charge and the beast. "Not anymore. He is redeemed!"

The serpent drew itself up, its rotting flesh sagging from its bony frame, and stood eye to eye with Jaav. Its brother watched with black, soulless eyes, its claws sinking deeper into Raya's mind.

Jaav glowed with the light of the Courts. "He is beloved of Elnai and you are no longer permitted to touch him!" His sword now flaming.

The fallen creature recoiled. It hissed its disgust, acidic saliva dripping from its fangs. It slinked back to Raya and twisted its talons deeper into Raya's heart.

ॐ◌ॐ

"You lie," Raya said again, spitting.

But, truth be told, she was scared. And she didn't even know why.

Maybe it was because she *did* remember. Or maybe it was because, though she did, she didn't want to. She had found long ago that if you repeat to yourself a lie long enough, eventually it becomes your reality.

Once again, she was consciously reshaping her memories to make it easier to live with what she deemed "necessary." After a while, she would know that her version of her past was altered, but she would continue to swallow it, painfully forcing it down, until *it* swallowed *her*. She would completely forget there was ever change.

Her lie would become her truth.

She had done it countless times before. Raya didn't even fully realize she was doing it any more.

But she did remember. Her own words and thoughts sounded foreign to her.

*What is happening to me?* "If you go after her, I will turn you in myself!" someone screamed at Damon. *That wasn't me.*

*Was it?*

The hurt in Damon's eyes held the answer.

"I love you, Raya," he said quietly. "I know I haven't said it, maybe ever, in the past. But you're my sister. You're my friend. We've been to hell and back together. Please—" His composure seeped away. His face broke.

Damon, unmovable, unreadable, unshakable.

Damon, her rock, the one who always kept his—and often times her—cool.

Damon, her brother.

Damon … crying?

This couldn't be Damon.

But it was. This was Damon. Broken. Weary. Cheeks wet with earnest tears, begging her to find the same peace he had. Tears he wept for her.

*For me.*

She wished with all of her being to grasp the hope he had found.

"*This is real*," he had said. "*This is everything we have been looking for.*"

"Raya, I love you. Love Himself is in love with you!" he said, unashamed. "I'm going to try to undo some of the wrong I have done. If you're going to turn me in, I guess I can't stop you. I guess I've truly lost my sister." His voice broke. He pulled his horse around hers and rode towards Reed.

After a short moment, he straightened his back, squared his shoulders, and lifted his eyes solely to the road ahead.

"Damon!" she kicked her mount. *I can't do this. I can't leave him. Maybe I can find what he has. Maybe there is yet hope.*

*No!*

Someone pulled up sharply on the reins. The horse stopped. Her vision blurred and swam. Someone was yelling at Damon again. The words were hard to make out with the ringing in her ears.

Her chest hurt. It felt like a sharp, cutting pain.

She felt the energy surge through her veins with every pulse of her heart. It was so painful … yet so exhilarating.

She licked her lips.

*This is power. This is truth. This is* mine.

"Stop, Damon!" someone cried. She realized it was her. "This is your last chance! I will turn you in!"

"I have made my choice," he said. "It's not too late for you to make yours. I'm praying for you."

She let loose a cry of outrage.

With a painful jerk, the energy was drained and her vision was once again pulled into focus. She looked around frantically. Damon was gone.

*What is happening? What have I done?* she gasped a sharp sob.

The energy spiked hot pain and left as suddenly as it came, *You are free.*

*I am free.*

*This is freedom. Don't chase after the chains.*

*Yes. This is freedom.*

౾

"They are tracking us," Riven said.

"We feared this might happen," Tim said. "They know—or at least suspect—who we are, but do they know about Musa's group? Do they know that we are prepared to fight?"

"I don't believe so," Riven answered, "but I cannot be certain."

"How many did you say branched out to follow each group?" Jay asked.

Riven's horse stamped impatiently, as if it understood the discussion. "Vincent and approximately eight hundred men have continued along their previous route due East."

"Presumably headed for District Ten, knowing that Haavene is there," Jay said.

Riven nodded. "Two groups of about two hundred each have branched northwest and southwest, following our groups. They seem to be just scouting us for the time being, but my guess is that as soon as they see that we are not only Resistance, but also armed, they will attack."

"We can still take them, with careful planning and the Maker's blessing," Jay said. "We still are over half a day ahead of them, and could put more distance between us. Since it takes longer to move twelve hundred than it does two hundred, we have an advantage. We can move more quickly."

"Also, as far as we know, they have no reason to believe we are armed," Tim said. "The Resistance has never done anything like this. Yes, we arm ourselves when going on missions to deliver the Books, but never anything of this scale. They don't realize that we have been training for this. They will not expect us to attack. In that way, we still have the element of surprise."

"We must go to prayer and discuss our course of action quickly," Riven said. "I sent Tristan with the news to the northwest group, but we need to get plans made quickly so we can get them to everyone in time."

"We must act quickly, before Vincent has a chance to. If we let them make the first move on their terms, we will not be able to survive. Even with the best laid plans, we will need the Maker's help to pull this off," Tim said. "We must attack when they make camp tonight. It will be dark in three hours."

"It will take that much time just to inform everyone of the plan—which we have not yet made." Riven said.

"We could be ready by midnight. That would be the optimal time to attack. We can be certain of the cover of darkness, and that they will have made camp and retired to their tents," Jay said. "Riven, did they have any guards posted throughout the night from what you saw?"

"One watching the horses several yards from camp, and three pacing about the camp," he replied. "Most of the men were in their tents, but there were a few out drinking themselves into a stupor."

"They obviously don't expect an attack," Tim said, then turned to Jay. "When you were a guard in Nazar's castle, how were the shifts?"

"It depended on your position and assignment," he responded. "Assuming it has not changed—and since Vincent is still general I doubt they have—the night watches would begin at dark, and change every six hours. Since it is Fewivmonth, midnight would be about mid-shift."

"Perfect," said Riven. "Now let us seek our Maker's wisdom and make plans."

As they continued to ride behind the southwest group, they lifted prayer to their Lover. Encouraged, they laid plans, and Riven rode quickly to inform the other groups.

Tonight, they would fight for their Lover.

Tonight, they would wage war.

ॐ∽

Musa could not sleep. Something was happening. She could sense it in her spirit.

*Holy Maker ... what do I do?*

Musa rose from her tent and woke all the others. Many were already awake—they felt it too.

"I believe we all feel something stirring in our spirits tonight," she said, her voice soft, but carrying a strength that reached every ear. "We all know that all around us there is an unseen but constant battle between the warriors of the Courts of Light, and the fallen warriors of the Shadow Void. Our actions, prayer, and worship factors in the outcome of each battle day to day. The outcome, in turn, affects us. But tonight, I feel this is far more than typical warfare. I feel the tension mounting. Something is shifting. War on the Resistance has long ago been waged, and now we have a small army to meet the challenge along with the warriors fighting for us. I feel that wars, both seen and unseen, are about to be waged—are being waged at this very moment. Can you feel the tension? There is a lot riding on this. This is a war we cannot lose." She scanned the crowd. "This is a war we cannot win."

Everyone was speechless at her statement.

"Not without our Lover. Not without our Maker. Not without our Savior." Louder, bolder, stronger: "We here will never win this war with swords, but we will fight!"

"For Elnai!" Janelle stood and shouted.

"For Love!" another cried.

"Let us fall to our knees and fight!" Musa cried.

As one the Lovers sank to their knees and lifted their hearts to the One who gave them life. Warriors. Lovers. In love with Love Himself.

Tonight, they would fight for their Lover.

Tonight, they would wage war.

❧

"Praise You, Holy Maker!" Baros Jakkiv said, breathing in the night air. He could feel strength and light pulsing through his veins. The Lovers were praising the Maker's holy name. Their prayers strengthened him.

"Thank You for Your strength. Please, Victorious Elnai, honor Your Lovers' prayers. They need Your victory this very night if they are to win this war."

৵৽৽৻

Nazar paced a trail in the floor of his quarters. Back and forth and back again. He was still fully dressed despite it being late at night. It was one of those nights again. The nights his dreams made him fear sleeping.

Those eyes burning bright and green in his mind. No matter how hard he tried to forget.

His heart skipped a beat.

Forget?

Did he want to forget? Forget the vibrant jade eyes and the way they pierced right through him in the best way. Forget the way her blond waves bounced about her shoulders. The way his heart swelled at her laughter, at her voice as she said his name. Forget the warmth of her body as he held her tight. Her soft lips as they pressed sweetly against his.

Forget her death.

Forget how she had left him that day. How he would have kissed her goodbye and held her close just a little longer if he would have known what would happen.

Forget how he let her go when he should have kept her safe. How he lost her.

*No, I didn't lose her. She was taken*—stolen—*from me! By* Him.

If he would have known that her so-called "Lover" would betray her. How *He* would let her die after she spent her life proclaiming His love.

Love. If this was love, then why did she die?

*He did this. He took her from me. He killed her.*

Maybe Nazar did want to forget. Even the good times. Because even remembering the good times didn't stop the pain. It would be so much easier to just forget it all. Because he couldn't fix it, couldn't make the pain stop, couldn't bring her back.

Yes. Nazar did want to forget. He wanted it to be over. Maybe he wanted *everything* to be over. Maybe breathing would not hurt so much if he didn't breathe at all.

Hot tears streamed down his face.

"This is all Your fault!" he screamed at the ceiling. "You are not Love! You are not Truth! You are a lie! You want to show me Your heart?" He grabbed handfuls of hair and raged through gritted teeth, "I have seen it! I don't want it! I know what You do to Your own Lovers! You call Yourself Love?" He gasped a rattled sob and threw a punch to the air. "What kind of Love, what kind of Lover forsakes those who serve You? She loved You!"

His voice dropped low. He took a deep breath, straightened his posture, and stared straight ahead at nothing. "And You betrayed her. You let her die. That is not love. I will prove that You are not the great Lover they praise You for. I will continue to kill Your Lovers and You will continue to simply watch them die. Watch them die as they praise You with their dying breath."

The room was perfectly still and silent.

"You took away the only thing that was dear to me, so I will take all You claim to be dear to You and watch as You do nothing."

# WARS WAGED

Raya simply rode. To nowhere at all. She just rode hard and fast, kicking her tired horse on. Damon had betrayed her. Damon had abandoned her.

*You cannot run away,* came the hiss. *Damon—He—cannot win, cannot be right. You must show Damon that his co-called "Lover" is blind and deaf if you want your brother back. Do what you must.*

Raya set her jaw and yanked her mount's head towards Reed.

*Yes. This is what I have to do. I have to save him. This is the only way. He brought this upon himself—he forced me! I am doing what I must to get my brother back.*

❧

Andrea floated just between the worlds of awake and asleep for a moment longer, savoring it. The dull, but ever present pain of the conscious world soon pulled her fully awake. Her blood still slowly seeped through the tattered bandages on her leg from going up and down the stairs. It hadn't had a chance to heal.

*And it may never get one.*

"Come on, Andrea."

She wearily pushed herself up and leaned on her left arm. "Ezra?"

"Yes?"

"Again? Nazar has already called us today. Is it already tomorrow?"

He hesitated. "No."

"Surely, we would know if …" Flora could not bring herself to say it, but everyone knew what she was thinking. It was ever present in each woman's mind.

They had discussed how he may kill them one by one or even a few at a time to get the others to talk. That he might think that would be more useful than a mass execution.

Today could be the day that Nazar started killing them. He only needed one person to give him the information he needed. They had assumed that he would take Tisha last, since she had the most information. They hadn't talked about who might go first.

Andrea had known it would likely be her. It would be the best way to get to Tisha.

"I love you. All of you," Andrea said, calmly.

"I love you," Tisha said, tears in her whispered words. "Maker's strength."

"No matter what happens," Rhoda said, shakily as well. "Remember His Promise. We are His Lovers."

"And He is ours," Andrea whispered weakly.

Ezra stood at her right and offered a hand to help her to her feet. She stood, slowly, shakily. The floor somehow jumped up to the ceiling, and Andrea somehow ended up spinning around and around. Or maybe rocking on waves? Maybe she was on a boat. Or the ceiling. She couldn't tell anymore. Just that it was dark and she hurt.

The world stopped spinning. Turns out she was not on the ceiling or a boat. Just the floor. It was cold, and her blood pulsed pain through the entire right side of her body. She tenderly reached to touch it. Her fingers came back red and sticky.

"I can't do it," she slurred. "I'm sorry."

Her stomach had long ago eaten itself and whatever was working in its place was eating the rest of her insides. She'd had very little water, and often awoke from the restless snatches of sleep she managed to get with her injuries throbbing or to Ezra summoning her. To top it all off, she had lost a lot of blood.

Ezra squatted down and studied her a moment, head slightly cocked, brows furrowed. Andrea was not sure what the other women were doing, she could barely focus on Ezra. He looked at her with pity, but Andrea also pitied him. She saw the fear, the questions, the confusion behind his dark eyes.

"I'm sorry," he said softly, "we have to go."

"I'll try," she managed. She pushed herself up on her elbows, and stayed there a moment, just breathing.

Without another word, Ezra once again scooped her up, turning sideways through the door.

Before he kicked it shut, Andrea looked back. In the shadows of the dungeon cell, she saw dirty faces smudged with tears and a few shaky smiles of encouragement.

"You have our prayers," Zania said.

Tears streamed down her mother's face.

She looked at Tisha, and whispered weakly, "I love you, Mother. Stay strong."

Ezra shut the door, but didn't bother putting her down to lock it.

Andrea felt very small, yet heavy. Her feverish head ached. She closed her eyes and just focused on breathing.

*Inhale, exhale. In, and out.*

"You amaze me," he said between breaths. "I could never do this. How are you so strong?"

Andrea turned that over in her mind for a moment. Here she was, being carried from her dungeon cell because she was too weak to carry her own pitiful weight, yet he called her strong. She could barely lift an arm to hold onto his shoulder.

"I'm not strong," she said faintly, her heavy eyes closed. "I'm weak. I'm scared."

"This … it doesn't make any sense."

"I know. I can't understand it either."

"How? How do you do it?"

"It's not anything I do. Any strength or courage you see is His." The corners of her cracked lips turned up faintly. "I'm scared. I am weak. But He is strong. I have hope in His Promise." She felt breathless just from the few words she said.

Ezra didn't speak for a moment. They reached the stair landing and the guard on the other side of the door let them through. Andrea let her arm drop, swinging with every step. Even though she was just trying to help Ezra support her, she didn't want to endanger him in any way. After they were clear, Ezra dared to speak again, knowing that someone could possibly overhear him as he walked. His words were slightly breathless from carrying her so far.

"His Promise you said?"

"It is what we place our hope in. What makes everything worth it." Her words were mumbled. She still kept her eyes closed; the world spun too much otherwise. "I was just about to tell you about the Promise yesterday, but Nazar came in."

Neither spoke again. They finally reached the little room and Ezra set Andrea in the chair.

Her head pounded, each hand grasped the side of the chair. She kept her eyes closed until her head stopped spinning. She blinked. It was dark. She could tell from the tiny rectangular window just a few inches below the ceiling. It was just above ground level and usually let in light from the prisoners' courtyard.

"What time is it?" she asked.

"An hour or so shy of midnight," Ezra responded.

Andrea felt an urgency to convince Ezra of the Truth before it was too late. "Ezra, please, you have to listen before it's too late." She shook her throbbing head, trying to strengthen her mumbled words. She turned in her chair to face him, and leaned on her right elbow on the table.

"You should save your strength—"

"No!" she was desperate, not to save her own life—but his. He was so close. "Short of a miracle, I am going to die tonight."

Andrea looked him boldly in the eye, breathing heavily. He looked stunned by the boldness of her statement.

"But let me tell you how good my Maker is: though my body may die, Nazar cannot kill me. I have found life in the Author of Life Himself." Her pain dulled as she was filled with a bold strength that cleared her words. She no longer could barely mumble half a phrase, but now was bursting with what she feared she would not have enough time to say. Though her voice was still a bit weak and winded.

"I'm at peace. If I die tonight, I know Who holds my soul. I know that I will enter into the presence of My Lover. No more fighting. No more pain or struggle. Just delighting in the light of His face, in love with Love Himself."

The last part of the dream played before her mind. She finally understood.

"*Drink,*" He had said.

"I have told you of the Holy Maker's perfect world, of how we scarred it with our own sin. How Elnai came down and gave His life in our stead. Now, when He looks at us, He does not see sin's black stain, but the red blood that Elnai shed to wash us clean."

Ezra remained silent, but held her gaze, simply listening.

Her hands dipped into the red waters. Power flooded through every atom of her being.

"Yet, even with Elnai's sacrifice, our world is still broken. That is why there is pain and struggle. Our hearts are reconciled to Him, but our world is still stained. There is death. There is sin. There is sickness, and pain, and hurt, and evil, and wrong in our dying world."

She spoke quickly, ever conscious of how little time she had. This was her last chance—she was almost out of time.

"The evil in this world hates the light of Elnai in the Lovers. People like Nazar—whether out of maddened jealousy, hatred of the truth that exposes their corruption, or deceptive ignorance—hate that light, and therefore wish to destroy it. That is why the Lovers are persecuted. Because in accepting Elnai's perfection, we are alienating ourselves from the imperfect world."

She closed her eyes and smiled as the word "*drink*" washed over her again.

"Now let me tell you what makes it all worth it. Let me tell you what gives me strength—the hope I cling to."

Ezra shifted nervously, but still listened.

"The Promise."

Eyes open. She laughed. It began weakly, then grew stronger. Even though the little motion of laughing hurt her wounds and made her stomach twist, she was filled with a bold peace. It was worth it.

*You are more than worth it.*

"The Promise that Elnai has not left us to suffer in a broken world. That, not only once we breathe our last here, we breathe our first in His Courts, but also that He is coming back! Elnai is coming in victory! In glory! In love! He is coming to rescue His Lovers, redeem the wronged, and restore our broken world." She closed her eyes, leaned her head back, and breathed deeply of the sheer bliss at the very thought.

She drew up the red waters and they were pure and clear once again. Restored. She drew it to her trembling lips and was swallowed by a beautiful feeling beyond description. One like she'd never known before.

"*This is but a glimpse,*" He had said. *He had promised.*

Andrea looked him in the eye. "Ezra, Elnai is coming back. He is coming in victory and in power. He is coming to rescue His Lovers and completely rid the world of sin and imperfection. He is coming to fulfill His Promise and usher us into His presence forever more." Looking at him, her heart ached. She longed for him to be reconciled to his Maker. To be free of the pain behind his eyes and discover the joy of being in love with Love Himself. Andrea's heart reached out, longing to touch Ezra's. It was Elnai's heartbeat in her own chest.

"But, Ezra, Elnai can't heal you if you refuse to let go of the chains. He has made the way! He offers you His Heart!" her voice broke as tears ran freely. "But He is not going to force Himself on you. He has given you a choice. I know that if I die tonight, I can go confidently into the Courts because it's His blood that makes me whole again. I've accepted His atonement for my imperfection.

"He *longs* for you. That is why He made a way. That is why Elnai lowered Himself down to us and conquered our sin and death after living a perfect life. But the Holy Maker is perfect and pure. His righteous majesty cannot be defiled by evil or imperfection. Therefore anything evil or impure cannot be in His presence. You have sinned. You have made mistakes. We all have. And since we're no longer perfect and whole, we—in our sin—cannot be in His presence. We were created as eternal beings. We were made to dwell in His wonderful presence forever. But we messed up. So Elnai in His loving grace has made a way.

"But if you don't choose to accept it, then you're not restored. You aren't pure. And you cannot be in His Courts. So you will have chosen to spend an eternity away from our precious Lover. You will be lost."

She still cried unabashedly. Her words now hoarse. "Please, Ezra, He loves you, He wants you, He created you, He redeemed you, He offers you His very heart, He has chosen you. Now it's up to you to choose Him. He longs for you to welcome Him in so He can bless you. Don't ever forget that." Hearing approaching footsteps, she wiped her tears. "Choose Him. Don't forget this. Don't forget the Promise. He's coming back. Are you ready?"

The door opened and in walked Nazar.

෴

Damon had simply showed the gatekeeper Nazar's ring, which he had "forgotten" to return, and he was allowed in. Raya had left him. He didn't know where she had gone or if she was coming back. But he had to stay focused on the task at hand.

As he walked down the dark streets of Reed and approached the castle entrance, his skin crawled. There was something different. A dark and eerie presence hung thick in the air. He could almost smell it. Rotting flesh.

*Elnai, give me strength,* he prayed. *And please forgive me for bringing Andrea and Your other Lovers here.*

"Back so soon?" the castle gatekeeper asked, recognizing Damon.

"I'm on urgent business," he snapped, flashing Nazar's ring as he strode by. "I have no time to make idle chat. Open the gate immediately."

Damon soon strode down the passages of the massive castle. He took the passageways that were least likely to be used and hurried to the dungeons.

෴

Nazar crossed the room in a few purposeful strides. "Last chance," he said, expression hard and unmoving. "Deny Him or forfeit your life."

"My life is already His," she said. Her words were confident, but she could barely sit up straight. "I will never deny my Lover."

He flew into a rage and jabbed his finger at her. "He is not Love! He is blind! He is deaf! He is dead!"

"He loves you, Nazar," she said softly.

He struck her and she hit the ground. Too weak even to cry out. She tasted blood on her lips.

"Get her up!"

She offered no assistance. She remained limp and focused on breathing. Yet, in even this she felt Elnai's supernatural peace more than ever before. Yes, she was in pain. Yes, she knew she would probably die tonight. Yes, she would not be in this situation if it were up to her.

But it was not up to her. Perhaps that was what she found most comforting. The peace in the surrender. Knowing that the Holy Maker of All Things was in control. When this season called life ended, true life began in eternity. She rested in His Promise. She was not panicked. She was ready. If Elnai chose to let her escape this, she would be thankful. But if He chose to take her into His Life beyond this world, she ached for that. Not for the death, but for the life beyond it.

*I am not afraid to leave this life behind. I am ready for the pain and fighting to end. Ready to bask in Your holy light.*

She was not afraid to die—she knew Who held her soul—but she was afraid of the journey to death. She hurt. It scared her to think it could get worse than *this*. But her pain and fight would be over and she would be ushered into her reward for all of the struggle she faced here. She found peace in that.

It was worth it. More than worth it.

She was now placed back in her chair. Her upper arms bruised from the many rough hands over the past week or so. She dug her fingers into the side of the chair, fighting to stay conscious.

"I will kill you!"

*I am ready, Elnai. I am tired of hurting. I want You.*

Nazar slapped his palm down on the table and spoke low.

"Your 'Lover' cannot save you. He turns a blind eye to His own people. After He lets you suffer, you would die for Him? In the Name of *Love*?"

Andrea took a deep breath and looked Nazar in the eye. Her voice was very soft and a little weak, but courage, peace, and strength seeped through her words. "He died for me, Nazar. He died for me in the Name of Love."

She saw pure panic in his eyes. His lips parted in a silent gasp.

He backed away a few steps as she held his gaze. "Don't look at me."

He turned his back to her. She noticed his heavy breathing.

He cried out in a groan, "This is not Love! He is not Love, Kyah!" *Kyah? Who is Kyah?*

Nazar swung around and grabbed her wounded leg. Tears streamed down his face, his words trembled and he crushed her wound. "You are not Kyah! I can kill you! I can! No Lover would do this to His own."

Andrea was too weak to fully cry out. She squeezed her eyes shut, hot tears streaking down her dirty cheeks. Her mouth open and teeth clenched in voiceless cry. She pushed up on the chair. A hybrid of a sob and moan escaped her.

Then, she was falling. She must have fallen for hours. Ages, even. The darkness swallowed her and she was lost to the conscious world.

അം

Riven looked to the night sky. Midnight. Everyone was in position. Leaving their horses and taking advantage of the Airissian terrain of rolling hills, one hundred Resistance fighters were closing in on Vincent's two hundred men who had been pursuing the group headed northwest. They now all slept except for two guards pacing a perimeter around the camp. Riven-Reau silently lay flat on the side of the hill opposite to the camp.

Footsteps.

Riven got ready. He listened until the guard had stepped just past them, then rose quickly to his feet. Before the guard had time to react, Riven stood behind him with an arm around his throat. The guard was unable to find oxygen to cry out. Finally, the smaller man went limp. Riven pulled him behind the hill, where the rest of Reau was waiting. They bound the man's hands and took his sword, then dripped some naxer into his mouth.

"Careful with the naxer," Riven cautioned. "We don't have much." He turned to Jac, who was peeking over, watching for Bennen's signal. "What do you see?"

"I see no one," Jac whispered back. "Wait. Yes, they gave us the signal both guards are down." Jac motioned back and then retreated back behind the hill.

Riven-Reau, Nev-Vax, and Med-Vax all proceeded silently to the camp from different directions. Tah-Marj and Nev-Marj readied their arrows and got ready on hills to the east and west.

Starting in the tents at the edge, the three groups spread out, swords drawn, moving as silently as they could.

Riven entered the first tent. The sleeping soldier began to stir. Riven gave him a swift knock on the head with the hilt of his sword. The man went limp, unconscious. Riven took his weapons and dropped them in front of his tent.

Before heading to the next tent, he glanced back at the southern hill where Dray's group was. As arranged, half of Tah-Marj was racing down the hill to retrieve the swords. He knew that Tori's group was doing the same on the Northern side.

Riven did the same with a second tent.

He entered the third. The man was sitting up, listening to the quiet, but unavoidable sounds of the attack.

"Resistance! The Resistance is—"

Riven knocked the man out and took his sword, but his cry had stirred half the camp

He rushed out to hear a few other cries cut short. The camp was now awake. Shouting began as men rushed from their tents, swords drawn to find sixty armed Resistance deep in their camp.

"We are under attack!" someone cried.

Riven, Bennen, and Carson signaled their men back.

Riven made sure his men were clear, then ran himself. Their confused enemies soon split after the three retreating groups. The Resistance fighters had disabled and disarmed at least half of the opposing army.

"Dray! You are clear!" he shouted.

Arrows flew through the darkness and thudded into the ground between Riven-Reau and their pursuers.

A few cries of pain mixed with other cries.

"Archers! Archers in the south! Retreat north!"

&#8766;&bull;&#8767;

Jakkiv fought hard alongside the Resistance. He and his warriors were fighting the fallen and stirring up panic within the hearts of Vincent's men.

They stirred up fear that took from them their ability to think clearly.

‰◦⊰

*Perfect,* Riven thought as Reau veered around to the west to further cover the panicked army. He heard Bennen shout to Carson and the whistling of arrows.

More screams of pain. More frenzied cries.

"Archers! More archers in the north!"

"They've covered the west!"

"Resistance fighters in the east!"

"Stop! Stop at once!" screamed the lieutenant in charge. "Find your heads! Silence!"

That calmed them some. They stopped running around in mass chaotic panic.

"We have you surrounded!" Riven shouted.

Tah-Marj and Nev-Marj were moving in closer, arrows ready at the string.

"You have barely half your numbers and some of you are injured!" Riven now had their attention. His strong, deep voice carried well through the quiet. "Surrender. You have been defeated. Lay down your arms and surrender quietly and you shall all live. We will even care for your wounds."

The lieutenant stepped out and jabbed his finger at Riven. "You think that I trust a dog like you? You will kill us! No surrender!"

"If we had wanted to kill you, we would have already. Did we slit your throats in your sleep? No. Have our archers sent arrows through your hearts? Or have we rushed you with swords now that we have you trapped?"

Murmurs erupted.

"Check your tents," Riven said. "Send ten to check your tents. You will find your companions unarmed and unconscious, but otherwise unhurt and breathing."

After a moment, ten stepped forward.

"Drop your weapons and you are free to pass," Bennen ordered.

They did, and went about the camp checking several tents each. They returned.

"Did my words prove true?" Riven asked. "Are they alive?"

"Yes. You spoke truly," one answered loudly enough for the others to hear.

"Lay down your arms," Riven said once more. "You have my word that you will not be harmed, and your wounds will be tended."

A few of them laid down their swords, and soon the others were following their example.

"Stop! I will have you marked for this!" the lieutenant screamed.

"Now get on your knees. We will come collect your weapons."

After a moment, the lieutenant was the only one standing. With a curse, he threw his sword to the ground and sank to his knees.

Their weapons were quickly gathered, then their hands were bound. Tori and Dray attended to the wounded, while the other Lovers sat the remaining men on the ground in groups of four and bound them back to back. Soon, all two hundred were awake and bound this way.

The five leaders—Riven, Tori, Dray, Bennen, and Carson—met afterwards.

"Any deaths on either side?" Riven asked.

"No, Maker be praised," Tori responded. "They suffered twenty-three injuries, but only four were serious. We tended their wounds and gave them moy-moy for the bleeding. They will live. Only three of us suffered injuries. All very minor."

"Thank Elnai," Carson said.

"Who are we going to leave with the prisoners?" Dray asked.

"We agreed on ten with the others." Riven thought a moment. "We will leave the three injured, Jac, and Liv for sure."

After riding for an hour, Riven, Carson, Dray, Tori, Bennen, and their groups met with the rest of the Lovers—save the twenty left with the prisoners. They brought each other up to date. Both groups had had a very similar experience.

Between both groups, they had only one death, six serious—but not life threatening—injuries, thirty-seven minor wounds among Vincent's men, and twelve minor wounds among the Lovers.

After thanking Elnai for a successful mission so far, they prayed for protection for the battle they were about to face. This time, they were attacking Vincent's main camp. They had the same plan—only this time it was not one hundred Lovers against two hundred enemies in two separate attacks, but one hundred eighty Lovers against eight hundred enemies in one camp.

They split up and moved to get into position. As they readied themselves, every heart held a silent prayer. This battle would not be easily won.

❧

"Do I look like some common dog like you?" Damon barked at the guard. "Do you know who I am? Do I need to remind you so quickly? I have the ring from Nazar's finger, I am the one who brought these witches in, who sat at Nazar's right hand at a feast in my honor only days ago, yet you question my authority?"

"I'm sorry, sir," the guard mumbled, clearly angry but knowing his place. "I didn't know. Forgive me." The guard offered him the keys.

Damon scoffed, "First you question me, now you insult me!" Damon growled, "I have half a mind to report you. Now open the door yourself, dog, before you fall completely from my good graces."

"My apologies, sir." The guard unlocked the door then descended the stairs in front of Damon.

Damon cleared his throat noisily.

The guard looked back.

"Do you expect that door to close itself?"

"No, sir." the guard ducked his head and squeezed past Damon to close the door. Damon took up much of the narrow stairway, but he refused to move. The guard had to turn sideways.

Damon didn't turn back, but heard the door close behind him. He proceeded down the stairs with the guard following behind.

He crossed his arms and glared once he got to the last door at the bottom of the dark staircase. The guard unlocked and opened the door. The dim light shone into the dark cell, revealing the women sitting in a circle, arms wrapped around one another and tears on cheeks. They had been praying.

"Thank you. Now I will be taking the keys," Damon said to the guard. The guard handed him the keys.

"You will be happy to know that I have decided not to report you."

"Thank you—"

Before he could finish, Damon delivered a hard right hook to his ear. The guard crumpled to the floor to the women's gasps.

He searched the shocked faces.

"Where is Andrea?" he asked.

"It may be too late," a Darrionite woman responded.

"Nazar took her a while ago," Tisha said.

*No. I cannot be too late. I have to save her. I have to make things right.*

"We have to go," he said, standing aside.

The women streamed out and Damon dragged the guard into the cell, locking the door.

"We have to hurry. We don't have much time. Do exactly as I say and maybe we can get out of this."

Damon came across a lot more confidently than he felt.

*I have to find Andrea.*

Damon flinched when he felt a hand on his shoulder. He was not used to this.

"Do you know who Ezra is?" Tisha asked.

"No," he responded.

"If we can find him, he may know where Andrea is. And he needs us. He will need to get out with us."

"Is he a Lover?" Damon turned to face Tisha.

Her face was a picture of shock. "No. But he is close."

"Stay here," he said once he reached the top of the stairs. "I will make sure it is clear."

Damon pressed his back against the wall and motioned the women into the shadows. They heard the heavy footsteps of the standard issue guard boots. The door opened.

Damon grabbed the guard and slammed his shoulder into him, pinning him to the wall, and shut the door.

He turned to knock him out.

"No!" "Stop!" "It is Ezra!" cried multiple panicked voices.

Damon still held the guard's shoulder with his left hand, pressing his arm across his chest and holding him securely against the wall, his right fist in the air, ready.

"Ezra?" he growled.

The boy nodded violently, eyes wide with fear and still gasping for breath after being slammed against the wall.

"Sorry." His voice was still low and threatening. He had to work on that. He released him. "I thought you were someone else."

"D-Damon," Ezra stammered, "you are the assassin that brought Andrea here. You and your sister."

Ezra's words pierced like daggers to the heart.

Damon looked at the floor. The knife twisted. He did this and his sister might turn him in for trying to make it right.

The heavy silence was almost more than he could bear.

"Yes." His deep voice still low.

"What are you doing here?" the boy asked timidly.

Damon took a deep breath. "Trying to fix what I have done." His dark eyes lifted to pierce into Ezra's. Ezra shifted nervously under Damon's hard stare.

"Where is Andrea?" he growled. He sighed and cleared his throat. He still had a long way to go. He tried again. Better this time. "Where is Andrea?"

"I-I-I don't know."

"Listen," Damon said, trying to take the threatening edge from his voice, but still sounding low and intimidating, "I'm trying to save her. Where is she?"

"Last time I saw her was when I dropped her off for Nazar to interrogate her."

"You mean torture her?"

"I don't know."

"Why were you coming here?"

"Because, uh …"

"We don't have time for this," Damon said, frustrated. "Speak!"

"I needed to talk to Tisha," he said, shifting nervously and shooting her a pleading glance.

"About Andrea?" Tisha asked.

He nodded. "And about something she said. But that is not important right now."

*She was trying to win him for Elnai. That is amazing. She still is so strong.*

"Listen, Ezra." His voice was still gruff, but softer. You could hear Damon's sincerity. "What Andrea was trying to tell you is the most important thing you will ever hear. It is the *only* truly important thing you will ever hear. Elani, the Holy Maker, is real. He is truth, He is freedom, He is love. He longs for you, He loves you, He is calling you. Don't *ever* forget that. But believe me, He's not going to force Himself upon you. You have to let Him in so He can heal you, so He can set you free. He has done His part, now it is up to you."

Several mouths hung open in shock. Everyone was stunned speechless.

Ezra's eyes brimmed with tears. "How did you know?"

Damon sighed. "Because she told me the same thing. It just took me a while to accept it. But trust me, if He can set me free, He can set you free. Don't wait any longer! I waited too long, and now we are here."

Damon looked away a moment, recomposing himself.

Ezra finally spoke. "I think Nazar is going to kill her tonight."

*Elnai help me.*

"Alright," Damon said, "here is what we are going to do. I need you all to listen carefully. We don't have much time."

❧⚜❦

Ezra and the women hurried along the seldom used passageway.

"We cannot leave Andrea," Tisha whispered desperately.

"We are not leaving her," Ezra whispered back. "You heard the plan. Damon said to hide outside the city, and he would get Andrea and find us."

Tisha still looked upset, but said nothing more.

"Alright," Ezra whispered, "the door to the prisoner's courtyard is just around the corner. Stay here."

Ezra nervously checked his uniform, then walked up to the guard at the door.

"The captain requests to see you immediately," he said, hoping the guard could not hear his beating heart.

"The captain?" the man asked. "I thought he was in Valrine this week."

"Well, he is back," Ezra said, "and he is angry. I would hurry if I were you."

"Angry? At me?"

"Very angry. Apparently, some prisoners escaped. Those prisoners were accused of aiding the Resistance." Ezra paused as if he were debating whether or not to tell him this. "Don't say where you heard this, but I am afraid he suspects that you had something to do with their escape. 'Resistance sympathizer' I believe is how he put it."

The guard's eyes grew wide. "No! I am not a traitor!"

"I'm only the messenger. I was sent to deliver the message and relieve you of your post."

The guard handed Ezra the keys and hurried away. Ezra's heart refused to calm down even after the man was gone. He looked around nervously before finally returning to the Lovers at a sprint.

"Come on," he whispered.

"It worked?" Flora asked.

"Just like Damon said it would. Now come on." His hands shook so hard he could barely get the key into the keyhole. He unlocked the door, took a deep breath and opened it.

He walked to the portcullis that served as an entrance and exit to and from the prisoner's courtyard, to Reed. This one led to the area where the executions were held. It was there to bring the prisoners to their executions without having to bring them through the main castle.

The guard was nodding off where he stood. Prisoners were not allowed out at this time of night, so there was not usually anything to see.

"I was sent to tell you that the captain requests to see you immediately."

"Hm?" he blinked the sleep from his eyes. "The captain? Is he not in Valrine?"

"Not anymore. Apparently, some Resistance prisoners managed to escape. You can imagine how Lord Nazar is breathing down the captain's neck. The captain is mad too."

The guard was definitely awake now. "They think I had something to do with it?"

"All I know is that the captain said something about 'possible Resistance sympathizers' and was so worked up that he would not wait until a decent hour." Ezra hoped his nerves didn't show through his voice. "I was told to deliver the message and relieve you of your post."

The guard handed Ezra the keys and rushed off. After the guard was gone, Ezra made sure that the door to the courtyard was left unlocked for Damon and Andrea, then opened the portcullis and left the keys in the cranks to hold it open.

They hugged the shadows as they hurried through the execution area.

Everyone breathed a sigh of relief. Though they never admitted it even to themselves, they had all feared that they might find Andrea's execution in progress here.

"How are we going to get past the city gate?" Rhoda asked.

"I'm not sure," Ezra said. "We will think of something."

"They will know to be watching for us. For me in particular," said Tisha. "We will have to tie him up or something."

When they neared the gate, the others stayed out of sight as Ezra went ahead.

"Hello?" He said.

Nothing.

He cautiously approached the guard-shack and peeked into the window. He gagged on his own bile and clamped a hand over his mouth. He ran back to the others. Eyes welled with tears, shocked.

"What is it?" Tisha demanded. "Ezra!"

He just shook his head, eyes wide.

Rhoda ran to the guard-shack and took a look. She quickly turned away, took a deep breath, and calmly walked back.

"The guard is dead," she said. "Arrow through the heart."

"Did Damon?" Zania wondered aloud.

Everyone considered it for a moment.

"I don't remember seeing a bow. Only a sword," Flora said.

"But remember how he took out that guard and nearly killed Ezra? He is a trained assassin. He is trained to lie. I would not be surprised," said one of the women.

Tisha was silent. Not meeting anyone's eyes.

"He didn't kill the guard. He knocked him out," Rhoda reminded them. "Yes, he was trained to be a murderer, but he was *created* to be loved by Love Himself. Besides, if he was lying, why would he let us get this far?"

"He seemed sincere when he spoke of Elnai. And he really did seem worried about Andrea. Do you think he's really changed?" Flora said.

"Have you forgotten that he is the reason Andrea was here? And in the state she was in to begin with?" another chimed in bitterly.

Zania was studying Tisha, who was lost in her own thoughts. Her brows furrowed over her green eyes, which avoided the others as she chewed at her cheek.

"What do you think, Tisha?"

Everyone quieted and turned to her. Tisha was obviously struggling with this. She looked up at each of their faces.

"I believe—" she sighed, exhausted and spent. "I think he has changed. I saw sincerity in his eyes. Felt it in his words. And he has helped us get this far."

Flora nodded thoughtfully. "He still has a ways to go, but are we not all imperfect? I love Andrea like a daughter and what he did was wrong, but I believe he has truly found love and forgiveness in the Holy Maker. If our Lover forgives should we not as well?"

"May I remind you," Rhoda said, "that most of us were already in that cell and Damon had nothing to do with it."

"While he did play a part," Tisha said slowly, "he was not the reason Andrea and I were there. He was a pawn. And if it would not have been him, it would have been someone else. Nazar and all powers against Elnai and His Light in us have been fighting against Resistance efforts ever since it was founded. I have to forgive Damon. If not because of me, because our Lover has forgiven him and us. I cannot ask for grace to cover my many sins if I cannot forgive a broken heart who has barely tasted the Love of Elnai."

She took a deep breath, feeling better. "I can forgive him. Because my Lover has and strengthens me to do so."

"So if Damon didn't shoot the guard," Ezra asked for all of them, "who did?"

"I don't know," Rhoda said, "but we have to keep moving. We have to get outside of Reed. If it's a trap, well we can't very well go back."

৵৽

Damon rushed along, hoping—praying—that he was not too late. He knew where she would likely be. He had thought to check here even before Ezra had said it was the last place he saw Andrea. He strode confidently up to the guard at the door, discreetly checking to make sure there was no one else around.

He stood, arms crossed expectantly, facing the door. He glared at the guard. "Are you going to make me wait all day?"

The guard looked angry, but then recognized him. "I'm sorry, sir. I didn't recognize you. I thought you were on a mission."

"I am on a mission," he growled. "Now, are you going to open this door or do I have to report you?"

The guard looked torn. "I'm sorry, sir, but Lord Nazar has ordered that no one but he is to enter under any circumstances."

"Do you know who I am?" Damon demanded. "I'm the one who brought the girl in. I am the one who sat at Nazar's right hand at a feast held in my honor only days ago. I also happen to be the one carrying Nazar's ring. Like I said, I have work to do. Are you going to do your job, or make me lose my already too generous patience?"

The guard, still unsure, unlocked and opened the door.

"Thank you for finally doing your job. I find things go easier when people actually do as they are supposed to."

"I'm sorry, sir."

"Stop apologizing. It is sickening."

Damon stepped into the small room and his heart caught in his throat. Andrea was limp in the chair, arms folded on the table, head in her arms. Her right leg looked far worse than it had when it had originally been injured. And there was a lot of blood. A large red handprint was on the table.

She was breathing, but he didn't know if she was asleep or unconscious. Her tiny frame shook with each breath. She had obviously lost weight that she didn't have to lose in the first place. She wore the same leggings, right leg ripped off above the wound, and the tattered and stained bandages were no longer recognizable. She had been given a different tunic; he recognized it as her spare from her saddlebag.

Anger and sorrow twisted in his gut. He could barely keep up the act.

"Wake her up," he ordered, his voice still low, but noticeably softer in both tone and volume.

"I'm not allowed—"

"Now."

The guard saw he had no other choice. He entered the room and walked past Damon, head dipped. Damon shut the door behind him. The guard looked at him curiously.

"You will be happy to know that I have decided not to report you," Damon said, closing the gap between them in three casual steps. "You will also be happy to know that I am giving you a nice shiner so you have an excuse. Just tell them I knocked you out."

"What?"

The words had scarcely left the poor guard's lips when Damon struck him with a left hook in the cheek, then swiftly followed with a hard right to the temple. The man dropped. Damon squatted down and inspected the man's face. His lip was busted and a large bruise was already swelling blue and green.

*Good*, he thought.

Damon took the guard's keys and then turned to Andrea. He froze. He did this to her. He swallowed the lump in his throat—something he had been doing too often in the past few days—and crossed the room slowly, as if walking on glass that would break under his weight. He squatted down next to the chair so that he was the one looking up to her for once and gently touched her shoulder. She might break too. Especially under the hand of a trained killer. The same hands that brought her here.

"Andrea, Andrea, wake up," he said softly; his voice sounded like it had melted. "It's me, Damon." *Some comfort that will be.* "I'm here to help you."

She stirred. Moving in slow motion, she lifted her head from her arms, gnarled waves of thick dark hair in every direction. She blinked slowly and turned to him, leaning on her right arm for support.

"Damon?" she slurred weakly.

"Yes. It's me," he answered. "I'm so sorry, Andrea. For everything. And you were right. I fought it for a long time, but now I see the truth. I have found the life you tried so desperately to show me."

Her emerald eyes glazed with tears, but she said nothing. He could not read her expression.

"I came back for you. I'm going to get you out of here. All the others are with Ezra. We are going to meet them outside of Reed. We have to hurry."

Andrea cut her gaze away from him. Damon could see the wheels slowly turning.

"Ezra?" she sounded so very small.

"He has not chosen Elnai's Love the last I spoke to him, but he was trying to ask Tisha questions. He is leading the other Lovers out."

She nodded, still deep in thought. She lifted a hand to rake her gnarled waves from her face, then swept her green eyes over him, studying his face before resting her piercing gaze in his eyes.

"This is true?" she asked. "Not another lie?"

"Yes. This is real," Damon said, almost pleading. "I know that you have no reason to believe me, but I am telling the truth. We don't have much time, we have to go, but let me tell you this—I have found my Maker—and I am never going back. I finally heard Him, I finally listened. This is living peace, Life Himself."

A weary smile curved her cracked lips. "I'm so happy that you found Him." Her weak voice was just above a tiny whisper. "I was praying for you."

That struck him hard. After he had put her through all of this, she still prayed for him.

"Thank you, that means more than you will ever know." He stood. "Now we have to get out of here. Can you walk?"

Andrea looked at her injured leg. "I can try."

He went around to her right side and gently took her right elbow to help her up. She grasped his arm with her left hand and stood slowly, putting no weight on or even fully getting her right leg under her. She closed her eyes and exhaled shakily through her lips. Her grip around his arm tightened as most of her weight was being supported by Damon.

Without another word, Damon released her elbow and swept her up in one swift movement.

She closed her eyes and winced, but didn't complain. Even though Damon was careful and gentle, there would be some pain.

"Can you open the door?" he asked.

Andrea reached out and did so, then leaned her head against him, her arms weakly encircling his neck to hang on. Damon nudged the door open the rest of the way with his foot, turned sideways through the door, and kicked it shut behind him. He walked quickly, almost at a jog. They didn't have much time.

Damon knew the guard's shifts, routes, and posts so he was able to avoid any confrontation for a while.

*What am I going to do if I run into a guard? I cannot fight him holding Andrea, and I am not sure I can talk my way out of this one.*

He glanced down at Andrea. Her eyes still shut tight, her brows furrowed together, breathing heavily. Each step he took shot hot pain through her body—he could see it, but do nothing about it.

He heard footsteps around the corner of the long hall he was walking.

"Someone is coming. Go limp," He whispered.

Andrea's arms slipped down, swinging with his every step, and let her head sag down.

"What is going on?" the guard ordered.

"I'm on our Lord's business. It is none of your concern," he answered sternly.

"It is my concern," the guard retorted. "Is that not the daughter of the Resistance leader? Where are you taking her?"

"What are you implying?" he glared. "That I am a Resistance sympathizer? Do you know who I am? I could have you marked!"

"You are one of the assassins."

"I'm in fact the one who brought her here. Only days ago I sat at Nazar's right hand at a feast held in my honor. You would be wise to check your words."

"Nazar has informed all the guards that if any Resistance prisoner—especially this one and her mother—is seen beyond the prisons without him giving notification, the prisoner is to be apprehended and it is to be reported immediately."

"Does the prisoner not look 'apprehended' to you? I was sent to get her. If you must know, I am taking her to her execution. She has gained too much public support to do it publicly. We are killing her quietly to avoid making a martyr out of her."

The guard still looked skeptical. "I was not informed—"

"What part of 'quietly' do you not understand? Is your skull that thick?" Damon growled. "If you must, escort me out to the execution yard. Then we will have a word with Lord Nazar."

"That will not be necessary—"

"Oh, but it is. You insisted." Damon started down the hall towards the door to the prisoner's courtyard. "Open the door and come."

The guard, defeated, walked to the door and opened it. "Strange," he said. "It wasn't locked. And where's the guard?"

"The guard is already in the execution yard," Damon said into the prisoner's courtyard. "Shut the door behind you and come."

Damon heard the door shut and carefully put Andrea down. She stayed limp as if unconscious.

"I see no one." Damon faced the guard, who turned to see that he had put Andrea down. "What are you doing?"

Damon casually closed the gap between them as he spoke. "You will be relieved to hear that I have decided not to report you."

"What is this-?"

Damon knocked him out quickly and watched the man drop.

"Ready, Andrea?" he walked back to find her sitting up, leaning back on her elbows.

She nodded. He lifted her into his arms once again. She held her head up and held on to his shoulder with both hands to help support herself.

"Can you carry me the whole way?" She asked.

"You don't weigh much," Damon answered.

"But you have to be tired."

"Don't worry about it," he insisted. "I'll be fine."

When they reached the portcullis, he found it closed.

"Do you see the keys?" His eyes swept over the walls in the darkness.

"No."

Damon bit back a curse. "I'm going to check the guard to see if he has it."

He set her back down and produced keys from the guard's pocket. He tried each key, but none of them worked.

Damon angrily threw the keys to the ground, biting back a string of profanity.

"Do you have to have the keys to open it?"

"No," he answered, pacing along the wall hoping he had simply missed the keys. "The portcullises are designed in a certain way to make escape difficult. There are two cranks for each of the gates, so you would need either four people to open the doors, or a key for each crank to lock it in place. Without the keys, I cannot open the doors alone."

"So how are we going to find the keys?"

"I don't know."

"Is there another way we can go?"

"There are many exits—but I am afraid that we would get caught if we tried any of them."

The door to the castle opened. Damon spun on his heel to face it, his hands clenched into fists, heart pumping adrenalin to face the threat.

"You've gotten sloppy, Damon. You didn't lock the door behind you."

"Raya." Damon breathed a sigh of relief, some of the tension drained from his muscles as his hands relaxed.

"If you want to get out of here alive, you had better follow me— and quickly." Raya offered Andrea a hand up.

"I have to carry her," Damon said. "Her injured leg is worse."

He lifted her up.

"Let me try to walk," Andrea said softly.

"Are you sure?"

She nodded.

Damon carefully lowered her feet to the ground. Andrea clung to his shoulder with both hands. She clenched her teeth and slowly put weight on her left leg. She stood a little straighter, although still leaning heavily on him for support.

"Alright," she said, a little breathlessly, "I'm ready."

Damon put a supportive arm around her and headed for the open door, where Raya stood waiting. Andrea limped badly with every step and relied on Damon, but managed to keep up a decent pace.

Raya hurried along a few paces ahead of them. "Quickly," she whispered over her shoulder.

*This does not feel right.* "Raya, where are we going?" Damon demanded.

"This way," she said, rounding a corner without slowing.

"This hall does not lead ..." Damon's words trailed off.

"Elnai, help us," Andrea whispered.

"Quite the heroic effort, Damon," Nazar said. "Especially for a murderer."

Raya was facing Nazar, back to Damon. Her head was slightly dipped.

A dozen pairs of heavy footsteps echoed through the hall. Damon heard the sound of metal scraping against metal as swords were drawn. He glanced behind him to see guards rounding the corner.

Nazar stood proud and tall, smugly taking in the scene. Damon was trapped in a hall between Nazar and a dozen armed guards. Andrea still clung weakly to his shoulder.

*Raya, did she?*

"Lift your chin, girl," Nazar said. "Take pride in your accomplishment. You are not having second thoughts, are you? Have you foolishly bought into the deception as well?"

Raya slowly lifted her head and turned to face Damon. Her back straight, expression hard.

"I'm no fool," she said coldly.

Damon felt icy daggers twisting in his heart. Raya had betrayed him. She was truly lost.

"Good." A grin twisted across Nazar's face; then he glared at Damon, who matched his hard stare. "Bring me the traitor's sword."

Raya marched over to Damon and drew his sword from its sheath, then handed it to Nazar without a word.

Nazar nodded, and the guards rushed forward. Andrea was yanked away from him. He heard her weak yelp as multiple hands grabbed him.

Damon jerked away. "Andrea!"

Sharp pain crashed through his skull and down his spine. He felt himself falling as the world went dark.

## CHAPTER TWENTY

# HARD WON

Ezra and the women waited outside of Reed for over an hour. Still no sign of Damon and Andrea.

"I cannot sit here and do nothing," Tisha said.

"We cannot go back," Ezra said. "Even if all of you were in perfect health, which you are not—you are weak, half starved, battered, and in desperate need of water—there would be nothing we could do."

"Well then, what do you suggest?" Tisha snapped.

"Tisha," Flora said gently, tears in her eyes, "I know you're upset, but the boy was only trying to help."

Tisha looked away, hiding her emotions. "I'm sorry, I just don't know what to do."

"As much as I hate to say it," Rhoda said slowly, debating each word, "I'm afraid that Ezra is right. If they did get captured there is nothing we can do and getting ourselves captured as well will not do anyone any good."

"What do you expect me to do?" Tisha's voice broke as her composure drained away. "I cannot simply do nothing."

For a moment, there was silence. Everyone was at a loss.

"Holy Maker," Zania began, "we need Your wisdom, Your guidance, Your comfort and peace. We are hurting. We are scared. We don't know what to do. We need You. Precious Lover, give us strength. Give Andrea and Damon strength and courage especially if they have been captured. Hold them tight and preserve them.

Help us—all of us—hold fast to You and Your Promise as we walk through this fire. Help us to rest in Your confidence and peace no matter what happens, no matter the pain. Our lives are Yours. If it is our time to enter into Your Promise, give us strength to pass through the trying journey from this life to eternity, give us hope in You. But if it is not yet our time, if it is Your perfect will for us to fight for Your truth another day, then help us to cling to Your victory. Help us to overcome this singing Your praises. We are not our own—but Yours alone. Give us peace in surrender. Give us strength to fight. Give us courage to speak Truth. Give us hope in the Promise."

Tisha and Flora were both crying unabashedly. Every eye was wet.

"I need to go home," Flora said after a moment. "I need to talk to my husband. I know he turned us in but I cannot give up on him. Before I leave with the Resistance, I must have one last discussion with him. If he still will not hear the Truth he will be kept in my prayers always, but I cannot stay there."

"We are praying for you," one of the women said.

"And I for all of you," she said, smiling shakily. "I must go now, but I will see you soon with an update on Judd and for good news about Andrea."

"We should head to Borrim," one woman said, "We could make it by dawn if we hurried. I know a Lover there who could offer us shelter for the night and possibly even be able to help us attain some horses."

"We have to get the children," Rhoda said.

"Is it safe?" someone asked. "What if we are recaptured?"

"We cannot leave our children," Zania said firmly. "We can take them to Borrim for the night, then we should ride to Darrion."

"We cannot go back home," said Tisha, referring to Haavene. "We must assume it has been discovered and that Tim alerted the others. They will have evacuated to Kimble and the northern districts of Darrion."

"Where exactly would the Resistance go?" Rhoda asked. "Maybe we can meet them somewhere."

"There are several routes and locations that the Council discussed," Tisha replied. "I'm not certain where they will be."

"We can go to District One," Zania said. "Only the inner city is fortified so we would be able to get in without too much trouble. I have family there that we would be safe with."

"What about you, dear?" Flora addressed her question to Ezra, who was staring at the ground and shifting on his feet.

"I have to run as well, am I right?" he asked softly. "I will be marked if they catch me. I can't return to the Outskirts."

"I'm afraid not," Tisha said sympathetically.

"I have to go back for my mother and sister," he said. "They rely on me. That is why I took this job in the first place—I was desperate. I have to get them out of Reed. Nazar will kill them."

"I will go with you," Tisha said.

"Really?" Ezra asked timidly.

Tisha nodded.

"Thank you," he said, sincerely grateful.

"Of course." Tisha smiled much more bravely than her heavy heart felt.

After a final prayer, goodbye hugs, and wishes of Maker's strength, they split into four groups.

Flora was going home to Cresso, hoping she could convince Judd of Elnai's Love, then leaving and meeting the others in Borrim on Fourth Bizivday in three days. And—depending on how her conversation with her husband went—deliver her decision about where she would go from there.

Rhoda, Zania, and three other women were returning to Valrine for their children—who had been left in the care of another Lover during their meeting—then taking their children to Borrim.

Tisha and Ezra were going back into the outskirts of Reed for his family. They would leave with Ezra's family, and hopefully Damon and Andrea, to meet the others in Borrim.

Everyone else was heading to Borrim immediately. They planned to leave for District One on Fourth Bizivday. Flora and Ezra were not sure if they would be going with them, and Tisha was not sure of anything. Not until she knew something certain about Andrea.

૭ન્ડ

Andrea sat in the corner of a fairly large room, her right leg stretched out and hugging her left knee. Her bright green gaze rested on Damon, who was sprawled out unconscious on his stomach. His wrists held by a short chain connected to the wall. He had been out about fifteen minutes.

Damon began to stir with a grunted moan. His eyes fluttered open and he winced slightly. The chains clanked slowly across the floor as he pushed himself into a sitting position, his back to Andrea. He pulled a heavy hand to his head. His fingers tenderly felt the matted hair and came away a bit sticky.

"It's not a bad cut," Andrea said softly.

"Andrea?" he twisted to face her. "Are you alright?" he tried to reach her, but was stopped by the tug of his chains.

"Yes." *Well, not really.* "They didn't hit me. They knocked you out with the hilt of a sword. You were out about fifteen minutes."

Andrea, unbound, scooted over closer to him. They both leaned against the wall staring ahead at nothing.

"Anything I should know?" he asked.

"They said nothing after they hit you, they just brought us here. Although I am quite certain they plan to kill us."

"Without a doubt," Damon said. There was no use in denying it. "I just am not sure how long they will wait. They may try to question us."

"They were going to kill me tonight. Nazar was interrogating me one last time, then they were going to kill me. Nazar was *questioning* me when I passed out. I woke up alone on the floor. I crawled into the chair and tried to sleep, I was—still am—exhausted. Then you woke me up. I assume that Nazar left to meet with Raya?"

Damon sighed. "I don't know. She told me that if I went back she would turn me in, but I didn't really think she would . . ." He met her eyes. "Something changed. I don't know what, I don't understand it, but you can just feel it. Raya is in need of her Savior, but I have never seen, felt, I don't know. She didn't even sound like herself." He looked away with wet eyes. "And I am not talking about words, her voice. She sounded different. I am worried, scared for her."

His words lingered in the silence for a moment.

"I'm sorry, Andrea," he said, voice thick. "For all of this, for everything."

Andrea closed her eyes and drew a teary breath, *What do I say? Holy Maker, I am scared. I am confused. I am hurt. Damon is part of the reason I am here, should I forgive him? Am I strong enough even if I chose to?* "Damon."

The sound of a key sliding into the lock. Damon and Andrea exchanged a glance, then looked to the door. A guard opened it and stepped aside to make way for Nazar. And Raya.

Raya wore a blank expression. Her icy gaze met Damon's.

Nazar looked hard and determined. Enraged. His eyes held a savage lust.

Lust for blood.

Andrea saw it. Damon saw it. There was no doubting it now. Short of a miracle, they would die this night.

Damon stood, his chains only allowing him to walk a few feet from the wall.

Four guards accompanied Nazar into the room, locking the door behind them.

Andrea felt at peace. Not at all afraid. She felt completely calm. She was ready. Was she suicidal? No. But she was ready. She accepted it. She was hurting and so very tired, she longed for her Lover. Her heart ached with desire to finally enter into His Promise. Into His Love.

*I am ready. I am Yours. Help me to be strong.*

"Last chance," Nazar said, looking at Andrea.

Andrea remained silent.

"Then you will die." He shifted his hateful stare to Damon. "Damon of Reed, once esteemed assassin, traitor to Airiss and your own blood, you are now stripped of all your former titles and the privileges that accompanied them. You are now marked."

Raya turned to Nazar sharply.

"Deny your supposed 'Lover' and you will live. Refuse, and you shall be executed with the witch."

"This was not the agreement," Raya said coldly.

"I said that I would allow him to live," Nazar said, matching her glare. "I gave him the choice of whether he lives or dies."

"You said you would set him free once he denied the Maker!" she argued.

Nazar backhanded her, she staggered back. Guards rushed around her, but waited for Nazar's order to seize her.

"I'm offering to set him free from the lie he has so foolishly swallowed!" Nazar roared. "Whether he accepts his life and freedom is his own choice."

Raya stood breathing hard with rage.

Nazar watched her carefully as he spoke. "Are you forgetting where your loyalties lie as well, Raya? Did you not yourself say that your brother was lost in his own foolishness? Surely you are no fool."

Raya spit blood from her split lip; a bruise was already discoloring the complexion around her mouth. She squared her shoulders and lifted her chin. "I'm no fool, nor am I a traitor."

Nazar studied her a moment before finally nodding to the guards. They sheathed their swords and backed away.

"Now, Damon," Nazar said, turning to him once more, "the choice is yours. Life or death?"

"Life," Damon said without hesitation.

Andrea felt her heart drop into the cavity that her stomach used to occupy.

"I have chosen Life," Damon said. "And I will never again deny Him. I will never again forget my Lover."

*Yes!* Andrea rejoiced inwardly. *Give Damon strength and boldness, Holy Maker.*

"Damon," Raya said, her voice low with rage, "don't be a fool. Forget His Name and spare your life. He is not real."

"Last chance, boy," Nazar hissed. "Admit that He is dead."

"If my Holy Maker is dead, then why do you fear Him?" Damon challenged.

"I don't fear Him! I am stronger! Because I can kill His people!" Nazar snarled.

Nazar rushed Damon and delivered a hard fist to the jaw. Andrea scrambled out of the way. Damon kept his head and recovered quickly. Before Nazar had time to react, Damon yelled, pulling against the chains, and brought a swift knee to Nazar's ribs. It made impact with crushing force.

Nazar staggered back, the wind knocked from his lungs.

A scream turned every head.

Andrea looked just as the lifeless body of a guard fell, bleeding from a chest wound. Raya stood over him with a scarlet dagger. She threw it at another guard who was unsheathing his sword, it struck his heart and she already had another from its strap on her thigh before his sword was half drawn.

Two guards were dead by Raya. The two remaining guards stood, swords drawn but not eager to rush her. Raya stood facing them, last dagger poised to throw.

All in five seconds since the first guard was stabbed.

Five seconds.

Nazar stood with his back to Andrea. She saw her opportunity. Andrea lunged for the dagger strapped to Nazar's right thigh. She grabbed the dagger with both hands. Nazar loosed an enraged cry and swung his right arm back at her.

Andrea gagged and fell back as Nazar's massive arm struck her in the throat. Her head hit the ground. Hard. Her vision faded.

The dagger clattered to the ground.

"Andrea!" she heard Damon's scream and tried to blink the black away.

The sickening sound of metal on metal filled her ears. Nazar was drawing his sword.

The sounds reached her in slow motion.

*Am I dying?*

Everything hurt. Her leg, her side, her head, her throat, her lungs.

*I have to get up.*

Andrea opened her eyes to see that Nazar had just drawn his sword. She saw the dagger beside her and rolled to her stomach and grabbed it.

Nazar had his sword in hand. He began the swing.

Damon, struggling against his chains, managed to plant a kick firmly in the back of Nazar's knee.

Nazar fell to his knees. Andrea barely had time to scramble out of the way, dragging her wounded leg behind her. Nazar grabbed her left ankle and yanked her back. The wind was knocked out of her as she hit the ground.

She heard Raya cry out. Damon was raging in vain against his chains. He could reach neither of the women.

Andrea could not look. One wasted second would mean death. She had to stay focused.

Ten seconds.

❧❦

Two guards were killed by Raya. The two remaining guards stood swords drawn but not eager to rush her. Raya stood facing them, last dagger poised to throw.

All in the five seconds since the first guard was stabbed.

Five seconds.

She quickly took in the situation. She had to save Damon.

Steadily growing pain surged through her veins.

*No, I have to fight it. This is not truth.*

One guard set his jaw and tightened his grip on his sword. He was about to advance.

*This is not freedom.*

Every muscle in her body tensed in anticipation of the guard's move. She had to act now.

*This is not life.*

The guard took one step.

*This is Death.*

*It* shrieked in fury.

Raya shrieked in desperation and threw the dagger. With a flick of the wrist, it left her fingers and spun through the air.

*You have chosen! There is no going back. It too late. You chose Death. You chose me. I own you.*

Without waiting to see if the dagger found its mark, Raya dove for the sword of the fallen guard at her feet. She grabbed it, and rolled to her feet. Ready. The last guard was coming at her.

Every nerve in her body spiked with pain. Her skull felt as if it was being pierced by invisible talons. Crushed by an unseen force.

Her lips parted in a cry of pain.

Ten seconds.

ॐ∞ॐ

Musa heard the unspoken Voice clearly. She stood.

Every eye turned to her. "Everyone, we must split into two groups immediately. One of you is to pray over the Resistance, and the other is to pray for a name that has been pressed upon my heart. I don't know who it is, but she needs our prayers desperately. We must pray for Raya."

Immediately every one of the Lovers in Musa's group went to war on their knees under the midnight sky and surrounded by unseen battle between warrior and fallen.

෨෴෧

Andrea twisted around, hot pain pumping with every beat of her pounding heart and stabbed desperately behind her. Andrea closed her eyes and bit back a scream as she felt the blade sink into flesh. She imagined it tearing into fibers, slicing through veins, the hot pain traveling through the arm, up and down the spine.

Nazar screamed and loosed his grip as the dagger pierced into his arm.

Andrea pulled it loose with a hoarse cry and scrambled to her feet. Her injured leg buckled and she fell forward, but managed to keep crawling on her hands and left knee.

*I dropped the dagger,* She could not stop to look for it.

"Hurry!" Damon cried. "Grab his sword!"

Andrea turned, grasped at Nazar's sword, which had fallen at his right side when he was kicked. Her fingers curled around the hilt, but Nazar wrapped his crushing grip around her hand.

Andrea cried out, startled, and acted in desperation. With her free hand balled into a fist, she repeatedly hit the bleeding wound on his arm.

Nazar cried out again and Andrea managed to pull loose with the sword. She reached Damon.

"Give me the sword!" he cried.

Just as it changed hands, Nazar was on his feet and charging them.

Andrea dove out of the way.

Nazar was rushing them with the dagger.

Damon backed almost against the wall to get more chain and jabbed the sword straight to Nazar's chest as far as the chains allowed. Nazar saw the sword and tried to stop, but he already had too much momentum. He slipped in the blood pooled on the floor and fell into the sword.

With a cry through clenched teeth Damon heaved the lifeless body to the floor.

Andrea looked away, blinking away nausea and tears.

"Raya!" Damon screamed.

She was backed in a corner, blocking a blow. The two swords were locked; the guard was leaning into it. Any second Raya would slip. She could not last much longer.

Damon took keys from Nazar's pockets and frantically began to work at his lock.

Twenty seconds.

☙❧

The warrior flew hard. He had been sent on the wings of Lovers' prayers. He had to help Raya. He zipped his way through the unseen battle in the streets of Reed. Everywhere you looked—if you had eyes to see—swords of warriors of Light and Darkness flashed. He charged, sword blazing with the cleansing light of the Courts, through a barricade of fallen creatures at the entrance of the castle. In a few powerful swings, the creatures were sent screaming into the Void.

Outside the door where Damon, Andrea, and Raya fought with flesh and blood, dozens of fallen creatures slithered about.

"You are not welcome here. We were invited here," they hissed.

"I'm under order and power of the Holy Maker! My Lord will not be denied!" Daniel responded.

All at once, dozens of creatures pounced on him. The warrior, empowered by the prayers of the beloved, cut through them quickly. And charged into the room.

Raya had a large fallen creature crushing her skull and another sinking its talons into her heart as an armed guard rushed her in the natural.

Brother spirits.

"In the Name of Holy Light, I command you to let her go!"

The creatures recoiled at the powerful Name and loosened their grip.

The warrior rushed forward, sword ablaze, and one of the fallen creatures threw itself at him.

The other refused to release her.

Wynn and Jaav were both fighting dozens each, but brother spirits were terrible strongholds to break. Daniel called on all his strength and fought.

Three more warriors burst in on the wings of the Lover's prayers. Two of them tackled the giant, fattened beast that had preyed on Nazar, the other charged the second brother spirit.

"In the Name of Elnai," the warrior cried, "I command you let go!"

The creature trembled at the Holy Name, losing its hold on Raya's mind. It whirled around, fangs bared in a snarl and charged the warrior.

Razor-like claws clashed with swords of light as the humans fought in the natural.

మ~ఆ

The pain in her skull momentarily lifted like a physical weight. Raya met the guard's sword with hers, blocking a fatal blow.

She was on the defensive. She could not get a counter in and turn the tables. And the guard was backing her into a corner. She could hear screams and cries coming from Andrea and Damon's direction beyond the clashing swords, but could not sneak a glance for even a second.

She had trained with a sword, but always favored bows and daggers, and left swords to Damon. This was testing not only her skill, but her strength. Her opponent was bigger than she.

She was now in the corner, their blades locked together. The guard was using his size and strength advantage against her.

Sweat poured down her face. She opened her mouth and gritted her teeth; her muscles quivering as she slowly gave way. The crossed swords inches from her face.

"Raya!" Damon cried.

She felt her sword slipping. Any second she expected the blade to end her.

*I'm going to die. I'm not ready.*
*I will be truly, completely dead.*
Twenty seconds.

మ~ఆ

Andrea didn't think. She just acted. She launched herself up with her good leg and crashed her right shoulder into the wall. Screaming into her teeth with pain. She ran—stumbled—forward. She threw her body into the guard.

The sound of sliding metal.

The smell of blood.

Distant, echoed yelling.

Falling.

Slowly falling.

Floating?

Ringing in her ears.

Pain.

Burning, dizzying pain.

The ceiling was spinning. Or maybe she was?

*Am I still falling?*

Raya somehow appeared over her. Raya was talking. Her mouth was moving anyway. No sound was coming.

Was Raya falling too?

The fuzzy world spun faster.

Was this real? It had to be.

*It hurts.*

*I know, beloved. It's almost over.*

*Elnai*, her world cleared a little at the thought of His name.

Damon was now leaning over her too. For some reason when his mouth moved, no sound came out either.

*Am I going to die?*

*Peace, child. You are mine. I hold you.*

The world cleared and pain washed over her. Raya and Damon were both holding Andrea's abdomen.

Their hands were scarlet.

"Andrea." Damon's voice was thick. "Can you hear me? She still is not responding, Raya."

"Yes," she said weakly; she could barely hear herself. She grimaced. "Ow, I can hear you."

"Thank the Maker," he whispered. "You will be fine, I will find some moy-moy, we can fix this."

"Damon." She smiled weakly. "It's alright. I'm ready."

"Andrea." His voice broke.

"I'm ready. I want to go home. I cannot wait to see Him, Damon." Her voice was barely above a shaky whisper. "Can you even imagine it? No pain. No more running or fighting. Just eternity in Light. In His love. I'm at peace. I'm ready."

Damon could not hold back the tears.

"Why?" Raya gasped, tears in her eyes and voice, her voice was almost angry through the emotion. "Why did you do that after all I have done to you?"

"Because I was ready …" she said, taking a deep, shaky breath. "You're not, Raya. You're not ready to face eternity. I want you to know Elnai's heart."

The world started to fade into darkness.

"Damon … Raya." She had to hold on just a little longer. "Don't hold on … Don't carry this. I chose Light. Darkness hated it. Don't …" she closed her eyes with a grimace. It was getting harder. She could feel herself … leaving.

"Andrea." Damon's voice was heavy with emotion.

"I release you to not hold onto this … I forgive you."

Damon broke down into sobs. Tears traced Raya's cheeks as well.

"I … I forgive you."

*Breathe.*

She breathed in, and out.

It was dark.

Falling.

Slowly falling.

Floating?

Weightless.

She was wrapped in Light. Peace. Bliss. Joy. Love.

No more pain.

She breathed in, and out …

Light.

*Welcome, beloved. Enter into your reward. Enter into Me.*

"Elnai?"

"I Am."

Laughter. Brilliant, perfect laughter that thrilled her to her deepest soul. Deeper still.

"Open up your eyes and see."

Light.
In love with Love Himself.

᠌᠍᠎᠏

Damon opened up the door to dozens of guards with drawn swords.

They seemed too stunned to attack.

Perhaps it was because there he stood, cheeks streaked with tears, covered in blood.

Nazar's blood.

Andrea's blood.

"Nazar is dead," he said loudly, voice still raw. "You don't have to live under him anymore. You are free from his cruelty. You can go home."

All but three—whether from fear, uncertainty, or relief—immediately turned and ran. The last three saw that they were alone and followed suit.

Raya stood by his side. Her right arm was badly wounded from the last guard. When Andrea had rammed the man, his sword had sliced into Raya's arm and he hit Andrea before Raya could recover long enough to kill him. She would likely never again be able to shoot a bow.

"What do we do now?"

᠌᠍᠎᠏

Ezra and Tisha were trying to convince Ezra's mother to leave when there was a commotion in the street.

Tisha peeked out the window to see countless guards running in all directions.

"Attention, everyone!" they called loudly. "Nazar is dead! We are free! Nazar is dead!"

Those loyal to Nazar cried, "Our Lord is dead! We must take arms or flee!"

Soon, all of Reed was in a frenzy. Nazar's few supporters mourned or ran away, while those who had long groaned under his tyranny lifted their voices in gladness.

Tisha could contain it no longer. She ran for the castle as quickly as she could.

She fought through the chaotic streams of people until she finally reached the prisoner's courtyard portcullis. Raya ran out and met her.

Tisha was wary at first. She looked the girl over carefully. Her arm was badly hurt and hastily bandaged. She supported it with her good arm. She was covered in blood. Even in the dull light, Tisha could see the tear trails down her cheeks.

"Raya?" Tisha said.

"I am so sorry." Her voice was weak and heavy with emotion.

"Where is Andrea?"

Raya bit her lip and looked away.

Tisha felt her heart tear within her. Tears flowed freely as a hand pressed firmly to her mouth.

"She saved me. She saved my life. I am so sorry. It's all my fault." Raya's voice broke as tears were wept once again.

Compassion, rather than anger, welled up inside of Tisha. Yes, she was hurting. Badly. But she could feel her Lover's heart beating within her chest. And she knew that Andrea was not hurting anymore. Andrea was actually to be envied by the Lovers. She had entered into Love Himself.

Tisha closed the distance between them; Raya still could not look at her.

"You have to forgive yourself, dear. You have to place your trust in Elnai." Tisha pulled her into a warm embrace, being mindful of the arm. At first Raya was stiff and uncomfortable, but she soon melted into it.

"Is your brother …?"

"He's fine. He's with her. He sent me to find you."

"Come. Let us go find Damon."

Raya turned to leave, but Tisha's soft touch froze her in her tracks.

"Raya—" Tisha's voice broke. "Andrea wouldn't have wanted you to feel condemned. She died because she wanted you to come to know the Holy Maker. You have to forgive yourself. She would have wanted you too."

"How are you so strong?" Raya asked.

"I'm not. I'm breaking." Tisha smiled tearfully. "But I know who holds my daughter. She has found her Lover and is rejoicing in His light. She isn't hurting anymore. She's free. I know the Holy Maker will give me comfort and peace. Even as He is now." Tisha sighed shakily. "And I have the Promise."

# EPILOGUE

Riven was about to motion his men to advance and take out the watchman, when a guard from a nearby town rode by wildly on his horse. The nearby Lovers ducked into the shadows. The guard didn't notice them. Whether from his frenzy or the Maker blinded his eyes, they would never know.

The guard rode into Vincent's camp screaming, "Everyone! Wake up! Wake up! We just received a messenger bird! Nazar is dead! Nazar is dead!"

He rode madly. The camp was plunged into chaos.

The stunned Lovers simply watched as the army fell into a frenzy, wildly leaping onto horses and running in blind terror.

Riven and Tristan looked at each other, mouths agape. Riven felt his lips spreading in a smile. "The Maker has fought our battle!"

Tristan threw his fist in the air and led the whole assembly in a cry of joy. The different groups of Lovers all came together once more, embracing and shouting for joy.

Riven was in awe. To see Elnai fulfill His Promise—even in a small part—overwhelmed him.

The Lovers laughed and embraced. The enemy army scrambled in all directions, not even hesitating as they passed the Lovers. Riven sank to his knees, closed his eyes, and breathed his prayers of gratitude. This was a small picture of the end days. Elnai would rescue His beloved and scatter His enemies once and for all.

*This was his Maker. This was his Lover. This was his Savior.*

*This was the Promise.*

*And what I say to you, I say to all: Watch!*

*- Mark 13:37 -*

*Watch therefore, for you know neither the day nor the hour in which the Son of Man is coming.*

*- Matthew 25:13, NKJV -*

# IMPORTANT NOTE

H i, I hope you have enjoyed the story of *The Promise*. I hope you laughed and cried with me as we followed our characters, but most importantly, I pray that I was able to make something perfectly clear—Elnai's Love Story to His people. Because while this story and its characters are fictional, I have done my best to paint a picture of Jesus Christ and His redeeming love through symbols such as Elnai and the Tree of Promise.

You see, God—our true Maker—has His own Book. Through the Holy Spirit, He gave us the Bible. And in the Bible, we can read from the beginning of time all the way to the end of it. Most important, I would think, is the part about Jesus. We can all agree that none of us are perfect and everyone has messed up at some point. Since our God is perfect and Holy, our sin and mistakes separate us from Him. We are not only the beloved creations of God, but we are also made in the very image of God.

> *Then God said, "Let Us make man in Our image, according to Our likeness; let them have dominion over the fish of the sea, over the birds of the air, and over the cattle, over all the earth and over every creeping thing that creeps on the earth." So God created man in His Own image; in the image of God He created him; male and female He created them (Gen. 1:26-27).*

When we sin or give in to selfish desires, we separate ourselves from the Holiness of God. He can no longer be with us. By choosing to sin, we are saying we would rather side with Satan and his kingdom.

This is where Jesus comes in. God created us. He loves us more than any of us can even begin to comprehend. It breaks His heart when we turn our backs on Him. He wants us to be able to live in His presence on this earth and then in eternity. But, being a God of justice, He could not just overlook our sins. He could not let us stain His image. So He sent His Son, Jesus Christ, to bridge the gap and redeem us.

> *For as the heavens are high above the earth, so great is His mercy toward those who fear Him; as far as the east is from the west, so far has He removed our transgressions from us. As a father pities his children, so the LORD pities those who fear Him. For He knows our frame; He remembers that we are dust (Ps. 103:11-14).*

> *For God so loved the world that He gave His one and only Son, that whoever believes in Him shall not perish but have eternal life. For God did not send His Son into the world to condemn the world, but to save the world through Him. Whoever believes in Him is not condemned, but whoever does not believe stands condemned already because they have not believed in the name of God's one and only Son. This is the verdict: Light has come into the world, but people loved darkness instead of light because their deeds were evil. Every-one who does evil hates the light, and will not come into the light for fear that their deeds will be exposed. But whoever lives by the truth comes into the light, so that it may be seen plainly that what they have done has been done in the sight of God (John 3:16-21).*

We see in the Gospels of Matthew, Mark, Luke, and John the life, death, and resurrection of Jesus Christ. Up until Jesus came, God's people would have to provide a blood sacrifice to temporarily cover their sins in the sight of Holy God. They were given the Law, which gave them rules and regulations to live by and very specific rules for making sacrifices. God knew that we could never live up to His stan-dards, yet He wanted to be with us so badly, so He sent Jesus. Jesus came to be the once-and-for-all sacrifice that would completely heal us of our sins and allow us to live in His presence again!

> *For all have sinned and fall short of the glory of God, and all are justified freely by His grace through the redemption that came by Christ Jesus. God presented Christ as a sacrifice of atonement, through the shedding of his*

*blood—to be received by faith. He did this to demonstrate his righteousness, because in His forbearance He had left the sins committed beforehand unpunished— He did it to demonstrate his righteousness at the present time, so as to be just and the One who justifies those who have faith in Jesus (Rom. 3:23-26).*

So Jesus came down, was born of a virgin, lived a perfect and completely sinless life, then gave Himself up to be crucified. Since He lived as a man yet was still absolutely perfect and flawless, He was the perfect sacrifice. He knew this, and because of His great Love for us, He offered Himself. He knew His sacrifice would redeem us. That is why in John 19:30 He said, "It is finished."

*And we know that the Son of God has come, and He has given us understanding so that we can know the true God. And now we live in fellowship with the true God because we live in fellowship with his Son, Jesus Christ. He is the only true God, and He is eternal life (1 John 5:20).*

God gave us free-will. He didn't want mindless puppets. We chose to turn away, and we have to choose to accept His gift of salvation and redemption. God wants a *relationship* with you. You were *created* to love and be loved! Now, just as Andrea discovered with Elnai, it is not enough to simply believe the truth about Jesus, but we have to act on it. We have to *choose* to commit our hearts to Him and declare our faith.

*You believe that there is one God. Good! Even the demons believe that—and shudder (James 2:19).*

So, what do we have to do to accept the gift of Christ besides believing? We have to *verbally confess* our belief in Jesus.

*If you declare with your mouth, "Jesus is Lord," and believe in your heart that God raised him from the dead, you will be saved. For it is with your heart that you believe and are justified, and it is with your mouth that you profess your faith and are saved. As Scripture says, "Anyone who believes in him will never be put to shame." For there is no difference between Jew and Gentile—the same Lord is Lord of all and richly blesses all who call on him, for, "Everyone who calls on the name of the Lord will be saved" (Rom. 10: 9-13).*

All we have to do to restore our hearts to God and live in His presence for all of eternity is believe in our hearts and then confess our faith. Part of confessing your faith is water baptism. Being baptized is something every Christian should be excited to do. To clarify—being baptized does not save you. You can be a Christian and never be baptized, and you can be baptized and still not be a Christian. But water baptism is part of *confessing your faith*. Think of it as putting on a wedding ring after getting married. That ring in and of itself does not marry you, but everyone who sees it knows that you have committed your heart to your spouse.

I am so thankful to Jesus for making it so easy for me. I think that is something worth celebrating! Because I never would have been able to willingly go through all that He did for people that had done me wrong. I wouldn't even have been strong enough to do it for myself.

Now, are you ready to accept Jesus and His gift? Are you ready to choose to commit your heart and life to God? When you pray, there are no special words to say. Just talk to God like He is in the room—because He is. I have put some words below to help you, but there is no magic prayer. All you have to do is admit you are a sinner and need redemption, believe in Jesus with all your heart, and confess your faith in him.

**God, I admit I have made mistakes and am not perfect. I know that I can never be enough on my own. Thank You so much for sending Jesus to die for me—to take my place and provide a sacrifice for my sins. Jesus, I believe that You are the only way to God and that You died and rose again so my sins could be forgiven. Thank You so much for saving me. I choose to commit my heart to You. I choose to live for You. Thank You that right here, in this very moment, You redeemed me. Amen.**

If you prayed that prayer, or one similar, for the first time and committed your life to Jesus, congratulations! I am so excited to call you my brother or sister in Christ! You now get to be called by His name—Christian. I encourage you to get into the Bible—Matthew, Mark, Luke, and John are great places to start—and get baptized. Find a church where you can worship with other believers and grow in Christ.

If you didn't accept, I pray that you will come to know Christ. Know that Jesus loves you—and He wants a relationship with you. Start looking, challenge God to reveal Himself, and I guarantee you that He will start showing up—even where you least expect it.

If you are already a believer, thank you so much for reading this. I hope it encourages you and strengthens your faith. Please join with me in prayer that this book and its message will reach those who need it. If you know someone who needs to hear the message of Jesus, please keep them in prayer. And if you think this book will be a blessing to someone, recommend it.

Finally, thank you so much! Whoever you are, no matter what walk of life you are from, I want you to know that I am praying for you. Yes, *you*. Lots of prayer has gone into this book and its readers. Sincerely, I pray that God blesses you and that you can come to know God.

Remember! Jesus is coming back! He is coming to bring justice and take the believers into His presence forever. This is our hope! This is our Promise! Are you ready?

*Hallie Jo*

*Look, I am coming soon! My reward is with me, and I will give to each person according to what they have done. I am the Alpha and the Omega, the First and the Last, the Beginning and the End.*

*- Revelation 22:13-14 -*

# APPENDIX

**The Airissians**

Government: Inhabitants of the Land of Airiss, which is one of the four powers of the known world, speak Common Tongue. Airiss is ruled by a lord, whose descendants precede him upon his death. The lord rules from a grand castle in Reed, the capital city, and appoints governors to live in specific cities to help him keep an eye on the people. Airiss is the center of most agricultural trade in the known world.

**Terrain:** Airissian terrain is mostly rolling hills perfect for farmland with a warm climate. To the north, near her border with the icy land of Lidian, there is a more snowy, mountainous terrain with cooler weather. To the east, near her border with the hot land of Darrion, there is a large mountain range. These mountains are tall enough that they create their own weather systems, causing frequent thunder storms and a large desert on the Darrionite side.

**Appearance:** The Airissian people generally are shorter, with lighter skin kept tan from working in the sun. The women usually are about five foot six inches to five foot nine inches tall, while the men are usually five foot ten inches to six foot tall. Their eyes are typically a shade of brown or hazel. On average, their hair is a shade of brown and straight. It is not uncommon for women to cut their hair short, and men keep their hair short.

**Beliefs:** Once all were free to choose their own religious beliefs, but under Nazar's rule he is making himself out to be a god and is persecuting all who refuse to bow to him.

## The Darrionites

**Government:** Inhabitants of the Land of Darrion, which is one of the four powers of the known world, speak Darroon. Darrion is governed by elected rulers and governors in each of the fifteen districts, who all answer to the elected leadership of Zain, the central and capital district. The Darrionites are infamous for their incredible abilities in war, and most of the cities—and even some entire districts—are heavily guarded and surrounded by massive walls. Many pay high prices for greatly sought after Darrionite armor and swords, as well as other blacksmith work, which is the country's main trade.

**Terrain:** Most of Darrion is very arid. To the west, there is a great desert below the mountains along the Airissian border that covers nearly five entire districts. To the north, near the Kimim border, it is more wooded.

**Appearance:** The Darrionite people are built tall and very strong, with beautiful dark skin. The women are usually about six feet tall, and the men typically are six foot three inches to six foot five inches. Their eyes are usually dark greens and browns or black, and their hair is usually always curled and dark brown or black. The women do many things with their hair, but the men mostly keep it cut short or in long dreadlocks.

**Beliefs:** Although the Darrionite people were never given as much religious freedom as the Airissians or Kimim, only in recent years the leadership has been prohibiting all religious worship, belief, or gathering. Most of the Darrionites now believe in nothing religious just as the leadership has been pushing, although many are very superstitious.

## The Lindianese

**Government:** Inhabitants of Lindian, one of the four powers of the known world, speak Lydeen. The four nations of the Lindianese people each occupy one of the Four Mountains. Each nation is led by an Elder and ten advisers that the Elder appoints. The four Elders and their advisers meet regularly and each of the Four Mountains take turns hosting the meetings. They live in, not on, the mountains. Their palaces, tunnels, and living quarters that they have carved into the deep caverns and cool rock are very extravagant and beautiful. They mostly choose to keep themselves completely separate from the rest of the world, but will allow Darrionite miners (they are too self-righteous to do it themselves, and the Darrionites don't mind the work and love the portion that comes with it) to mine the precious jewels from the mountains around the Four. The jewels and resources from their mines are their main and nearly the only trade or even relations with the "outsiders." Their relationship with the Darrionites is good on strictly business terms because of the mining arrangement.

**Terrain:** Very cold and snowy. It is a very mountainous terrain with an extremely frigid climate.

**Appearance:** Built tall and slender with snow white skin. The women are usually about five foot ten inches, and the men average six foot one inch to six foot two inches. Their eyes typically are deep grays, purples, and blacks, but will occasionally be a dark blue. Their hair is almost always perfectly straight and silky black. Women never cut their hair and usually wear it with or in elaborate braids. The men keep their hair long as well, but cut it.

**Beliefs:** They are a very solemn people. Religion of any kind or form is strictly, and really always has been, prohibited. They devote themselves to the pursuit of knowledge—to the point that it becomes a religion in itself. Their ever-growing library contains thousands upon thousands of books, scrolls, ancient writings, maps, and documents. They teach Ancient Tongue in their schools and pride themselves in their vast knowledge. They study and document everything and are constantly making copies of the information they already have. They are particularly fascinated with the stars, and have several holidays devoted to their study.

## The Kimim

**Government:** Inhabitants of Kimble, one of the four powers of the known world, speak Kimim. Each tribe has its village Chief, but there is technically a king. The king, like the Kimim people as a whole, has always been very laid back and mostly lets each village chief run his own affairs and the King runs the Capital city (a town by any other standards) and keeps the peace as well as unites the tribes in times of war. The tribe chiefs take a portion of the profits that their tribes make and bring it to the King in regular meetings. The King then uses those things in foreign trade and gives each tribe a portion according to how much they chose to contribute as well as a small portion for himself. The Kimim are gifted woodworkers and huntsman. Their trade with the other lands is often beautiful clothing, woodwork, and furs and meat as well as other things they get from the wild game they hunt and trap. The Kimim are a very simple and mostly carefree people, who always seem to have some sort of village gathering or other festive event.

**Terrain:** Thickly wooded with a cooler climate near Lidian and a warmer one near Darrion.

**Appearance:** The Kimim are a smaller people built hardy with bright eyes of blue and green. The men are usually five foot seven inches to five foot nine inches tall, and the women are often five foot to five foot three inches tall. Their hair is light, almost white blond to light brown, and is usually playful waves or bouncy curls. The men's shaggy hair grew over their ears and the women typically keep theirs just below the shoulder.

**Beliefs:** Happy and easygoing, but not afraid to work, the Kimim never had an official religion or any restrictions. For the most part, many Lovers could often be found among the Kimim. In recent years, with the other three powers banning or restricting worship of the Holy Maker, Kimble has begun to follow their lead. Soon, the Lovers worry, it will be completely banned there as well.

## Darroon

The language of the Darrionite people is a very stern and blunt sounding tongue. It is spoken in all fifteen districts as the primary language, but as is the case in the other lands, Common Tongue is a second language to many.

Adding "nn" to the end of a word makes the "ing" as in eating (Eat—Dyrt; Eating—Dyrtnn)

If the word already ends in "n," add "dnn" as in killing (Kill—Cahn; Killing—Cahndnn )

Adding "us" to the end of a word makes the "ed" as in quieted (Quiet—Dray; Quieted—Drayus)

If the word ends in a vowel, add "s" as in received (Receive—Evise; Received—Evises)

Adding "ox" to the end of a word makes it plural as in swords (Sword—Vax; Swords—Vaxox)

If the word ends in a vowel, add "x", as in pigs (Pig—Jai; Pigs—Jaix)

Adding "un" to a word makes the "er" as in wiser (Wise—ujay; Wiser—Ujayun)

If the word ends in a vowel, just add "n" as in faster (Fast—Zo; Faster—Zon)

| Haavene—The name of the ancient city which is now the ruins that serves as the main Resistance base

| Yipoc Raj—Room in where copies of the Book are made

| Zann Raj—Room in where the Lovers gather for large meetings or fellowship

|Narik Raj—Room in where weapons training takes place

|Tuary Raj—Room that serves as a hospital

| | | |
|---|---|---|
| Ain—Us | Bree—Then | Dray—Quiet |
| Anni—You | Broh—Than | Drayund—Silence |
| Annis—Your | Cahn—Kill | Drayus—Quieted |
| Avitom—Stop | Cahndnn—Killing | Dyrt—Eat |
| Aw—As | Cahnus—Killed | Dyrtdnn—Eating |
| Bar—Have | Ce—Are | Elihim—Like |

Ene—Or
Ert—Do
Evice—Recieve
Fain—Die
Gi—Not
Haavene—Fortress
Hev—Him
Hiv—He
Ilt—To
Ina—I
Ingo—Price
Jai—Pig
Jaix—Pigs
Kaziim—Portion
Kogh—Must
Lene—For
Les—No
Mage—Damage

Marj—Arrow
Mayah—Bring
Mayahx—Brings
Nai—We
Narik—Train
Ne—Will
Nylra—That
Odo—Much
Ogg—Go
Payryl—Brother
Qui—My
Quil—Me
Raj—Room
Reau—Scout
Ree—When
Savine—Dog
So—From
Tiv—Sell

Tuary—Sick
Ujay—Wise
Ujayun—Wiser
Um—Food
Vax—Sword
Vaxex—Swords
Veast—Starve
Wa—Of
Widnai—Spirit
Xaiv—Friend
Yain—The
Yas—See
Yipoc—Copy
Za—Meet
Zain—Capital
Zann—Meeting
Zo—Fast
Zon—Faster

## Lythrainial

Lythrainial is the Holy language spoken in the Courts of Light. Not many are fortunate enough to hear it with physical ears on this world, and even those who do rarely are granted understanding. The Language—like its Maker—is a mystery. The language gives praise to Elnai in every word and is very songlike and beautiful. In fact, in the Courts there is no difference between spoken word and song. Everything brings worshipful glory to the Holy Maker of All Things.

Adding "ese" to the end of a word makes the "ed" as in praised

Example) Praise—Ini; Praised—Iniese

Adding "al" to the end of a word makes it plural as in tongue

Example) Tongue—Lyth; Tongues—Lythal

| Writhrial Tose Ra Lindrene—Lythrainial name of the Book

| Lythrainial—Name of the language of the Courts

| | | |
|---|---|---|
| Baros—Second | Lindrene—Light | Ra—Of |
| Everindel—Word | Lyth—Tongue | Tose—Heart |
| Inial—Praises | Lythro—Song | Vinai—Over |
| Jakkiv—Strength | Ny—Place | Writhrial—Holy |
| Lavin—Jealousy | Nyese—Placed | Yosim—Defense |

## Ancient Tongue

Ancient Tongue is now a dead and mostly forgotten tongue—with the exception of its use in the dating system. Up until the Third Age, when other languages began to develop, it had been the only language spoken. Besides the dating system, the Lidianese have taking great pride in learning their people in Ancient Tongue. They write their documents in and continuously work to translate their vast library into Ancient Tongue for the sole purpose of taking pride in the fact that the other nations will not be able to understand it. The Lidianese also work to decipher ancient documents of the Second and Third Ages. Even so, the Lidianese still have much to learn of the Tongue of their ancestors.

Note: The Common Tongue number system is used in every land. Weekday and Month names—although in very formal occasions and documents all the dates are in Ancient Tongue—are the only exception, where Ancient Tongue numbers are used in front the word day or month. For example, "Salmday" translates "Firstday". There are seven days in a week, twenty-eight days in a month, thirteen months in a year, and 364 days in a year. This is the system used in every land.

Note: If the number ends and the add-on begins with a vowel, drop the vowel from the add-on.

Adding "Lm" to the end of a number makes the "st" as in 1st

Adding "s" to the end of a number makes the "nd" as in 2nd

Adding "iv" to the end of a number makes the "th" as in 8th

Adding "ec" to the end of a number makes the "rd" as in 3rd

Adding "soar" to the end of a number makes it a teen as in 13

Adding "ah" to the end of a number makes it a number from 20 to 99

Adding "Daus" to the end of a number it makes it a hundred as in 200

Adding "Ahdaus" to the end of a number makes it a thousand as in 4,000

One—Sa
Two—Bia
Three—Tah
Four—Nev
Five—Med
Six—Biz
Seven—Da
Eight—few
Nine—Dray
Ten—Sour
Eleven—Ary
Twelve—Lil
January—Salmmonth

February—Biasmonth
March—Tayecmonth
April—Nevivmonth
May—Medivmonth
June—Bizivmonth
July—Daivmonth
August—Fewivmonth
September—Drayivmonth
October—Soarivmonth
November—Aryivmonth
December—Lilivmonth
13th month—Tahsoarivmont

## Common Tongue

Common Tongue—the language of the Airissians—is practically the primary or secondary language to everyone. International trade and meetings are done in Common Tongue. It is taught in homes and schools in all three of the other powers. Its number system is the only accepted one in any and all schools and business, and all written word—the exception being those written before the Fourth Age and some in the Lindianese Library—is in this tongue.

## Kimim

The language of the people of Kimble is now primarily spoken only by the more remote tribes of the wooded land. It was a playful sounding tongue full of many clicking sounds and many variations between tribes. There are around twenty Kimim tongues spoken widely, as well as many others spoken only by one tribe. The Great War of the Fourth Age demanded unity among the scattered tribes in order to survive and assemble their National Army. The Common Tongue became a bridge between the language barriers and ever since, many now speak it as their native tongue. Although the king never made Common Tongue the official language, now many of the people have never known Kimim. It is now only spoken among a few old and remote tribes.

## Lideen

The Lidianese's native language is called Lydeen and is fluent and elegant. Very few besides the Lidianese people themselves understand, read, or speak it because it is jealously guarded from all deemed "in-superior."

# ABOUT THE AUTHOR

Hallie Jo finished writing The Promise: The Lover's Heart at the age of sixteen. She is an avid reader and loves all genres, from fantasy to suspense to poetry. Some of her favorite authors are Francine Rivers, Frank Peretti, and Ted Dekker. She is a passionate lover of Jesus and has plans to serve on the mission field. Her writing is heavily influenced by this calling, and she prays that this book will be the first of many used to share the gospel. She is currently a homeschooled junior in high school and plans on attending Bible College. She has always been actively involved in her church and loves spending time with friends and family.